Tutelary Presences

Other Works
by Johann M. Moser

Verse

Most Ancient of All Splendors

Late Autumn at Dumbarton Oaks
And Other Poems

Farewell … and If Forever
And Other Poems

Prose

The Ivory Fount
A Novel

Love of the Blossoming Hills
New England Stories and Sketches

The Song of the Eternal Aeons
A Phantasmagoria

Translations

O Holy Night
An Anthology of Classic Nativity Verse

Devoutly I Adore Thee
Prayers and Hymns of St. Thomas Aquinas
(with Robert Anderson)

Johann M. Moser

Tutelary Presences

And Other Stories

The Diamond Ledge Press
Sandwich, New Hampshire

For more information, please contact us at:
https://diamondledgepress.com/

978-1-964001-03-6 (hardback)
978-1-964001-04-3 (paperback)
978-1-964001-05-0 (ebook)

Library of Congress Control Number: 2024904673

Contents

"Feed It to the Birds"

This year, as usual during the Christmas season, Francine devoted special attention to the small flock of cardinals that gathered to feed on the nuts and raisins she would spread for them in the backyard. She liked to stand by the dining-room window and admire their scarlet plumage, so bright against the snow and ruffled a bit in the cold. For her, the scene was Christmas itself in all its warmth, serenity, and animation—so different, it must be said, from that "other Christmas" whose tensions were taking shape in the household around her. She envied the cardinals; they didn't revel in the feasts of the holiday season; and they were—were they not?—very happy.

Francine's mother, Marianne, was busy in the kitchen with her Christmas baking, but the kitchen radiated neither warmth nor joy, nor anything else, except for the atmosphere of an embattled camp. In fact, it had been in a state of siege for two days. Now, on Christmas Eve, Marianne was entering into the final phase of her annual baking project: the production of an elaborate French-style *bûche de Noël* in all its decorative grandeur. During this time, all normal use of the kitchen was suspended, and Francine, pressing her forehead against the cold windowpanes in the dining room, reflected on how she and her father, Derek, had to scavenge for their meals on those rare occasions when it was safe to trespass into the potential crossfire of the kitchen.

The kitchen itself was a site of devastation: flour and sugar covered the floor, the counters, the shelves; piles of broken eggshells were scattered among bowls and utensils; and the top of the electric range was blackened by a huge stain of scorched chocolate. In one corner were the slumped carcasses of four *bûches* that had failed at some stage or another of preparation. Enshrined in the midst of this culinary wasteland was Julia Child's *The French Chef,* opened to a page titled *"Bûche de Noël"* and splattered with meringue, brownish vanilla spots, and other adornments more or less impossible to identify.

Marianne, naturally, was frantic.

She was frantic because things kept going wrong and she wanted her masterpiece to be perfect; and she was frantic because the effort expended on the *bûche* prevented her from attending to the other activities of the season, and she felt that Francine and Derek resented this. She, in turn, resented this imputed resentment, as well as their occasional appeals for a cease-fire which she would only interpret as a further sign of their ill will, to say nothing of their cultural obtuseness. After all, the *bûche* had become her regular Christmas gift to the Marlboroughs, who lived on the neighboring block. They had lived for many years in France. As far as Marianne was concerned, they were the epitome of good taste and cultivation; they knew what a *bûche de Noël* was and could appreciate it. For them it must be perfect, exactly *comme il faut,* no matter how many *bûches* had to be abandoned along the way, for they would know the difference.

As Francine continued to watch the birds fluttering around the backyard, she heard her father enter the kitchen. She knew he had a plan in mind to divert her mother—a "diversionary tactic," as he'd referred to it the previous evening. Derek, at first, silently reconnoitered the dreadful state of the kitchen and of Marianne's nerves. She paid no attention to him. However, she was somewhat calmer than usual, since she'd finally managed to "roll" her latest *bûche* without allowing it to split. Meanwhile, Derek moved cautiously across the kitchen to the far counter and began to nibble discreetly on a piece of one of the defunct *bûches.*

"Say, this is pretty good," he remarked.

Marianne didn't answer. She was occupied in making meringue toadstools for the decoration and was squeezing the fluffy egg-white mixture out of a pastry tube onto a sheet of wax paper.

"They were too dry," she replied finally without looking up. "They broke when I tried to roll them. Now would you please be so good as to get out of here!"

Derek nibbled a bit more at the thin, dry cake. "Surely," he said, "there must be something we could do with these discarded cakes. Perhaps we could cut them up into little squares and frost them and put sprigs of holly on them and …"

"Nothing of the sort! I've no time for that!"

"Don't worry. I'll do it. Francine and I shall do it."

"Get out!" she retorted, looking up angrily from the toadstools.

Derek backed away from the counter and stood by the swinging door that led into the dining room. He began his prepared speech: "You know, Marianne, Francine and I would really love to help. Together, we could all make a *bûche* for our own family Christmas. They're awfully good and make such a wonderful centerpiece for the table. You're an excellent cook; you do realize that, don't you?"

Marianne glared at him.

He continued, "You could be so much more relaxed about all of this. It would be a family enterprise. And we wouldn't mind at all if it wasn't absolutely perfect. We probably couldn't even tell the difference," he chuckled.

"You just bet you couldn't tell the difference. That's the whole problem," she yelled and grabbed for her Julia Child cookbook while Derek, having been on previous occasions the target of an airborne *French Chef*, ducked through the swinging door.

Again, she yelled, "I'd rather feed it to the birds!" as the book flew through the door on its return swing, slid across the dining-room table, and collided with a bowl of fruits and nuts. The door swung shut. Walnuts, oranges, and apples rolled over the surface of the table and dropped to the floor; and the birds outside flew up into the trees in alarm.

Francine looked at her father.

"It didn't work," he said and went back into the living room to untangle the Christmas tree lights. Francine turned around to gaze out the window again. She tried to imagine the droll sight of her cardinals pecking away at a *bûche de Noël*. Then she began to pick up the fruits and nuts that were scattered about on the floor and table.

By midday the *bûche* had been frosted, and the frosting had been scored to make it look like bark. Little branches of frosted cake were added around the sides. Then the toadstools were placed in small clusters on the surface of the bark and sprinkled with cocoa powder to make them look mottled and authentic. Finally, glittering spun-sugar moss was added, and the entire *bûche* was lightly dusted with powdered sugar to give it a snowy appearance. Derek was pressed into cutting off a few inconspicuous sprigs from the Christmas tree so that evergreens could be artfully arranged around the rim of the silver platter upon which the *bûche* had been placed.

The effect was enchanting. Both Derek and Francine admired it. It evoked all the mystery of a dark, wintry forest. In its wonderful tranquility and rich aromas and delicate solemnity, it was redolent of so much that was best and most meaningful at Christmastime. It reminded Francine of her little flock of cardinals. And how very real those toadstools looked! Perhaps, she thought, it was worth doing this after all.

Marianne readily accepted the praise of her family and joined in their admiration; then she carefully wrapped the *bûche* in transparent plastic wrap, put her coat on, and bore the magnificent gift off to the Marlborough's house on the next block.

Nancy Marlborough answered the door and, upon seeing Marianne with the *bûche* on the silver platter, clapped her hands and chirped with delight.

Marianne sang out, "*Joyeux Noël!*"

"*Oui oui! Non non!*" Nancy sang back.

Marianne hopped over the threshold, the *bûche* held up at shoulder height, and began to bounce up and down in a stiff-legged little jig, singing all the while: "*Joyeux Noël! Joyeux Noël!*"

"*Oui oui! Non non!*" Nancy sang in return and began to jig in the same style with her arms waving around.

James Marlborough, sitting in an armchair by the fire, lowered his newspaper to witness the strange events in the vestibule. Marianne called over to him, "*Comment ça va, mon vieux?*"

He mumbled something in return, which she couldn't hear, but assuming that he'd asked her how she was, she shouted back cheerfully, "*Très bien, merci!*"

Meanwhile the cake had changed partners, and now Nancy held it at shoulder height while the dance continued. "Thank you so much for such a lovely cake," she cried out.

"*Je t'en prie,*" Marianne replied.

"*Oui oui! Non non!*" Nancy rejoined.

Marianne suddenly hesitated and looked curiously at Nancy. She was always mystified when Nancy went into this absurd "*Oui oui! Non non!*" routine, but she quickly resumed her dance, hopping out the door and crying out again.

"*Joyeux Noël!*"

"*Oui oui! Non non!*" Nancy trilled after her and closed the door.

James lowered his paper once again and stared at Nancy as she placed the *bûche* on a side table. "Not another of her damned *gateaux*?" he asked. Nancy nodded, looking disdainfully at it and annoyed that James had used the word *gateaux*, which she didn't quite understand. James laid the newspaper on the floor beside the chair and nodded in return.

"For years, I cajole, manipulate, deceive, do anything I can to get transferred back to the States and out of France and now I have to be reminded of it constantly by that fiendish Francophiliac friend of yours. Tell her, Nancy, that we loathe French cuisine to the marrow, even to the very aspic of our bones. Tell her we loathe . . ."

"I can't tell her that—it would kill her."

"Not such a bad idea," he answered. "Anyway, what are we going to do with it?"

"With what?"

"With that 'boosh' or whatever they call it. Who would think that a cake made up to look like a rotting log in a forest, covered with several species of fungi, could be an attractive thing to eat on Christmas Eve? That entire cuisine is infatuated with rot and decay and slime and mold and who knows what else. Think of those cheeses buried in dung, those wines festering in damp, musty cellars, those interminable mushrooms, those black clammy truffles unearthed by slobbering snouts of hogs and embedded in crocks of greasy goose liver!

"On a diet like that, no wonder it was a French scientist—Pasteur—who discovered bacteria! Ugh! I wouldn't touch that 'boosh' even if you threatened to toss me into a pit with a thousand live *escargots.*"

"What's that?" Nancy snapped back.

"Snails," he answered. "Those slithery, creepy things they like to eat. Why don't you simply dispose of the cake?"

"How?"

James hunched up his shoulders and lifted the palms of his hands, contorting his face in what he supposed was a mimicry of a French facial expression: "*Donnez-la aux oiseaux!*"

"What?" Nancy snapped again.

In her six years in France, Nancy had never learned more than two French words, *oui* and *non,* and she figured that if she repeated both of them in the singsong way she did, she'd pretty well covered all linguistic contingencies she might have to face. In any event, she hated to have French spoken to her, especially by James, since she always suspected that some insult was intended by it.

James, contorting his face into yet another shape, exclaimed, "Feed it to the birds!"

"*Oui oui! Non non!*" Nancy tweeted gleefully, hopping once more in that strange stiff-legged jig and flapping her hands.

On the following morning, a beautiful Christmas day, Francine spread the nuts and raisins for the birds and went inside the house to await their arrival. She'd provided them this morning with a very special treat—an entire bag of pistachios—their favorite, but rather too expensive to be given out on ordinary occasions. This was their Christmas gift. But they didn't swoop down as they usually did as soon as the door was closed. In fact, they didn't come at all, and Francine was disappointed. She felt lonely without them.

Suddenly, as she was about to turn away from the window, a single male cardinal, brightly hued in the morning sun, flew over the back fence and alighted on the snow just beneath the windowsill. He was carrying something in his beak that he now placed on the ground, glanced at momentarily by tilting his head, and began to peck. It was a toadstool. Francine was surprised. She didn't know that birds ate toadstools. Also, it seemed odd to her that toadstools would be around this time of year.

She called to her mother, who was in the living room, sitting among piles of Christmas wrappings and ribbons, and who was absorbed in a new book about French cuisine that she'd received as a present from an aunt. Marianne wasn't interested at the moment in pursuing speculations about the eating habits of birds, but she did call back, "Of course, toadstools must grow in winter. Why else would facsimiles of them be placed on *bûches de Noël?*" Then she turned to her book and said to Derek, who was examining some new fishing tackle, "Derek, there's a wonderful recipe in here for a special kind of *crêpe* for New Year's Day. Don't you think it would be nice to invite the Marlboroughs over for a special French *soirée* with champagne and all that?"

At the window, Francine watched the cardinal devour the toadstool and fly over the back fence without even noticing the pistachios. The bird glided up and down over the various fences and hedges of the block and across the street, to where he landed in the Marlborough's yard.

The other birds there were busy. They hewed and pecked and fluttered around each other. They made little chocolate footprints in the snow. They reveled in their holiday feast, and they were — were they not? — very happy.

The Story of My Life

S ure, there's room. I'll squeeze over a bit. There's plenty of room. Sit
down. Make yourself comfortable. Where are you getting off? How's
that? Fifty-Seventh Street? Great place to get off—Tiffany's, Bonwit
Teller, Carnegie Hall, Russian Tea Room! So, which one are you going to?
A dentist? Yeah, I bet you are! Really? Well, that's no great place to be going,
is it? Can't you just feel that drill already boring down into your teeth! I can
feel it, even though I'm not going.

Me? I'm getting off at Thirty-Fourth. Empire State Building. I'm just going to look at the view. For about the hundredth time, I think. I like looking
at the view. I love New York, and I love just looking at it.

So, what's in the paper this morning? I don't read the *Times*. It's got too
many ads.

I'm not being a pest, am I? I guess if you buy a newspaper, you buy
it to read it. Never mind me. I run on a bit now and then. But I'm not
like one of those guys who sits down next to you on a bus and insists on
telling you the story of his life. Heck no, I'm not like that. I can't stand
that kind of thing.

Eighty-Fourth Street. Museum! I spend a lot of time there. What a great
collection! Still got a long way to go, don't we? You see that fat guy in that
seat over there? He's taking up two seats, isn't he? Why doesn't he have to
pay two fares? Now you answer me that.

Sorry! Didn't mean to interrupt you. Hey, that looks interesting about the D.A.'s office. Excuse me, I'm just trying to catch that one word in the crease. Yeah! Got it. Thanks.

But don't let me disturb you; I mean, don't put away the paper on account of me. Well, if you must. Excuse me again, if I stand up and look for Cleopatra's Needle as we pass. Yeah, okay, it's great. Cleopatra's Needle is great. But you can't really see it well from here anymore, now that they built that big extension on the museum. That's too bad. But I still look for it anyway. Just a habit. I love those ancient Egyptians. Do you love them? Ancient Egyptians—they're my kind of guys. Excuse me, I'll just squeeze down again.

I love this time of year in New York. Early March. Pretty soon they'll be painting the green stripe down the street for the St. Patrick's Day parade. I love that—all those crazy things, those people carrying along Fifth Avenue banners saying, "England, get out of Ireland." We all need a cause, don't we? Makes life more fun.

Me? No, I'm not Irish. Come on, now: do I look Irish? I mean it, do I look Irish? Who ever saw an Irishman who looked even remotely like me? What Irishman has a nose even half as long as mine?

No, I'm . . . Well, I'm not going to tell you. No, I'm not telling. No, sorry, I'm not. Well . . . maybe I will. People always get such screwy looks on their faces when I say it. So here it comes. Ready? Sure you're ready?

I'm Montenegrin.

I knew you would get a screwy look on your face. Everybody does. They're positively embarrassed. Montenegrin? Montenegro? What is it with this guy? Is that some place in a comic strip—the kind of place the Phantom would hang out in? Or Mandrake the Magician? Or a vampire of some sort? There's no such place. Maybe he's talking about Monte Casino, or the Count of Monte Cristo, or something like that?

Of course, some people know, I mean, like there actually is such a place, and then they act even more screwy. Montenegro! No one comes from Montenegro! I mean, it's impossible. Where the heck is it, anyway? You surely know it's tucked away in a corner of Yugoslavia—the former Yugoslavia, to be exact, right next to Albania. Don't you? You don't. Well, now you do.

And, if you do know, isn't that the place that has been cut off from the rest of the world for the last hundred years—provided, of course, that it ever was connected with the rest of the world anyway, ever in its history? Isn't that the place where people run around in crazy robes and hit each over the head with glinty sabers all the time and discharge long-barreled flintlocks with fancy carvings right between their neighbors' eyes? You get the picture? It's no great picture.

Seventy-Ninth. Hey, that fat fella got off. The bus feels like it rose up three inches, doesn't it? I'm not pestering you, am I? I know I run on.

Now about this Montenegrin stuff, I always like to say that Montenegrins are one of the most ancient peoples of Europe. But I don't say that. I mean, I said it, but I don't usually say that. I figure someone might say, "Ancient? Yeah, and they stayed that way!"

So, I don't say it, even though I said it. You understand. You would never come back with a dumb crack like that, would you?

I knew you wouldn't.

Now, what do you think it was like for me as a kid? I grew up in a small college town in New England. It was one of those real preppy places—no place for a Montenegrin, let me tell you.

My father ran a grocery store where the college kids bought all their beer. It did a great business. So, of course, I was, in addition to being Montenegrin, a "townie." You know what a "townie" is? A "townie" is just about the worst thing you can be—a kid who grows up and lives in a college town.

But everything got even worse. I did really well in high school, and they gave the best student in the high school each year a free tuition to the college. Now don't get the impression that, because I did so well, I'm smart or anything like that. Immigrant kids always do well, because they're too stupid to know yet that goof-offs are the ones who really get ahead in life. Gee, mister, you must have done really well, what with that expensive suit and reading the *Times* and all, but I bet you were no goof-off, were you?

The college was rolling in money, so this business of giving a scholarship was its little gesture of goodwill to the local people. Goodwill? What goodwill? After being a "townie," the next worst thing is to be a "townie" enrolled in a college in whose town you're a "townie." I mean, that makes you Mr.

Jerk from Dorkville, even though all these students are paying astronomical bucks to spend four years of their lives in that town too. Do you get that?

And heaven forbid you should ever get a good grade in a college course. "His father sells under-the-counter booze to the prof's perpetually crocked wife; that's why he got the A."

Of course, I didn't want to go there. No luck! My father tells me, "Here, or nowhere!" Little did he realize that "here" and "nowhere" were the same place in a situation like that. But Montenegrins do what their fathers tell them to do. The saber. The flintlock. You get the picture? It's not always a pretty picture. Anyway, kids whose fathers run grocery stores don't turn down free tuition, even if it's from the University of West Hell.

Seventy-Second Street! The model boat pond is not far away. You know, Conservatory Water. And the statue of Hans Christian Andersen. I love Hans Christian Andersen. I love those stories. Do you love those stories? Hans Christian Andersen — my kind of guy!

College was as bad as it could have been. It may have had a fancy name and reputation and all that, but it *was,* for all purposes, the University of West Hell. One day I tried, Mr. Jerk that I am, to invite a pretty co-ed from out of town to my house for a special family occasion. Why did I forget? How did I forget? When Montenegrins have dinner on special family occasions, the women eat in the kitchen and the men eat in the dining room. "Hey, honey, you in there with the women, me in here with the men! Of course, none of them speak English. But you'll get by. They'll keep smiling these big smiles at you and pushing big slices of spinach pie in your face. By the way, don't expect their teeth to look like American teeth. And don't spill your spinach pie!" That went over like something else! She never spoke to me again. A Montenegrin and a "townie" all at once — it was too much.

I'm not boring you, am I? This bus sure is crowded.

But one day something really bad happened. Maybe it wasn't so bad, but it was bad. Well, there was this fraternity. Maybe you don't know what a fraternity is. Maybe you do. Maybe you belonged to one? Well, don't answer that.

A fraternity is a house where lots of kids crowd together in some murky basement room outfitted like a tavern or whatever and hang out all day — kind of like bats that like to hang upside down, all jammed together in a dark, drippy cave.

Now, this fraternity had all these kids who must have been kings or something because they all had "the Second" or "the Fourth" behind their names. They decided to throw a party—I think it must have been some charity idea, to have a party for people whom they would never dream of inviting to a party—people, in other words, who didn't belong to some fraternity or other or who were social misfits of some kind. People, in other words, like me.

It was a big college weekend, so they were putting themselves out to let their place be used like this. It was supposed to be a costume party. You come in some kind of crazy get-up—you know the kind of thing—pirates, ghosts, whatever.

Well, I'm up to this, and I accept the invitation. What an idiot!

I go home and tell my parents. What an even greater idiot!

And what do you think? Well, they go clear out of their minds. They'll get me into a costume like no one ever saw before. People's mouths will drop. I say "no"—I'll just go as a tramp, or something simple. I heard that everybody goes as something simple. Some of the people might not even be in costume at all—that's the rumor that was going around. But my parents won't accept that: kids at a big-deal school like this being so unimaginative!

"You just don't know them, Poppa! Being unimaginative is the name of the game. Why else do you think they tank up on so much beer?"

But, as I told you, you don't argue. I mean, not much. A musket ball right between the eyes if you argue. You get the picture? As I said, it's not always a pretty picture.

The next thing, I know I'm dragged up into the attic, and big trunks are opened up that I never knew were up there. And what's in these trunks? You got it. *Montenegrin stuff!*

The stuff is pretty musty—who knows how long it's lain there? But it's gorgeous. I mean, I've never seen such gorgeous things. It would make your Montenegrin blood dance to see such things—if you had any Montenegrin blood, and, mind you, I'm not trying to suggest that you do.

Pretty soon I'm outfitted in a get-up that makes me look like a Montenegrin warlord fresh out of his fortress on top of some great marble mountain.

And that's not all. Over a gold-embroidered coat of flaming red my father straps an immense, clanging saber, and a thin, long-barreled flintlock whose stock is inlaid with ivory and walnut and is embossed with silver and brass. Then he puts this crazy turban on my head.

I never saw such a smile on my father's face. I never saw such a smile on any man's face. And my mother—she's beside herself. She immediately goes down to the kitchen and makes some spinach pies—you know, in order to celebrate or something like that.

Well, that's just an initial test. Many other things are tried on, aired out, cleaned, mended, polished. On the day of the party, my parents work all day on the costume. By evening, I'm arrayed in something like I'm sure no college town in all of New England has ever seen or will ever see again. My mother even cuts off a lock of her own hair (her hair matches mine), which my father fashions into a huge curving mustache and affixes to me somehow with great skill.

My parents are so proud. My father even photographs me in the costume. When I look at myself in the mirror, all I can think is, "I sure wouldn't want to be someone who runs into me in the dark of the night."

Unfortunately, that's how some other people feel, too, later on.

Sixty-Seventh Street! Look at all the traffic!

Maybe I'm boring you. Maybe I should stop. Go back to the paper.

Well, well.

Hmm. Hmm.

So, you know what happens? I knew you'd be interested. I knew it when you didn't pick up the paper. Right?

Okay. I go to the party. I don't want to startle anyone, so I take a shortcut through the woods to the fraternity house. Well, that's a typical "townie" thing to do, anyway—take shortcuts through the woods. "Townies" always know everything there is to know about shortcuts through woods. Then I approach the brightly lit windows of the frat house and take a peek in.

Somehow, I suspected it, but I never believed it: there they all are, guys and girls, some solitary with hunched shoulders and haunted eyes searching for the nearest corner to squeeze into and disappear, others clustered nervously into tight little intimidated groups. Misfits all, just like me. Everyone socially paralyzed. No one having any fun. And *no one* in costume.

Then it dawns on me. The frat boys wanted to see who would be so dumb as to show up in a costume. I guess they would parade in at just the right moment and get a big laugh out of it. At least the others got that much figured out.

Well, there was one guy dressed up sort of like a clown — either that or that's the way he normally dresses. Anyway, he edges closer and closer to a door, embarrassed, as clownish as indeed he looks, waiting for an opportunity to make his escape.

I'm mad. Mad at myself. I want to draw my saber. I want to load and fire my flintlock. Actually, I couldn't. I don't have any ammunition. The ramrod is broken. And my saber is blunt.

I know I can't go home because my parents would be so disappointed. I can see them, sitting together at the kitchen table, nodding their heads, stupendous smiles on their faces, imagining me moving like the prince of the mountaineers though the admiring faces of the pale flatlanders, however titled and kingly they might be.

And here I am, a great big idiot, peering through the windows, with tears coming down my face and gradually washing away my mother's mustache — I mean, the mustache made of my mother's hair. But I stick it back on again, so that no one will recognize me.

I slip through a back door of the fraternity, just so that I can say I actually went in, grab a bottle of something or other from a table in the cocktail pantry — I think it was scotch — and go out into the orchard behind the row of frat houses. I know I can't go home for at least several hours. I climb up into an apple tree, drink that scotch, and get drunk. Then, laying myself out on a broad, flat bough, tucking my saber underneath my leg, and bracing the musket against my shoulder, I fall asleep.

Sixty-Fourth Street! The zoo! Hooray for the zoo! I like to visit the orangutans. I love them! Do you love them? You do? You don't? No opinion on the matter? Well, it's not important. I'll try to remember not to ask you again.

Orangutans are my kind of guys! Did you know that an orangutan is seven times stronger than even the strongest human being? Isn't that something! Someone told me that. You should know that, just in case you ever get it into your mind to push an orangutan around. Sometimes I even wish

I were an orangutan, though I wouldn't want to be in a zoo with all kinds of crazy people gaping at me. I mean, I wouldn't even want me looking at me.

Which brings me back, incidentally, to sleeping up in tree boughs—you know, like orangutans do. Anyway, I was asleep for a while, right up there in the tree bough. Later on, I'm awakened by some kind of quarrel going on underneath me. It's really late now, and there are these three couples directly beneath me and illuminated by an automobile's headlights aimed across the lawn and through the orchard. They're all arguing with one another. Sometimes it's the three guys against the three girls, and sometimes it's one guy and two girls against the two guys and one girl, and sometimes it breaks up into little separate arguments. Eventually, it's every combination you can imagine. Have you ever known these groups of couples that always hang around together and act like one big couple? I don't know why. I always figure one couple is enough of a problem.

So, on goes this argument. I think it's about cars or something. Who drove whose car and where and why and should they have and so on. They must have been psychology majors or something like that, because the argument is full of psychological words and accusations. I guess there are many different kinds of nuts in the world, and these people know all the names for them and how to apply them in a situation like this.

Now, one fabulously cute girl, or so it seems from where I'm perched, is wearing this really low-cut evening dress. Remember, I'm seeing this all from above, craning my neck as much as I can to get a view. Of course, now the view is rather a bit more interesting, so I crane my neck even more, and . . . I fall.

Yes, I fall.

I fall from the bough right into the middle of them. What's worse, I land upright on my feet, my mustache bristling, my saber clanging in its scabbard, and my musket following me down and, almost magically, slapping into my open palms.

There's this horrible shriek and jostling and pushing. One girl faints and falls to the ground, and two guys and two girls rush toward the nearest frat house—to get the "posse" or the "vigilantes" or something like that—while the other guy, who must have been some kind of football player, grips my neck with one hand while he bends over the fainted girl and shakes her with his other hand.

I didn't know what to do. I meant no harm. But I have to get away from there. So, twisting myself around somehow in the iron grip of that guy, I grasp the musket by its barrel and slam his gigantic crupper so hard with the flat of the walnut and ivory stock that he loses his grip on my neck. He dives down over the poor girl, and his head practically digs into the ground.

Then I see a crowd streaming out of the frat house like … like … well, just like a swarm of bats fluttering out of a cave, you know, the way they do when it gets dark. I make a quick check to see if the girl is still alive under that enormous, bulging hulk. She is. In fact, she's regained consciousness, stares at me for a second from below that colossus, and begins screaming.

Satisfied that she's okay, I take off though the woods, running like hell and holding on to the musket with my right hand and the scabbard of my saber with my left hand so it won't clatter at my side and give me away.

As I told you, I knew all the shortcuts through the woods and neighborhood backyards and was soon safely home, creeping into the cellar through a low window so that my parents wouldn't know I'd returned. I could just imagine them still sitting upstairs at the kitchen table, dreaming about what a dashing figure I was making at that party.

By the way, I have to confess that there were moments early in my escape when I thought of turning around, taking a stand, and engaging in combat, single-handedly, with the whole pack of my pursuers. It's just the sort of thing a Montenegrin mountaineer would have done, which is why, I understand, there aren't all that many Montenegrin mountaineers still left around to do it anymore. But I didn't do that. The craven townie in me prevailed over the valiant mountaineer.

I never told my parents what happened.

My father wanted to hang that photograph, immensely enlarged, of me, fully costumed, and surrounded by an enormous and ornate brass frame, in a place of honor in the grocery store where acres of six-packs are stacked ten feet high—you know, exactly the place where everyone in the college always goes and would be sure to see it.

It took a lot of work to dissuade him from that. I actually had to argue with him—not a safe thing to do, as I've told you. Anyway, it would have been curtains for me, if he'd done what he wanted to do, because talk of what happened spread throughout the campus and the frat guys were busy sniffing out the guilty culprit, whoever he should turn out to be. They never did recognize me. Luckily, I'd kept my mother's mustache on at the time. And the turban helped too.

So why do I tell you all this? Because this *is* the story of my life. I mean, my whole life has been like this. I'm not complaining or anything like that. I love my life. I love who I am. I love what I am. I love being Montenegrin, and I revere my ancestors. They were noble people. But I just have a way of always being—you know, as they say—"overdressed for the occasion." Of dropping out of nowhere into the middle of someplace or something where I should not be. Of being in the wrong place at the wrong time. Of putting myself out for something or some people I shouldn't be putting myself out for. Of talking to the wrong guy about the wrong ...

Fifty-Ninth Street! I love looking at the horse carriages with the Plaza in the background. It looks like something you might see in—well, in Montenegro. You know—a royal palace or something like that, with horse carriages in front because they don't have automobiles yet or whatever. Just kidding! But I don't really know because I've never actually been there.

Hey, where are you going? This isn't Fifty-Seventh yet. This isn't your stop. What are you doing? You forgot your paper! What's the hurry? Hey ...!

Hey!

I've done it again.

I've done it again.

Hmm.

Sure, sit down. I'll squeeze over a bit. There's plenty of room. Make yourself comfortable. Where are you getting off?

Wobbly Jane

I called her Wobbly Jane because, when she walked along the street, she wobbled. She was tall, willowy, and — yes — remarkably sure-footed, and she walked with a short, brisk stride. Still, her head and shoulders had a funny little wobble in them as she walked. It made her look — I'll admit it — just a bit goofy, but it was an attractive kind of goofiness.

She always smiled, and her eyes were always smiling, too, as if the world was never anything less, nor anything more, than an amusing to place to look at. People, even the most complete strangers, smiled back when they saw her — smiled in a kindly way, but I don't think she was ever quite aware of that. I never knew what she was aware of.

I'm not sure she was ever really aware of me — except for one occasion, and I've always thought that that one occasion lasted for all of about two seconds.

She worked as a librarian in the New York Public Library on Forty-Second Street. She had a desk tucked away in a wood-paneled little alcove on the side of one of the big reading rooms. It was lit by a small, shaded lamp. I was never sure exactly what she did, but patrons of the library approached her desk, talked quietly with her, and were sent off in one direction or another. Whatever they came for, they got. An atmosphere of warmth and trust and cheerfulness seemed to emanate from that alcove. Even a kind of awe was there: I once saw some cocky but bright-looking college boys approach that alcove and be instantly tamed, if not quite subdued, by its curious aura.

I first saw Wobbly Jane one day when I was working in the library. I was at a reading station not far from her alcove, and she was returning from her lunch break. I saw her wobbling walk and pretty face and cheerful eyes. Then day after day, and week after week, I came to do my research and, more importantly, to look at her. I was continually trying to think of things that I could ask her about, but they always seemed so trivial that I never did approach her desk about them. I was conducting a research project in chemical engineering, and I felt awkward about asking for information on that subject. I wished I were a literary type, or something to that effect; then it would have been much easier.

I didn't actually make her acquaintance until I noticed her on the street one day. I recognized her from a block away by her wobble. No one else in the world wobbled like that. She was walking up Fifth Avenue to the Schrafft's on Forty-Eighth Street. I followed her. I would later learn that this was her regular place to go for lunch. She would sit at the soda fountain and almost always have the same lunch: a toasted cheese sandwich, a pickle, and a cup of tea. Sometimes she had a turkey sandwich with lettuce and mayonnaise, but the pickle and the cup of tea never varied. The regular soda jerks seemed to know her well, but I don't think she knew them. Anyway, I followed her into the restaurant and was lucky enough to get a place next to her at the soda fountain.

When we'd been served, and she was eating her sandwich by opening it up and pulling out one piece of turkey at a time, I started up a conversation. I asked her if she was going to see the St. Patrick's Day parade that would march up Fifth Avenue the following day. She didn't seem at all surprised or taken aback at being addressed by a stranger. Perhaps she was accustomed to it by working at her desk at the library. Anyway, she replied that she was planning to see the parade and that she never missed it.

I don't remember where things went from there, but I walked back with her to the library after lunch. I think we talked about everything. She told me, from memory, all the Major League Baseball scores from the previous day. I acted as if I was surprised at some scores, and disappointed by others, but really all I cared about was that she was telling them, because I have no interest in baseball, or in any other sport, for that matter. But I figured she did. Later I would come to know that she had no interest in baseball either, or in any other sport. But she always knew the scores, and she always told them to me. I wonder if that was one of the things people approached her for at her desk in the library. She never told me much about herself, her family, where she went to college, or how she came to work at the library, but I figured she was in her late twenties, though I never really knew.

Over the several years that I knew her, I accounted myself very fortunate if I could see her perhaps once or twice a week for lunch, or sometimes for dinner—but that was rare. On occasions we would walk together in Central Park. She knew all the statues in the park and made a special point of visiting each one of them regularly as if they were old friends. Especially she enjoyed the statue of Shakespeare, the busts of Schiller and of Balzac, and the statues of Sir Walter Scott and of Alexander von Humboldt over by the Museum of Natural History. And so many others. Balto, the husky who took the serum to Nome, was another favorite.

She loved New York in all its seasons, and I came to see New York through her eyes. She loved the Christmas decorations in the store windows—especially the big colorful Santa Clauses with wonderful sleds and dazzling reindeer pulling at the harness. They were particularly good if they were mechanized so that the figures tipped back and forth slowly, but with slightly—well, wobbly—motions. She seemed to have a peculiar attitude toward Santa Claus—as if she actually knew him as a real person and found it intensely amusing to see a familiar old friend portrayed in such comical guises. She also loved to gaze at the Christmas tree at Rockefeller Center and the skaters on the rink below. Often, we watched the children visit FAO Schwarz with their parents, but that was when FAO Schwarz was on the other side of the street and much smaller and a lot less showy than it is now.

In the spring and the fall, we watched the parades together. We went to the museums together. She was an endless source of information about everything we saw, and she was enchanted by it all. But somehow, in quite another way, none of this was really there for her. She saw things—but she didn't see them—as if she looked right through them at something else. That's the way she saw me too. She looked right through me, never at me.

I loved the way she dressed. Her clothes didn't look like anybody else's clothes. When she went out on the street, she wore narrow, creased garrison caps of the sort soldiers wear, except that her caps—she seemed to have quite a few of them—were very colorful and were worn jauntily tipped to the side of her head. She must have pinned them in some way to her fluffy brunette hair, or else I don't see how they could have stayed on her head, especially with that little wobble of hers. She also wore colorful scarves that matched her caps.

The effect was remarkable. No wonder everyone noticed her. The rest of her attire was simple and didn't change at all with the tide of fashion over those years, though it always looked fresh and crisp and impeccably clean. It occurred to me only after I'd known her for a while that she made all of her own clothing, and that's why it didn't look like anybody else's. Also, she wore no jewelry and very little makeup. She did have a thin golden chain around her neck with a tiny golden cross suspended from it. I never asked her about this, and she never brought it up.

I have to confess to something awful.

I have to confess to wishing, sometimes, that some little harm would come to Wobbly Jane—nothing big, you must understand, just a little thing like an unpleasant patron at the library, or spilled tea on her blouse, or, worst of all maybe, a sprained ankle at some curbside on her walk back to the library. I wanted anything that might make her seek out some sort of help—from somebody, from anybody, but especially from me.

How I longed to be of service to her, to aid her in a moment of crisis, to lift her up if she had slipped in a puddle, to fix something in her apartment, to stand heroically between her and a potential assailant, to wrest her rights from a penny-pinching landlord, to dry her tears with a fresh Kleenex extracted ever so expeditiously from a pocket where it was being faithfully stored for no other purpose than this.

It never happened.

For all her wobble, she never tripped. She never fell. She never needed me for anything. She never needed anyone for anything. If you'd poised her on a high, narrow pinnacle and tried to lure her off with all the promises the world can give, she would never have budged or even lost her balance for a moment. That's how she was.

There was one time when she actually invited me over to her apartment for lunch. This was on a day off. I was really quite surprised by the invitation. I'd never been in her apartment before, and this was for lunch! In fact, as I approached her building, practically dancing like Gene Kelly on the street, I flattered myself by thinking that I was at a critical turning point in our friendship.

Then, when I got there and she had let me into the apartment, I discovered that she'd completely forgotten about the invitation. I sat for a while in her sitting room as she busied herself with something in another room.

Like her alcove at the library, the apartment was warm and cheerful and filled with books. There were also flowers and little statues and some fine porcelain neatly displayed on shelves. Meanwhile, she suggested that I look into the refrigerator to see if there was something we could have for lunch. In the refrigerator I saw cartons of milk and orange juice, a package of Kraft American cheese slices, a few apples, a jar of pickles, an open can of Campbell's turkey noodle soup, and a loaf of Pepperidge Farm white bread. I noted especially the loaf of bread because I didn't keep bread in a refrigerator and because it was the same brand of bread that I buy.

Also in the refrigerator were several books and a purple scarf. If this had been anybody else's refrigerator, I would have been surprised by these latter items. But, as it was her refrigerator, I was not.

The kitchen seemed to have no other food in it. We ended up going to a Floxie's on Third Avenue, the place that has the "Hamburgers with a College Education." I was still in an exuberant mood, so I ordered their specialty, the Hamburger with the Ph.D. (it's also called "Professor Burger" and has onions, bacon, and cheese on it), and she had her usual toasted cheese sandwich with a pickle and a cup of tea.

I never quite knew what Wobbly Jane did on Sundays. She had a way of disappearing. Or, at least, she didn't answer her phone and was never available for anything. I could never figure it out. She didn't seem to have any relatives, or at least anyone she ever spoke of. She didn't have friends either.

Where did she go? What did she do?

Perhaps she just vanished like some fairy princess into that world of books that surrounded her. Was there a magic king somewhere that she sought out? I could see her, like the characters we see sometimes in a movie, stepping into a page of a book and appearing on the other side in a land of enchantment. With what a funny wobble would she take that step! How I would have followed her — followed her anywhere!

One time when we were talking about something, we got on the subject of St. Louis. There was a curious confusion that ensued, when she said some things that didn't make any sense to me. She talked about going to visit St. Louis. I thought we were talking about the city of St. Louis, so I got going about the great arch and the Mississippi and whatever. Then something about a St. Michael got in there too! St. Michael? Where's that? Is there someplace called St. Michael? We never did get around to clearing up the confusion.

Only a long time afterward did I realize what the misunderstanding was all about. I'd stepped into St. Patrick's Cathedral one day to get out of the rain and found myself exploring the interior of the church. In the aisle that runs around the back of the choir and the main altar, I discovered a little side altar dedicated to St. Louis, the king of France. On one side of the altar is a statue of St. Louis; on the other side is a statue of St. Michael the Archangel.

Why did that side altar remind me of the alcove in the library? Of her apartment? Of her?

Did she come here? What did she do when she was here? Was St. Louis another one of her friends? Was this the magic king sought out by the fairy princess? But I knew in truth that she wasn't a fairy princess and that the king she sought wasn't magic. St. Louis was a friend — just a friend and that was all.

Once, and only once, in a conversation, I — how should I put it? — "declared" myself to her. Is that the expression? I told you I'm not a literary type, but if that expression seems a little awkward, it's nowhere close to being as awkward as what I actually said to her. The occasion was in a restaurant somewhere. We were sitting together at a table, so that we were facing one another. That was unusual because Wobbly Jane always preferred to sit at soda fountains. I don't remember what we were talking about, but suddenly, out of nowhere, I said the stupidest thing that, in the history of the world, any would-be courting gentleman ever said to his fair lady.

I said, "You know, I think you're a *humdinger*."

How could I have said that?

I swear to you, I'd never used that word before in my life. I've never used it since—except, of course, to tell you what happened. I don't even know where I could have gotten it or how it could have entered my vocabulary. But there it was, popping out of my verbal reservoir like the plucky head of an otter out of a silent, woodland lake. In retrospect, I figure it was just the sort of whimsical remark that Wobbly Jane could be most expected to appreciate. But I was embarrassed, instantaneously.

Wobbly Jane cocked her head just slightly like a little puppy and looked at me for about two seconds. I think it was two seconds. I think that during those two seconds she was really looking at me—that is, really seeing me for the first time and not looking through me at something else.

Despite my embarrassment, those two seconds were the best two seconds in my entire life. In fact, those two seconds were better than my entire life has been, or ever will be. Then she said something that changed the subject, and she didn't see me anymore.

When I received a job offer in Seattle, I thought that, at last, Wobbly Jane might take some serious notice of me. Certainly, she would regret that I was leaving New York, perhaps never to return. Certainly, she would protest and try to get me to change my mind. But I don't think she regretted it one bit. Instead, she congratulated me and wished me well. She never protested, and she never even hinted I should change my mind.

When I said goodbye to her on the steps of the public library, she stood on a step higher than mine, framed in my line of vision by the great sculpted lions at the portals, and good-naturedly leaned over and kissed me on the bridge of my nose.

It's the only time she ever kissed me, and it's the only time I've ever been kissed on the bridge of my nose. I've seen people kiss dogs on the bridges of their noses, and she might as well have been kissing a dog goodbye.

That was the end of it. I watched her wobble up the stairs and into the library.

She never looked back.

From Seattle I sent her Christmas cards every year. I went through a special effort to find what she might like—big colorful cards with jolly

Santa Clauses on them. I even found one on which Santa's beard was made of real cotton and stuck out from the card in a little fluff.

But I never received a card in return. I figure she probably loved the cards but just forgot to answer them. One year the card came back still in its envelope. It was stamped by the post office. It couldn't be delivered, and there was no forwarding address.

A few years later, I came to New York on a business trip. I tried to look her up, but she was gone. The alcove in the public library was occupied by someone else. The Schrafft's where she had had her lunch had been turned into a boutique for fur coats.

I even went to her apartment building and spoke to the landlord — the landlord I'd once hoped to defend her from. But he was a very nice guy. He said that one day she just left.

What about her stuff? I asked. She sold everything she had, he said, didn't take it with her, gave the proceeds of the sale to a poor family several blocks away. He had no idea where she went.

I wonder where she is now. I can't imagine her being away from her alcove in the public library, or away from Fifth Avenue, or away from New York.

Did she finally wobble off forever into one of those books of hers whose pages she turned with such delicacy and affection?

Did she find in an ivory palace somewhere a Royal Spouse, adorned with gold and anointed with frankincense and myrrh, whose mysterious and beautiful realm she was always gazing at through the appearances of this world?

I hope I'll see her again someday.

Maybe I will. I think I will. But all of this happened so long ago.

I don't think I've ever loved anybody as much as I loved Wobbly Jane.

Le Danse du Diable

Byron Langley was not the first in his affluent suburban community to discover between the pages of a glossy mail-order catalogue some strange and initially inchoate resuscitation of a long-forgotten dream. Indeed, the very merchandising principle of many such catalogues depends upon producing precisely this effect in their unwary customers. You may never have actually engaged in homesteading in Alaska, or in climbing a Himalayan peak, or in managing a tropical plantation, or in breasting the ice-cold waves of an arctic sea in your private windjammer; but you can purchase the appropriate outfit for doing so, even if it's to be worn only on a Saturday excursion to the liquor store and even if the setting is no more exotic than a comfortable and exquisitely landscaped suburb of New York City, such as that of Upper Paragon, New Jersey.

Many of Byron's neighbors had succumbed, at one time or another, to the temptation. In fact, Milton Barnaby, an eminent Wall Street lawyer who lived only three houses away from the Langleys, purchased an entire lumberjack's outfit, along with a huge double-headed axe of Paul Bunyan vintage, in order to fell a dead rhododendron bush in his backyard. Across the street from Milton Barnaby, Jonathan Birdsell purchased an Australian field jacket to go with his new Land Rover, a vehicle he needed for the presumably arduous journey over the rugged outback that separated his commodious "shack" from the local supermarket. Yet another neighbor, whose name discretion forbids us to mention, had the custom, during autumnal windstorms, of standing for long periods of time on his back "deck" dressed in a Norwegian fisherman's outfit as he scanned, with a brass telescope, little more than the brook that babbled down from his neighbors' yards and past his house, all the while sipping hot tea laced with potent naval rum from, of course, an appropriately weather-beaten tin cup.

An advantage of the so-called anonymity of suburban life, as well as of the copious leafage of trees and hedges with which we conceal our dwellings, is that we can indulge such private fantasies without too much public attention to the fact, though such attention, implicitly and finally, is the point of it all. Our neighbors may have to make quite an effort to see what we're up to, but it's important that such an effort be made and that it be, in any case, well rewarded.

In Byron's case, the long-forgotten dream was stirred by what might be described as a particularly undistinguished and, in one sense of the word at least, "modest" article of clothing to be found in the pages of L.L. Bean — a pair of red-flannel long underwear.

Byron probably had little idea of why he was so attracted to this underwear; but, after all, long-forgotten dreams are like that. The clear, imaginative, improbably detailed pictures of youth are replaced only by the longings connected originally to them. We struggle with these longings, often — though in vain — trying to define them, and even more assiduously trying to repress and restrain them, especially when they arise at some inconvenient time, such as in the middle of a business conference or while we're trying to negotiate some particularly tenuous agreement. But then again, everything in our environment perpetually urges us to give in to such impulses, to "throw off our fetters," to be outrageous, to indulge, to buy.

It all comes down to the same thing in the end.

Byron, however, did struggle with the temptation for several years. We must give him credit for that, but the insistent arrival of catalogue after catalogue, in season after season, broke down his resistance at last. He felt, finally, a devilish streak coming out in him (and how ominous is this talk of "temptation" and "devilish," considering the outcome of all of this). In any event, he said, as we all finally say when submitting to a whim, "Why not?"

Byron's wife, Midge, was consulted. She was a little surprised by his desire for this odd item of clothing but had no objections. The item was ordered.

Several weeks later, Byron came home on the evening commuter train from New York, where he pursued a mildly successful career in international investment banking. There he found, leaning against his front door, a large brown shipping envelope from L.L. Bean. He picked it up and carried it into the living room, where he laid it on the long maple coffee table. Midge arrived home a few minutes later. Byron didn't hurry to open the parcel. Instead, he waited until he'd changed into his casual wear and until both Midge and he could settle down for their cocktail hour with tall, cool high-balls propped before them on the coffee table. When all was ready and calm, he ceremoniously pried open the end of the envelope. A small plastic bag with the bright red garment tightly folded up inside it slid out onto his lap.

His initial reaction was, as one suspects it often is in these situations, one of acute disappointment. For part of a reverie has abruptly materialized with agonizing literalness, all neatly folded in an antiseptic and paltry-looking plastic bag.

Where is the rest of it? Where are the glaciers, the wind-blown sea, the banana trees sweltering in the tropical sun? Why are they not in the package too? After all, the catalogues show these things, if not always to the eyes, then at least to the spirit. Aren't they part of the bargain? Did they forget to send them along?

"Well," Byron asserted, as he was accustomed to do in such matters, "you take what you can get." That was one of his favorite expressions.

After the initial letdown, Byron removed the garment from the plastic bag and, lifting it up, allowed it to unfold before him. A long vertical row of small white buttons, contrasting sharply with the brilliant red of the flannel, secured the two sides of the garment all the way from the neckline down to the crotch. Suddenly, Midge giggled.

"What's the matter?" Byron asked, a tone of alarm in his voice.

"Look at the back! Turn it around!" she cried.

He swung the garment around and discovered a long slit in the back end, held together—demurely, you might almost be inclined to say—with a single white button. He was awestruck! This startling aperture seemed at once to galvanize for him some part of the long-forgotten dream. Obviously, this was the perfect garment to wear in the middle of the night to some remote outhouse perched precariously on the edge of a jagged cliff.

It all came to him now—or so he thought—a smoky cabin high in the Ozarks, the hound dogs, the moonshine, the hogs submerged in their own swill. How he would stun and horrify the neighbors! How jealous they would be to see him lolling about in front of his house on hot summer evenings, dirty, chewing tobacco, barefoot, with nothing on but a pair of old overalls, held up by suspenders over his red-flannel long underwear, which would soon be splotched with sweat, dust, and streaks of tobacco juice that, not successfully expectorated across the yard, had been drooled down over a crudely unshaven chin and onto his chest. Even Milton Barnaby would be thoroughly abashed, his lumberjack duds ignominiously reduced to the status of slick professional wear.

Byron let out a whoop—what he presumed to be, no doubt, some version of a rebel yell—downed his highball in one great gulp and lunged from the couch into the bedroom to try on his new underwear. Meanwhile, Midge sat nervously in her chair and listened to Byron's voice expostulating on his newfound role in life.

Suddenly there was a long, studied silence. Not a motion, not a sound from the bedroom! Then, just as suddenly, Byron appeared in the doorway.

Midge shrieked. His tall, angular body, frozen into a contorted posture that resembled a Picasso *saltimbanque*, straddled the doorway in its blazing red, skin-tight outfit. His eyes had the look of wild astonishment in them, and his mouth was held tautly open as if he were in the throes of some monumental decision. The decision, whatever it was, was made. With a single grandiose movement of arms and legs, he bounded into the center of the room, almost hitting his head on the ceiling, and came to a perfect rest in a *demi-plié*.

"Byron!" Midge screamed. "You look like . . ."

"I know! I know!" he declaimed. All thoughts of outhouses, hound dogs, and little brown jugs had been instantly banished from his mind.

"I'm the Devil!" he shouted. "I'm the red Devil, come to accuse the world of its sins!"

At this juncture, you might be impelled to inquire about the long-forgotten dream. Did it all have its origins in the frustration of a little boy who didn't get the costume he wanted on some teary-eyed Halloween of yore? Such a conjecture might well be reasonable, except that the sporting of this marvelous devil apparel quickly assumed dimensions inexplicable by such a simple hypothesis.

For Byron, after his dramatic leap into the center of the living room, proceeded to engage in a very bizarre sort of dance. It resembled initially an odd combination of ballet, kickboxing, and mime. He glided across the living room into the dining room and back, his arms and legs flailing in every direction. Now and then he would shake his fists, parrying and jabbing like a boxer.

At last, he broke into a whirling Russian folk dance, kicking his legs out and shouting, "I accuse. I accuse. I am *diabolus*. I am the adversary. I am the Devil who accuses the world. *J'accuse. J'accuse.*"

With that, his leg hooked by mistake around the leg of the coffee table, throwing it over, breaking the highball glasses, and pitching him over the couch where he landed in the narrow space between the picture window and the couch. Midge jumped from her chair and ran to the couch. She saw him reclining there, flat on his back, with a huge, if fatuous, smile on his face.

"How do you like it?" he asked.

"Like what?" she asked in return.

"My dance. My Dance of the Devil."

"Well ..."

"I'll call it, *Le Danse du Diable*. Sounds classier in French."

"Why not *El Danza del Diablo*?" she suggested with a laugh. "Sounds more ferocious, more intense ..."

"And like some kind of tequila drink with hot peppers in it," he replied quite seriously.

"Or how about *Der Tanz des Teufels*? You know — Faustian, Walpurgisnacht, and all that."

"Too Teutonic. Too Wagnerian. Not for me."

"Then *Le Danse du Diable* it is. Now let's have dinner and forget about it as soon as possible. I'll have to clean up these broken glasses, since I assume you're in too distracted a state to do it yourself."

Midge went to get a broom to sweep up the broken glass while Byron still lay behind the couch, wrapped in deep thought. When she finished, he was still there. She urged him to get dressed for dinner, but he didn't seem to hear.

As she went into the kitchen, she kept thinking about the chaotic dance she'd just witnessed. Of course, you could regard it as a kind of a travesty, a grotesque mimicry, a satire on dance; she'd seen Byron do this kind of thing before, but never with the energy and persistence he'd just exhibited.

Midge had trained as a dancer in her girlhood and had kept up a lively interest in it ever since, though she prided herself on her ability to keep a critical distance from the fads and obsessions that, in her view, so dominated and diminished the seriousness of the dance world.

Byron, on the other hand, never professed anything but a deep contempt for dance as an art, never lost an opportunity to ridicule it, or to assume, at the oddest moments and in the oddest places, some hideous and contorted variation of a conventional dance move. Midge always felt that he did this at times to amuse her and at other times to tease her about her abiding interest in various dance styles. But now, for the first time, he'd executed an entire dance routine before her eyes.

As improvised and absurd as it was, Midge was nevertheless deeply troubled by it. For in the process of the dance and between bouts of the most frantic whirling of arms and legs, Byron again and again, for only split seconds at a time, executed moves that only a professional dancer would know how to do. Further, even in the wildest of gestures, he always seemed to have an almost perfect control over his movement and an innate sense of how to blend one movement into the following one, no matter how incongruent the subsequent movement happened to be.

Well, there was an explanation after all. At the Upper Paragon Racket Club, Byron was rather well known for his ability to do imitations. He did imitations of how fellow club members walked, how they lifted a glass of beer, how they got in and out of cars, and how they played tennis. Nor did he need to devote much study to their movements prior to the convincing imitations he could render of them; some brief observation was sufficient to enable him to do it naturally and spontaneously.

He also did the most astonishing imitations of animals — of elephants eating foliage with their trunks, of moths beating around light bulbs, of dogs throwing up, of cats licking their paws, of daddy longlegs slowly picking their way over a garden fence, of cobras coiling upward out of some basket to the tune of a reedy pipe. His hilarious and most popular imitation was that of a matador locked in mortal combat with a raging bull wherein he mimicked both the movements of the matador and the movements of the bull *simultaneously.*

Anything that moved he could imitate; it made sense, then, didn't it, that he could imitate, with startling grace and demeanor, the positions of classical ballet, as well as the gestures and modes of other dance styles?

The crowd that had watched him in the bar of the Racket Club found his antics to be the most wonderful entertainment. His mimicry of flamenco and the tango had his audience practically hurting with laughter. He could imitate the tap dancing of Fred Astaire, the leaps of Gene Kelly, and the gyrations of Elvis Presley.

Midge, naturally, found most of this to be rather embarrassing for her; nevertheless, she was frequently just as surprised and amused as the rest of the audience by what Byron could do, and there never seemed to be an end to what he could do.

She only regretted that his contempt for dancing prevented him from engaging in any ballroom dancing with her. She loved ballroom dancing, and the only time she'd ever danced with him was at their wedding, where social propriety and an insistent, even if brand new, mother-in-law had forced him into it. But, to her surprise, he knew the dances and executed them with a perfection she'd never experienced in a partner before.

She also regretted that she had to seek out her old friends in the dance world to accompany her to the performances in New York that she so treasured and delighted in. Her teacher, Madame Schernovsky, had retired recently from her studio in New York to an adjoining township, and Midge enjoyed staying in touch with her and renewing her enthusiasm for the dance through sharing her occasional companionship.

She'd succeeded only once in compelling Byron to attend a dance performance — and that with the promise of a good restaurant that she'd discovered near the theater. He'd been restless throughout the performance, shifting in his seat and shielding his eyes in the most brazen way so that he could not see the stage. He even was the source of some mortification when, at one point during the performance, he burst out loudly, "They don't know what they're doing!" The people in the surrounding seats turned to glare angrily at him, while Midge hid her face in her hands.

The problem was: she'd already, at that point, realized that the dance company was a sham, and the performance was incompetent. Byron, for reasons that utterly defied any explanation, had been right in his judgment.

So much for *Le Danse du Diable*, she thought. It's come and gone, like all the rest.

Perhaps it had something to do with her. Perhaps some malevolent spirit really had entered into Byron under the guise of that long red underwear to accuse not the world but her of insufficiently dedicating herself to an object of artistic devotion, of having prematurely abandoned a demanding and uncompromising vocation.

Dance, in its demonic mode, had arisen to reproach her through the antics of her husband. She decided to put aside these questions and ponder them no further.

But *Le Danse du Diable* didn't go away.

On the following day, at the time of the cocktail hour, a reinvigorated Byron donned his red-flannel underwear once again and flailed across the living room floor, kicking and jabbing, stabbing and bolting, swirling and flaring. This time he had pushed aside any potential obstacles to the dance, such as the coffee table. Once again, the dance was accompanied by sporadic outbursts of accusations leveled against just about everything in the world.

Midge watched this spectacle from the safe distance of the door leading into the kitchen. She held a highball in her hands and sipped from it. She noted a new set of variations introduced into the dance that seemed to have some relationship with oriental martial arts, including karate, tai chi, and samurai swordplay.

She decided to play the role of critic and declared that the chops and swings didn't match well with the Russian folk-dance motifs that were occasionally resumed. Without ceasing to dance, Byron shouted back that her remark was "insensitive" and "philistine" and that he was trying to create a "disturbing, disjointed" image that would cause people to "rethink their lives and values."

Midge laughed; yet she was slightly shaken by this mention of "people." Was someone actually supposed to look, someday, at this?

After a few more whirls around the room, Byron shouted again, "I'm synthesizing Eastern and Western Man in my dance! I'm creating a universal language!"

Midge shouted back, "Don't forget about Ancient Man and Renaissance Man, and Neanderthal Man and New Jersey Man and Peking Man! Or was it Peking duck?"

Byron was undaunted by this challenge. "Don't worry! I'll get to all of those in time."

On the third day, Midge was startled by yet another set of innovations. Byron took up a number of very odd positions, puffed out his cheeks, rolled his eyes, and rocked his head back and forth on his neck. He pounced backward and forward, flapping his arms and slapping his bare feet against the floor. His fingers moved rapidly through dozens of complex formations as he danced.

"Hindu temple dancing!" Midge thought. "Or at least some preposterous version of it! How would he know how to do that?"

She called out through the kitchen door, "Indra fights the great dragon, Vrtra! The monsoon rains are coming!"

Byron stopped short. "Not at all!" he shouted back, after a hesitation. "I am Shiva, god of destruction. I stamp down the demons of the underworld. In my cosmic dance, I contend with the powers of darkness."

"I thought you were a demon, the Demon King himself, the Erlkönig, the power of darkness personified."

"So I am. So I am. I dwell in paradox and ambiguity!"

"The ironic Mephistopheles!"

"Whatever!"

He resumed his dance, waving his arms so quickly through so many gestures and positions, his fingers and palms twisting into a rapid succession of precise "mudras," that it looked as if he had, indeed, six arms like the god Shiva himself.

Then he began to point wildly in one direction after another while shouting, "I accuse you, and you, and you, and you, and you!"

He stopped again.

"Midge," he cried, "what can I do in this dance that would really offend an audience, really bring home its complicity in socio-, politico-, cosmological evil?"

The mention of an audience was a bit disconcerting; but she answered, "I do have a suggestion, but you may not like it."

"I'm open to all suggestions."

"You know that opening in the posterior of your costume?"

"Yeah."

"Well, at the climactic point of the dance, you just turn your back to the audience and ..."

"Midge! You're not being serious about this at all!"

"Is anyone being serious about anything?"

"I'm no longer open to suggestions."

The dance now shifted to something like an Australian aboriginal shuffle, filled with abrupt stops, a frozen position held for a few seconds, and, just as abruptly, a resumption of jagged, up-and-down movements, as if Byron had an imaginary spear in his hand and was shaking it at some recalcitrant kangaroo in the bush somewhere.

Midge retreated to the kitchen. She'd come to detest *Le Dance du Diable* and to regard it as something distinctly—well, diabolical.

Two months after the arrival of the accursed parcel, the dance had, as the expression goes, "taken over their lives." It was always the first thing that Byron did when he arrived home from work. He danced his silent, savage dance until he was exhausted. Eventually, he took up the dance on weekends as well, spending much of Saturday morning engaged in his—as he claimed—"perfecting" of it. Only on Sunday did he consider it appropriate to desist, perhaps out of some deeply residual, if subconscious, respect for the Sabbath.

Midge could no longer stand to watch or even be close to it. She found somewhere in the house, or out of the house, to be away during its daily performance. She no longer noticed the almost infinite permutations it passed through, though she did become aware that it transformed gradually into a quieter dance with less thumping and banging in its process. Meanwhile, Byron was neglecting his lawn and garden work and had given up playing tennis at the Racket Club.

Midge finally decided to take action. One evening at dinner, while Byron was ravenously slurping up his cream of artichoke soup, Midge calmly inquired, "Byron, don't you think it's time to give a performance of your work?"

"H'mm," he answered without looking up from his soup. "I perform it almost every day."

"Yes, but I mean a public performance—before a real audience. You don't want to go around accusing imaginary people. You need to accuse real people."

"I'm not ready for that yet. The dance must be perfected."

Midge stirred her soup for a moment. She said, "Well, Byron, I understand why you think that. Every true *artiste* strives for perfection. But I wonder if an *artiste* can truly perfect something without some exposure to a public. That's a way of finding out, sometimes, if an *oeuvre* is working or not."

"Sometimes!" Byron replied, looking up from his soup. "That's the catch. You can't trust an audience. Audiences mostly have the standards that someone else tells them to have."

"Perhaps. But an art needs a public resonance of some sort." Midge responded. Then she added, somewhat dramatically, "If it's pursued purely in private, it will ultimately turn in on itself and wither and die. *You wouldn't want that to happen, would you?*"

Byron eyed Midge suspiciously. He looked down at his soup and scooped out an artichoke leaf with his spoon. "There's a spike on the end of this leaf," he said. "It could catch in my throat, couldn't it? A person could very well choke and die on it, couldn't he?"

Midge continued. "Actually, Byron, I've made an arrangement—nothing too ambitious, you understand ..."

"An arrangement! What arrangement?" He pushed aside his soup with the potentially deadly leaf left floating on its surface.

"For a performance—you know, at the annual Racket Club Talent Night next month."

"What?" Bryon rose out of his seat, his mouth open, his eyes bulging. Midge was glad he wasn't wearing his devil outfit at the moment. The eyes of the Accuser were supremely accusatory.

"The Racket Club Talent Night? *Le Danse du Diable* at the Racket Club Talent Night? Are you crazy?"

"Byron, it's already on the program. It will be wonderful!"

"Midge, this is serious work I'm doing. Am I going to be sandwiched in between Bee Bee Hagen's rendition of the Nocturne in E-Flat and Kim Dougherty's slides of India?"

"Bee Bee does a very nice Nocturne in E-Flat. After all, it's the only piece of music she knows."

"She always messes up the trill at the end. And as for Kim Dougherty—why does she think that hideous photographs of Bombay prostitutes are somehow artistic, just because ..."

"They're 'socially relevant,' my dear. She trying to accuse us of something with them, thinks they make us feel somehow responsible—the same thing that you're trying to do."

"Not quite, actually."

"Anyway, she's back in India right now."

"Photographing more prostitutes, in Calcutta maybe ...?"

"She won't be on the program. In fact, yours will be the last performance, the highlight of the evening, so to speak. It's all very exciting, don't you think?"

"This is absurd, Midge, out of the question! I won't do it."

Byron sat down again and glared at Midge from across the table. "Besides, what sort of audience would that be? It's the very heart and soul of consumer society. New Jersey Man is Consumer Man."

"Just the audience you're trying to reach!" Midge retorted. "You take what you can get, as you would say. If your message isn't effective here, it won't be effective anywhere."

"But they'll hate it!"

"Isn't that what you want—for them to hate it?"

Byron's eyes brightened at the suggestion. "I could really give them hell, couldn't I?"

"You certainly could. Your choice of words is most apposite, in more ways than one."

"It will be *Le Sacre du Printemps* all over again. A riot. A storm of protest. I could make them feel really guilty."

"Yes, and they'll love how guilty you make them feel."

"But then they won't hate me."

"They'll hate you because they'll hate themselves for loving to feel guilty, and that will make them feel even more guilty, and then they'll blame you for making them do something they love to do."

"That doesn't make any sense. I won't do it." Byron fell into a resentful silence.

Midge had one final ploy left. "Byron, do you know what I think you need?"

"What?"

"A grant."

"A grant?" he repeated. The word had a certain ring to it.

"That's what I said—a grant. What *artiste* these days is without a grant? And conversely, without a grant, how can you be an *artiste*? You see my point, don't you?"

"I suppose so, though the purpose of these grants seems to be to ensure that any art form is as bad as it can possibly be."

"That may be true. But in any case, to get a grant, you need some kind of performance record. And you know that everybody has to start somewhere. The Racket Club is as good a place as any. After all, these people, despite whatever shortcomings they may have, are the support of the arts in our time, the patrons of the modern age. Look at all the paintings they lavish all that money on in New York galleries! Their toleration for the ugly is limitless."

She winked as she said this, but Byron missed the innuendo.

"Okay," he said. "I'll do it. But there's a problem with the costume. I can't simply go out on the stage with a pair of long underwear on, especially with that opening in the back."

"Don't worry. By the time we're finished working on the costume, no one will recognize it as a pair of ornery long johns fresh in from Dogpatch. We'll sew up the back, add some lace cuffs to the collar and to the sleeves, and . . ."

"Yes, and I can cover my face with some kind of red paint with a black stripe coming down over my forehead, nose, and chin, giving me a kind a 'divided' look." Byron leapt from his chair and assumed a series of his official "marionette" poses, his arms and legs lifting and falling in weirdly contorted gestures, as if pulled by strings, and his head bobbing mechanically up and down.

"And your hair can be spiked up into horns …"

"Well, we'll have to think about that."

"And music? How about Tartini—you know, 'The Devil's Sonata?'"

"I don't think I recall that."

"Or Stravinsky—'The Triumph of the Devil' from *L'Histoire du Soldat?*"

"Too fast. Too noisy. Too much drumming."

"As if you know the piece! Nobody knows it!"

"I do! Only too well. 'The Devil's Dance' in it is more subdued."

"I guess you do know it!"

"But I don't care for that either. No music anyway. I require silence." Byron waggled his head raffishly while twirling about, stooping, and twirling about again.

"You would have made a great Petrushka," Midge exclaimed.

"I did, apparently."

"You did? You did what?"

"There are those who said I did make a great Petrushka," Byron shouted back as he whirled once more. "Just not great enough for … for me."

"What are you talking about? You're really crazy! How do you come up with such complete nonsense? I can't believe a word you say," she laughed.

Byron sat down at the table again, and they finished their meal. Midge was satisfied with the plans. But she knew the risk she was taking. An unusually large audience would probably flock to the Talent Show to see Byron. They would expect his performance to be—and understand it as—an immensely funny satire on avant-garde dancing. They would laugh throughout the dance and perhaps even shout and make jokes.

She was still not certain what was going on in Byron's mind about the dance; she continued to suspect that the dance was some kind of enormous ruse calculated to result in precisely the hilarious outcome it would have on the evening of the Talent Show. It wasn't inconceivable for Byron to think up and carry out just such a practical joke on her and on everybody else in the community.

She could just see him, at the end of the dance, assuming some Dying Pierrot gesture with a silly smile on his face and his arms twisted grotesquely around his neck as the audience roared with laughter and the curtain dropped ridiculously, calamitously, on top of his head.

And yet there was something else involved that she couldn't understand. Much of Byron's life was a mystery to her. He never spoke about his college years. She'd no idea what he had studied or what had done. It was as if he were hiding something from himself, as well as from her.

After college he spent three or four years abroad, in France mainly. She always assumed that he'd studied international finance there or had worked for some multinational organization in Paris or Strasbourg or Brussels, though a recent vacation in Paris had revealed his rather deep intimacy with that city.

But he never discussed those years either, though his fluency in several foreign languages had helped him to land a reasonably good job with the international division of an investment bank on Wall Street. Curiously, however, he never expressed any interest in his job; he just did it.

The only thing he ever seemed to enjoy was … to put it simply, to move. Just to move — like a cat walking along a picket fence, like a swallow darting through the evening air, like a cheetah, lithe and lean and swift, gliding and swerving across the African veldt. To watch Byron play tennis was a source of wonderment for anyone who happened to be a witness of it. Unfortunately, though, he couldn't hit the ball.

And now there was this dreadful, chaotic dance. Midge didn't know what to make of it.

Byron intensified his efforts at developing the dance, especially in the final weeks before the performance, when he took his annual vacation solely for this purpose, destroying Midge's plans for a tour of Austria. But she was willing to make this sacrifice. She was convinced somehow that one performance would be sufficient to bring *Le Danse du Diable* to its predestined and certainly cataclysmic finale. She thought of Berlioz's *Damnation of Faust* and the hectic ride of its doomed protagonist through the belching, sulfurous, cacophonous grottos of Hell.

The performance was scheduled for an evening in late June. The stage at one end of the ballroom at the Racket Club was ideal for performances of various kinds and was often rented out for children's piano and dance recitals, as well as for occasional professional and amateur groups, such as jazz bands, string quartets, choral societies, and the local Gilbert and Sullivan Association, which used the facility for its annual operatic fête.

As Midge had anticipated, the Talent Show drew an unusually large audience. Word had gotten around. Who would want to miss seeing Byron Langley in a full-scale travesty of modern dance? It was a fine, warm evening, and the audience was in a buoyant mood; its only challenge would be to survive most of the performances that would precede the notorious *Le Danse du Diable*, which, even though yet unseen, had a reputation that had burgeoned beyond all bounds in the imaginations of its prospective audience.

Even Madame Schernovsky showed up, much to Midge's mortification. She motioned to Midge as she entered the ballroom. "I hear your husband is just too amusing," she said. "I look forward so much to seeing him." She went off to her seat with a little backward wave and a chuckle.

The sequence of acts proceeded with the usual results. A slightly bored, restless, inattentive audience managed, more or less, to suffer through the various performances, though there were bright spots, such as the country music trio of the Emory sisters, all corporation lawyers, who sang and hooted through a number of Nashville pieces while swirling their fluffy orange skirts; the magic show of Ruddy Lindstrom—invariably delightful for all its mistakes, including Ruddy's having to chase his rabbit up the center aisle of the ballroom while the audience both jeered and cheered him on; and Dick Oleander, who did a seriously fine Cajun banjo routine. Bee Bee Hagen played her usual Nocturne in E-Flat, sighing, rolling her eyes, and swaying her body as if wafted away in some ethereal ecstasy. She messed up the long trill at the end, as everyone could predict she would. The audience now braced itself for the event of the evening—*Le Danse du Diable*!

Midge had worked assiduously on the costume and, on the evening of the performance, helped Byron with his red and black makeup. His hair was left natural. When everything was in place—Byron standing ready behind the curtain and the lights ready to flash on as the curtain opened—Midge exited the stage area from the back door and fled across the lawn to the clubhouse tavern. It was closed. She remembered then that it was always closed during the Talent Show to keep people from sneaking out during the performances for surreptitious drinks.

She sat on the steps and decided to wait out the horror that was about to ensue. She could imagine Byron there on the stage, the bright lights aimed on him, the red underwear with the lacy cuffs, the wild pointing and gesticulating he would do.

Sure, he might be funny, and yet it was all so awful anyway. She suffered for him, and she suffered for herself. She wished, for once in her life, that she smoked cigarettes, for that seemed the appropriate thing to do in situations like this. She also wished she could disappear for a while, vanish into a fairy forest, be out in the middle of some vast sandy steppe dining voraciously on locusts and honey, be secluded away in a shed built atop a giant baobab tree in Tanzania with baboons clustered on neighboring boughs and screeching their hearts out . . .

A roar of laughter ripped through the ballroom. The curtain must have opened! Midge wanted to run away. "Run," she thought. "Run, Midge, run." There was more laughter a few seconds later, though now not quite so loud.

Midge got up to run. She would run out to the tennis courts. There she would be safe from all the humiliation. A bit more laughter — though now hesitant and nervous. Several seconds later a single loud guffaw echoed from the ballroom and was cut short by its own guffawer.

Silence.

Absolute silence.

Deathly, still, stony silence.

Midge was still, too, listening to the silence, although images of running still flooded her head. She saw herself running down a wet Parisian street in the depths of the night, fog curling through the dark alleyways and around the lamp posts, running, running, to a bridge over the Seine, where underneath its arches the black foamy waters eddied and swirled, the dark Parisian night, Paris, the silence . . . !

The silence.

Suddenly something in her screamed: "He was a dancer once! He was a professional dancer! That's what he was doing when he lived in Paris! How did I fail to see that all these years?"

Just as suddenly, she wanted to see what everybody was so silent about. Instead of running away, she ran to the entrance of the ballroom and slipped into the rear of the audience.

The audience was spellbound. It was locked in a breathless panoply of crooked necks, torsos bent forward, tilted heads with mouths open, and eyes hypnotized by the spectacle in front of it. The angular figure on stage, glaring red in the stage lights, looked twice as big as life. Midge could hardly believe it was Byron.

He moved slowly, rhythmically, through a set of modulated gestures, every limb and sinew blending together in a perfect synthesis of bodily form, a kind of sculpture in kinesis, fascinating in every detail of slant, dimension, and control, confinement and freedom, rhythm gathering into architecture and resolving back into rhythm again.

Midge was astonished. She'd never seen anything like this before. He was doing things, combining movements in a way and with a complexity that she'd never envisaged was possible. Every movement flowed with perfect necessity and yet with utter unpredictability from its preceding movement, drawing out and perpetuating the quintessence of its form while transmuting it into something fresh and startling.

And there was no sign, no hint, that he even thought of an audience in front of him, no crazy posturing, no accusations, no message to be delivered. It was just pure design exquisitely internalized, exquisitely folded in on itself like the play of refractions in a lucid gemstone as it's turned around in the light of the sun.

Too soon it was over. She'd missed most of it. The curtain dropped as he assumed a final pose.

After a short period of dead stillness, the audience seemed to awaken from a trance, and a genteel, subdued applause passed through it. The curtain didn't come up for a bow, and the audience slowly began to rise, look around at one another, faces bewildered and mystified, and file out in silence, not talking or laughing or having much to say to one another. There was no rush to the tavern, which was just opening its doors; the people went to their cars and drove home.

Midge was at the back of the ballroom and, as friends and neighbors passed her, pushing through the exit, they looked strangely at her.

Bee Bee Hagen went up to her and took hold of her hands. There were tears in her eyes. "I'm so embarrassed," she whispered. "I'll never play my Nocturne again. After that, how could anyone do anything again?"

The once and future Norwegian sea captain, whose name we dare not mention, stopped by her, looked her in the eye, and said, "I've never seen anything so beautiful, not even a narwhale arcing through the icy floes of an arctic sea." This was high praise from a man who had never been anywhere close to an arctic sea.

Dick Oleander, carrying his banjo case, commented, "You should have told us. It was remarkable. It was more than that—it was great."

Midge cringed when she was approached by Madame Schernovsky, who looked hard and puzzled at Midge. "How long have you known about this?" she asked.

"Known about what? I don't know what you mean," Midge responded.

Madame Schernovsky shook her head. "I've never seen anything like it. Give me a call in the morning. We must—*we must*—talk." She walked off to her car.

The usual socializing and banter that followed Talent Show was neglected. The tavern opened and then closed shortly afterward because no customers came.

Midge found herself alone. She turned and worked her way back through the remaining crowd in the ballroom and up to the stage, where the curtain was still closed. She groped for the center of the curtain and pushed her way through.

Byron was sitting cross-legged on the floor, his head bent, his hands in his lap, the stage lights still illuminating with sharp intensity his bright-red costume, which was now darkened by large, round stains of sweat. Long streams of sweat from his hair and brow had run little crevasses through the red and black greasepaint on his face. He seemed to be so exhausted that he could not move.

Midge came up to him and knelt down beside him. "Byron, do you realize what you have done?"

He didn't reply. He sat as if in a trance, looking straight before him. Finally, he said, "Yes, I know. It was awful."

"Awful? Byron, it was great! The audience was stunned by it, reduced to gaping idiots by it. You took them out of themselves. But it's more than that. Byron, you've made a revolution. It's like the invention of polyphony, like the discovery of the triadic chord; nothing will be the same again."

"It was awful, that's all."

"Byron, I tell you this was a moment in dance history, a …"

"Midge, did we throw out that catalogue from the place in Seattle?"

"What? What are you talking about?"

"You know, the catalogue from the Yukon outfitters. I thought I could pan for gold in the brook that runs past our backyard. They have all the stuff you need …"

"But *Le Danse du Diable*!"

"I won't need these anymore," Byron proclaimed as he stirred into action and ripped the white cuffs off his sleeves. "My red-flannel underwear will be perfect for a 'forty-niner' *redivivus*!"

"Byron," Midge shouted. She jumped to her feet, pursed her lips, and raised her fists in a militant gesture, suggestive of old Soviet posters. "Down with global evil! Don't give up the ship! Damn the torpedoes! Don't tread on me and all that! *Le Danse du Diable* will change the world! With a few refinements, it will create riots in every capital city in the world! There's no end to whom we can accuse! The new order is coming!"

"I'll need a floppy, wide-brimmed hat and some high boots."

"Down with consumer society!"

"Quit it, Midge. You know as well as I do that dancing has nothing to do with all that nonsense. I've no one to accuse—except myself."

Byron, now refreshed and his spirits lifted, sprang nimbly to his feet. His face twisted into the sharp-eyed leer of a Hollywood actor impersonating the archetypical ruthless business tycoon about ready to close an unscrupulous deal. "Midge, you and I are going to make a million. Panning for gold is just the beginning."

"But *Le Danse du Diable*!"

"Just wait and see all the stuff we're going to consume." Byron glided off the stage and into a back room to change.

"*Le Danse du Diable*," Midge wailed.

The following morning, Midge waited to make her call to Madame Schernovsky until after breakfast, when Byron had gone out to the yard. As she dialed the number, she noticed Byron pacing back and forth on the lawn and occasionally going over to the brook at the far end of the yard, as if studying it for some obscure purpose. Madame Schernovsky answered her phone but didn't have a chance to say much until after Midge had impetuously summarized the events of the past few months, including the post-dance denouement. When Midge finished, Madame Schernovsky was silent. Midge could hear her carefully measured breathing over the phone.

Finally, she spoke. "About the professional training, of course—that we can find out easily enough, if he hasn't, for some reason, changed his name. I doubt that he has. It's quite inconceivable that there would not be people who would remember him—remember him perhaps as the most extraordinary dancer they had ever encountered—and who would not, even to this day, feel about him as I feel now—an unspeakable sadness. I could almost die with the sadness I feel. And yes, I do remember some curious gossip that once wafted through the downtown studios and lofts where we worked—it was so long ago. Just a mention ... just a hint. A great Petrushka, it was said ... discovered in Europe ... Someone whose name no one seemed to know ... Forgotten about soon enough."

"Madame Schernovsky, I just don't understand what you're saying, I don't ..."

"Ah, my dear, I've seen this kind of thing perhaps only once or twice before in dancing. I've heard of it in the other arts as well, and I imagine it happens in everything that humans do. So often we're under the illusion that when there's a person endowed with a great intelligence for some activity, an innate sensibility beyond anything most of us can imagine, it will express itself naturally and irresistibly. But nothing could be further from the truth.

"I suppose there may be a hundred reasons why such an intelligence fails to flourish as it should, but the saddest of all is this: in some people, its penetration of an activity is so prodigious and so complex that it paralyzes the person's ability to pursue the activity. Where we ordinary mortals see moderate success at least, even sometimes great success, such people see only devastating failure, in themselves and others. Where we're willing to abide, to be patient with, to a greater or lesser extent, all the mediocrity, the sham, the pretentiousness that goes on in any art, they are not; they're simply too embarrassed, too disgraced, too ashamed by it.

"I think this is the case with your husband. Such people become exiles; exiles from the art, exiles from themselves. It's a deeply tragic thing. And the loss to the art itself is beyond all calculation. I wonder if I've ever seen, except among a few of the greatest *artistes*, a genius for bodily movement such as your husband has, as trained or untrained as it may be. He's a 'natural'—and you know well enough, Midge, how guardedly I use an expression like that, as committed as I am to the discipline of training. But that's not all; what we saw last night was simply extraordinary. There was a whole new definition of dance there."

"The audience was mesmerized by his performance," Midge protested.

"As it should have been," Madame Schernovsky replied. "It will probably not see its like again. Audiences often have an intuitive sense for what is good, and sometimes they recognize it when they see it. The problem is that they have also been conditioned to distrust their own perceptions, to submit to the opinions of cultural mandarins and to accept bad things as good. That's the problem. In the last analysis, however they may respond to a work in the immediacy of the situation, they can't put that response together with a larger, a more total picture.

"People like your husband know how arbitrary it all is, because for such people, none of it is arbitrary at all. They understand what is involved. They grasp the foundations of it, the essence that pulls it all together. You said that, originally, he wanted the audience to hate him; but, in reality, it's the audience that he hates—hating it for its fickleness, its lack of steady discrimination. Even more, he hates the dance world for having made it that way. He also hates himself because he cannot do what he thinks he should be able to do and gives it up in frustration. He cannot live up to his own standards."

"And this stuff about accusing the world, consumer culture, all the rest?"

"It's not at all unusual for someone like your husband to express himself in the most ridiculous and irrelevant fashion about something at one level that he really only understands at another level, that is, in terms of the practice of it. If there was any 'statement' in that dance at all initially, it was directed at the world of dance itself. That was the object of accusation. And all that clowning, that irony, that preposterous rhetoric—are these not signs of his own alienation from what he loves best?

"But statement or no statement, he created an artistically beautiful dance of unbelievable richness, and that's all that matters; and under all that silly chatter he knows that that's all that matters—which is the core and heart of his tragedy. In the final analysis, he sees through the rhetoric of art with remorseless accuracy, even as he can mimic it with remorseless invective. I know that I'm saying very direct things to you, Midge, and perhaps you don't want to hear them, but it's my own sorrow that urges me. I love my art and grieve for anything that fails to make it as good a thing as it can be. I know it's difficult, ultimately, to conjecture a thing like this, but the world may have lost, in him, one of the greatest dancers in its history."

"Then you think there's nothing we can do, nothing that can salvage the situation."

"Nothing. Nothing at all that I know of. Genius, Midge—even the most extraordinary sort of genius, such as I'm convinced your husband has—is one thing; quite another thing is the motivation and confidence and will-power and circumstances efficacious to make that genius flower as it should."

After Midge had hung up the telephone, she watched Byron out in the yard as he continued to study the course of the brook. He seemed to be making plans for the gold-panning operation. Then he backed up from the brook, braced himself, and began to run toward it. "He's going to jump across the brook!" Midge gasped.

As he approached the edge of the brook, he rose from the ground in a perfect *saut de chat*, his arms outstretched, his head tilted back, one leg curved beneath him as he sailed in a tall arc above the glistening waters, and landed, gracefully, flawlessly, on the bank beyond, where he stood for a moment, his arms curved down by his waist and face bent backward, radiant and serene in the glow of the morning sun.

He turned to study the brook momentarily and then as quickly lost interest. Once again, he backed up several yards and ran toward the brook. Halfway across the brook, suspended almost, as it were, in midair, he executed a triple pirouette and descended lithely on the other side on a single leg, his other leg and one arm extended together in a perfect symmetrical curve.

It was a perfect finale, a perfect finishing touch, Midge thought to herself. She laughed. Could it really be any better than this?

"You take what you can get," she said to herself, and she was content.

Poet-in-Residence

In a dark corner of the college tavern, the poet-in-residence sat on a stool at the far end of the bar, stroking the cold, damp sides of a glass of beer with his left hand and drawing deep inhalations from the cigarette clutched in his right hand. His ashtray was filled with dozens of cigarette butts. His hands were long, bony claws. His thin, tall body, his small, balding head, his flat, deeply ridged forehead and stooped back gave him the appearance of a serpent coiled in the shadowy aperture of a cliff. Narrow reptilian eyes, deeply set in a pinched, sallow face, squinted steadily in front of him at a fish tank mounted on a shelf over the bar.

In the tank, several small fish undulated through the pale-yellow light of the water and in and out of the windows of a miniature sunken ship. Next to the ship was a treasure chest spilled open to reveal a mound of tiny golden coins, and leaning against the chest was the skeleton of a drowned pirate still garbed in its pirate clothes as its plastic skull jerked up and down in rhythm with the bubbles that periodically squirted out from a little hose behind its neck.

The poet exhaled his cigarette smoke as he watched the tiny skull lifting and falling, its slack jaw opening and closing at the same time; occasionally, the poet emitted a rumbling groan from somewhere deep inside his throat. Otherwise, he didn't move, except for the rare raising of the beer to his lips, the slow, methodic gulping of the cool liquid with eyes appreciatively closed, and, before he set the glass down, the contemplation of the remaining beer held up high in front of him with the spectacle of the drowned pirate refracted through the rich golden brew.

The poet's name was Randy Bellows. It was early evening, just an hour or so before the boisterous college crowd would begin to arrive at the tavern.

For an undergraduate at the college, Doreen was a bit early this evening. She was a nursing major and came into the tavern to relax after a grueling afternoon in "clinicals." She was a pleasant, if ordinary, young woman, a bit overweight, with pretty brown eyes. She was still dressed in her student nurse's uniform, though she had a light-blue sweater drawn rather tightly over it.

Doreen saw Randy on his lonesome perch in the shadows at the end of the bar and vaguely recognized him. Doreen rarely came into the bar section of the tavern, and this certainly was the first time she'd ever come in alone; but, whenever she'd come in, she'd seen this gaunt, lonely figure sitting in the far corner and staring into the yellow glow of the fish tank with its tiny pirate skeleton nodding in the deep-sea currents, presumably for the rest of eternity.

In this instance, however, there was a deeper recognition, one that Doreen felt impelled to investigate. She was hardly a shy young woman. She walked the length of the bar and climbed up onto the barstool next to him. She gazed at him, almost breathlessly, and said, "Are you …? Could you be, by any chance …? I mean, you're not, in fact, Randy Bellows, are you?"

He took another long draw on his cigarette and stared pensively into the bubbly light of the fish tank. "I am," he replied solemnly.

"Oh, how delightful!" she chirped. "Oh, the real Randy Bellows! I recognized you from the college newspaper. They had an article about you last month. So, you're a real, live poet! It must be delightful to write poetry!"

His only answer was a deep-throated groan.

"What do you write about?" she asked.

He didn't answer for a while. He stared at the sluggish yellow undulations of the fish in the tank. Finally, after two more puffs of his cigarette, he muttered, "Life."

"Life?" she asked.

"Life."

"But what about life?"

"Just life."

"You mean like, '*Life is a bowl full of cherries,*' and stuff like that? Oh, how exciting!"

Again, he was silent. A look of blistering contempt curled his upper lip, revealing for a moment two elongated venomous teeth at either side of his mouth. He lifted the glass of beer to his lips and slowly drew in the cool golden liquid with long, languorous swallows that suggested that even this, yes, even this act of drinking a beer in a college tavern was akin to imbibing the divine nectar of the gods, the healing waters of life itself that alone could console the ineffable pain in the depths of the human heart.

After examining the rich brew in the pale light of the fish tank, he set the glass down on the bar again and, still staring straight ahead of him, said, "I don't write about what life is; I write about what life is not."

She stared at him. She could see that here was a person utterly unlike anyone she'd ever known before. At last, now a bit timid with awe, she ventured to say, "That's just amazing. That's the most wonderful thing I've ever heard. Oh, I knew you were a genius. Could you recite something for me, something you've written, just a single line of poetry perhaps?"

He groaned again.

"Please!" she implored.

He gazed into the depths of the watery silence of the fish tank, waiting, watching, peering into the twilight gloom of an eternal sea with its grimacing visage of death, the jaws gaping and snapping shut in speechless reproach, luring, cajoling. Then he uttered, "Few people realize the emotional investment any artist makes in a work. It's very difficult to expose such deep things to the obtrusive glare of the common day. You must understand . . . you must understand . . . the pain."

"Please, please, please," she cried, "I do understand. I'm a nurse; I understand pain." She cocked her head slightly to the side, beamed, and clucked: "I'm into pain management, you know."

Another seemingly interminable silence followed. Randy screwed his eyes up into a tragic mask of the most implacable intensity. A slow rumbling began in his throat. It rose higher and higher. His mouth opened, discharging curling and ominous wisps of oracular smoke. And, in a scratchy voice, he chanted, slowly and plaintively:

"*Life is*

"*Not*

"*A bowl*

"*Full*

"*Of cherries.*"

He was silent again.

She was stunned. "You wrote that?"

He nodded his head and took another draw on his cigarette.

"That is, I mean that really is, I mean really, you know, profound. I mean the way you took a … a … cliché, and kind of stood it on its head. I mean that's really meaningful. It's just so dark, and creepy, and, you know, existential, and stuff like that. It's given me a whole new way to look at life. Wow! So, life is *not* a bowl full of cherries. Wait 'til I tell that to Mom. She won't like that one bit. Not one bit, believe me! She always goes around saying that life is a bowl full of cherries." Doreen giggled.

He acknowledged her adulation with a modest but painful tilt of the head and took yet another deep draw on his cigarette, staring into the quivering light of the fish tank. The pirate skeleton continued its spasmodic nodding, as if to show its approval as well.

"Anything else?" she went on.

"What do you mean?"

"Anything else you've written about what life is not …? Could you say some more lines?"

He was silent. He took another long drink of his beer and returned the glass to the table with a clunk, this time without examining it.

"That's all that I've written," he said despondently.

"All?"

"Yes, all. I wrote that six years ago."

"But why haven't you written more? Surely there are other things that life is not. Surely you haven't exhausted the subject! There are lots of things that life is not … life is not … a … a … life is not a potato chip! Life is not … a … a … a coconut cream pie!"

He turned his head slowly toward her for the first time, rolling it around on his long, leathery neck in a snakelike motion and fixing his reptilian eyes blinklessly on hers. His face seemed suffused with a fiery, though muted passion.

"Poetry doesn't happen simply because you want it to happen. It has to come of its own. Your whole inner being has to heave and shake, and the poem erupts out of you, arising from the depths of your soul and swirling through your throat and exploding out of your mouth into the blazing light of glory and infamy."

"That's how '*Life is not a bowl full of cherries*' came?"

"That's precisely how it came!"

"Gosh! It's kinda like getting sick and throwing up, huh?"

He continued to gaze at her for a few moments with unutterable contempt. He turned again to the fish tank, his cigarette, his pirate, and his beer.

Doreen gazed at him. "Now I know why poets are called the 'unacknowledged legislators of the world,'" she said. She cocked her head again and smiled: "I learned that in an English course."

He nodded gravely. "It's a terrible, terrible burden. People just don't understand."

"I must go now. I have an early class tomorrow morning. I'll never forget this. I mean, I'll never see life in the same way ever again. I'll never see bowls full of cherries in the same way either, not with all that erupting and swirling and vomiting and whatnot. How can I thank you?"

He softly waved away the smoke that had gathered in front of his face. "It's nothing at all. I'm just doing what destiny has compelled me to do."

"And which the college is paying you to do," she added with joyful and innocent eyes.

He was a little shaken by this remark. His serpentine eyes actually blinked. "Even poets must put bread on the table," he pronounced.

"And beer in their bellies!" she exclaimed, as she skipped off the barstool. "I think it's just wonderful—wonderful, wonderful, wonderful! Goodbye!"

He said nothing.

She left the tavern. He ordered another beer.

When it arrived, he took a long draught, held up the glass before his eyes to examine the depths of the golden brew, and, after setting the glass on the bar again, lit up a cigarette. He squinted inscrutably into the pale yellow light that undulated hypnotically, monotonously in the fish tank before his eyes. He watched the skull of the drowned pirate dip, jolt upward, rise, and dip again. Then he groaned as the exhaled smoke of his cigarette wrapped his head in a wraith of impenetrable gloom.

The Knights Templar of
Eighty-Fourth Street

Running into Ollie Johannsen at a café on Third Avenue was enough of a shock, if I may say so. I hadn't been in New York for years — and I mean years, twenty-five years or so, though I don't live all that far away. I knew that the old Third Avenue El had been gone a long time now, but I still thought of Third Avenue as the cavernous, sunless, littered place it used to be, punctured now and then by those trains shrieking on that huge, rusty trellis overhead. Now all these spiffy shops and outdoor cafés serving espresso and French croissants! It was just too much of a change from the whiskey joints that I recall where a skittish kid could steal a glance through the door for a second or two at a Dodgers game on the round black-and-white TV screen mounted at the far end of the bar before some husky-voiced drunk chased him away.

As for Ollie — well, he recognized me before I recognized him. He jumped up from his little marble table and ran over to me, shouting, "Marty! Is that you? Marty Sadowski, do you remember me? I'm Ollie! Ollie the Viking! You know, Ollie, Chief of the Varangian Guard! Don't you remember me?" So I gaped at him the way a person who has forgotten his glasses tries to scan a menu or something like that, trying to read what is front of him through a watery film of floating images and blurred figures until he finally gets it.

Yes, through the trim, graying beard, through the face with its lines and bumps and altered coloring, I gradually saw the fierce little blond-haired kid I once knew, Ollie himself, the self-styled Viking and Chief of the Va-rangian Guard.

"God Almighty! So that's you, Ollie!" I said. We shook hands, and he invited me to join him at his little table. And guess what! He ordered for me one of these coffee cappuccinos along with some—what he calls—"biscotti," but which look to me like children's teething biscuits, except with nuts and who knows what else in them.

Actually, this kind of situation is pretty awkward, if you ask me. If I'd known in advance that Ollie was sitting there and would recognize me, I would probably have dipped off into a back alley and avoided meeting him, just like one of those kids in the old Tully gang so long ago. Then again, dipping off into back alleys was a way of life for them, and our guys never really knew how to do it; and, even if I'd mastered that art, I don't think an adult could pull it off quite as—well, gracefully—as a kid could.

So I sat with Ollie, having one of those conversations that's like talking to a person though a thick wall. But things got better as we went along. He was very excited, what with his trim suit and neat beard and haircut that all seemed so unlike him. I thought that he would have matured into a taller and stockier man, but he was slender and short and looked as if he spent a lot of time jogging and doing things like that. Our conversation brought back a lot of things from the past, and he really wanted to talk about them.

He told me he'd been a "flower child" in the late sixties and early seven-ties—kind of late for him, I would have thought, since he would have then been close to thirty years old. He was "into the whole scene," he said. Now he worked for a publishing company—glossy magazine fare mainly, the kind of stuff that, he admitted, should make any normal person feel sick, if there were any normal persons left. He was an editor. He'd been in and out of a marriage and had no children. And there were all kinds of things he didn't feel too good about. The MacPherson twins, Robbie and Scott; both dead in Vietnam. And other stuff like that. He asked me if I'd known about Robbie and Scott. I said I did.

"How did you know?" he asked.

"I was in Washington on vacation. I took my family there. I figured that if any of us might have ended up on the Vietnam Memorial, it would be the MacPherson brothers. And there they were all right, early on in the war too. Later I made some inquiries. They were in the same unit, killed in action at exactly the same time and place. They were together. Their names are inscribed together on that wall."

"I know that," Ollie said. "They were real warriors. The only real warriors among us. They would have saved our honor—the honor of . . . ," he hesitated.

"The honor of the Knights Templar. They did save it."

"In a way. But we were not equal to it."

Who is ever equal to anything, I thought. But I saw vivid images in my mind of that time so long ago, of the great battle in Central Park, of the clouds of dust, the tears, the blood, the crying and the shouting and the jeering, and the two MacPherson brothers marching with arms locked into the heart of the enemy, their voices raised in a marvelous keening we had never heard before: voices like bagpipes over the highland moors. They turned the tide of battle; they put the enemy to flight.

Ollie must have read my mind.

"What voices they had! Do you remember that, Marty? Do you remember the Solemn Vesper services on Sunday afternoon, the Palestrina and the Monteverdi and the Josquin, the shrill treble voices of those angelic brothers rising up out of the basses and tenors and spreading through the medallioned vaults of St. Ignatius? Could we have known anything finer than that? Where is all that glorious music now, Marty? Does it fertilize some swamp grass in the Plain of Jars along with their blood?"

I thought more about all that. Of Robbie and Scott MacPherson, identical twins, I thought. Of Danny Jacobiwitz. Egon Kola. Hernando Silva. Hermann Gessner. Ollie Johannsen, who sat across from me. Tony Santini. Mike Lehmann. Mark Spaghnum, who was the traitor. Florian Dupré. Jimmy Osperti. Li-San Lu. And myself. Fourteen of us.

We were in the sixth grade at St. Ignatius Loyola School on Eighty-Fourth Street between Park and Madison. We were altar boys at the baroque church on Park Avenue—all of us, except for the MacPhersons, who sang in the choir. It was a demanding task in those days—a daily routine in which, in the early morning hours, several dozen Jesuit priests, resident at the parish and teachers in the educational complex of schools that surrounded it, fanned out from the sacristy to the multitude of tiny side altars in both the upper and lower church, all of them needing the prompt and exact ministrations of a small army of acolytes. Then there were the official daily parish Masses at the main altar, the big Masses on Sunday, and, most wonderful of all, the Solemn High Mass at 11:00 and the Solemn Vespers at 3:00, in which we could swing the golden censor while listening to the stupendous strains of the great organ and the choir's rendition of glorious Palestrina.

We were all proud of our ability to recite or sing in Latin, which we had never formally studied, though, in fact, we understood quite a bit, and I've never been able to figure out how we knew as much as we did. We were the best students in the sixth grade. *We worked hard to get things right.* That was our motto, our purpose. We were Scottish and German and Italian and Polish and Hungarian and Filipino and Norwegian and Chinese and French. Danny was part English and part Jewish, though he was being brought up a Catholic. Mark Spaghnum — the one who betrayed us — was sort of nothing that we could ever figure out. Maybe that's why he betrayed us. *Most importantly, none of us were Irish — at least not completely Irish.*

We were the Knights Templar. We were sworn by solemn oath and covenant to defend the Holy Roman Catholic Church against the Saracens. But there were no Saracens around. Therefore, we were sworn by solemn oath and covenant to defend the Holy Roman Catholic Church against the Irish.

No easy task, that! We were awash in a sea of Irish — the nuns who taught at the school were Irish, the Jesuit priests and brothers who ran the parish were mostly Irish, 80 percent of the students at the school were Irish. Actually, we really didn't have anything against the Irish. In fact, many of us were partly Irish. We did have the impression that the Irish had something against us. Who else was there for us to be opposed to? And, if we were protecting the Holy Roman Catholic Church, that meant, in effect, that we were protecting the Irish against — well, for all purposes — the Irish. There was something a bit awkward about that.

So ours was a lonely calling and a solitary destiny. Were we ever proud of it! We liked to think that we corresponded with those posters mounted so prominently over the blackboards in our schoolrooms that showed kids from every nation and race holding hands together. Like the Knights Templar of old, we were an international society.

Our only difficulty was what to do about St. Patrick's Day. At the time of our formation, in October of our sixth-grade year, we decided, against our deepest desires and inclinations, to forgo its celebration. We had to assure St. Patrick, of course, that it had nothing personally to do with him and that we would continue to invoke his aid in worthy projects, especially when we prayed for the conversion of the Irish. After all, we must pray for our enemies. Isn't that what we're commanded to do?

Only three of us were actually foreign born. Florian Dupré was the son of a French diplomat at the United Nations, but he spoke English flawlessly and acted, for all purposes, just like an American kid. Hernando Silva was a Filipino who spoke with a heavy accent of some sort; he was rather obese and had the somewhat unnerving habit of wanting to hug and kiss us at the most embarrassing moments.

Hermann Gessner was different. A tall, heavily built boy, he was a few years older than the rest of us because he could barely speak English and therefore was several grades behind where he should have been. He was the only student I ever knew at St. Ignatius whom the sisters actually seemed to be afraid of. We heard that in wartime Germany four or five years earlier he'd been pulled out, barely alive, from underneath a pile of dead kindergarten children so charred on top, so reduced to oozing flesh beneath, that they were no longer recognizable. That happened after one of the great firestorms in Hamburg, and it was only the beginning of what he's suffered. Both his parents had been killed in the war. He was sent by some kind of agency to live with an aunt in New York.

The nuns feared him, I think, because he'd survived the kind of life-threatening, "final" experiences that so preoccupied their imaginations, especially in their favorite martyrdom stories, and that fact gave Hermann some special kind of power over them. Also, as doggedly patriotic as the nuns were, they felt both remorse and compassion for the victims of civilian bombing during the war.

The rest of us were second or third generation. Li-San Lu's family had been in America for many generations, but he could speak some Chinese. Egon

Kola's parents had come from Hungary before the war, but he knew only a few words in Hungarian. He was short, dark, and thickset, and his favorite habit was to approach a person suddenly from the back and whisper in his ear, "Meet me tonight in the Casbah!" None of us knew what this Casbah business was all about, but we figured it was a line that he'd picked up from a movie. In any case, the Casbah must have been a very secret place. For Egon was full of secrets: he always talked of secret codes and secret hiding places and had objects, especially plastic cereal-box rings, with secret compartments in them.

Mike Lehmann was different from the rest of us. He came from a wealthy family that owned a lavish apartment on Fifth Avenue filled with rugs and paintings and highly polished furniture that reminded us of the sorts of things that were on exhibit in the Metropolitan Museum of Art. He, more than anyone else, exercised a kind of leadership role in our group, and many of our official "chapter" meetings were held around the immense carved table in his parents' dining room — a proper table for Knights Templar. Over the table hung a huge chandelier that sparkled with little lights and hundreds of gleaming crystal pendants, and one entire wall of the dining room was covered by a seventeenth-century Gobelin tapestry depicting a dark, thick-leaved forest with shepherd girls in a clearing and high-plumed cavaliers on prancing steeds. During the meeting we drank wine-red cherry soda out of Mrs. Lehmann's silver goblets.

We were all fascinated by the United Nations, so that, at times, we mimicked its deliberations by having one person speak in gibberish while another engaged in an apparently simultaneous "translation" of this gibberish into English. In effect, this meant, of course, that the one who was doing the "translation" was the one who was actually expressing an opinion about something. Only Florian, Hermann, and Hernando spoke a real foreign language, but the practice of supplying a totally irrelevant translation was still in force. At other times, garbed in curious renditions of medieval capes supplied by old silk tablecloths and satin curtains, we conducted our meetings in a ceremonial, pseudo-liturgical fashion marked at all stages by formalized gestures and by pompous, though randomly evolved protocols.

In contrast to Mike Lehmann, the MacPherson twins lived in a cramped apartment overlooking the El on Third Avenue. Their father was old enough to be their grandfather. Their mother was deceased. They had two brothers, quite a bit older than themselves, who had been in the Marines during the war and whom we often saw in church acting as ushers for the Solemn High Mass at 11:00 each Sunday.

We all loved going to this cramped apartment whenever we could. We enjoyed seeing their enormous German shepherd, which liked to lounge on the fire escape in front of the apartment and watch the El trains screeching noisily by; we relished the stories told by their kindly old father, who was long retired from the New York City Fire Department; and we were thrilled by the wartime adventures of the older brothers whose gentleness and calm were so unlike the nervous lives of many of our own parents. They had been at Iwo Jima and Okinawa.

Once some of us had seen a movie about fighter pilots battling Japanese aircraft in dogfights, and we were eager to tell them about the movie and about how funny and insulting the comments were that the American fighter pilots radioed to the Japanese pilots before they blasted their cockpits with machine gun bullets, killing them and shooting down their airplanes.

The brothers didn't think it was funny; in fact, it made them angry. They told us that those soldiers on the other side were there for the same reason the American soldiers were there: they were bound by honor to stand with their fellow countrymen. Governments, not soldiers, were responsible for war. Soldiers, even enemy soldiers, were not criminals and not to be treated or regarded as such. Anyway, they said soldiers should always respect their adversaries. After that, we were pretty tame about that kind of thing.

Another place we liked to go was Tony Santini's. His father was a shoemaker. The entire family—his mother and father and Tony and four little dark-eyed sisters—lived in a few small rooms behind the shoemaker's shop on Second Avenue. Nothing in the world ever smelled like that shop—the leather, the oils, the waxes and glues and polishes—it was great! From the other end of the shop—the door leading into the living quarters—came aromas of the best food in the world, and did we ever have plenty of that, while Tony's little sisters stared at us from behind doors leading into the bedrooms!

The Santinis were poor, but Mrs. Santini felt a need to feed copiously any stranger who entered their private world. Mr. Santini, too, was an object of no little amazement. He wore a leather apron and moved through the tangled mass of shoes and boots and handbags with cheerful skill, tapping on heels and soles with his little hammer and listening all day to an Italian radio station that played operatic music.

Among us, only Mike Lehmann and Jimmy Osperti were familiar with this music. Jimmy's mother was a singer in the choir at the Met, and his father was a violinist; he knew a lot about this kind of music but didn't seem too interested in it.

Mike, on the other hand, seemed to know it quite well. Whenever he came into the crowded little shop, he would try to identify what was being played. "From *Il Trovatore*, first act," he would shout. Mr. Santini would beam with delight, even if he got it wrong (and my impression was that he usually got it wrong). Mr. and Mrs. Lehmann, and many of their friends, often sent things to be repaired by Mr. Santini, whom they said could make and remake shoes better than anyone else. And Mike took every opportunity he could to bring a parcel full of shoes to be mended and to talk with Mr. Santini about the opera.

Mike would also tell us sometimes about Lohengrin and Parzival and Montsalvat and the Grail, and we thought that this was the neatest thing we'd ever heard, though we were not too enthusiastic about the music that went along with it. But the MacPherson twins liked to hear the music and compare it with Josquin des Pres and the kind of things they sang in church. And we did like to listen to two pieces that Mike Lehmann insisted on playing for us on his high-fidelity before we began our meetings: "The Entrance of the Gods into Valhalla" and "Siegfried's Rhine Journey."

Li-San Lu was the quiet member of our group; he tagged along with us, always finding everything somewhat perplexing, if also amusing, and rarely said very much; we never saw his family or learned much about them. And as for Mark Spaghnum—he was just who he was, that was all, though he came from a well-off family and was the only one besides Mike Lehmann who had a television set, so we often went to his apartment to watch Hopalong Cassidy movies.

The last member of the group was Danny Jacobiwitz. His apartment fascinated all of us because the walls were painted a deep purple, except for yellowish patches where plaster had fallen off. In the midst of the obscure shabbiness of the various rooms, however, were low, cushiony pieces of furniture draped haphazardly with the most brightly colored pieces of cloth we had ever seen. His mother was a spare, tall, anxious woman who spoke with an English accent and who always fussed over us and made us eat over-cooked and dried-out hard-boiled eggs, which we hated but which we would manage to choke down for Danny's sake.

His father was the real marvel for us in that apartment. He was always at home, silent, somewhere in the background, a heavy, dark man with a massive bald head and a great beard who never said anything to us. He seemed to live in another world. He wore a hooded robe with stripes of many colors and curiously shaped slippers and a tiny, round, bejeweled cap on the back of his head that looked like the small cap worn by bishops and cardinals and the Pope under their miters. His name was Abraham.

We didn't quite know what to make of this; after all, we figured we were, as the nuns had told us, the children promised to the original Abraham — as numerous as the stars in the sky and the sands of the desert. Moses and David were our forebears, our ancestors; we were — were we not? — the Chosen People. Who were these others who claimed that same inheritance?

No story ever captivated us so fully as the story of Joseph and his coat of many colors. So, was this man, this Abraham Jacobiwitz, sire of Danny, a latter-day Joseph, sitting at the entrance of his purple tent "in the cool of the day," wrapped in his marvelous striped robe and gazing silently over his herds and flocks and into the depths of a parched wilderness? He was the very image of ancient and imperturbable repose, like those dark, somber figures that looked out at us from the mosaics and the murals half-hidden in the shadowy alcoves of St. Ignatius Church.

In another sense, too, he reminded us of the young, bearded men in black suits and black hats carrying black briefcases who strode energetically across Central Park in perfectly straight lines, ignoring the sidewalks, looking neither to the right nor to the left of them, and cutting right through people's softball games and picnics. We figured they would walk right through a tree and out the other side if it happened to get in their way. Someone once told us that they were "young rabbis" or rabbinical students. But so was Jesus, we thought. We tried to imagine Jesus in a black suit and a black hat with a briefcase striding forcefully across Central Park. What was this all about?

It was from Sister Bridget that we first learned about the Knights Templar. Indeed, she knew how to keep quiet and attentive our classroom of fifty riotous boys, seated in five rows of ten desks apiece. One of her methods was sheer terror — her ability to see and to pounce on any disruption with a speed and force that defied all description.

Another method was flattery; she told us how superior sixth grade boys are to any other class, as if being in the sixth grade represented the highest point of life, and we loved to hear that, oblivious to the fact that, in the following year, we were bound to fall back into the ranks of the reprobate.

She also told us, pointing rather sarcastically at the girl's section of the school, how silly girls were and what silly games they played, and we loved to hear that, too, especially now that we were deeply troubled by beginning to find them interesting in a way we had never found them interesting before.

Most of all, she was inclined to interrupt some lesson in long division (long division and fractions being her specialties) with the most entrancing stories of heroes from the past — knights of King Arthur, Samson and Joshua and Esther and Judith, George Washington and Daniel Boone and Abraham Lincoln and Mother Seton, St. Louis of France and St. Joan of Arc and the Jesuit martyrs of North America — all jumbled up together, as if they had known one another and had been the best of friends.

On the Knights Templar she had particularly strong views, praising their military prowess in protecting the pilgrims to the Holy Land and inveighing against their outrageous treatment at the hands of jealous monarchs and gullible, cowardly churchmen who were all too ready to believe any misrepresentation put before them.

She also noted, with no less forcefulness, how internal traitors and opportunists equally helped to bring them down. Sister Bridget had a sharp tongue, all right, and never ceased to remind us that fickleness and weakness of heart are things we could all count on at critical moments in our lifetimes, even as St. Peter, the Rock himself, the Keeper of the Keys of the Kingdom, had denied Christ three times when heroic resolve was most demanded.

But we took to the Knights Templar and learned everything we could about them. They were our models—though more our models in our talk than in our action. In a curious way, our fascination with the Knights Templar got fused with our devotion to that old Basque soldier himself, St. Ignatius—yes, St. Ignatius, whose armored and wounded figure in the midst of the great Battle of Pamplona, portrayed in a mosaic arching over the right side of the main altar in the church, never ceased to incite our admiration and wonder.

Every weekday, during school hours, Eighty-Fourth Street between Madison and Park was closed to traffic, enabling it to be used as a playground for the students at St. Ignatius during recesses and lunch breaks. From 11:30 to 12:15, grades one through six would have their lunch break. The girls, dressed in their blue uniforms, congregated at one end of the street, toward Madison Avenue, where they would play hopscotch and jump rope as they chanted their curious little songs and jingles. At the other end, toward Park Avenue, the boys would cluster in their white shirts and blue ties to play tag and shoot marbles, flip and exchange baseball cards, but mainly to circulate in small groups that were perpetually involved in one kind of intrigue or another among themselves. Sixth graders, of course, as the oldest group, dominated the scene. It was here that the Knights Templar could exercise their power.

Our only rivals were two other groups. One group was "the Shamrocks"; they were led by a fellow named Donny Groghan. Donny was a favorite of the sisters. He brought silly-looking plastic flowers for Our Lady and cute little presents for the nuns; he acted and looked like an angel; he was very holy and darling; he could recite everything that was in the catechism perfectly; and he was certainly pegged as a future priest, though he wasn't an altar boy. The rest of the Shamrocks were also like that. Sister Bridget was always cooing over them, though she was annoyed that they couldn't get very good grades.

We figured that the Shamrocks were too stupid to be altar boys, and anyway, we knew the catechism better than they did; it's just that Sister Bridget didn't call on us, because she knew that we could recite it *and* explain it. By the way, we brought flowers for Our Lady, too, but they were real flowers, appropriate for the season, and were really beautiful.

I don't know what the Shamrocks did after school or where they went, but we always imagined that they were either at home playing with their sisters' dolls, playing tiddlywinks, or else being taken to something like the Peanut Gallery on *The Howdy Doody Show*, though sometimes we did see them at special kids' Saturday matinees at the Trans-Lux theater on Eighty-Fifth Street and Madison. We had one opinion, and one opinion only, of the Shamrocks: they were soft and sneaky.

The other group on Eighty-Fourth Street didn't have a name but, because they traipsed around after a kid named Shaun Tully, we just called them the Tully gang. They were a slinky, surly lot who lived in shadows and dark places. In fact, during the lunch break, we rarely saw them. We knew that they smoked cigarette butts they salvaged from parental ashtrays or picked up in the streets and then came to class smelling like tobacco.

They didn't bring lunches in lunch boxes but carried greasy paper bags in which the remnants of old and foul-smelling bologna sandwiches were carried around for days and were munched on now and then when some presumably desperate hunger drove them to it. They were often the recipients of the sisters' wrath, were sent home from school for using bad language, and were the sort that eventually got expelled from school. On the rare occasions when they were active on the play street, they grabbed candy bars out of the hands of third graders, attacked columns of first graders on their daily walks around the block, ran off with and tangled up the ropes the girls used to jump rope with, shouted insults and obscenities at just about anyone, and harassed elderly adults who were passing by.

Shaun Tully himself was a short, puffy kid, already marred by a bad complexion that looked like a sort of perpetual chicken pox, and he often looked swollen and bruised, as if he'd been beaten up by some older person — maybe a father or mother or a sibling. At school, he was a bully.

His best friend was named Buckley — we only knew him by his last name because we called him "Buckley the Kicker." Buckley tagged around behind Tully and, in conflicts of various sorts, often threatened to kick an adversary by drawing back his leg and bending over in an aggressive fashion, ready to deliver the kick. He rarely did kick, but sometimes he did, and we always regarded that as the lowest of cowardly acts. I don't know what the Tully gang did after school, but they seemed to vanish into the great labyrinth of dark passages and alleyways that perforate the monolithic-looking blocks of Manhattan. We also figured they hung out around the banks of the East River, for there was something curiously aquatic about them, something wet and slimy, something associated with sewers and puddles and the stuff that gathers over blocked drains. We had one opinion, and one opinion only, about the Tullys: they were mean and ratty.

The Knights Templar met on weekends or after school, either at one of our apartments or in a small triangular nook of Central Park that we came to think of as "our territory" and that was wedged in between the Eighty-Fifth Street Traverse on one side, the long high fence of a playground on another side, and a sidewalk bordered by Central Park Drive on the third side. Today it's a carefully groomed grove of trees making up a far section of what is called the "Ross Pinetum." Back then, it was a tangled, wooded area with a grassy clearing in the middle that we called "the Battlefield." Directly in the center of the clearing was a dry, dusty patch of ground, particularly useful for stirring up the clouds of dust we considered appropriate for combat and which sent us home so filthy that prolonged and agonized scrubbing by angry mothers in blackened bathtubs was scarcely sufficient to make us ready for human concourse once again.

The dense woods and underbrush surrounding the clearing were fretted by a network of small footpaths, dotted here and there with little thickets where you could be safely concealed from the prying eyes of the world. We prided ourselves on the deftness and speed with which we could negotiate the maze of paths. Most wonderful of all was the playground side of our territory where two long parallel lines of forsythia bushes arched over each other and created a tunnel where a person, in the right season of the year, could run full-speed for fifty yards without being seen from the outside. We were convinced that we were the only people who knew about this natural wonder, and we called it "the Magic Tunnel." But, in all, our wooded nook was a very private place, invaded only now and then, and to our unspeakable mortification, by the occasional couple who came in to lie down in the grassy clearing and sun themselves or to wrap themselves around one another in the most unseemly fashion.

We used our territory as a base for our excursions throughout Central Park, which sometimes extended all the way down to the Central Park Zoo, to the ponds and lakes we liked so much, and the rocky cliffs, which we climbed, and the wooded areas, the Ramble, which we regarded with the awe of Arthurian knights adrift in the great enchanted forests of Brocéliande. We loved to watch the horses cantering by on the bridle paths throughout the park and often discussed the horses we would like to own and what names we would give them, though only Mike Lehmann had ever actually ridden one.

We also loved the human monuments—Alexander Hamilton, so sagely meditating the Metropolitan Museum of Art; Cleopatra's Needle, propped up on its massive greenish-bronze crabs; the "castles" and "forts" and arcades of the park; the splashing fountains and arching footbridges; and the narrow, cobbled walkways twisting capriciously through the luxurious fronds of the Shakespeare Garden.

The most exciting thing of all was at the east end of Turtle Pond: the great mounted statue of King Jagiello with two gigantic swords raised and crossed over a head of stern features with a leonine mane of hair magnificently flaming out from underneath his armored crown. The occasional winter snow brought us out with sleds to careen perilously down the slopes of Cedar Hill just south of Seventy-Ninth Street.

Often, when we didn't meet at our apartments or go to the park, we went to the movies together at the RKO or at the Loew's on Eighty-Six Street. Several museums were our favorites as well: the Museum of Natural History, where we loved the animal dioramas, the dinosaur bones, and the huge canoes of the Northwest Pacific Indians; the Metropolitan Museum, where we spent hours studying the suits of armor and the collections of swords and crossbows and halberds and muskets, though occasionally we strayed into the Egyptian and Assyrian collections or admired the immense terra-cotta warriors still displayed among the Etruscan antiquities before they were discovered to be fakes and removed from the museum; and the Museum of the History of New York. where the old fire-fighting equipment was of special interest to us. Often we planned a major trek to the Cloisters at Fort Tryon Park, but never fulfilled that ambition.

We also loved the old classic comics — the renditions of the *Iliad* and *The Three Musketeers* and a dozen others; and we looked forward every Sunday to reading the great, full-page spread of "Prince Valiant" in the old *Journal-American*. It was from this source that Ollie Johannsen discovered his Viking identity and styled himself, after those intrepid Norse warriors who took up garrison duty for the Byzantine emperors, Chief of the Varangian Guard.

And, of course, there were the books we loved and shared and imitated: *Treasure Island* and *The Black Arrow* and *Robin Hood* and *Tom Sawyer*, and a multitude of others, many of them garnished with the richly colored illustrations of the elder Wyeth. They bespoke a world of the real and the imaginative that was manifold and splendid and wonderful.

Soon after we'd formed ourselves into the formidable company of the Knights Templar, two of us, Mike Lehmann and I, were summoned to the principal's office. She was Mother Eileen McKay. A summons to her office was as welcome as a summons to a dragon's lair. We were terrified, and rightly so, as we stood at attention in front of her desk, because, in the buzz and confusion of what we were able to hear in her initial tirade, we heard the terms "ringleaders" applied to us, and we knew that such an accusation could not help but have the most severe consequences.

When she finished, we were silent, and she glared at us with eyes like a double-barreled bazooka that could have punched holes through the armor of a tank. Then Mike Lehmann, arching slightly forward and with his eyes just a bit closed, as if he were leaning into a powerful wind, declared, "But we have done nothing wrong, Mother Eileen."

Mother Eileen retorted, "Now, that's not what I've been hearing. Is it true that you've been meddling with Donny Groghan and his crowd?" She tapped a pencil compulsively on her desk, at times jabbing its point through a hole on the soiled paper ink blotter in front of her.

Mike said we'd never done anything like that. We'd never meddled with them. I nodded my nervous assent. After a brief silence, and to my horror, Mike added that, if they meddled with us, however, we certainly would meddle back. I nodded again, but only after a marked hesitation.

Mother Eileen stared at the hole she'd made in the blotter. She leaned back in her chair. She said that she had figured that might be the case. Anyone with a head on his shoulders, she said, would know what Donny Groghan and his crowd were like. Donny Groghan was a little sneak, if ever there was one. He's one of those fellows who lie whenever it suits them to lie. The world is filled with people like that. We couldn't believe she actually said that to us.

After another hesitation, she stated her purpose. "You know, boys, it's my decision to turn over the governance of the recess period to you. Between 11:30 and 12:15, the Eighty-Fourth Street playground is in your keeping. I expect you boys, the Knights Templar, as you call yourselves, to protect it and keep it safe and in good order. I know you won't fail me."

We couldn't believe our ears. We felt as if some feudal queen had consigned the defense of her realm to our charge.

"What's more — remember this! Don't you ever back away from an Irishman — or an Irishwoman either. It'll get you nowhere, and they'll hate you when you do that."

She dismissed us. As we walked toward the door, she asked us to stop and said, "You'll change your mind about the Irish someday. Some of them are going to be your friends, and some of them are going to be your enemies, just like everybody else in the world. The only thing that matters about persons is the goodness of their souls."

Mike Lehmann looked directly back at her. "We know that already, Mother Eileen."

"I'm sure you do," she replied. "Why else would I have consigned the play street to your charge?"

"Anyway," he went on, "I'm half-Irish."

"I know you are," she concluded. "And I know your mother well. We went to school together. Her people came from Skibbereen, as mine did also."

We took our mission seriously. Stealing from younger kids, bullying, using bad language, pushing people around — all vanished soon enough under our governance. We provided escorts for the first grade when they went on their class walks and couldn't help but think, in this context, of the Knights Templar protecting the pilgrims as they progressed through the Holy Land.

We even watched out for the girls and made sure nobody interrupted their games or called them names, and that was an awkward thing for us to do. And yet, in some sense, few things gave us greater pleasure. It had not escaped our notice that knights were supposed to have a special protective relationship to ladies. So everything went well, and the Tully gang seemed to disappear more conspicuously than ever before from the street.

In late April of our sixth-grade year, we decided to have a Grand Chapter meeting. We got that pretentious title for a meeting by reading up about the Knights Templar. Several key issues were beginning to affect our group. We held the meeting, as usual, at Mike Lehmann's apartment, and after the opening ceremonies — of a rather prolonged nature this time — we settled down to business. We decided to dispense at once with simultaneous translations. A few matters of lesser importance were resolved without much discussion. Then Jimmy Osperti arose. He announced that he'd been approached by two classmates who had asked for admission to the Knights Templar. "Who are they?" the group shouted. He said with just the slightest diffidence on his part, "Tommy Shanahan and Kevin O'Kelly."

The group was stunned. Jimmy continued, "They're both neat guys. They're smart. Tommy's father is a doctor. Kevin's father knows how to fix televisions." We were especially impressed by the latter information; television was still a rare thing in our lives, and knowing how to fix one must be an extraordinary skill indeed.

Scott MacPherson rose too: "Tommy Shanahan is in the choir. *He works hard to get things right.*"

"And Kevin O'Kelley serves the seven o'clock Mass every weekday for grumpy old Father McCracken. Now that takes guts, because Father McCracken constantly forgets where in the Mass he is, and he doesn't like to be reminded, especially by the altar boy," Jimmy Osperti added. Both Jimmy and Scott sat down.

Hermann spoke up, "*Ja,* I sink ve admit sem, not so?"

"But they're Irish!" Hernando declared.

"So what?" Scott replied. "Some of Tully's gang actually aren't Irish, and even some of the Shamrocks." Mark Spaghnum shifted uneasily in his seat when he heard that piece of information.

"Why don't they join those other groups?" Ollie the Viking said, his fierce blond hair catching the glint of the huge chandelier that hung over us.

Scott protested, "There are lots of kids in the class who are Irish, and they won't have anything to do with either the Shamrocks or the Tullys. They're not mean and ratty like the Tully kids, and they're not soft and sneaky like the Shamrocks. They're like us. We should want them on our side."

Mike Lehmann rose to address the group. He assumed the posture that he was fond of on special occasions and that Florian Dupré, with a bemused smile on his face, liked to call "*la grande maniére de General de Gaulle*," though none of us had the slightest clue as to what this meant. "We are a consecrated fellowship of the valorous," Mike Lehmann commenced in his most sanctimonious tone. "It's up to us to extend our guardianship over all creatures who cry out for justice. We answer only to the King of kings; and all peoples, beyond all boundaries, beyond all nations, are under the protection of our noble company. We make no distinctions of race or kindred."

An uncomprehending silence followed this curious pronouncement. I rose to speak: "Anyway, there were chapters of the Knights Templar in medieval Ireland. There were many Gaelic knights in the Order. They were brave and spirited warriors." I sat down again.

Danny Jacobiwitz contributed his bit to the argument: "Just think of Sister Bridget. She's as Irish as you can get, yet she loves to talk about the Knights Templar. They're her heroes."

One by one the Knights assented. Egon Kola seemed especially pleased that he would now have some new people to meet secretly in the Casbah. But we were all aware that the mission of the Knights would have to change—the Irish could no longer be identified as the Saracens. We didn't seem to have much of a problem with this; it never really did mean much anyway. Now we could celebrate St. Patrick's Day again, and everyone was wildly in favor, greeting that resolution with an impromptu and boisterous snatch of "McNamara's Band." Furthermore, such a change was more than compensated for by the fun there would be in designing and carrying out some elaborate induction ceremony. We decided to conduct the ceremony on the final weekend in May, the weekend after Ascension Thursday that year.

As it turned out, the induction never happened. We didn't know, as we sat together at that Grand Chapter meeting, that, by the final weekend in May, only a month away, the Knights Templar of Eighty-Fourth Street would no longer exist. Thus does sudden and unpredictable disaster hang over all great human projects and aspirations.

Mark Spaghnum brought up the final issue of the day: smoking. The Knights were astonished by the introduction of this subject; after all, smoking was forbidden by the school, and it was unthinkable that the Knights should go off to their Central Park retreat, even if into the coverts of the Magic Tunnel itself, and puff furtively on a few cigarettes. But Mark didn't rest his case too easily. After all, in their own neighborhoods the Tully gang smoked quite openly on the streets. And yes, the Shamrocks smoked, too, though secretly.

"Where do they get their cigarettes?" Ollie asked.

"From the Tully gang," Mark answered, with a knowledgeable assurance of the inner workings of the Shamrocks that should have made the club members vaguely suspicious of him.

The debate ended on that note. The Knights Templar rejected the smoking proposal. The fact that the Tullys and the Shamrocks engaged in smoking was sufficient reason for not doing so. Mark Spaghnum sulked by himself for the rest of the meeting and was the first to go home. It's curious that no one thought to ask Mark about what he knew and why he knew it; it's even more curious that no one paused to note that, if Mark were correct in what he said, the Shamrocks and the Tullys had a stronger connection than any of us had suspected.

The following Wednesday the Knights Templar were astonished by the most disruptive news in their short-lived history. Mark had defected to the Shamrocks, had taken up smoking in the alley behind the school, and had, as his price for acceptance into the rival group, revealed the secrets of the Knights Templar to the derisive smiles of the Shamrocks. The august ceremonies of the Knights Templar were openly mocked on the playground.

That afternoon after school, the Knights Templar met in their enclave in Central Park to respond to the crisis. There we made our biggest mistake. We allowed ourselves to become a band of predators, intent upon securing title and turf by submitting them to the whimsical fortunes of the field of combat. The passion of wrath gave force to our conviction of righteousness.

We declared war.

The decision was not unanimous. Hermann Gessner opposed the decision (he knew, apparently, something about the unforeseen consequences of war), as did Hernando Silva and Li-San Lu. But they agreed to stand by us anyway.

Of course, we didn't really expect anything to happen; it was a bluff, after all. How ironic in retrospect! It turned out to be a bluff all right, not of ours but of others turned against us, and it would destroy us.

On Thursday morning, Ollie the Viking, as emissary supreme, approached Donny Groghan during recess and laid down the terms for satisfaction: deadly engagement on the Battlefield at three o'clock on Saturday afternoon. Mark the traitor would know where this was.

On Friday, somewhat to our surprise, the challenge was accepted. We heard about the acceptance early in the morning as the message was passed from one Templar to the next, sometimes even during the various Masses we served and interspersed into the Latin responses themselves, much to the chagrin of the priests who occasionally noticed what was going on. We should have thought about that acceptance and from whom it was coming. But warlike as we were, we were no longer thinking.

Friday afternoon and Saturday morning were times of the most fervid preparation. An imposing array of household implements was pressed into service. Dishtowels became war banners, steel mixing bowls became helmets, trash-can lids became shields. Jimmy Osperti transformed a grid for storing phonograph records into a truly convincing armored visor for his face. Plumes and lace appropriated from mothers' hats were converted into proper knightly adornments, and knitted afghans took on an uncanny resemblance to chain mail. Leather gloves pirated from parental troves became the most redoubtable gauntlets, and even old graying spats, leather boots, and vests that Tony Santini found among the piles of discarded materials in his father's shop were reconfigured as greaves and breastplates.

A particularly barbaric touch was added by several fox-skin stoles of the sort women used to wear and which so fascinated children in church as they studied the little beady eyes of the dead foxes with their tails held ever so demurely in their tiny muzzles. These wraps, just recently out of fashion and now available for pennies in the pawnshops, made several of us look like suitable henchmen for Attila the Hun.

Several red American Flyer wagons of the sort children always seemed to get for Christmas in those days became our "transport" and were filled with cone-shaped cardboard orange-drink containers that could be picked out of the trash cans in the park and filled with dust, resulting in "dust bombs" that could be heaved, with the requisite sound effects supplied by the heaver, spewing their dust in the air or ripping open on contact with person or ground and creating a huge puff of lethal Central Park dust.

The most important contribution of all was the collection of genuine Marine equipment that the MacPherson brothers had in abundance, even though it didn't match the strange medieval outlays that most of us managed to produce. But it gave a certain authority to our venture. We only regretted that we lacked the two new members whom we had agreed to admit to the Knights Templar, but events had moved too quickly for that. Tommy Shanahan and Kevin O'Kelley would have been welcome support troops for our army.

At three o'clock, our combat formation was ready and stood at alert on the dusty patch in the center of the Battlefield. Seven of us made up the first line, heavily armed with forsythia switches and our armored regalia. The MacPherson twins, dressed in their Marine helmets and ammunition belts were at the center of this line. Ollie the Viking and Mike Lehmann secured the flanks. Ollie was wearing a dashing red cape and a thick woman's hat with a hollow plastic horn sticking out of it, of which he was particularly proud.

The second line consisted of five Knights Templar accompanied with the "transport" and poised to fire the multitudinous dust bombs, the pinecones, and the acorns we had collected. Li-San Lu stood in this line, not quite sure of what was going on, but put in charge of a collection of acorns and a slingshot to fire them with. Hernando was a wagon puller, and Egon was a Special Bombardier, Class IV (why Special Bombardier and why Class IV we couldn't quite figure out — it was a secret he didn't care to divulge); his head was wrapped in a strange Moorish-looking shawl, suitable, no doubt, for a clandestine meeting in the Casbah. Both Danny Jacobiwitz and I were at the center of the second line, providing backup for the MacPherson twins and dressed in some of their Marine paraphernalia.

The third line was Hermann Gessner, standing alone and somewhat unwilling to participate. He was unarmed and lacked any battle gear. He carried a first aid kit in a little knapsack on his back and had attached some kind of Red Cross insignia to it. With all this, we considered ourselves to be an unconquerable army.

But the Shamrocks didn't show up.

We waited for fifteen minutes and began to break up the formation when Dinny Milliken appeared at the edge of the Battlefield. He was a meek little kid who just kept to himself in the Eighty-Fourth Street play area. We realized at once that, although he wasn't a member of the Shamrocks, he'd been sent to us by them. We immediately took him hostage. He told us that the Shamrocks were ready to meet us at the west end of Turtle Pond beneath the Belvedere Castle. We promptly let him go, and he vanished as abruptly as he'd come. We never saw him again that day.

We were troubled by having to take up an engagement on fairly unfamiliar terrain, but, then again, we were quite ready to acknowledge that, after all, the Shamrocks had a right to neutral ground. So, the procession to Turtle Pond began. We decided not to advance directly across the Great Lawn; instead, our armed column proceeded southward behind Alexander Hamilton, past Cleopatra's Needle, and turned to the right near the King Jagiello statue.

I think that the various strollers in the park that day must have been startled by that militant-looking band of children, armed to the teeth, pulling loaded battlewagons behind them, wearing the oddest assortment of household implements adapted to various knightly purposes and bearing pennants and flags of all kinds. A passing policeman studied us rather closely and followed us for a while, deciding eventually that this was nothing to be worried about.

Of course, in principle, he was right.

We expected to meet the Shamrocks frocked in similar array and going through a rather elaborate ritual somewhere between play-acting and a mild scuffle in which no one would be hurt, though a few tears might flow from someone who imagined he was hurt. The winner would be the side that held out longer in a pompous exchange of sorties and retreats, escalated by the occasional flying acorn or dust bomb and climaxed by some obscure action that, finally, for no apparent reason in the end, put the other side to flight.

At the far western end of Turtle Pond, there were no Shamrocks. Again, occupying the locale where years later the Delacorte Shakespeare Theater would be built, we stood in formation awaiting the enemy and were just breaking up when an unfamiliar boy, certainly not a St. Ignatius boy, in any event, appeared out of the bushes at the edge of the pond and told us that the Shamrocks had changed their mind and had gone over to the Battlefield to meet us there. The boy slid away into the bushes and almost, as it were, into the pond, like a long, slithery water snake, and we wondered who he was.

We should have taken note of this ominously aquatic quality in him, but I think that our brains were no longer functioning properly. We should also have wondered how a complete stranger like that would have known our word, "the Battlefield," for a small clearing in an obscure corner of Central Park. In a similar procession, we returned to our territory, made our way through its woody perimeter, and lined up on the Battlefield, but there was still no sign of the Shamrocks.

Then we heard a loud whoop. Our formation tightened, but we could see no enemy. Suddenly a band of boys burst out from the end of the Magic Tunnel where they had been concealed and, screeching obscenities at us, came ripping down through the woods and out into the Battlefield. It was a shock for us that anyone but ourselves would know about the Magic Tunnel, and we knew then how deeply our secrets had been betrayed. But just as quickly, we realized we were outnumbered.

There were boys there we had never seen before, who didn't go to our school. None of them were Shamrocks. None of them wore simulated battle costumes, but most of them were armed. Some carried fresh-cut forsythia switches, and others brandished sticks and jagged boards. Leading the band into action was Shaun Tully and Buckley the Kicker. It was the Tully gang. They were not there to play games. They were there to fight. Really fight.

They launched into us with such speed and fury that we scarcely knew what was happening. We found ourselves punched, thrown to the ground, kicked, slashed with forsythia branches so hard that it tore our skin. Our regalia, our flags, our armor entrapped us so that we couldn't defend ourselves.

Ollie got tangled up in his flamboyant red cape and fell to the ground while some kid snatched the plastic horn off his hat and began to pommel him with it, breaking it into splinters, and only his mother's old-fashioned thick hat saved him from serious injury.

Our first line collapsed so rapidly into the second line that the Tullys were grabbing our wagons and turning our own dust bombs against us, hitting us full force in the face with the dust and blinding us and making us scream. Hernando was utterly unprepared for an assault like this; Florian fell into his arms, and both of them pitched backward. Florian's face was already bruised and swollen. Li-San Lu actually did manage to get off a few acorns with his sling, and Tully howled as an acorn slapped forcefully into the center of his forehead. But Li-San soon found himself a victim of the terrible Buckley the Kicker and was sent rolling in the dust in front of a cascade of savage kicks.

We scrambled, we fell, we tumbled over each other under a hail of fists and sticks and dust bombs and all the projectiles we had taken so much time to accumulate, as the Tullys yanked off our chivalric garb, tossing it around and laughing and shouting. We fell back in complete disorder to the third line.

And there Hermann Gessner held his ground. He stood with his arms outstretched, not fighting but seizing and throwing back anyone who tried to pass him while they punched and kicked at him, threw dust in his face, spat at him, and shouted obscenities and threats at him. He would not move. They dropped back, puzzled by this. Of course, he was physically enormous. Our whole group sprawled on the ground behind him, momentarily safe. He'd broken the force of the enemies' attack.

Dust swirled around us; we were bleeding and aching; many cried and tears streaked their dusty, bruised faces. Ollie lay in a heap under his red cape and didn't move; Hernando looked as if he was about to vomit; Mike Lehmann showed signs of an incipient black eye; and Jimmy Osperti was gripping his bleeding thigh where both his pants and his skin had been slashed open by a particularly vicious application of a forsythia switch.

Then the MacPherson twins went into action. It was their moment. They hoisted themselves up behind Hermann, threw off their Marine helmets and ammunition belts, and, coming out from either side of Hermann, locked arms and walked directly through the swirls of dust and into the Tully gang, as they chanted that weird song of theirs.

The Tully gang divided, leaving a corridor of filthy, suddenly intimidated gang members, through whom the two brothers marched directly up to Buckley the Kicker and Tully himself. Buckley tried one of his famous kicks, and Robbie MacPherson grabbed the end of his foot and flipped him around. Buckley dove into the dusty ground and smacked his head against a small stone. He let out a terrible scream.

Tully turned to run, but Robbie grabbed him and swung him around by the shoulders, and Scott slammed his fist directly into Tully's face, causing blood to spurt from his nose. Another well-aimed punch sent Tully sprawling to the ground, where he scrambled backward on his heels and his palms for a moment, flipped over, jumped up, and ran into the woods, holding on to his face. The entire Tully gang, seeing their leaders running off, went into flight as well.

With the exception of the MacPhersons, the Knights Templar could not rally to the pursuit, though Tony Santini had recovered himself and, with fists flailing like a shadow boxer, would have followed them in their retreat. The rest were defeated and humiliated, sitting or standing now among their childish things strewn all over the Battlefield and realizing how foolish they had been, how pretentious, how vulnerable.

Hermann Gessner went from one Knight to the next, picking them up, helping to brush them off, applying bandages to wounds, and wondering why any of this had happened. The MacPhersons were edgy, ready to continue the fight. Everyone was grateful to them. At least the Tully gang had been prevented from gloating over its victory and walking away with trophies.

On the following day, the Fourth Sunday after Easter, St. Ignatius parish was ministered to by the most bruised, scarred, and crestfallen collection of acolytes probably ever seen in the history of ecclesiastical institutions. The priests were alarmed, the deacons mortified, and the congregations astonished at the black eyes, the bandaged faces, the scraped hands and wrists.

Those of us whose ears were tuned to the Latin of the epistle for that Sunday, according to the old rite, may have heard, *"Ira enim viri justitiam*

Dei non operatur" — "For the wrath of man does not work the justice of God." The voices of the MacPherson twins were stronger than ever, and, at the Alleluia verse, filled the church with their angelic song: *"Dextera Domini fecit virtutem: dextera Domini exaltavit me"* — "The right hand of the Lord hath wrought power; the right hand of the Lord hath exalted me."

During the subsequent week, efforts to revive the Knights Templar were fruitless. We were too ashamed of ourselves — before the school, but especially among ourselves.

The Shamrocks, of course, were cowardly and beneath contempt and everyone knew that now, though there were those few, as I guess there will always be, who admired their cunning in bringing the Tully gang up from the wharves of the East River and into Central Park and luring us so perfectly into the trap that destroyed us.

Of course, without Mark Spaghnum's expert advice, none of that would have been possible. Mark himself suddenly seemed to have taken ill; he didn't show up at school again that year.

As for the Tully gang, they truly vanished into their hiding places and perhaps dissolved as much as we did. Tully with his broken nose and Buckley with his badly bruised forehead never came back to St. Ignatius. They had been brought down by the courage of the MacPherson twins alone and, as leaders, were disgraced.

Things went reasonably well on Eighty-Fourth Street during recess, nevertheless — perhaps because the year was over and everyone's mind was on something else. Mother Eileen McKay did give some of us a rather odd look. I don't think she was aware of precisely what had happened. And Sister Bridget was poised to drop us into the bottomless abyss of non–sixth graders, where we would cease to have any meaning or importance for her.

But the Knights Templar could not regroup. The fantasy — or was it the understanding — that made us work was gone.

Mrs. Lehmann, knowing from her own son's black eye and tearfully sputtered account that disaster had struck, tried to revive our spirits by inviting all of us to have lunch together at a restaurant, followed by a matinee in a real live theater downtown on Broadway. We saw Mary Martin perform in *Peter Pan*. Tommy Shanahan and Kevin O'Kelley were asked to join us for this event. The efforts of the gang of lost boys in Never-Never Land to repel the evil pirates were not lost on us, and we all wished we could fly around through the air as Mary Martin did in the role of Peter Pan. If we could have flown around like that, Tully and his crew would have had something more serious to contend with. Anyway, we enjoyed the afternoon, and we enjoyed the company of our new friends, but we didn't revive.

Perhaps it was just as well. It was the end of the school year and, once we advanced into the seventh grade, the playground, and our mission there, would no longer be part of our lives. Many boys left the school that year too. My family moved to New Jersey; Florian Dupré's family was recalled to France. Hermann Gessner's aunt decided to move to the Midwest and some of us, many years later, heard of him when he emerged as a defensive linebacker on the Notre Dame football team. It was said that nobody in his zone ever got past him. Jimmy Osperti, for all his lack of interest in music, followed in his parents' footsteps anyway, took up the violin, and entered the world of symphony orchestras.

Mike Lehmann went on to a New England prep school and then to Harvard, where he chanced to run into none other than the contemptible Mark Spaghnum, whom, after he'd identified himself cheerfully as a fellow collegian at a reception for new students in Dunster House, Lehmann practically punched right there and then in front of the resident house dean. None of us ever heard again of Li-San Lu or Hernando Silva.

Danny Jacobiwitz, I'm told, donned a robe and flowing beard like his father, but his robe was gray and cinched at the waist by a cordelier. As a Capuchin friar, he has worked among the poorest of the poor in the darkest corners of the earth. Tony Santini went to Regis and became a Jesuit. They say he's the old kind of Jesuit — no nonsense, tough to the core, an Ignatian trooper to the end.

The MacPhersons' voices soon cracked, and the choirmaster of St. Ignatius Loyola Church on Park Avenue complained that he'd lost the best treble voices he'd ever had. They were great ends on the Cardinal Hayes football team. They graduated from Fordham and became second lieutenants in the Marines just as Vietnam heated up. Of course, they never returned.

Me?

I, Marty Sadowski, am an electrical contractor in Paterson, New Jersey. The only member of the original group whom I've maintained contact with has been Egon Kola. He runs a restaurant in nearby Passaic.

"No, no, no! Don't tell me!" Ollie shouted at me across that marble table in the café on Third Avenue, when I told him about Egon's restaurant. "Don't tell me it's called The Casbah!"

"As a matter of fact, it is!" I laughed. "And it specializes in exotic couscous dishes and skewered lamb."

"I suppose it's full of dark corners and hidden alcoves where you can have any manner of clandestine assignations with mysterious strangers in the cloak of utmost secrecy."

"I think you're right. At least it has the right setting for it."

"Does it have doorways with beads hanging down over them, through which you can catch a glimpse of enchanted, glowing eyes following your every movement?"

"Well, not that I'm aware of. But I'm sure such a deficit could be easily remedied with just the right suggestion to the proprietor."

Ollie wanted to order me another cappuccino, but I declined. "Frankly," I said, "I'd prefer a beer." He resisted that.

"What about Mike Lehmann," I asked. "Whatever happened to him?"

"You won't believe this, Marty, but he became the real thing—I mean he became a high-ranking member of one of those chivalric orders that does charitable work in the Near East—you know, running hospitals and schools and things like that. He lives between Jerusalem and Rome."

"I guess you need to be loaded to do work like that," I said.

"It helps. But he's on no lark. It's not just an honorary thing for him—a pretext to walk in grand processions sporting a sword and a plumed chapeau. It's his life. *He works hard to get things right.* That's what I hear."

Ollie gazed down into his empty cup for a moment. "So, who won in the end?" he asked. "Who are the winners now?"

"I don't think I understand."

"Just who won? The soft and the sneaky, the mean and the ratty, or the just and the valiant?—though maybe not quite so valiant in the end, most of us, and not so just either."

"I don't know."

"Who won in the Church? Just think of it, Marty! Where's the Latin now? The glorious liturgy, the Palestrina, and the Josquin des Pres? Where are the sacred motets, the Solemn Vespers? Now we have 'Let's hold hands with Jesus'! The soft and the sneaky won that one, no doubt of it. Donny Groghan is probably in a diocesan chancery somewhere, pulling down a comfortable salary on others' charity, the soft and the sneaky pulling the wool over everybody's eyes, mocking the people who pay them, just as they always do."

"Is that why you're estranged?"

"What do you mean?"

"Estranged, in self-imposed exile, apostate …"

"How can you …?"

"It's all too obvious, Ollie. Is it because of people like Donny Groghan that you've abandoned the connections people need in their lives, including the one people need the most?"

"Maybe. Don't press the point, Marty. I already feel bad enough about it."

"What about the mean and the ratty? Where are they? Where's Tully and his bunch?"

"They're either in prison, or they're running the city, maybe even the country. In either case, they won—I mean, they ended up where they always wanted to be: running amok in the back alleyways and slimy gutters of this world, in the dominion of the absurd, the dominion of treachery and violence."

"I wonder if you don't make it sound more fearful than it really is," I inserted.

"Perhaps," he said. "But I take the fallen principalities and powers pretty seriously. It's the one thing I do know something about. Actually, the amazing thing is that Tully himself turned out to be all right. I think that Scott MacPherson's punch may have bent his nose, but it also straightened him out—either that or some special dispensation of divine grace. Or maybe Scott MacPherson's punch *was* the dispensation of divine grace. Anyway, he runs an upscale bakery on Lexington and Seventy-Fourth Street where he sells organic olive-artichoke bread to brain-dead glitz-peddlers like me. *He works hard to get things right.*"

"And the just and the valiant?"

"The just and the valiant—the real ones, just think of that, Marty. Those beautiful voices: *O ces voix d'enfants chantant dans la coupole.*"

"What's that? I don't understand."

"A line by a French poet. His name was Verlaine. T. S. Eliot quotes the line in 'The Wasteland.'"

"I don't know stuff like that, Ollie. What does it mean?"

"It means, 'O those voices of children singing in the dome.'" Ollie almost choked when he said this; he lowered his face, and his eyes watered with tears.

"I think you're taking all of this too hard, Ollie. These things happened so long ago. It's time to forget," I replied.

"Do you think they walked that way—the way they walked into the Tully gang—but now into the dust and smoke of the Plain of Jars, arms gripped together, singing their immortal battle song? Or was it a 'Gloria' by Palestrina they sang, resolutely, forever faithful, *semper fidelis*, as they walked through the portals of their death? I wonder what got them in the end—the Cong, the North Viet regulars, friendly fire from their own aircraft, or maybe fragged in the back by some of their own men who resented their discipline and courage and wouldn't follow them where they were going—*just the way we did.* Does it make any difference?"

"Forget it, Ollie! I mean, you remember there was a lot of ambiguity about that war and people defined their responsibilities accordingly."

"Yeah, but I don't know where there isn't ambiguity about everything people are asked to do, especially when the mean and the ratty and the soft and the sneaky are running the show. Anyway, some of us managed to manufacture as much ambiguity as was convenient for us, but the irony is that we were the least ambiguous of all and the most self-righteous—after all, we thought we knew absolutely what was right and wrong, even though we knew practically nothing.

"Now, in retrospect, I don't know, Marty, what was right and what was wrong about that situation. The point is that so many of us, even if we disagreed about the cause, didn't have the decency to stand by our compatriots in their travail, either in spirit or in compassion. Many of us rooted for the guys who were shooting at them. I joined up with the soft and the sneaky, just as old Mark Spaghnum did. And I've stayed there ever since. It's just that I don't feel very good about it. But the just and the valiant did the honorable thing. The MacPhersons did the faithful thing and lost their lives doing it. They stood by their countrymen.

"What a big deal the rest of us make out of our lives, Marty—our careers, our professions, the things we have, our sacrosanct 'identities' that we nurture with all the attentiveness lavished on a spoiled child; and the bigger and bigger a deal we make out of ourselves, the thinner and flimsier we become. Then we go to therapists, whom we pay to pump up our egos even more than they are already, so that, in the end, we'll vanish into nothing at all. I wonder if that's what Hell is—getting puffed up so big that you're finally vaporized and disappear into a noxious cloud. The more you're concerned with your identity, the less of it you have."

Ollie looked puzzled. "So how come you didn't go to college, Marty? I mean, that's what I heard about you. You were the smartest kid in the class. How it used to annoy Sister Bridget to have to announce, 'Marty Sadowski got the highest grade again.' But she got you to write the Christmas play, and it was a great play. You were our bard, after all, our singer of tales. Our scholar too, our communal memory. Remember when Father Sullivan visited the class one day to talk about the Mass and asked what the Minor Elevation was, the 'Remembrance of All Nature,' as they called it back then, and you recited the whole thing in Latin from memory and then went on to tell him what it meant, where it came from, and what its function in the Mass was. Sister Bridget practically dropped dead on the spot, and Father Sullivan's eyes bulged a foot out of his balding head, and I figured he might have swooped on you right then and there like a hawk and carried you off 'up the river' to Sing Sing or to that seminary in Yonkers or some dreadful place like that."

"*Per ipsum, and cum ipso, et in ipso,*" I said. "You see, I still recall those words.

"Through Him, and with Him, and in Him," Ollie translated. Then he added "*... est omnis honor et gloria ...*"

"Is all honor and glory," I translated in turn. "But you left some of it out, important stuff."

Ollie stared at me for a moment. "You see, I can remember too. Does anybody ever forget something like that? Least of all someone like you. You seemed to know the entire Ordinary of the Mass by memory—in Latin yet—and taught many of us how to be altar boys by simulating the entire priest's role in the privacy of our homes. All you needed was a table, and a big book of some sort, usually a dictionary, a wafer and a cup, and some carafes of grape juice and of water, and a little bell we could tinkle, and nothing could hold you back. You were better at teaching us how to serve the Mass than the priests were. You could imitate the whole thing, do it sometimes more convincingly than the real people could. How you could speak the words of the Consecration! I've never heard it done like that, the way you uttered it as if the entire universe itself revolved around each word: *Hoc est* ..." He hesitated.

"*HOC ... EST ... ENIM ... CORPUS ... MEUM,*" I finished.

"FOR THIS IS MY BODY," he said.

There was a long silence after that. We just sat at the table together and watched the traffic and the crowds on Third Avenue trundling by: the trucks, the cabs, the automobiles, buses filled with passengers, the pedestrians with their children and baby carriages, their packages and briefcases, the honking of horns, the shouts, the laughter, a dazzling and motley pageant, the *processio creaturarum* of this world in all its variety and bustle.

I finally broke the silence. "We were good at what we did. All of us!"

Ollie nodded his agreement. "I think we were. Remember poor Florian Dupré! He was assigned to serve the Masses of that tall French Jesuit who came by from time to time. That priest said the Mass so fast and with such a strange way of pronouncing Latin that none of us could follow him except Florian. I've heard his books, later on, were influential for a while in the Church. Something about the evolution of the universe, about the biosphere and the Omega Point or whatever—I don't remember what it was. I ran into some of that when I was at Villanova but didn't pay much attention to it."

"I don't know much about it either. Such things come and go, but why they come and why they go can be pretty important. Anyway, I'm all right, Ollie. I didn't go to college because I had other things—more important things, frankly—to do. My father died, and I had to support the family. But everything, by and large, has gone well for me. I have a great family of my own and a great business. I work hard to make things right for my customers. I try to figure out what they need and give them that. I do the same for my family and for my friends. I would do that for you too. That's enough. So don't worry about me.

"The problem with you, Ollie," I said, "is that you've subscribed to the idea that life is supposed to work out in certain ways—according to some socially prescribed script that gets written by—well, I don't know by whom, and that's part of the problem, too; and in the end, it's the script that is really supposed to look good, not the life. But by whomever the script is written, life just doesn't follow it. There are just too many surprises—many of them fairly unpleasant, many of them downright horrible, though quite a few of them are more wonderful than we have much of a right to expect them to be."

"I won't worry about you, Marty," Ollie remarked. "How could anyone worry about you! You know, I'm one of those people who write that script. I know how false, how fabricated and contrived it all is. Its purpose is to sell stuff. Or to get power so that you can push other people around—*libido dominandi*, as that old African saint once said, the lust to dominate, the source of all evil. But you have to admit, in any case, that the days of our honor and glory have passed."

"That's where you're wrong again, Ollie," I said. "It wasn't *our* honor and glory. It never was. That's not what we stood for. Sure, we were a bunch of kids playing a game. But, for better or worse, we were the Knights Templar; don't forget that. *We were the Knights Templar.* That's who we were. There were things we believed in, and I figure we got a lot of things pretty well botched up, and we knew we did, and regretted we did, like everyone else does most of the time, like all that nonsense about the Irish being our enemies. But chivalry is always there, even if there's no one around who's chivalric. And I don't mean the chivalry of blood and bluster; I mean the chivalry of service and sacrifice. Such things don't pass away; they never pass away. They don't belong to us; they're gifts we receive; they belong to someone else—"

"*Cujus regnum non erit finis.*" Ollie interrupted, "whose Kingdom has no end."

He gazed at me for several moments. "How often do you think I get to hear something like that?" he said. "You were not just the bard and scholar among us. You were the prophet too."

"Hardly a prophet," I protested, "just someone trying hard get something right, as difficult as it is. All good things are difficult to get right. Anyway, that's beside the point. You know what you're missing in your life, Ollie. You wouldn't have called me over to this table to talk to you if you didn't."

I prepared to depart. I was eager not to drive back to Paterson in the evening rush hour. Ollie gave me his business card. "Look me up sometime. Come into the city for dinner—I mean, you live so close. Why stay away for twenty-five years?"

"Maybe, but you know how twenty-five years passes—like a watch in the night, like a dream, like grass on the meadow," I said, looking at his card. "How come it doesn't say, 'Chief of the Varangian Guard,' on the card?"

"It should, I guess. What it does say is almost as fanciful and pretentious, except that at least the older title had a certain nobility to it. Take care, Marty!"

"Take care, Ollie. Remember me to Shaun Tully when you go into his bakery to get a loaf of that organic olive-artichoke bread."

"Count on me!" he said in reply. "And I'm sure that Tully will be pleased to know that you're thinking of him."

"You're kidding!"

"I'm not kidding. He's not the same person you remember. He's a fine person—generous and cheerful and forthright. Not like me. He probably turned out better than most of us."

The drive back to Paterson wasn't at all bad, despite the traffic tie-up on the ramp leading up to the George Washington Bridge. I was glad to have seen Ollie. I would like to see him again. I would even like to drop in someday at that bakery on Lexington and Seventy-Fourth and pick up some items. I wonder if Tully makes a good old-fashioned loaf of rye bread, organic or not. If he does, I bet it's the best rye bread in New York City.

But I was glad to be getting home. It's always good to get home, wherever that is; and that makes it kind of the same for all of us, doesn't it? I mean, we're all, after all, going in the same direction, and I think that's pretty good too.

Don't you think so?

Leander Baxter and the Foxtowne Races

Leander Baxter, all my sports-car-racing friends would be quick to agree, was possibly the ugliest man who has ever lived. His head was shaped like a clothes hanger held up vertically and on its side: it was narrow and was flat in the back, and, in front, both a receding forehead and a nonexistent chin slanted backward from an immense arched beak of a nose. The top of his head rose to something about as close to a point as you can get, and there a single tuft of hair stuck obliquely out of a mass of hardened furrows and sclerotic veins.

The rest of his body was a short, scrawny bag of bones dangled loosely from that head. No belt ever designed could be so meager as to fasten anything around that waist of his, so his baggy pants were supported by a set of suspenders that hung from the tiny spurs of his shoulders—though, to be sure, his pants were sometimes also secured by what looked like the snippet of a worn-out automotive fan belt tied into a knot at his waist.

For all this, however, Leander was not without a certain charm, if I may be permitted to stretch the meaning of that term a bit: he was a cheerful, good-humored, gentle sort of fellow. And though his smile revealed little more than a mouthful of long, yellow, rodent-like teeth, he had two little emerald eyes that glittered and bulged when he spoke in that twangy cockney accent of his, and that gave him a certain curious animation, especially when, as he was so often prone to do, he stretched out his suspenders with his spidery fingers and allowed them to snap back against his shrunken chest.

One other feature of his commanded attention, and not infrequently solicited a respect well beyond what anyone was, at least initially, ready to offer: his forearms, usually visible because Leander always wore his shirts rolled up to the elbow, were built like Italian salamis—just as thick, just as mottled and ruddy, just as, I should add, peppery and sharp for anyone willing to risk the force of their thrust. For his fingers could contract into bony hammers of unbelievable hardness, and, at the end of those powerful forearms, they became weapons that many regretted having ever provoked.

That scene, I'm sorry to say, was a familiar one—or at least it was familiar to drivers, mechanics, team owners, sundry camp followers, and other riffraff who frequented the racing-car hangouts along the East Coast, especially in Florida. I said I was sorry about this, and I'm sorry that there was something about Leander Baxter that made him the target of any bellicose stranger who happened to be passing through and who happened to cross Leander's path at an inopportune moment—inopportune, I might add, in the final analysis, for the stranger and not for Leander.

But I'm not sorry about the inevitable outcome, for it was invariably amusing, invariably welcome to all those who had the good fortune to observe it. In fact, there was no small amount of jealousy among the habitués of the aforementioned hangouts as to who had been privileged to see what and when and how.

Imagine, for a moment, our bellicose stranger wandering into a bar and becoming gradually soused beyond what's prudent for anyone, in such circumstances, to become. Imagine him fixing his hostile glare on the diminutive, warped figure of Leander Baxter and getting annoyed that such a disfigured exemplar of the hominid species could get away with existing and could, moreover, under such obviously adverse circumstances, dare to exhibit some traces of relative contentment, especially when things are not going too well in the stranger's own hopelessly and undeservedly befuddled life. He approaches this unlikely creature and proceeds to rough him up a bit—you know, just shake him around a little, call him a revolting little creep, or whatever befits the more or less insidious predilections of our bully-boy gentleman at the time.

What follows needs to be seen—or rather, needs to be heard—to be believed (one rarely sees it, for it occurs rapidly and without warning). The relative serenity of the hangout is shattered by an unearthly, high-pitched sound—a snapping sound of the most extraordinary intensity and precision, so sharp indeed that it makes your own head involuntarily whip backward. It sounds as if someone has slapped a bamboo shaft violently against a table. Then our hapless stranger either turns around and walks out of the bar, or else, without waiting for that particular formality, sinks in a heap to the floor, right then and there. In any case, he doesn't get far before collapsing. He's lucky if the tip of his chin hasn't been broken clear off the end of his jaw and is not sagging loosely in the flap of skin just beneath it.

Leander's aim is just that precise and just that powerful. His bony hammer of a fist rises in a lightning-fast uppercut, like the piston of a Formula One car, with the palm of his hand upward, as in a softball pitch. It's not the knuckles but the part of the fingers below the knuckles that makes contact with the tip of the chin. It's a blow that maximizes all the leverage and all the strength of his right forearm. Needless to say, there's never any further contact. Leander meanwhile, unperturbed and imperturbable as ever, returns to whatever gin concoction he's been nursing for the last half hour or so and gives the incident no further thought.

I guess we all regard it as something of a favor to have seen this sort of occurrence at least once in our lives—it gives us status; it places us within a particularly noble niche in the sports-car hierarchy to have been a witness to one of Leander's notorious knockdowns; but the greatest privilege of all was to have seen it happen at the banquet dinner that followed the Foxtowne races, and the observers of that event constitute, quite frankly, a kind of aristocracy to this day among their less-favored peers.

There Leander Baxter knocked down his man, as he was accustomed to do; but in doing so, he succeeded—unintentionally, of course—in knocking down the pretensions of an entire city. The supremely pompous and parvenu municipality of Foxtowne fell at the edge of Leander's bony fist. It was a marvel to see, and the aforesaid municipality has never, at least to my knowledge, recovered.

Leander was famous in quite another way as well. He could, if given sufficient time, a good place to work, plenty of solitude, and several cases of a good-quality British gin, transform any automotive wreck you gave him into a reasonably well-functioning racing car, if not into a contraption of demonic speed and dexterity—and I use the term "contraption" quite deliberately here, for such creations, however capable of the most stunning feats, were as deformed and ungainly as their unfortunate creator.

Some people—people prominent in the world of sports-car racing—thought Leander was perhaps the best automotive mechanic they'd ever known; but this was a difficult hypothesis to test. He didn't like to work with new cars, he detested any kind of team organization, and the whole commercial side of racing was, for some reason, anathema to him. As a result, he was never connected, at least officially, with any of the spectacularly successful teams and car firms, and efforts to recruit him into a position commensurate with his abilities were always tenaciously resisted.

Consequently, it was difficult to assess the extent of his skills. He was more interested in turning junk into speed.

Rumor has it that when he lived in Coventry, England, during the war, he was given the job of taking variously damaged military aircraft and making them fly again. It's said that he was very good at this. It's said that he was the only one who was good at this. After the war, when he became a racing-car mechanic, this sort of perverse talent was transferred to automobiles. But, as good as he was, no major racing team could ever interest him, and no brand-name car attracted his attention ... unless it already had the status of scrap metal conferred officiously upon it by someone who should, presumably, know what he was talking about. This is where Leander came into his own; he was the master of desperate cases. And yes, he could make them work—work beautifully—for a while.

In the early 1950s, he immigrated to the United States.

Rumor had it that he suffered some tragedy early in the war, especially as the result of the great bombing raid on Coventry during the Battle of Britain. He kept his former life a secret, however, though on rare occasions, when deep in his cups, his face suddenly drawn and haggard and his glittering emerald eyes momentarily dulled by some inscrutable suffering, he might, quite unexpectedly, be heard to mumble, half to himself, half to his ill-prepared listeners, "In Coventry, durin' the war ..." But that's as far as he ever got. He would slosh the remains of his gin around the bottom of his glass and mumble again, "In Coventry, durin' the war ..." There was never anything more than that.

No one presumed to press him on the matter, to ask him to continue, to plead for an explanation. We all supposed that perhaps a once reasonably presentable young man was dragged from the smoking ruins of an exploded hanger, transformed into the gnarled and broken human corpus we all could identify to this day as poor Leander.

Whatever military hospital he'd ended up in for a while had not been able to do for him what he'd been able to do for those wrecked aircraft he'd so gallantly and skillfully put into service once more. Or maybe it had. No one had ever claimed that Leander's salvaging operations looked very good, but they certainly worked. The situation with Leander himself was, unfortunately, all too analogous.

Now, I should point out that Leander's arrangement with Bill Hennessy, Palm Beach multimillionaire and international *bon vivant*, was ideal. Bill was a tall, portly, barrel-chested man with wide, roundish cheeks that curled up into large apples when he smiled his cherubic grin. Hennessy was interested in racing cars—that is, in both the cars themselves and in ferreting them, at very high speeds, around racetracks in the fellowship of like-minded colleagues; but though he was enormously wealthy, he wasn't interested in paying exorbitant sums to buy expensive equipment. Furthermore, he fancied that he had a certain ability to design cars and was always dreaming of making some sort of hybrid automobile that would stun the world by combining, in some extraordinary way, the parts of many different well-known racing breeds.

This suited Leander perfectly: he could collect the parts, most of them bent and burnt from whatever catastrophe had put them out of commission; work on them at leisure in the roomy Spanish hacienda-style garage in Palm Beach that Hennessy let him use and that had a small apartment attached where Leander could live; submit to the verbose, but luckily infrequent, discourses delivered by Hennessy on his hybrid dream car of the future while limitless bottles of gin were opened, emptied, and tossed into a mound of hollow motor-oil cans and rusty auto parts; and, several times a year, roll out of the garage some patchwork monstrosity that was bound to outrun anything that you wanted to put up against it, at least until Hennessy, in his inimitable way, had destroyed it—a feat usually accomplished by the fifth lap of any race he entered.

For Hennessy, if I may be permitted the liberty of passing on gossip that everybody knows already, destroyed everything he touched: the theatrical shows he sponsored always closed a day or two after opening night; his marriages foundered, one after another, leaving behind a costly wake of alimonies; his multitudinous hunting and fishing expeditions had a singular way of never producing the desired quarry (it always got away, for some, usually absurd, reason); his harebrained schemes to increase his already enormous inheritance generally resulted in its sizable, if momentary, reduction, even as it enriched every high-level confidence man (and woman) operating within the New York–Palm Beach axis; and his car racing was a series of disasters.

Yet he found all of this very amusing.

Hennessy reveled in failure with an enthusiasm and a *joie de vivre* as intense as his equally bedeviled and now deceased father had reveled in success. In fact, every failure was the source of some hilarious joke that Hennessy could tell at a dinner party. He had lots and lots of these jokes. And when he guided the smoking remains of a racing car into its first and final pit stop, its clutch ground to powder, its gears stripped, and its brakes practically red hot, he laughed deliriously with triumph as he yanked off his goggles, revealing an island of crinkled white skin and jocular blue eyes in a face besmirched with oily fumes.

After all, who did lead the pack—I mean really lead the pack—until the car came apart?

Hennessy was one of those men who love machines but don't understand them, don't understand that they can endure only so much stress and no more, and consequently are excessively brutal with them, quickly pushing them to a premature demise.

Leander, I think, was probably always just a bit depressed by this outcome, even though he knew in advance that it would happen. But that's when he would really go to work—no longer on Bill Hennessy's car, but on everybody else's, wandering up and down along the pit-stops of the racing teams and pitching in to help them out, often solving problems with a speed they couldn't match and putting their own cars back on the course in crack running order. Oddly, this skill was never envied or resented by other mechanics. He intervened only when he was asked to, he carried out the task with humility, and he walked away without expecting anything in return. Least of all was he looking for someone's job. Hence, his arrangement with Hennessy was ideal. There was nothing else he wanted.

Now, all of this brings me back to Foxtowne.

Some cities, like some people, grow faster than they should, and it gives them odd ideas about themselves. The municipal elders of Foxtowne, at the pinnacle of its glory—which is to say, before it was brought down by Leander—decided it was time for the city to make a name for itself; after all, it was, of late, no longer a mid-Florida shantytown surrounded by vast snake-infested swamps and inhabited by a few dozen contentious, tobacco-chewing alligator hunters.

In its own perception, it had grown, it had blossomed—if I might here be allowed to invoke a florid rhetoric befitting the object of hypothetical praise—into ever the most exquisitely burg-like of all burgs in this burgish world, with boulevards and highways, fast-food strips and shopping malls (though without the best stores, to be sure—a problem certain to remedied, however), and acres of tiny houses and patterned driveways stretching endlessly over the Floridian savannas and baking like little tin pastry trays under the remorseless Florida sun.

To celebrate its transformation into a major municipality, the Foxtowne elders decided to add an "e" to its original name of Foxtown and to build a gigantic, and utterly pretentious, recreational center with a cheaply constructed banquet hall as its crown of glory. But the city elders, having achieved the erection of what was, after all, a monument to themselves, conceded that there was one final problem that needed to be solved. No one used the banquet hall, because no one came to Foxtowne. Somehow the town needed to become justly celebrated throughout the world.

Well, like some other Floridian townships, Foxtowne had nearby a series of landing strips used as Air Force supply dumps in the past and now abandoned to clumps of swamp grass, scorpions, and waddling possum families. Like these other townships, it conceived the idea that it could convert these strips to some novel purpose: Why not use them as the basis for what might turn eventually into an international racing track? After all, world-famous Sebring, not too far to the north of Foxtowne, had originally done something of the kind and had made of itself an astounding success. Certainly, Foxtowne could do the same.

But it would start off modestly — that is to say, with minimum invest-ment of either city money or city intelligence, both of which, it may be said, were in short supply — and invite the Palmetto Sports Car Association of Southern Florida to hold its annual weekend convocation at what would be touted as a new and exciting racing facility. The two days of events would be highlighted by a grand banquet on Saturday evening specifically for the racing teams in the magnificent new banquet hall.

Frankly, I don't know what made the governing board of the Palmetto Sports Car Association accept this proposal without looking into it more carefully than it did. That it holds its biannual meetings in the cocktail lounge of the Sunny Vistas Hotel in Miami didn't help matters too much. Anyway, whatever firm the Foxtowne elders hired to do the public relations pitch did a great job; I understand that no one from the firm had ever actually been to Foxtowne or ever planned to go there; but they sold it as heaven on earth, and the gradually more and more inebriated members of the governing board believed every word of it.

As a result, in late spring of that year — an inauspicious time, for that's when Florida begins to get too hot for an event of this kind (or, arguably, for an event of any kind) — hundreds of racing cars on trailers and thousands of sports-car devotees descended on the hitherto obscure little city of Foxtowne. Hennessy was among them, driving a large, well-equipped RV camper and towing behind him a trailer with Leander's most recent fabrication — a bashed-up version of a Lotus with a dozen parts borrowed from other cars packed variously into it. Hennessy had hoped to enter it at Sebring, but it was finished too late for that, and the Foxtowne event, though largely an amateur affair, would be a good testing ground. Leander was somewhere in the back of the camper, taking a nap because, as he often did, he slept during the day and worked at night.

In one sense, the details of Hennessy's race were largely unexceptional. As usual, he took off like a rocket but destroyed the car before the third lap by running into a cinder block that had been carelessly left by the side of the track and that others were swerving to avoid and that Hennessy, for some odd reason, was convinced he could clear if he was going fast enough, though his Lotus hybrid was the lowest-slung car he'd ever driven. The block ripped out the bottom of the car, and it returned, sputtering and bleeding oil, to its pit stop with its entrails dragging along the ground like some wounded and savagely gored picador's horse in a Spanish arena.

Hennessy was bellowing with laughter, as if he'd just had the funniest experience of his life. Apparently, he thought somehow that the car would jump over the block as if the car actually were a horse and he was racing it in a steeplechase event. Leander was noticeably disconcerted by such idiocy, as he always was; but that was the price he paid for the freedom he wanted. He muttered something and walked away to see what he could do for other drivers and their cars.

The cinder block was, in its own way, merely an exemplary case, if I may use such a lofty expression to describe such a paltry thing, of what the whole weekend was like. The racetrack was a horror. Failure to consult the right people, coupled with the determination to spend the minimum of money, had left behind a clumsily demarcated obstacle course, filled with dangerous potholes, bumps in the corroded concrete surface, right-angle turns almost impossible to negotiate at any speed, bad visibility, and sections of slippery molds and fungi where the original landing strip had become partially immersed in the surrounding swamps.

Animals wandered onto the track at will: one old hound dog was killed early in the race, and an entire possum family was reduced into a furry blood slick upon which cars skidded and swung out of control. One car avoided hitting a miniature Key deer by leaving the track and swerving off like a swamp craft over an adjacent wetland until it sank finally into the muck and fronds, leaving no trace behind except for intermittent bubbles popping up through the mud and a swearing driver jumping up and down and frantically pulling leeches off his drenched racing jacket. He was lucky; he didn't have to deal with the deadly water moccasin that yet another driver noted coiled up sleepily in his bucket seat just as he was about to hoist himself into the cockpit.

Needless to say, accident followed accident, and fortunately none of them were too serious because the good city fathers had provided almost nothing in the way of emergency fire or medical equipment. Further, tickets to watch the race were expensive, and this expense was compounded by additional fees that spectators had to pay to move from one section of the track to another, which fees were again charged if they retraced their steps. Getting to and from the limited and utterly lamentable toilet facilities under these circumstances could turn out to be a costly venture, so much so that gradually even the most obsessively modest among the day's sports-car aficionados found themselves drifting off to nearby clumps of mangrove or other barely adequate cover in order to heed the call of nature.

Off the track, things were even worse. Foxtowne wasn't prepared for the huge influx of people who planned to spend at least one or two nights there. Camping areas had been set up, but they were situated on such poorly drained land that countless cars and campers sank into the wet ground and had to be pulled out by the curiously abundant tow trucks available around the perimeters of the campgrounds. Pegging tents in such marshy terrain was out of the question; sanitary facilities were absent; and at night clouds of mosquitoes arose from the swamps, making the barbecues and other traditional festivities of the racing weekend utterly impracticable.

In town, businesses raised their prices to the highest level they thought they could get without causing a riot. Meanwhile, the local police force, reinforced for the weekend by droves of officers brought in from surrounding towns and by a group of not altogether reputable citizens deputized especially for the event, managed to post No Parking signs in every location it was necessary to park, as well as to create on every road leading to the racecourse special speed limits that were impossible not to violate unless you were piloting a three-year-old's tricycle along such a road with at least one of your legs in a cast.

The result of these measures, added to a traffic-control system as chaotic as it was rigidly enforced, was a level of police harassment that quite defied anyone's memory of an occasion that could equal it. Furthermore, the ramshackle and as yet unrenovated Foxtowne courthouse, an unsavory relic of a juridical past better left unremembered, remained open throughout the weekend and late into the night, staffed by a succession of magistrates, each more surly and imperious than the one who just vacated it. Local authorities wanted to be sure that no one left town without paying their parking and speeding tickets. Accordingly, throughout the weekend a parade of racing fans was dragooned through the unpainted hallways of the sweltering building, often made to wait for hours, threatened with being clapped into a crowded cell if the charges were contested, and forced to pay an inevitably hefty fine before having their impounded cars returned to them.

On the racetrack, matters were not helped by a violent thunderstorm that passed over the region in the late afternoon. In the steamy aftermath of the storm, the first day's final race was conducted by a few dispirited drivers who no longer cared what was happening. When the checkered flag was brought down on the final race, a young, unknown driver in a Jaguar glided into victory, his car and his energies, much to his own surprise, being among the few that survived the day. He apparently didn't mind spinning and sliding around huge palm fronds, plastic trash bags, and Styrofoam food receptacles scattered all over the track by the storm and left there by the negligent maintenance crew (who, in fact, had already gone home).

In a damp, scarcely noticed little ceremony, he was awarded a monstrous, gold-painted plastic trophy for his pains, presented along with a wet, lip-sticky smooch from a local beauty who sported possibly the loftiest bouffant of peroxide-blonde hair the world has ever seen and who represented the Foxtowne Chamber of Commerce.

He also was forced to listen to a long harangue from the mayor of Foxtowne extolling the virtues of his municipality in setting up such a public-spirited event, while a photographer from the *Foxtowne Bugle* snapped several photographs and took down some notes. He asked the victor if he was deeply grateful to the good people of Foxtowne for all that they had done for him (this gratitude obviously having not been volunteered); the victor mumbled something that neither the reporter nor anyone else heard, but the reporter wrote down a gushing reply of his own invention to flatter the readers of Sunday's newspaper. During all of this, the spectators drifted back to their soggy encampments and prepared to settle down for the night.

The next day, the rally, the gymkhana, and the acceleration tests were supposed to take place.

None of this happened. It couldn't happen, not after Leander had done his … his job, or whatever you want to call it.

The paramount event for the weekend, of course, was to be the banquet on Saturday evening. It had been heralded as a black-tie affair, and wet, exhausted, soiled drivers and their mechanics found themselves in the awkward situation of struggling into rented white dinner jackets and the accompanying apparel without showers or appropriate places to change. Gradually they began to converge on the banquet hall itself, mainly on foot.

The facility was only about a mile away from the track, and they realized that to drive might take an hour or more as they were marshaled by traffic control along some circuitous route that would wind inexplicably through the entire city, as well as possibly incur an infraction of some draconian traffic rule that could land them in the courthouse for hours. As it turned out, the decision to walk there had benefits later on, which no one could have anticipated.

The banquet hall was a curious combination of something contemporary in style with something traditionally Southern. Its front entrance was set off by a colonnade of ornate classical pillars molded out of plastic. Behind them, glass doors led into a large, gymnasium-like area where exposed girders and cooling ducts laced back and forth high over the dining area and supported garish chandeliers that dangled below. At one end of this cavernous edifice was a stage. A twenty-member dance band, dressed in a pale-pink livery, had set up their equally pale-pink music stands and their brassy instruments and made ready to entertain the honored guests.

In front of the stage was a large buffet table covered by a floor-length tablecloth and by that sort of display of food — of pineapples and frosted hams and spiny Florida lobsters and other items — that is familiar to anyone who has had the nauseating experience of viewing such gustatory outlays on cruise ships and in gambling casinos and that, for some reason, despite the smiling chefs who stand behind these exhibits, never gets eaten by anybody. In this case, an attendant with a white tunic and slicked-back hair hovered unctuously over the display. His job was to keep people away from it.

On the left side of the stage and buffet was a long bar where several bartenders awaited what they figured, and correctly so, would be a heavy demand for drinks. Between that bar and the stage were two sets of swinging double doors that led into the kitchen. On the right side of the stage and buffet were two doors, quite close together, one labeled "Ladies" and the other "Gentlemen."

If you looked toward the opposite end of the banquet hall, you saw a colossal mural in chalklike pastels, covering the entire wall, of Ponce de Leon discovering the Fountain of Youth, backed up by his band of astonished conquistadors. They had good reason to be astonished, for squirming around in the fountain was a bevy of the most lascivious-looking nymphs, or mermaids, or whatever, that have ever been painted in the history of the world. I've never known what the word "fleshpot" actually means, but in this painting the Fountain of Youth was certainly depicted as a pot of flesh.

The banquet hall wasn't, however, without a touch of elegance, for on the far side of the hall was a series of tall French windows with delicately fashioned fans over their doors. These doors, however incongruent with the décor of the hall, were wide open and led out to a spacious and manicured lawn behind the building. The lawn itself was bordered by a dense woodland of cypress and tamarind, all hung dramatically with long swaths of Spanish moss.

The banquet commenced.

The band, known as the Baying Hounds, began to play a kind of swing music from the thirties in a whiny "country-western" style—just the sort of the thing intended to regale an over-eighties crowd, if such a crowd happened to be there and could stand to listen to it. The sports-car teams filed in and looked for places among the garishly decorated tables.

The banquet was free, supposedly, the tab being picked up by the Foxtowne Chamber of Commerce, but hidden costs began to emerge. For example, the drinks were not free, nor were, as people found out too late, the bowls of chips and pretzels and other comestibles served up with them. Since dinner was intentionally delayed for as long as possible, and, since the price of everything was astronomical, the teams found themselves paying lots of money out of pocket.

Naturally, a great deal of drinking went on. The long bar near the kitchen doors was kept busy for a full hour or more as waiters rushed trays of glasses back and forth, delivering well-diluted but still, over time, potent drinks to the impatient customers. The sight of the food on the buffet table, counteracted by the rancid smell of its preservatives, served only to exacerbate their appetite with a mix of attraction and repulsion.

The arrangements for the banquet were presided over by a short, rotund *maître d'* in a pink dinner jacket, a white ruffled shirt, and a little black bow tie. He had a remarkable resemblance to one of Walt Disney's three little pigs — the industrious one who made the brick house — and he kept, not quite appropriately, given the characters in the original tale, huffing and puffing up and down the lanes between the tables, giving orders and rebuffing the complaints of the sports-car teams with comments both contemptuous of them and self-pitying of himself. The waitstaff was a strange lot. Were they migrant waiters on loan from the toughest seafood joints from higher up on the East Coast: from Atlantic City or Asbury Park or Coney Island or wherever unpredictable and dangerous customers might be expected to convene?

The *maître d'* had also presumed to hire a staff of bouncers in case anyone became too boisterous. This staff was provided by an assembly of thugs, about fifteen of them, enlisted from the local motorcycle club and stuffed into ill-fitting evening clothes. They sat in a special room reserved for them behind the kitchen, read magazines, pulled up their sorely strained cummerbunds and dress shirts so that they could display and study each others' belly tattoos, and waited to be called into action, if such action were ever, at any point, deemed necessary.

The great repast was finally served: canned fruit cocktail with a splotch of melted lime sherbet as a garnish, followed by a plate of prime rib au jus, so fat and so overtenderized that it looked like a clump of whale blubber floating in puddle of greasy beet juice. It was accompanied by a white slippery mound of whipped something or other, presumably potatoes. And carrots diced up with peas — you know, I'm sure, that mutually incompatible concoction, especially when the carrots are undercooked and the peas are overcooked. The meal was eaten in silence as the "hounds" of the band "bayed" on and on with relentless monotony.

Dessert? There never was dessert. Maybe dessert was that chocolate cake and the other confections that ended up all over the place. Who knows?

Now listen. Here it comes.

It was never, under any circumstances, a pleasant thing to eat close by Bill Hennessy. Yes, in the proper setting, Hennessy was something of a gourmet. Indeed, he'd partaken of much of the finest cuisine that the world can offer in its finest restaurants; but he was also something of a gourmand, and vile food, somehow, induced him into what resembled a consumptively maniacal state. The viler the food, the viler became the barbarian relish with which he slurped it up. He attacked his roast beef and whipped potatoes with unbridled passion. Indeed, I think that the entire slab of roast beef went down in one piece. It's amazing he didn't choke to death on it.

Leander, having finished God only knows how much gin and needing to put a little distance between himself and the monster of consumption at his side, decides to make the perilous journey to the men's room. Why perilous? Because he's in no condition to go anywhere.

He gets up and starts his walk. He seems to be lost. He swerves back and forth, bumping into tables, chairs, people, even a waiter or two. Several accommodating gents, figuring out where he's headed to, give him a little shove to get him turned back in the right direction.

Everyone begins to watch. They laugh.

The waiters and the *maître d'* begin to watch. They scowl.

The band stops its baying. They watch, too.

The attention of the entire banquet is now focused on Leander as he maneuvers his way to the front of the hall. He gets himself poised about twenty yards from the men's room door, squints to make out the word "Gentlemen" on it, aims himself accordingly, backs up a bit and then plunges forward. His trajectory veers off course. In he goes through the door marked "Ladies."

The banquet hall erupts into applause—clapping, shouting, hollering anything and everything you can think of—which breaks the gloomy demeanor of the sports-car teams.

But the unctuous and decorative attendant behind the buffet table doesn't have the same reaction and is no longer quite so unctuous and decorative anymore. He dives through the ladies' room door a moment or two after Leander and reemerges, holding Leander practically suspended in the air by the back of his collar and shaking him, so that Leander looks not altogether unlike a freshly snagged pompano flapping back and forth as it's lifted up on a line out of the Gulf Stream and into someone's fishing net. The attendant then lowers Leander to the floor and, still grappling him by the neck, begins shouting obscenities at him.

Leander has his footing again. That's a bad thing (for the attendant, that is).

Leander has his footing again. And that's a good thing (for Leander, that is).

He's anchored.

The entire banquet hall falls into silence — a silence of breathless anticipation. They know what's going to happen.

Suddenly it comes — the sound of a bullwhip snapping, or a tree cracking violently in a hurricane hitting the Bahamas, or a bat hitting a baseball with unspeakable force.

The quondam warden of inedible frosted hams and plumed pineapples rocks back and forth for a few seconds, his eyes glazed and his tongue lolling out of this mouth, sits down on the floor, rolls his head around once or twice, and, with one shoulder and hip propped up in most awkward way, pitches over and lies motionless.

The audience is almost as stunned. In a stupor, Leander gazes down at his most recent victim, as if he doesn't quite know what's happened.

A waiter bolts out from behind a nearby table and lunges at him. He never gets close. From somewhere in that banquet hall a plate filled with prime rib au jus and whipped potatoes rises up to meet the attack. The waiter falls back, wiping gravy and slippery potatoes from his jacket and threatening to "kill" the guy who did that. The *maître d'* quickly motions together a squad of tuxedo-clad shock troops and advances on Leander. He snorts as he struts, huffing and puffing his way toward Leander. "Ah knew it, ah jus' knew there'd be trouble, ah knew ..." He's cut off by a martini glass that whizzes past his nose. More plates rise up to block his squad. Bellowing and booing and hurling plates come from every direction in the banquet hall as the squad, hunched down and with arms over heads, retreats to the kitchen doors under a shower of flying utensils.

Leander, meanwhile, disappears.

After this, there's a short respite. The drivers and mechanics, roused at last from their dispirited torpor, joke with one another, stand up and make impromptu speeches, offer toasts and challenges, and call out noisily to friends at the other end of the hall. Seeing Leander pull off one of his famous knockdowns in such a particularly spectacular setting is a cause of no little celebration. They're elated. They jump up on their chairs and whoop and shout and dance, turning around in little circles and wrapping bunches of plastic flowers on their heads. Leander has just enacted for them a kind of collective revenge for everything that has gone wrong in Foxtowne. Meanwhile, all the banquet personnel evacuate the scene while the Baying Hounds creep down behind their music stands and instrument boxes and keep out of sight.

But trouble's brewing, and the more perspicacious members of the crowd begin alerting their fellows to what's about to happen and to get prepared. For when the kitchen doors swing open again, discharging a wild mob of waiters, cooks, busboys, dishwashers, and the gang of thugs hired as bouncers, the attack is met by a solid wall of flying plates, silverware, ice cubes, bread baskets, vases with plastic flowers in them, glasses, beer bottles, and chairs.

The noise of the first onslaught thunders and reverberates through the dining hall, as its impact pins the opposing army to the walls by the kitchen doors and drives many into the kitchen again, while others scramble over and hunker down behind the long bar. The *maître d'* makes a rather late entrance, comes huffing and puffing through the doors, and tries to stop his own people from counterattack. To no avail. He's hit in the face with a slab of roast beef and sent reeling and gagging back through the kitchen doors.

The counterattack takes place. Banquet hall personnel explode out of the kitchen again, now armed with pots and pans, ladles, mixing bowls, brushes, brooms, sponges, scouring pads, and other projectiles that they fling through the air, while their comrades, pinned against the wall or behind the bar, begin picking up and throwing back the things that had initially been tossed at them, contending all the while with the bottles of booze whose short careers have come to an end as broken glass in alcohol-reeking puddles.

The sports-car teams immediately flip their tables over to use as barriers facing the enemy and then return the fire. Soon enough, by linking table to table, they create a series of trenches and cross trenches in which individual combatants can move back and forth into different positions as the battle demands.

Meanwhile, a group of waiters manage to take possession of the stage and, with the now eager participation of the Baying Hounds, is able to use it as an ideal spotting position to fire downward at the drivers below. Several waiters even drop into the space between the stage and the buffet table and shower the drivers with the food display. One driver is hit full in the face with a frosted ham, while another is gashed on his wrist by the claw of a careening lobster.

It's then that one of the more notable acts of martial bravery takes place, one that is especially fortunate, as it turned out later, for Leander. A gaunt figure, probably six foot five with immense shoulders, rears up from among the tipped-over tables, and, in the full force of the flying objects that filled the air, begins to chant the Marine hymn as he leads an assault on the stage. He's followed by ten or so young stalwarts.

Accompanied by the cheers of the entire assembly, they drive off the waiters posted behind the buffet tables and mount the stage, where a furious battle ensues. The Baying Hounds retreat in frantic disorder, leaving their instruments behind. The waiters are tougher and hold out to the last before they're driven off. The victorious Marine snatches up a trumpet that had been stashed under one of the chairs and blows a series of harsh, loud blasts over the hall. Everyone hollers their approval, while in a far corner of the hall several voices are lifted in a Notre Dame football chant.

Bill Hennessy, meanwhile, kept looking for Leander. He figured Leander must be under that buffet table and hidden from sight by its floor-length covers. He knew that Leander could be in serious trouble and that he should get him out of there as soon as possible. It would be only a matter of minutes before the police would show up. He began to crawl through the network of trenches, encouraging the pockets of combatants as he went, until he reached the front line, where the exchange of projectiles was most intense. The space between the front line and the buffet table would be perilous to cross, but now at least he had cover provided by his colleagues on the stage. The floor was littered with broken glass and slippery with food. He eyed the stained and battered buffet table and took the plunge. A moment later he was underneath the table and surrounded on all sides by the heavy table coverings.

It was dark there, and curiously silent as well, as if the coverings filtered out most of the noise, even though there were regular thuds and muted explosions, as an object hit the top of the tables or the nearby floor and shattered into little pieces. It was like … It was like being in a kind of bunker or in some kind of bomb shelter.

In the darkness at the far end of the table he saw Leander, sitting, his back stooped, his head just barely touching the bottom of the table, legs folded, his hands in his lap. His face was drawn and haggard. The light had gone out in his eyes. He gazed emptily into the darkness.

"You all right, Leander?" Hennessy asked.

He nodded. His body rocked just a little bit back and forth.

He mumbled something Hennessy could not hear. He moved closer.

"In Coventry …" Leander began.

He hesitated.

"In Coventry, durin' the war …" he said again.

"Yes," said Hennessy, crawling up to Leander and sitting down in front of him, though he had to stoop his head low to be in a sitting position. "Tell me what happened in Coventry during the war, Leander. Tell me about it."

There was a long silence. The thuds, the breakage, the uproar outside continued in full force around them, though muffled by the heavy tablecloths. One large piece of pottery smashed on the table right over their heads.

"Yuh know, boss," Leander mumbled. "I'm 'earin' some blokes say I got ta look the way I do 'cause a' somethin' that 'appened ta me durin' the war."

"Yes, Leander, I've heard people say that."

"Well, fact is, I was born this way. Me dad neva saw me 'cause I was born aftah 'e went away to Flanders in the first big row, and 'e did'na survive that. Me mum used ta say 'e was a lucky man for all a' that. 'E would'a found 'is grave any'ow the first moment 'e seen me, says she. Better lookin' down the snout a' one a 'em Hun machine guns than at me, says she. That's me own mum who says that. That's how bad it was, Mr. 'Ennessy—when yuh own mum makes a point, now and again, a tellin' yuh how ugly yuh are."

"I think I understand—maybe just a little bit."

A series of shrieks and cheers reached them from beyond the tablecloths. Some major attack had begun, but it died down quickly. The attack had obviously been repulsed.

In the darkness, Leander still stared down at his hands in his lap. "But there's anotha thin' that's even more difficult to understand, boss. Yuh see, one day I be meetin' this girl, and 'er name is Alice. Alice ain't no ordinary girl; she's a real beauty, I mean she's a real special girl. And she goes for me. I mean she luvs me. Can yuh figure that, she actually luvs me? And I luv 'er."

Leander looked up and gazed at Hennessy through the shadows of the tablecloth.

"Yuh know, if yuh're born lookin' like some kinda bloomin' mistake, and the prettiest girl in Coventry takes a fancy to yuh, that's no small thin'. I mean, no small thin'. Course, the otha' blokes in town, what with all their preenin' and all their charmin' ways, dunna take to this all that well. That's 'ow I learned to knock a fella down — it was for 'er sake. They gave me a lot a' trouble for 'er sake. And they gave 'er trouble too."

A heavy crash on the tabletop above them suggested that someone had jumped from the stage onto the buffet table. Footsteps slammed along the tabletop, followed by another loud thump as the bounder leapt off to the floor and ran away.

"What happened to Alice?" Hennessy asked.

Leander looked down again at his hands in his lap for a moment before he answered.

"It was'na me, boss; it was she got dragged out from a buildin' afta' the big raid on Coventry. They could'na save 'er."

Leander shook his head slowly, resignedly.

He explained, "Yuh know, a fella like me does'na get a second chance, even if 'e be wantin' it. Aftah Alice, I did'na even want it. Nothin' could be the same as 'er. It's been a lonely life evah since."

They sat together in the darkness, sat in each other's presence, ignoring the riot going on around them. Hennessy, perhaps for the first time in his life, was able to join seriously, if but momentarily, in another's grief. Then he shook himself, as from a stupor. The sounds of the battle had taken an ominous turn.

Hennessy said, "Leander, we need to get out of here. The fun-and-games part of this situation is pretty much over. Now the serious part will begin, and you'll be in big trouble if the police get hold of you. They'll blame you for the entire thing."

Life flickered back into Leander's eyes. He looked up. "Then we'd bettah be on our way, had'na we?"

Hennessy lifted the tablecloth and peered out. "We could wait for a lull, if it ever came, but we should go right now. At least we know we're protected from the back."

The situation in the banquet hall was worse than ever. A new sortie from the kitchen doors, led entirely by the motorcycle gang, armed with fire extinguishers and spraying foam wildly all over the place, was repulsed by a thunderous salvo of dessert plates, each with a piece of chocolate cake or some other pastry on it. These desserts, hundreds of them, stacked up on dollies, had been discovered by some of the more enterprising drivers reconnoitering for fresh ammunition. They'd been distributed just in time for the new onslaught from the kitchen.

Of course, they're picked up and returned with equal force, many of the pieces of cake ending up as black splotches on the great mural of the Fountain of Youth. The fleshpot of squirming nymphs no longer looks all that enticing, and Ponce de Leon's beaming visage has been effaced by a splatter of key lime pie.

In the meantime, a number of chandeliers either had gone out or been torn down from their roosts, leaving behind intimidating gaggles of live electrical wires and plunging the banquet hall into an eerie twilight darkness.

Hennessy and Leander scrambled out from underneath the table, jumped to their feet, and, accompanied by the whoops and cries of their confreres, ran across the debris on the floor to the first line of tables, leapt over the first table, and stooped down just as a barrage of cooking items clattered against it. The surrounding combatants promptly returned a volley of dinnerware.

Crouched behind the same table was a rather jovial man, stout, wearing a captain's hat and sporting a thick mustache, who had collected a copious supply of glass ashtrays, which he'd stacked up in a column. Ceremoniously he lifted one ashtray after the other from the column, lobbed it in a high arc over the no-man's land, and whistled in imitation of a mortar shell as the ashtray disappeared with a soft thud behind the bar, usually followed by a flood of obscenities and a raised fist or two shaking above the bar.

Leander and Hennessy realized they had no time to linger over this curiosity. From table to table they crawled, getting pounded on the back or having their hands shaken by the combatants as they went. They had just reached the French windows with their wide-open doors when sirens were heard in the distance. They were the first ones to escape from the hall and to run across the adjoining lawns to the woodlands beyond.

A stampede followed. In one great surge, the entire banquet hall was evacuated. Drivers and mechanics bolted over the network of tables, tripping and falling, and just as quickly springing to their feet again. Banquet personnel squirmed out of their hiding places and raced across the room in pursuit, though they didn't anticipate the terrain they would have to cover and began to slip, stumble, and collide with each other. Realizing how difficult it would be to go beyond the first line of tables, they stopped and began to mill around angrily in the front of the hall.

The police, significantly delayed by their own system of traffic control, arrived. They burst through the front doors as an armed phalanx, swinging their billy clubs, mistaking, in the dim light of the hall, the waiters and cooks and bouncers for the diners. The police lit into them with their clubs; the banquet personnel fought back; and it took a minute or more of savage clubbing and screaming to clarify the mistake.

Then the police tried to run through the hall. The turned-over tables, slippery food, fire-extinguisher foam, and mounds of eating and cooking utensils littering the place were difficult for them to traverse. They had scarcely reached the windows as the last few men vanished over the far lawns and into the woods. One policeman actually drew his revolver and fired several shots into the woods before another officer stopped him. It was lucky the drivers and mechanics had walked to the banquet: now they didn't have cars to retrieve from the parking lot and were able to melt into the crowds of campers and fans that jammed the town and the outlying fields in every direction.

Nobody, frankly, knows how the fire got started.

Yes, that was next.

Theories abound to this day. Some attribute it to the torn electrical connections of the chandeliers, others to something that may have happened in the kitchen with stoves left burning during the melee, and yet others to the sudden appearance of a flaming acetylene torch in the hands of a rabid motorcyclist bound on revenge for having received the full impact of a heavy glass ashtray directly on top of his head. In any case, the depletion, at this point, of usable fire extinguishers and the traffic tie-up in town preventing rapid access of the fire department, resulted in one final and lamentable outcome.

By morning, nothing was left of the banquet hall, or the recreational center, except a smoking heap of tangled ducts and girders and the remains of the plastic columns, which had melted down into grotesque caricatures of classical architecture of the sort you would see in a surrealistic painting. The glory of Foxtowne was gone.

Further, a nighttime ensued of policemen frantically tramping through the soggy camps of the sports-car fans, shining flashlights into the faces of sleeping campers, hustling hundreds of unsuspecting victims out of their cots and sleeping bags and through the paint-cracked halls of the courthouse and submitting them to threats and interrogations. The search narrowed down to one individual whose name could not, quite oddly, be remembered by anybody but who could be easily identified as a scrawny little fellow with a huge, hooked nose and pointed head whose equal in ugliness the world had never known.

Just before dawn, Hennessy awoke in his camper with a start. Where was Leander? he thought. What was he doing? He looked out the window. The fields were still dark, although a slight glow of red stretched along the eastern horizon and a heavy mist hung over the cars and trailers and encampments spread over the wet grass. A few people here and there had risen and were preparing pots of coffee and toasting bacon over campfires and small portable stoves. Slowly, the camp, which resembled a nomadic army, was coming to life in the early dawn. Hennessy doubted that the events scheduled for the day would take place, especially after the previous evening. There would be a massive exodus. It would take place soon.

He exited the camper and walked around to the back, where the trailer was attached. He and Leander had already loaded up the Lotus on the previous afternoon, soon after the race. And there was Leander, standing on the trailer with his body already bent over into the car's engine cavity. He was rapping gently on some engine part. The car's hood was propped open and stood up against the ruddy eastern skies. Leander looked up momentarily. "Mornin' ta yuh, boss. There's fresh tea on the stove," he said.

"Thanks anyway," Hennessy replied, "but I think we need to go. Right now."

"One or two more details ta attend ta, and I be finished." He kept tapping into place whatever it was he was tapping. Hennessy clambered up onto the trailer and looked down into the engine compartment.

"I think that can wait. We don't have a moment to … Good God, Leander, hide yourself! Get under the car! Something!"

Out of the roseate mist of the heavy dawn emerged two state police officers not more than forty paces away. They squished slowly through the marshy ground with high boots. They wore wide-brimmed hats, thick leather belted holsters with immense forty-five-caliber revolvers tucked into them, and, despite the low light, huge round sunglasses. Hennessy heaved Leander up by the back of his suspenders, turned him over, and squashed him down into the engine compartment, slamming the engine hood on top of him.

"Uh! Did yuh 'ave ta …?"

"Shut up!" Hennessy whispered loudly. He rubbed his hands as if he was finishing off some little job and turned to face the officers.

They stood about ten paces from him.

"Good morning, officers!" Hennessy said cheerfully.

They eyed him silently, hands cupped over the glossy hilts of their revolvers.

"Mechanic, huh?" one of them asked.

"Me? A mechanic? Oh no, I don't think so. But I could use a good one. Do you know any?"

"Smart-ass!"

"We're looking for one too — a fella, they say, who looks like someone put him through a wringer on one of those old-fashioned washing machines. You seen him around?" the other officer inquired.

"Yeah, a shrimp with a nose like a fishhook and with forearms, they say, that look like Popeye's," the first officer added.

Hennessy appeared to think for a while. "The description's familiar. There's a guy like that around. I've seen him. But I don't know what his name is or where he is at the moment."

The officers had heard this story before, again and again, throughout the night. They smiled sarcastically at Hennessy. They demanded that he step down from the trailer, examined his driver's license, and took down his name and number. One of the officers took a rather strong interest in the peculiar looking car on the trailer. He mounted the trailer.

"What a mess!" he exclaimed. "How could anyone race in a broken-down rig like this?"

"I told you I needed a good mechanic," Hennessy clucked nervously.

"Let's take a look under the hood," the officer demanded. "I want to see what makes this thing run."

"Really, there's nothing there to ..."

"Open the hood! I want to see what's in there!"

Hennessy leaned over the trailer, reached into the cockpit of the car and released a catch. The hood sprang slightly open. The officer grabbed it and swung it all the way open. He looked down into the engine cavity, at one point bending over and moving his head close to the machinery. He stood up straight again and laughed. "I guess you have your problems, all right, mister. That engine is the ugliest mess I've ever seen."

"I hit an obstacle on the track, a cinder block ..."

"I guess so. And I've seen some pretty smashed up cars in my time." He slammed the engine hood down. He didn't hear the muted "ouch" that accompanied it. He clambered down from the trailer. "You let us know if you see that fella we're looking for."

The two officers ambled slowly off into the misty plain, their boots pressing bubbly footprints into the soggy grass.

"Lemme outa 'ere," Leander moaned.

"When we're ten miles down the road," Hennessy answered. He climbed into the RV, started up the engine, and slowly guided it over the field, avoiding the scattered encampments and the especially wet patches of ground, and onto the road. He turned toward the sun, which was now a glowing orange ball in the east, suspended in a thick gray fog.

Fifteen minutes later, he pulled over to the side of the road, went back to the trailer, and released the hood. Leander popped out of the engine cavity and stretched himself. He snapped his suspenders against his chest and smiled.

"What the hell happened back there?" Hennessy asked.

Leander shook his head slowly. "Got me, boss. That bloke was lookin' right in me face. In fact, he lowered 'is big mug inta strikin' distance. I was ready to let 'm 'ave it, ta tell the truth. But then 'e draws back and laughs the way 'e did. I guess there are times in life when lookin' like a piece of bloody machinery 'as its advantages. Course, I was 'alf wrapped around that engine, so maybe ..."

Hennessy let out a roar of laughter. "Leander, get into the RV. Let's go home. You know I can't stand being this far away from the ocean, and that sun is promising to turn this place into a frying pan by midmorning."

They got into the RV. Leander went into the back to catch up on his sleep. Hennessy drove home, a big smile on his face. He rehearsed in his mind how he would tell this story at the next big dinner party, chuckling to himself as he reviewed one incident after another.

And that's how I heard about much of this story, though I actually saw some of it —witnessed it myself— especially what happened at the Foxtowne banquet hall. I'm the one who got his wrist slashed by the flying lobster claw. I can show you the scar if you'd like to see it. And I share the privilege of having been present at Leander's greatest knockdown ever, along with a few hundred other guys. I'm proud of that. It's a story to tell my grandchildren.

The rest of it, as I said, I heard from Bill Hennessy, who dominated an entire luncheon party at the Belle and Bauble Club in Palm Beach with his account of what happened—of what happened under that table, of what went on afterward. Hennessy laughed his way all through that story, except for the part about the conversation he had with Leander under the table. That he took seriously—which was rare for Bill Hennessy, who couldn't take very much too seriously.

All of this happened quite some time ago. Foxtowne, I understand, after recovering as much as it did—which took a while—turned its attention to becoming a center for an annual national quilting convention. But it never rebuilt its banquet hall, and the landing strips have been returned to permanent occupation by their rightful inhabitants: the possums and egrets and water snakes and whatever else.

Leander Baxter has departed for a habitat somewhere that none of us know about. Maybe he went back to England, back to Coventry, back to where he'd plucked from a ravaged life the few real moments of happiness he'd ever known. He's only a memory for us now. If he was the ugliest man we ever knew, as ugly as those high-tuned contraptions he patched together, he, like them, had the soul of a sleek Ferrari blasting through a turn at Monte Carlo at two hundred plus. That's what we saw in him.

Maybe that's what Alice — Alice, the prettiest girl in Coventry — maybe that's what she saw in him too.

The "*Grand Oeuvre*" of Ilya Moshevitz

I cannot say, unequivocally, that I looked forward to the visit of that young man, Brian Seldon. I knew what he was searching for, and I knew equally well that I couldn't give it to him, that it didn't exist, at least not in the form that he could find even remotely acceptable or, better said, even remotely endurable.

An erratic fellow he was and is: mid-height, lean — skinny almost — with dark, greasy hair that never gets combed, dressed perpetually in khaki pants and a green blazer with leather patches at the elbows and so threadbare that, up close, it almost looks like a tweed fabric; a brilliant fellow perhaps; one of those rare but unruly students who show up at public city colleges with absolutely minimal entrance standards because they failed so many of their high school courses — failed them while they spent so many precious, and, in this case, precocious, adolescent years haunting the New York Public Library and reading things, erudite things, that most of us, even at our august and privileged universities, have never heard of and never particularly want to hear of either. You could say that such a fellow, such an *ungeschämte Kerl*, has an indomitable nose for sniffing out the arcane, the eccentric, the esoteric; and that, I might say, is precisely what brought him in the first place to Ilya Moshevitz.

Ilya was anything but that. Indeed, by contrast with Ilya, everything else in this world can be considered arcane, eccentric, esoteric. If I've ever known anyone who stood, in a sense, at the center of the world, it was Ilya Moshevitz. What a surprise it must have been for Brian Seldon to find himself at a lodestone, a still point, as it were, of a world gone lavishly wild, when he must have fancied himself the wildest thing in it!

Now that Ilya has passed from this world, poor Brian Seldon, uncouth and impoverished as he is, must all his days bear with him such inexplicable richness, such intellectual splendor, that you might almost think he would perish from it. He won't, of course; he's a tough New York kid, "streetwise" as the expression goes, a "survivor." He'll see it through, but it will be very tough for him — tough because he's come to me seeking something that doesn't exist, except perhaps … except perhaps in himself.

He comes to my office in the dead of winter, sits nervously in the reception room and tugs and pulls, with raw, cold hands, at the green blazer that is stretched precariously over his incredibly bulky ragg-wool sweater — the usual winter variation of his standard attire, so I've been told. He watches the department secretary as if she were about to push some button that would result in nothing less than his summary and acutely embarrassing dismissal. It's clearly not the sort of place he's accustomed to be in.

He's jittery, sits at the edge of his chair, notes a tuft of sweater sticking through a hole in his blazer and pokes it back into place with an impulsive jab of his finger, and glances around from time to time as if anticipating the sort of pompous attendant who suddenly shows up and asks the obvious parvenu to vacate the premises.

Yes, I remember waiting once for somebody in an exclusive, marbled hotel foyer downtown — he was a wealthy alumnus of my prestigious institution — and expecting any moment that an emissary of the hotel management might ask me to leave. Imagine that — a man in my position, holding a professorial chair at a top-ranked university, terrified of being expelled by a fellow whose bellboy livery would give him such authority in just that set of circumstances and none other!

Such a fellow, too, I must say, to my deepest shame, would have succeeded, without much of a protest on my part, in throwing me out.

But my task, of course, was to ingratiate and inveigle the gentleman who kept me waiting. Why had the alumni office asked me to do this? What did they know about me that maybe I didn't even know well enough about myself—or was unwilling to acknowledge about myself? What, for that matter, do they know about all of us?

Brian's task was infinitely more earnest than that. He'd tried for months to arrange this meeting; I'd tried for months to avoid it. Yet for all his diffidence as he sat squirming in that waiting-room chair looking like a seedy character out of a Gogol novella who anticipates an unpleasant meeting with "Mr. Big Man" or some other such eponymous personage, he knew that it would take a virtual host of adversaries to expel him from this alien turf, and this knowledge itself served merely to increase his anxiety.

If there were going to be a fight, there would be a very big fight. That much I could guess about him—he was frightened, but in no manner submissive to his fear.

Of course, no incipient adversaries lurked behind the doors, and I would be, and was, as it turned out, as friendly to Brian as it was in my nature to be friendly to anyone, and I always am. This would be my first formal meeting with him, my first conversation, though I felt I knew him already. Ilya had mentioned him to me on several occasions when we met at the café on Eighty-Sixth Street in Yorkville, which served the Viennese pastries that Ilya occasionally indulged in. Ilya spoke of him only in incidental allusions now and then—as if I knew Brian already.

I did see Brian from time to time, at a distance, when he showed up at a variety of academic conferences in recent years—especially when he knew that Ilya would be there—dressed as ever in his threadbare green blazer but without the required official conference name tag attached to it and without the neat folder and program that everyone else bore politely in their arms, indicating, as I always suspected, that he'd probably circumvented the reception table, to say nothing of the conference fee.

He would sit in the back row, jumping up on occasion to leave the room, returning just as abruptly, sometimes waving his hand wildly during discussions and question-and-answer sessions without ever being recognized by the moderator, never attending the dinners and social hours that so often accompany these occasions, and fleeing off into the outside world at the strangest moments, as if suddenly stripped of his garments and leaving them behind, like that young *schlemiel* in the Christian gospels who ran away naked into the dark Jerusalem night.

As I said, I'd never met Brian before in a formal sense. His telephone calls, which began only a month or two after Ilya's death, were always brief, impulsive, peremptory. I finally agreed to meet with him.

I was Ilya's literary executor. It was through my influence—perhaps gained by my successful mulcting of that wealthy alumnus's ego and bank account so long ago—that Ilya's collected papers and notes, all but a tiny portion of them unpublished, were gathered into twenty-eight cardboard cartons and ensconced in a dark corner of our university archives. It was the least I could do for Ilya, even if the best I could do was to corral for his life's work a remote spot in the gigantic underground repository where the slag and jetsam of the previous century, being removed already from the stacks, was accumulated in huge and inaccessible heaps.

I had the sense of depositing what I vaguely knew was an incalculable treasure inappropriately into some rubble-choked corridor beneath a pyramid—a pyramid of papers and documents whose insufferable weight and ultimately indistinguishable interior mass had become as much an obstacle to learning as an aid to it and whose mute and enigmatic density might not be penetrated for centuries, for millennia even, if ever at all. It was about those literary remains that Brian Seldon had come.

Yet I, too, was afraid. That's because Brian Seldon knows something that I don't know, that I still don't know, that I will never know.

My fortunes and the fortunes of Ilya Moshevitz always ran remarkably close to each other. We grew up together in Kraków and attended that venerable and ancient university, the Jagiellonian; we communicated during his Warsaw years; we were together in Vienna, in Berlin, in Heidelberg; then there was Paris and New York. We weathered together, survived, barely escaped, the unspeakable calamities of our all too calamitous century—calamaties whose scope and breadth our present age still hasn't even begun to reckon with, and probably never will.

Later we began to go in different directions, though we remained close friends at all times. I married, had a family; he remained too engaged in his work to give such a prospect more than a passing thought. I understood quickly what you had to do to get ahead; he understood that, too, but wouldn't do it.

I spent some time at Chicago, later at Berkeley, before my final appointment in New York City. He stayed in New York, went from the New School of Social Research to a Jesuit college and then to one of the city colleges. That's where he remained. He produced only a minute body of written work—some essays in Polish journals and also a few scattered among German, Israeli, Spanish, and English periodicals whose editors, puzzled and stunned by the enormously rich and dense conceptual style and figuring that something important was going on in them—although they didn't know what that was—agreed to accept them for publication.

Needless to say, these essays are never cited and have had no impact on the scholarly world, except in a curiously negative way. As much as I can understand them myself, they appear to reposition, to redefine so radically the issues and subjects that they treat that the scholarly world they potentially address is left holding the proverbial "empty bag"—an "empty bag," I should add, that that same scholarly world is perfectly content to keep on holding.

At Ilya's final college appointment nobody paid much attention to him either—his classes were always small, his participation in collegial life minimal; he was a lonely hermit in one of the biggest educational systems in the world. That's perhaps as it should have been. The small stream of students who passed, usually for one semester only, through his classes in political theory regarded him as a wizened old gent with a heavy accent who mumbled things they found generally incomprehensible.

Then there were the occasional students who came along and who had—how can I say it?—their world turned upside down for them.

Who actually signed up for a second, a third, and a fourth course with Ilya!

Who knew that, after Ilya, nothing would be, could be, ever satisfactory anymore!

None of them—perhaps no more than five or six such students over the years—persisted in the scholarly life. You might say that they had little option to have done otherwise. One student, a young woman, went into academic administration and soon became an associate dean in Ilya's college. I believe she did this for one purpose only: to create, as in fact she did, a protective cover for Ilya, a bulwark against the local groups and individuals who, while never understanding in the least the issues and conflicts involved in Ilya's situation, had been so influenced by academic politics that they'd come to share, to a greater or lesser extent, fear of Ilya and sometimes even hatred of him.

Brian Seldon was merely the last of this group of special students. Like all of them, in one sense, he wasn't truly "qualified" to be the recipient of what Ilya had to say. He simply didn't have the education that would be required, the extensive and exacting knowledge of languages, the access to the multifarious worlds of thought and culture that these languages gave, the encyclopedic historical sense that went along with this, as well as an intimate familiarity with the work of great minds of the past whose names and books are now largely unknown even within the most erudite of modern academic circles. Indeed, you can't even find many of these books unless you're willing, in a given case, to trek into the hinterlands of, let's say, Slovenia, where the volume in question lingers, sole survivor of its kind through a tumultuous half millennium, in a quasi-ruined monastic library where you need to have the linguistic, to say nothing of the paleographic, training requisite for reading it. Ilya did a great deal of that trekking.

I shared some of these accomplishments with Ilya — nowhere near as fulsomely as Ilya possessed them — and part of our friendship was based on this. But these few students, and Brian Seldon especially, managed to get hold of something I could never really fathom except at a distance — the immensely subtle and complex philosophical substratum that welded all of Ilya's knowledge together into — I'll call it — a "fearsome" coherence, "fearsome" in its illumination, its depth, its understanding of things, aspect by aspect; its bedazzlingly multiform grasp of social and political realities; its freedom from the oceanic wash of clichés and falsifications that tend to dominate almost any academic discipline.

There's something about actually knowing a thing that strikes terror in the heart — a *mysterium tremendum*, if I may use, for the moment, a theological term. That's why, perhaps, I was always afraid to know what Ilya knew and why I always evaded the effort of really trying to find out. My own failure to possess this knowledge may also be why I'm inclined to rhapsodize about it: those who do possess it are stunned into silence, or, like Brian Seldon, inflamed into a mute but ferocious incandescence they scarcely know how to contain. I cannot help but think of one of those underground clefts filled to the core with searing lava: all that massive release of energy beneath the surface of the earth, undetectable in one sense and yet sending tremors through the entire globe.

So I was afraid for good reason—of him; of his seeing how little I know; of my own pettiness before such a marvelous and awesome thing as the intellectual power I knew he would possess, and yet would be so unaware that he possessed it.

I'll admit that I sat in my office for a while, sometimes gazing at Brian through the thin slit of the door, which I'd left deliberately ajar for this purpose, and sometimes swiveling around in my chair to stare out the window at the street below. It was late afternoon in mid-January; a pale, winter sun was already hanging low over the New Jersey Palisades beyond the Hudson. A few shops along the street had turned on their neon storefront lights, and, at the corner of the block where the street intersects with Broadway, I noted that the Christmas decorations, still belatedly festooned in a newspaper store window, began to flicker.

In my sundry ruminations I'll confess to making Brian wait a bit, as I also had in answering and returning his calls; I don't know why. It's the sort of thing "Mr. Big Man" just routinely does. I guess we academic people enjoy exerting the small amount of power we have. Or maybe I expected the meeting to be too unpredictable. I'm used to students who are like me, who are like the rest of us: poised to assess the situation, to second-guess as perspicaciously as possible the particular rules of the immediate game (or perhaps to apply general rules to the particular exigencies of the immediate situation) and act accordingly, to "play the angles," as they say, to do whatever is necessary to promote your own advantage.

Brian wouldn't be like this. Even if he'd wanted to be like this, he couldn't. It was too late for that. After Ilya, there was going out—departure, exile even—but no going back.

I pushed the buzzer on my phone. Brian jumped. The secretary answered the phone and directed him into my office.

"Anything I can get you?" I asked him when he slumped down into the large leather easy chair in front of my desk. This capacious and somewhat ludicrous chair had the effect on him that it's intended to have on students and other occasional visitors. It gives the illusion that the visitor has conferred upon him the place of honor, while making him feel passive, tired, and vulnerable.

My desk is my fortress, my bulwark, my Mount Horeb, my Miltonic "throne of royal state" from which I can peer down with inscrutable authority at the person sunk helplessly in the encompassing and oppressive leather folds of that chair. The large rectangular window behind my desk, at just the right time of day, frames me as an imposing and imperious silhouette, shrouded in darkness but encircled by a radiant nimbus of light. I also take notes during an interview—though I'm only pretending to do so; that little diversion always manages to blunt any aggressiveness or any fortuitous glints of something resembling moral courage on the part of my interlocutor that could, but almost never does, arise.

But, as I said, Brian would be different, unpredictable. I had to be prepared for anything. Still, the sudden torpor that settled over him as he settled back into that monstrous and consuming chair may just have been an expression of a momentary reprieve from all that tension he'd expended in trying to see me these many months. He rubbed his thin hands, still chapped red with cold. Clearly, he could use a pair of gloves. Anyway, he refused all offers of coffee, tea, or sherry that I made. I would have thought that grasping a hot mug of coffee at least would have warmed his hands; and it would have given me the opportunity to fumble around in some dark niche of my lair while the preparatory clatter of cups and spoons broke the resolute silence that I was already finding difficult to sustain.

Brian didn't come directly to the point. I think he just needed, at the onset, to talk about Ilya; after all, he'd never had the chance to talk about his mentor to anyone other than a few students who had studied with Ilya, and what they knew about his personal life was even less than what he knew. Ilya's professional colleagues at the city college were of no help either. They were, by and large, scarcely acquainted with him or his work, though a few were subject to the pernicious rumors about Ilya that from time to time wafted into their often sordid and beleaguered world from the higher, though equally sordid and beleaguered, elevations of academia. I was the only person Brian knew who had a long-standing friendship with Ilya. Certainly, my being appointed executor of his estate was confirmation of that.

Furthermore, as I figured, Brian may have had an image of Ilya leading an intensely eremitical existence, surrounded by books and (as he may have imagined) dusty old parchments and manuscripts somewhere in a basement apartment. Actually, Ilya occupied a small but rather elegant and airy penthouse apartment on Riverside Drive that featured a balcony garden that overlooked the Hudson River and was furnished with an assortment of Biedermeier antiques, Bohemian crystal vases and decanters, and in his living room a particularly rare Iranian carpet. He'd received, in spite of everything, a good salary at the city college where he worked and had little to spend it on. He also was the recipient of a small cluster of heirlooms that came to him, rather belatedly after the war, from Kraków. All of his possessions were now in storage awaiting shipment back to Europe, specifically to Maastricht in the Netherlands, where Ilya's sole relative, a niece, was living. I was in charge of that.

Nor was Ilya's life as solitary as Brian conceived it to be. He had many friends outside academic circles (outside that "dreadful academic ghetto," as he sometimes called it): people in the theater, music, and art worlds, as well as habitués of local culinary establishments whose ingenious eccentricities Ilya savored with no little pleasure.

As is so often true of our times, I'm inclined to think that what appears to be at the fringe is precisely what was central throughout our history, and what now appears to be central is precisely what was ever peripheral in that past. But I shouldn't get into this. What I'm getting to is that the initial stages of my conversation with Brian were devoted to personal reminiscences of Ilya; I imagine that that's how it should have been, under the circumstances.

"You might have the impression," I continued in my somewhat diffuse discourse about Ilya's personal life, "that Ilya was a solitary man by nature. Indeed, it was exactly the opposite: a more gregarious fellow you could scarcely find, even if what, for him, was constitutive of a 'like-minded society' was frequently unusual at best, for his life was a kind of persistent dialogue with persons who lived centuries ago and whom he regarded in approximately the same way as neighbors who lived down the hall or as confreres who regularly gathered at the same park bench each day after a volatile, if also hearty, luncheon together.

"As you know, Ilya made a point of frequenting many professional meetings. He knew as well as I did, and as I suspect you do too, how much these meetings serve as arenas for self-promotion, for academic grandstanding of the worst sort. But he was always, within these arenas, a model of civility, of gracious deportment, reserving himself ever for the polite but well-turned *bon mot* that sent not a few budding intellects, I suspect, scurrying back to their academic burrows to reconsider some word, an expression even, that was used carelessly or inopportunely.

"I often wonder how much effect, in the long term, such a practice really did have on anyone. To make a given term precise, even to think that such a term should be precise, sometimes requires that you change your thinking about virtually everything.

"More to the point, what Ilya often detected, though he cloaked such detection under the guise of a mere rhetorical consideration, was the use of a term that blurred a distinction with some other term being used in the same paper and, in doing that, violated the axiomatic foundations of the exposition itself, thereby introducing a contradiction that, quite literally, collapsed the entire paper into an exercise of verbal ingenuity at best, or, at worst, a heap of sophistical fatuities.

"Perhaps it was sufficient, as Ilya would say, that you be simply 'haunted,' not by the specters that ordinarily are taken to 'haunt' us but by reality itself, which is the most 'haunting' thing there is. But it was the least that Ilya thought he could, and should, do, and he always did it in good faith, even as he understood as well the relative futility of his gesture.

"Furthermore, Ilya was quite committed, in principle, to the social dimension of higher learning: higher learning must be a communicable learning, he liked to say; but he would add a point, which I'm not sure I really ever understood, that one feature that makes such learning distinctly 'higher' is that the intelligibility of its object shapes, as far as it can, the communicability of the discourse, rather than is shaped by it."

"It also means," Brian added impatiently, "that not every communicative context will be appropriate for such discourse—in fact, there may not, nor ever may be, an appropriate communicative context for it. Since the discourse is not prepared for the audience, the audience must be prepared for the discourse. There's no control you can exercise over that; what is radically contingent must be respected for what it is."

"That may be," I said. "Ilya always said that the addressee will allow itself to hear as much truth as it wants to hear." I was somewhat abashed by this rejoinder. It wasn't the only time in this interview that Brian Seldon, however inadvertently, would remind me of how much more he knew about Ilya's mind and thought than I did. I was also embarrassed by how much Ilya's apothegm applied, archly, to me.

"But for all this," I went on, "Ilya didn't always manage to stay out of trouble. Mind you, he never looked for it, never wanted it in the least. Indeed, he was deeply offended by the atmosphere of arrogant contentiousness, of scoring points, that all too often characterizes academic debate. But, on a few occasions, he really did strike out at an opponent, and it was especially painful when it happened in an academic field that Ilya, at least 'officially,' didn't belong to.

"There was a time when a young professor from—well, I guess it was a Midwestern university somewhere—delivered a paper that applied a few concepts of the school of Bachofenian infra-generative linguistics—it was very popular at the time—to some questions of social theory. In the discussion period, Ilya raised some very minor objections. That was his customary thing to do—to raise a minor objection, as we have noted, usually about the use of a term. The young professor, breathlessly exuding his gratitude (just in case the unknown person with the heavy accent in front of him should end up someday on a tenure review committee or an editorial board that would determine his fate), duly wrote it on the margin of his paper without quite realizing that this minor objection, once carefully considered (if it should ever be carefully considered), would bring down his entire project.

"But someone in the audience did realize the implications of the objection, and that was Professor Bachofen himself, who, somewhat late and unnoticed, had entered the conference room. This, I might add, was his accustomed way of doing things: he rarely showed up at these shindigs, and when he did, he entered secretly and waited for just the right moment to reveal his sacral presence, rather like a Homeric god appearing suddenly amid the action on the dusty plains of Troy, greeted by all the requisite phenomena of shaking knees, chills racing down the back, and hair standing on end.

"In any event, he now rose unexpectedly to the defense of his presumptive protégé. The audience gasped. He stood there, as heavyset as the stump of a tree, his face lifted up, his eyes closed, and lips smiling in a kind of pained rapture, and delivered a carefully articulated but utterly obscure set of comments, while with one hand he stroked the air in front of him as if to shield his face from a cloud of buzzing flies circling around his head.

"Professor Bachofen didn't actually reply to Ilya's objection but rather gave the impression that he had. The point was to make the audience forget what the objection was in the first place, for to reply to the objection would serve not only to remind the audience of what it was but also to open up even new avenues of criticism in what Professor Bachofen must by now have realized was an easily assailable position.

"Ilya took the floor again, rising up against the effort of the moderator to change the subject and move on to a new questioner. Professor Bachofen's eyes bolted open in sudden alarm, and his head jerked in Ilya's direction. Now, of course, he recognized, more or less, who was making the objection, knowing Ilya more by reputation than personally, but knowing enough to realize that this obscure voice represented a serious and deadly adversary. Ilya addressed Professor Bachofen's irrelevant and distracting observations with a short disquisition that, for anyone sufficiently informed about the matter, exposed the false premises that supported the structure of Bachofenian linguistics and collapsed the entire enterprise into a detritus of triviality and nonsense."

"What happened then?" Brian practically shouted. This was the sort of academic street fight that I was sure Brian would appreciate. He was sorry he'd not been there to witness it.

"Well, you know very well that, in a sense, nothing happened. In an audience of — let's say — three hundred people, about ten or so will stare at the floor with amused smiles on their faces. They not only know that Ilya has been correct; they had come to the same conclusion a long time before, for exactly the same reasons, but just didn't want to be the ones to have said it publicly. After all, they're in the same field as the Bachofenian entourage and figure they would have to deal with the untoward consequences of their statements for, possibly, the rest of their days.

"Another, even smaller group—let's say two or three—have understood and are genuinely surprised. They'll try to hunt down Ilya after the meeting is over and find out who he is and what else he knows. But he gives them the slip.

"Rightfully so: as soon as they return to wherever they come from, a stack of eighty exams, followed by four committee meetings, will obliterate anything they learned. Further, they'll quickly realize that to subscribe to anything this alien presence proposes will destroy their careers.

"But even worse, one of them is bound to be, in an inverse sense, an incipient Bachofen, a Bachofen *in ovo* who wants to overturn the Bachofenian empire and establish his own regime and is looking for any ammunition he can find to further that end. As for the rest of the audience—they don't understand and don't care. The modern university is, on the surface, an eclectic affair—*chacun à son goût*; and we're not talking here about *bon goût* either, just enough *goût* and of the right kind to get you permanently admitted to the great academic cocktail party."

"What about Bachofen? What happened with him?"

"He retained his composure, if that's what you mean. He either failed to understand Ilya's *ex tempore* disquisition or else—one hates to think this—understood it, or even always knew that such a refutation of his work was not only possible—it would be, once proffered, decisive—but that consideration could not be expected to have any impact on what had become one of the more successful academic enterprises in the postwar period.

"Do you actually think that Professor Bachofen would relish the loss of that long train of twenty or more courtiers who, now informed of his attendance, would trail around behind him through the hotel corridors for the rest of the conference—all for the sake of a few observations made by an obscure fellow whom the profession had pegged as a specialist in the political thought of medieval Islamic Spain and who attempted to teach an assortment of no-account students from various ethnic minorities a few points about the nature of human communities?

"And especially when such an obscure fellow spoke out in a field where he had no recognized voice or authority to be speaking?

"Ah, specialization is the way we ensure that any really comprehensive mind will be locked away in its own appropriate cell, so that we may pursue our eclectic business quite unimpeded by the threat of actual intelligence.

"But you can be sure that Professor Bachofen could scarcely be expected to forget, even less to forgive, such an affront, incurred in public no less; you can be sure that he instructed his entourage of sycophants to carry his outrage into every niche and corner of the academic world. Professor Bachofen was a classic example of what Ilya would describe as an academic who doesn't *study* his subject as much as *use* it for his own advantage."

"But as for specialization," Brian intruded, "Professor Moshevitz did believe in its importance, did he not?"

"Of course he did. It's just that he thought you could not be genuinely, as opposed to speciously, specialized unless you knew, in fact, a very great deal outside your own area of specialization. Otherwise, you are, in a sense, misinformed even, and perhaps especially, about your own field and in a really very serious way. Further, academic specialization is scarcely a license to be an ignoramus and a vulgarian, as I'm afraid it's often taken to be. You still have the obligation, especially as a member of a community of scholars — of a universal and transhistorical community of scholars yet — to be a learned and cultivated human being." I was glad to be the one who could make this point about Ilya.

I proceeded, "But to return to my story: in the meantime, of course, Bachofenian linguistics has perished, not because it's false, which it so clearly is, but because people got bored with it, or else departments had absorbed as many Bachofenian adherents as they could, so that it no longer gave access to the sort of career people were looking for.

"On the other hand, such incidents could be dangerous for Ilya. As in so much else in life, a handful of disaffected spirits can spread the most poisonous malaise through large groups of people who don't even know why they're responding and acting the way they do. Crowds, even elite crowds, are intellectually credulous and morally weak. Knaves know this, almost by instinct, and act upon it. In a way, it was fortunate that Ilya found as obscure a niche as he did, for that protected him from a great deal of harm. But even there, he wasn't always safe. It was good that Janet Schafer—"

"Yes, she was helpful. A fine person, an outstanding mind, and an excellent associate dean of the college where Ilya worked."

"I don't know how the antagonism got into your college in the first place. I think it had a lot to do with Professor MacCollody James in my department."

"I know who he is, that imbecil—" Brian burst out.

"Please! Remember where you are." I lowered my voice. "Professor James was terrified of Ilya. He should have been terrified of me, too, but he never was, even though he was aware, or must have been aware, that I knew what Ilya knew, at least in regard to the matters that concerned him. But I guess he just realized that, for my own comfort, I would never 'blow the whistle' on him. Of course, he was right. I'm not the sort of person who would 'blow the whistle' on anybody. But about Ilya, he could not be so certain. He'd seen Ilya do his occasional demolition job."

"What did Professor Moshevitz know?" Brian asked. "He never said anything about Professor James, except that we should not depend on his work—that his translations were flawed. I drew my own negative conclusions about Professor James independently—just seeing him in action on a few occasions. In fact, I never quite understood Professor Moshevitz's cordiality to people like him."

I laughed. "Ilya was cordial to everybody—until, at least, they transgressed too grievously a limit of impropriety that Ilya could no longer abide in good faith. As for Professor James, he promoted himself as the leading authority on medieval Islamic political thought in the English-speaking world. But ..." I leaned forward to Brian and almost whispered to him, "He doesn't know any Arabic—except for what's necessary to order a carafe of coffee in a Cairo café."

"But the translations!"

"Done by a few graduate students under his supervision. They were native Arabic speakers who didn't know English very well and who certainly didn't know the richness, or the history, or the subtlety of their own language either. We often assume that those who have grown up speaking a language actually know something about it; in fact, they rarely do. I doubt there was any scholar in this field or any related field in the United States or in Europe who had the command of classical Arabic that Ilya did. He knew that Professor James was a sham—a sham from top to bottom. Professor James did everything to discredit Ilya within our department, and generally in the field of medieval political studies, as if to fend off some future possible challenge to his reputation. His attempts at disparagement spread from here to other places. It was dreadful to be around that sort of thing.

"I would voice my concerns about this to Ilya from time to time, but he, imperturbable as ever, would say, while he stirred the tea in his tall Russian glass, 'Never mind. MacCollody is throttling his own prolifically ovulating golden goose—and panicking as he does it.'

"A catastrophe almost happened last year. A Fulbright exchange scholar from Riyadh signed up for one of his classes. He's an intelligent young man who's also a potential Islamic scholar of real merit. The story goes that in class he challenged Professor James about the translations. It was an embarrassing moment for old MacCollody, so I've heard. Needless to say, the student was immediately declared *persona non grata* and was discouraged, in the most vigorous way possible, from continuing in the program. Apparently, an anonymous note sent to the State Department suggesting that he was a security risk didn't help him out much either. He was sent home before completing the end of the Fulbright year."

"Professor Moshevitz often spoke of the importance of Arabic."

"Of course he did. It's one of the great learned languages of history. It gave him access to, among other things, a transmission of Greek thought based on older and more accurate versions of the original Greek documents than were preserved for the West in later Byzantine redactions of these same documents. His knowledge of classical Greek allowed him to discern the original subtexts of these Arabic versions. And then his knowledge of Hebrew—"

"And almost every major language of Western and Eastern Europe ..."

"Well, he knew only a few words and expressions in Hungarian, even though Budapest was one of his favorite cities, and he had a curious predilection for Hungarian wines. But he never knew any far-eastern languages, much to his regret. I could add that he's the only person of Central European Jewish descent I've ever known who could, for some bizarre reason, read

Gaelic. I assume he shamed you into learning some languages. That was one of his more endearing traits."

"He did. He gave me, one day, his own annotated copy of a Kantian text and told me to read it. It was in German. The annotations were in a mixture of German, English, Polish, and something I took to be Hebrew but later found out was Yiddish."

"It was not unlike Ilya to formulate a proposition in several different languages, one right after the other, just to see what it looked like in each language and to see if that made any difference in understanding it."

"That may have been true in this situation, though it was difficult for me to judge. In any case, I told him I couldn't read German. He expressed astonishment. He threw up his hands; he wailed, 'Oy, oy, oy, you don't want to be provincial, do you?' I said, 'What's wrong with being provincial?' He said, 'Nothing, if you're a provincial. But if you're not a provincial, everything. If you don't know German, you're provincial. How provincial do you want to be in the end? If you're unable to listen in on a major part of the intellectual conversation of modernity in its original language, what can you possibly expect of yourself?' He told me to learn it and get back to him in three months."

"*Hast gemacht?*"

"*Naturlich.*"

"*In drei Monaten?*"

"*Das war nicht leicht.*"

"Any other languages?"

"Latin. He said, 'You don't want to be *illiterate*, do you?' Actually, I already knew some Latin, having had several years of it in high school."

"And Greek?"

"I'm pretty embarrassed about that. I know only a few technical terms in Greek. I'm partly Irish, so one time Professor Moshevitz reproached me for not knowing Greek by saying, 'I thought all Irishmen knew Greek!' I guess all the Irishmen he worked with at St. Edmund Campion's knew Greek. I received a Jesuit education, in a manner of speaking—that is, after the Jesuits had abandoned just about everything they stood for. That's why I didn't know much Latin either. By the way, I knew about the Gaelic. He tried that out on me once. That was embarrassing too. I know as many words in Gaelic as appear on the flags of the Fifth Avenue St. Patrick's Day Parade."

"Did he say anything else about Greek?"

"Yes. He said, 'Do you expect to walk around without feet or legs? If you don't, then learn Greek.'"

"I figured he would say something like that."

"At least I could read French and Spanish. What would he have said if I hadn't known those languages?"

"He wouldn't have said anything. He would have thought you were a hopeless ignoramus and thrown you out of his office."

"I guess he would have. He did wonder why, if I'd gone to the trouble of learning French and Spanish, I didn't know Italian and Portuguese as well."

"So did you ever go to that trouble too?"

"I did. It wasn't any trouble. Every language is a treasure. I learned that from him. But about the Greek, I guess I still don't have my feet or legs. I'll correct that. I shouldn't have gone to a Jesuit school after all. If I'd come from a wealthy family, I could have gone to one of those fancy New England prep schools where they still teach Greek. Why do rich Anglo-Saxons get the privilege of learning Greek when they have the least use for it, except to be able to identify names of college fraternities?"

"Well, I can't answer that. As for the Jesuits, Ilya told me that he'd witnessed a great number of institutional and societal collapses in his life-time—most of which had disastrous consequences. But he witnessed few so rapid and so unexpected as what happened to the Jesuits."

Our conversation finally turned to the question of Ilya's literary remains. This is what I'd dreaded; this is what I'd tried to avoid, or at least delay as much as I could. I excused myself for a moment, rose from my chair and went to a cabinet on the other side of the office. Here I extracted a cigar from a small mahogany box. "Would you like one?" I asked Brian, waving the cigar around a bit like a baton.

"No thanks," he replied.

He'd managed to pull himself out of the soft folds of the leather chair and to prop himself up by leaning an elbow on the right arm rest and pushing with his knee against the left side of the chair. A huge tuft of sweater erupted from underneath the leather patch on his left elbow. I wondered how long he could remain in this awkward position.

I returned to my seat at the desk, lit up the cigar, and emitted several great puffs of smoke. There's nothing like that, I tell you, to get things off course, but it didn't work. Brian pursued the question of the literary remains.

"Notes mostly," I repeated several times. "A folder with offprints of his published pieces, another folder with several unpublished papers, and, besides that, enormous amounts of notes. Thousands and thousands of pages of them. Written in a dozen languages. I couldn't even make an initial inventory of them. I don't understand their pattern. In any event, I think it would take several years simply to catalogue them properly."

Brian stared at me incredulously.

"I don't even understand how you could use these notes," I said. "Some are obscure, almost I would say, cabalistic, in their mode of utterance. That wasn't typical for Ilya. He didn't like to indulge in that sort of thing. He found it pretentious in others."

Brian finally recovered from his incredulous silence. "I think he spoke like that (and only rarely did he speak like that) when he was talking about himself—maybe to himself, but in front of others," Brian retorted. "What's an example?"

"I'm not sure I can ..."

"Professor Moshevitz told me you have the best memory of anyone he ever knew."

"He said that?"

"He did."

"I'll take that for the moment as a compliment. He told me once that he knew people whose intellects, he thought, were destroyed by their power of memory. It delivered them, according to their own lights, from the necessity of thinking. I know that seems paradoxical, and I won't try to explain it. But I hope he didn't intend to draw me into that particular net, though I know myself well enough to imagine that I fit in there anyway."

Brian nodded in a strange diagonal way, as if neither affirming nor denying what I'd said. I figured he understood all these matters as well as, if not better than, I did. I hesitated and said, "Well, I think I remember one statement that went something like this — and it strikes me as really quite a remarkable statement: *If what is for Hobbes, according to Hobbes's way of thinking, a Kingdom of Darkness, it should for us, according to our way of thinking, necessarily be, as it were, a Kingdom of Light."*

You might have thought I'd just delivered a blow to somewhere just below Brian's midriff, for he doubled forward in his strange perch at the side of the chair, pushing his wrists in on his stomach, and rocked backward and forward for a moment until he threw himself into the depths of the chair with a great sigh of what I might be inclined to call resignation — if it was really that at all. The chair emitted a great puff of air.

"Well, of course!" he exclaimed. I could tell that, underneath his mode of resignation, he was extremely agitated. "Now, why would you chance to remember that particular one?"

"I don't understand it, but it sounds like something, as I've said, distinctly remarkable," I commented after several moments. "It was, like so many such apothegms, written by itself on a separate piece of notepaper — just that one sentence."

Brian didn't reply. He seemed to have his gaze fixed anxiously at some invisible point in the middle of the room. I drew in and then exhaled a monumental cloud of cigar smoke, a sort of Jehovah-on-Mount-Horeb gesture, if I may say so, and extinguished the cigar by punching it several times into the ashtray on my desk. I inquired, "To start with what I take to be a fairly minor issue, what can an expression like 'necessarily — as it were' possibly mean?"

"The entire statement is clearly metaphorical, a trope in the broader sense —" Brian began.

"Ah, a 'trope,'" I interrupted. "I know that term had a special meaning for Ilya, and presumably therefore for you —"

"Special, in a way," Brian interrupted in turn, "and yet not special at all — not special in the sense of idiosyncratic or esoteric or merely stipulated, though it would be easy enough to perceive it that way; but certainly special in the sense that it 'specifies' what others vaguely mean by it, yet in a way that's much more precise."

Brian's former distress seemed to vanish almost as soon as he began to unravel an intellectual problem. He continued, "Yes, a trope — indeed, several of them, superimposed one on top of the other. That's why it's so unlike Professor Moshevitz, who was, ordinarily, wary of such language. He's building on, and inverting antithetically, a metaphor of a sort, appropriated from Hobbes, the 'Kingdom of Darkness,' with another trope, I assume of his own invention, the 'Kingdom of Light,' and identifies each with a contrastive way of thinking—that of Hobbes and that of what he can identify as his own. But then he introduces what seems to be an implicit logical rule into this complex trope with the word 'necessarily,' as if to say that Hobbes, deriving such a conclusion from his premises and assumptions, logically entails, even necessitates, someone else, Professor Moshevitz himself in this instance, deriving a contrary conclusion from his own oppositional premises and assumptions.

"But there's no real logical rule involved here; its purely hypothetical, probabilistic status is confirmed by 'as it were.' It's also curious that, by using first-person-plural pronouns, he doesn't refer only to himself but rather to himself as a representative of a like-minded group, both a part of a whole as well as a part who is the whole, who would share the same convictions—not just several metaphors but a complex, many-layered synecdoche you might say. It's a very strange statement."

"How well you remember it after a single hearing, I must say—after all, to engage in such an analysis," I remarked. "I'm not the only one around here with a good memory. But frankly, I don't have the slightest idea of what you're talking about."

I resisted the temptation of accusing him of indulging in obscurantist jargon because such an accusation ran the risk, as I was aware it so often does, of actually being a confession of ignorance about a legitimate technical vocabulary that someone might be using with great penetration and accuracy. And I knew that this would hold true especially in this case. Ilya always insisted very strongly that no academic pursuit has advanced to becoming an authentic "discipline" until it had developed its own rigorous technical lexicon. He also knew how easy it was for sham vocabularies to be developed and genuine ones to be corrupted.

"It doesn't matter," Brain responded. "The function of a statement of this kind isn't really to tell you much of anything—it assumes you already know everything it says. In this particular case, the statement makes no sense at all if you're not well acquainted with the work of Hobbes alluded to, in this case *The Leviathan*, to say nothing of whatever is meant by 'our own way of thinking.' It just combines purportedly familiar things in a special way with the purpose of asking us to *do* something. That statement is, in its own way, a very private note, a sort of 'remember to do' note: such as 'remember to pay the electrical bill.' But it has also been left behind for some reason. It's a prodigiously complex directive. It leaves me, for the moment—immobilized."

"Immobilized? Now, that's a curious effect of a statement that is asking you to do something."

"It immobilizes because, if you take into account all of its implications, it asks you to do something so … so drastic."

"Then what *does* he want?" Actually, I didn't really want to know, especially if it were so drastic. I detest drastic things. I've avoided them all my life. As it turned out, I wouldn't find out anyway. Brian made sure of that.

"He wants us to know and act on the truth, and nothing else, and to find out for ourselves what that truth is."

"Ah, truth! We live in a world of suppositions, don't we, none much better than any other. The modern university is a catafalque of suppositions. Anyway, you speak in riddles; you keep speaking in riddles—"

"Actually, I'm not speaking in riddles at all. I think you have the impression that I'm talking to you in riddles because, among other reasons, I'm not really talking to you at all."

"Then to whom are you talking?"

"I'm talking to myself."

"Maybe we should change the subject altogether," I remarked in exasperation.

We did. Or rather Brian did.

Still slouched back in the leather armchair and tugging the sleeves of his blazer down over the bulky sweater that protruded at the wrists, he resumed the subject I knew he was most interested in. "I had the impression that Professor Moshevitz was working on a major book, a treatise that would bring together all of his work. A '*Meisterstuck.*' A '*grand oeuvre.*' Something meant for posterity."

"A '*grand oeuvre*'?" I repeated.

"Yes," he affirmed.

"A *magnum opus*? A *summa*? A multivolumed compendium of all that he knew?"

Brian nodded.

"What gave you that impression? Did Ilya ever say so?"

"No—at least not in any definitive way. But there seemed to be a 'thing' he was working on. A project—something with defined features—not just a series of notes. Did you find any such work among his papers?"

"Brian, there's no such thing among his papers. No '*grand oeuvre*,' nothing of that kind."

"You're sure of this?"

"I've sorted, in a manner of speaking, through the entire collection. An immense compilation of notes, as I told you, ranging all the way from a few words on a single page to short disquisitions of several pages, but no '*grand oeuvre*.'"

Brian was puzzled. "I don't understand. I was certain there would be such a work—perhaps not completed, but mostly there. The completeness that he'd seen, the core insight radiating through all that historical knowledge … certainly he put it all together somewhere in writing!"

"I can give you a pass that will allow you to enter the archives," I remarked. "One of the assistant archivists will help you find the materials. You can look through them yourself. But unless you discover something I didn't see, there's no such *magnum opus*, no '*grand oeuvre*,' as you call it."

Brian shook his head in disbelief. "Yet he asked you to preserve these notes. There must have been a reason."

"I think so, but I don't know why. It would be difficult for almost anybody to know what to do with them."

Brian pulled himself up out of the deep leather chair and paced around the office several times, staring at his hands and punching his right fist again and again into his left palm, as if conditioning a baseball mitt. He stopped suddenly and blurted, "The pass! You will get me the pass?"

"Leave your address with the secretary on the way out. The pass will arrive shortly in the mail. Use it whenever you want and as long as you want to use it. But I can assure you, you will not—"

"I'll find out for myself," he interposed. "I'm sure that I'm not ready to deal with those notes, either, and I may never be, but looking through them will help me at least to make some preparations. Thank you … thank you for your time. I do appreciate it."

"And if I can be of any further help …" But he'd already bolted through the door, which he left partially open. I saw him stop at the secretary's desk, scribble something on a pad of paper, rip the sheet of paper off the pad, leaving behind a good quarter of the sheet still attached to the pad, and poke the jagged remnant of it at her with a brusque little nod.

As he turned to leave the reception room, he almost collided with a tall, slightly stooped man with long and dramatically combed-back hair, curled in little wisps at the back of his neck, who was entering the room from the hallway outside and who cradled a prodigious assortment of manila folders in his arms.

Professor MacCollody James lurched backward and glanced with some alarm over his half-glasses at the tattered young man in the overstuffed green blazer who retreated into the hallway and, clearly too impatient to wait for the elevator, descended the stairs with such short, quick steps that he appeared to be sliding downward into the stairwell. In a moment he was gone.

"My goodness," MacCollody exclaimed, "Whoever let that waif in here? He looks like as unsavory a chap as has ever weaseled his way through these hallowed halls."

I rose from my desk, went to my door, and peeked out at the secretary and at MacCollody with an embarrassed smile. "Don't worry, MacCollody," I said. "Nothing bad will come of him."

"Well, he looks like the perfect little arsonist to me."

"How apposite an observation, MacCollody!" In an unwonted display of temerity, I declared, "He could, if he wanted to, set the world on fire."

" 'Set the world on fire'? Now what historical personage of note most infamously bequeathed to us that preposterous expression?"

"No one whom you would be apt to recall, I imagine."

"Well, a barbarian at the gate, in any case!"

"You needn't worry," I replied. "The barbarians occupy the city. Now and then a civilized man knocks at the door, but the barbarians won't let him in. In any event, I wouldn't lose any sleep about it, MacCollody. We might be reduced to cinders, but we wouldn't know it, and life would go on as normal—a life of plunder and rapine, such as it is."

I wished him good evening and closed the office door. My eyes blinked in bewilderment. Had I actually said what I'd just said? I'd better be more cautious in the future. Did some of Brian's "grit" rub off on me for a moment? I went to the window and stood there, wiping away some of the condensation, waiting to see when Brian would appear on the street below.

In some peculiar sense, I thought, our young man may never have fully grasped who Ilya was. He may think Ilya was a brilliant, if neglected, intellectual and scholar of our age, of our specific historical milieu. But "brilliant" is just not the correct descriptive epithet, and he was not "of our age." Our universities are filled with "brilliant" men and women. That they lack intelligence—intelligence in the wonderful ancient way that Ilya used that term—has little to do, one way or another, with that brilliance that they possess and that serves just as often to blind them as it does to guide them.

For brilliance is the ability to make things up, the ability to shine with an inner light, to be the mastermind in your own elaborately contrived, artifactual world, to add to a set of established professional protocols an ingenious twist that appears to redefine those protocols while, in fact, it merely belabors and confirms them, to draw attention to the self above all.

But intelligence is the ability—oh, however more prosaic it seems—to see what is front of your nose, to conform your mind to the reality that confronts it. How difficult it is to do that, yet how much more luminous it is, finally, for all the brilliance of the universe is in it—a brilliance that outshines our paltry inner glow as the sun outshines a candle.

What was it old Aristotle had to say about all this?—that we're like bats, unable to see what is most evident because our eyes are blinded by the sun, by the light of the real itself. Ilya used to say that the universe perpetually speaks to us; how important it is for us to be silent for a while just to hear its speech, its logos, its word. An infant becomes a child when he stops making noise and starts listening; a child becomes an adult when he listens with all the seriousness that's due to the voice that addresses him.

Listening to the cosmos, we become like it: "*Vult autem anima totum mundum describi in se*," Ilya liked to say to me, quoting one of his innumerable medieval mentors at the most inopportune moments, when I would be trying to concentrate on a delectable slice of Linzer torte — "the soul craves to have the whole world inscribed upon it." In that very adulthood, we preserve what is authentically childlike in us forever — our wonder, our perpetual surprise, our tender watchfulness extended to the entire universe itself.

And then just consider what the presence of that irrepressible *eros* says about the soul itself — yes, that it was made expressly for that inscription. For, as Ilya might add, if the soul desires to have the whole world inscribed upon it, it's equally true that the whole world desires to be inscribed upon the soul; that it was, wonder upon wonder, made expressly for that purpose.

As for "of our age": it was precisely because Ilya was so superior to our age that he could immerse himself so deeply in its details — details often gruesome enough — and with a thoroughness and perspicacity that the rest of us cannot even dream to manage because we are the age, in all its baseness, in all its intractable obtuseness. That's part of the reason why he was neglected — though, that, to be sure, is a weak way of putting it.

He wasn't neglected.

Perhaps it wouldn't even be correct to say that he was ignored or shunned or feared, though all of these claims may have been partially true.

He was just incomprehensible to most of us — yes, to me as well, which is why I could never help him, except in this one final way. I could, after all, gather up his things, put them into storage, engage in yet one more feat of collection (certainly the most important of my life), and indeed, act as his "executor."

I'm glad that our friend Brian Seldon doesn't see — doesn't yet see, but he'll see when he tries to go through those notes, each of which, like a nugget, refracts a light of such intensity — just how utterly different Ilya was from the rest of us. The agony could be too great to bear. It's hard enough for him as it is. Imagine carrying around the knowledge that he must have — the knowledge that Ilya imparted, the knowledge of Ilya himself. How shall he contain it? Those words of — is it Jeremiah? — echo in my head: "... within me a burning fire, within my bones; I'm weary with holding it in and I can no longer ..."

As for me—I would give anything to know even a part of what it's all about, *if I could give up my privileges*. Which I cannot. Things are just … too comfortable for me. I'm glad to be an "executor." That's what I've been in everything else I do, and I think I do it well. That's what we here all do in our own way—we shuffle papers; we see to appointments; we burrow and store things; we gather immense amounts of information—as a resource for people like Ilya, should they ever happen to come around. And one did come around. *Thank God, one did come around.*

Sometimes I'm inclined to believe that our whole university system, our entire structure of higher learning, exists for no other purpose than this: to prepare a seedbed for the dozen or so Ilyas who happen to come along from one century to another, if we're lucky enough. And only those who are lucky enough to move within the ambit of an Ilya for some fleeting moment of their lives know who they are or that they're even here.

But that, in itself, is good enough. That, in itself, is more than good enough. That, in itself, is *shekinah*, a presence of something that far transcends us, that leaves us speechless with awe. Meanwhile, rest assured, we shall continue, with all due diligence, to ply our hobbies and secure our trades.

Ilya left no '*grand oeuvre*' in the ordinary sense. He, more than anyone else, recognized how useless that would have been, that it would have been even, in some subtle way, a betrayal of his own work. He left notes, for he knew that those who could use those notes, those who could see the coherence and could work out the connections, would be the only ones who could share his knowledge. He left a living heritage. I, and my colleagues, are bound, ineluctably, in chains, in the appurtenances of the dead—not the dead who have died but the dead who make of life a living death. How did the poet Rilke put it?—that the eyes of the dead roll around in their sockets and now look only inside, no longer beyond themselves.

For all that, Ilya Moshevitz, that old fox, left a "*grand oeuvre*" nevertheless. How could it have happened otherwise?

I gazed through my office windows, now frosted at the rims, as the chill New York evening settled in. I looked down the narrow street and saw the dark, shadowy figure of Brian Seldon already at a distance, standing at the corner where the street meets Broadway, waiting for the streetlight to change. Brian pulled his threadbare jacket around himself, hugging himself and tucking his bare hands under his arms in an effort to keep them warm. I wondered if I shouldn't send him a pair of gloves—a belated Christmas present, an offering of peace. I could get the address he left with the secretary.

Overhead, the black silhouettes of a flock of pigeons darted and swooped through the street against the cold orange sky, and the sun set beyond the trees of Riverside Park, beyond the Hudson River and the crowded ridges of the Palisades. I watched as the streetlight changed and Brian crossed over Broadway with his strong, nervous strides and then vanished around the corner into the brightly bedazzled night of that illustrious avenue.

I said to myself, "I'll probably never see him again. But it's good he doesn't know the one thing I do know. He may never know it."

I collected a number of bulletins, announcements, and papers that accumulated on my desk and sorted them into several groups. Ah yes, just the kind of thing I know, finally, how to do. I'm "Mr. Big Man," like so many other "Big Men," squeezed into a world so diminutive that nothing I've ever done will count for much—except for this, *except for this*. I've collected and stored the papers of Ilya Moshevitz.

I turned again and looked through the window at the long, empty street, now dark except for the streetlamps and the lights gradually blinking on in the entrance lobbies below and, higher up, in the kitchen windows of the surrounding buildings.

Yes, Brian doesn't know that it is he—he himself—who is the 'grand oeuvre' of Ilya Moshevitz.

Harry Wiedenhausen

"Good-for-nothing lout!"

That's what Juliana Wiedenhausen howled at her husband when she kicked him out of house and home. Harry, whatever else he may have thought about the slightly awkward situation he now found himself in, was puzzled, not by the substance but by the tone of her—in fact, quite warranted—reproach.

"By God," he mumbled to himself. "She's right. But I thought that's what she liked about me."

And in what sense was it a reproach, anyway? He was proud to be what he was. "Amused, complacent," as our old bard of Camden, Walt Whitman himself, might say, Harry took everything in stride. He always did.

So there he was—flushed out of domicile, marriage, a way of life, it seemed—everything Juliana and he had shared so seamlessly the past thirty-five years. You would have thought that his own dear spouse, steeped in the crucible of his luminous imagination for all that time, could rise to a more eloquent dismissal than that. Grand and beautiful years they'd had together—easy, relaxed, playful, intimate, and yet not so intimate that each partner was not able live a life of his or her own: Juliana devoted as she was to her innumerable pastimes and forays; Harry devoted as he was to being something of a fixture at the Dolphin Beach Club, where, in its plush lounge facing out over the sea, he presided over the supreme languor of Florida afternoons.

But something had changed. Maybe it would be unreasonable to expect less, now that prosaic little Gregoire, with his sandals slapping ever fitfully over the terrazzo floors of their spacious villa, had become Juliana's mentor of late, her arbiter of taste. He gave her unstinting attention, which is what she now craved.

He was young, a bright-eyed elf with the brains of a toad, waiting in the bush for the properly pre-senescent butterfly to snag with his garrulous tongue. He wrapped his carefully tanned but knobby, depilated legs in a pink sarong and was forever shoving furniture here and there, fluffing pillows, and rearranging potted plants; and he ferreted Juliana through chic little shopping malls, where they gobbled down exotic snacks while on the run to nowhere, laughing and stuffing themselves with passion fruit and Mongolian yogurt.

He was what every Palm Beach matron dreamed of, at one time or another, to console her amid the converging infirmities of incipient old age. Pathetic little Gregoire! If that's what she wanted, she was welcome to him. Harry smiled: anyway, the "*affaire*," as only a hopelessly naïve observer would call it, would not last long.

He packed up his antique Rolls-Royce — one of those enormous, black, big-fendered, and glassy coaches that still sported old-fashioned carriage lanterns mounted at the sides of the back doors — with those few things he actually owned in his own name, which wasn't much, depending on the context you put it in. He tossed his expensive wardrobe wherever he found space in the roomy passenger compartment. He scraped together his collection of gold tie pins, diamond cuff links, and absurdly expensive Italian watches into a leather satchel; and, with some care, he carted down from his bedroom the little oak casket with brass fittings that he called his "pirate's chest."

He'd saved it, as a kind of joke really, for a "rainy day," thinking he would never need it. It was filled to the brim with shiny Krugerrand gold coins. He may also have had about five hundred dollars in his wallet at the time.

All of this would be, to say the least, a goodly loot for the average citizen — worth, all told, perhaps, three or four hundred thousand dollars; but in Palm Beach, needless to say, such a sum was paltry, negligible, virtually parsimonious.

With this "sparse" patrimony, Harry was well aware, as he took his place in the chauffeur's niche and navigated the stately vehicle down North County Road and past the Dolphin Beach Club, that the only route for him to take was the one directly out of town. Exclusion from Palm Beach society was as rapid, as inexorable, and as capricious as was its inclusion. If you had money, you were in; if you had none, you were out. Exceptions were made for the ability—well, let's say, the willingness—to provide certain "exceptional" services. Any effort to circumvent these barriers, the slightest hint of deprivation, the slightest vagueness or prevarication in your explanation would lead to immediate branding of social leprosy, however genteel its expression might be. Didn't he know? Hadn't he seen it done more often than he now cared to think of?

Accordingly, reaching the Breakers Hotel and the Royal Poinciana Way, he took a right turn, drove westward toward Lake Worth, and crossed over the bridge into mainland Florida. To those not familiar with the geography whereof I speak, from the perspective of that long, slender, offshore island luxuriously crowned with palm groves and with the crested mausoleums of the rich, mainland Florida is synonymous with disgrace, with destitution, and with despair (unless somewhere, over those shimmering plains, you also own a ranch well stocked with thoroughbreds and polo ponies and the manicured stables to keep them in). And since Palm Beach has no hospitals, it's the mainland where one goes, not just spiritually but also physically, to die.

Yet somehow Harry, in his all-so-endearing phlegmatic way, knew he wouldn't be gone too long. Someone, he knew, would need him. It was just a matter of time.

Harry had one other asset, a little secret he'd closely guarded all these years. It was a remarkable item for a man of his social stature (as ambiguous as that had always been) to possess, and yet nothing in this world could have signified more perfectly who Harry was and where he came from. Harry visited it from time to time, and, like so many who withdraw to mountain or monastic retreats of various kinds to rediscover who they are, there Harry was refreshed and renewed again in precisely that identity that Palm Beach society at heart so delighted to see in him.

The item in question was an old scow moored, among other, not-too-dissimilar craft, in a mangrove swamp about an hour's drive from Palm Beach: a dirty, paint-chipped, utterly disreputable little barge with a small cabin fore and a warped, corroding deck aft — absolutely, I tell you, the best place in the whole world to hang out on a blisteringly hot afternoon, a fishing rod dangling negligently over the side, a chest of cold beer readily accessible, and a lethargic pelican perched on the faded gunwales, waiting patiently for the occasional fish that it knew Harry would eventually toss in its direction.

Rarely, it must be said, did Harry actually spend the night there; but the cabin, outfitted as it was with a cot and stove and dining table, was always ready to receive him in its penurious manner — after a brief inspection for, and consequent dispossession of, big hairy spiders and other unwelcome inhabitants. So Harry had a place to live, a roof over his head after all, a shelter from the ferocious noonday sun and equally ferocious downpours of the evening thunderheads. He was as much at home here, frankly, as in those lushly terraced palaces he normally occupied.

He might, of course, have to explain his altered situation to his neighbors in the surrounding boats. There was Al, the ruined stockbroker, who mumbled incoherent figures all day long; the Prophet Dan, a Seminole half-breed who spent his life reading the book of Daniel over and over again and who had three old hound dogs, one yellow, one black, and one white, named, respectively, Shadrach, Meshach, and Abednego (though collectively he called them the "races of man"); Hiram and Jessy, the elderly black couple who caught and sold enough crayfish and prawns to make a small living from it; and Dillon, the ex-Marine, who kept reliving in his vociferous dreams the assault on Iwo Jima.

But Harry was quite satisfied by all of this — as strange as it was to see his Rolls-Royce drawn up to the old dock and still crammed with his assorted stuff. His impoverished neighbors accepted him graciously as one of their own, without flattery or resentment or interest in his apparent riches.

At this point, no doubt, you're all ablaze with questions: and I don't mean to ingratiate you when I call those questions "philosophical," for they touch, in a way, on those fundamental issues that tell us something about who we are and where we're going as a civilization. But don't worry, I'm not going to — sorry, I amend that — I'm not *yet* going to present you with a philosophical disquisition apposite to our subject. I'm simply alerting you to a significance whose intimations you may already have discerned.

For Harry, you see, is all of us. He's what and who we really want to be. As the old bard of Camden would say, speaking for so many of us: "I lean and loaf at my ease, observing a spear of summer grass." But more about that later.

Life, I should say, was as good for Harry on his impecunious scow as it would have been anywhere else in the world — and that's saying a great deal, for Harry had indeed been many places in the world and had tasted generously of those myriad paradises that the world holds out in such profusion but that so few of us ever have the requisite time or resources to visit. On top of that, every place was a kind of paradise for him, or at least readily adaptable to whatever paradisal longings he may entertain at the moment.

For the passage of time was for Harry a kind of pageant whose every detail he noted and relished to the highest point. Take, for instance, the stillness of a white egret fishing in a nearby lagoon, with the dawn spreading its soft rose and amber hues among the dark-green mangrove. Or the glide of pelicans over the surface of the water, or the circling of buzzards high in the morning light, or the buzz and hum of colossal bees among the palmettos and the scraggy riverbanks. Or the sluff of little waves against the hull of the scow when, half hidden under the brackish waters, an enormous manatee sluices lethargically by on its way to its feeding grounds and the little flotilla rocks up and down, the boats scraping lightly against each other.

The Prophet Dan always rose early to chant, in low mumbly tones, his curious oblations; Shadrach, Meshach, and Abednego would surround him, waiting for breakfast, whimpering, curling around, and pawing and scratching their ears. At midday, Al and Dillon might share the day's news together, talking to each other from across their bows, gesticulating and pointing to the piercing blue of the sky and the sunny cloud banks drifting overhead, as if that was where everything was happening, calling to Harry on occasion, soliciting his opinion on this or that story in the papers. In the evening, Hiram and Jessy would sometimes pay a short visit, bringing with them a pot of steamed rice and shrimp and a spicy creole sauce in a small ceramic dish. Harry would reflect, in such a case, that he'd not eaten better in some of the greatest restaurants of the world. He meant it too; and Hiram and Jessy knew he meant it, as they laughed and clapped their hands.

Harry, then, might stay up until late at night, as he was inclined to do, when the stars blinked large and bold over the tropical marshlands, all of them clinging to the deep, sloe-black skies like summer insects to a windowpane. He would gaze for hours into the tender hollows of the universe, which churned melodiously around him, presumably for the sake of his sole pleasure and delight.

Now, Harry had hardly had much time to "settle" in (I use that term advisedly—there really was nothing to "settle" into, and Harry was always "settled" anyway) when, one day, a large, lividly pale-green automotive monstrosity rolled out of the early wetland mist and up to the dock where Harry's Rolls-Royce was parked. Shadrach, Meshach, and Abednego barked wildly until the Prophet Dan, assuming a magisterial Mosaic prominence, rose up with his staff and stilled the unruly multitude of "the races of man."

Meanwhile, the vehicle sat there for a minute. The door swung out. A pair of thick, hairy legs in yellow pants, but barefoot, also swung out and rested there for about a half minute, the almost round feet with tiny, appended toes suspended in midair. Then a pair of loafers were dropped noisily on the ground, the feet tilted downward and slid heavily into the loafers, and a figure stood up, huge and portentous. He wore a salmon blazer and an open green shirt. A shark tooth was suspended from his ruddy, many-layered neck with a thick golden chain. Harry, alerted by the yapping of the dogs and happening to catch some of this action from down below through a "porthole" in his little cabin, quickly recognized Bartolf Pearson, manager of the Dolphin Beach Club, and emerged from the cabin to greet him.

Harry helped him over the short gangplank and into the scow, which tipped precariously as Pearson sat down on the lid of a bait box. He looked at Harry and nodded with a smile, "Well, old Harry Wiedenhausen! Gone just a few weeks and already we need you back, you old son of a bitch, Harry Wiedenhausen."

Now, you can imagine that this encounter might be a bit awkward — for, in a sense, Bartolf came as an emissary from a higher world, lowering himself to the dregs of this marginal society, a potential bestower of good or evil. But it wasn't like that at all: he came, instead, as a suppliant. He came like an imperial eunuch seeking, in a remote mountain cave, the sole ancient warrior who could save a kingdom from its final dissolution.

Ha! How odd to think of Harry as a warrior! But Harry sat on a gunwale opposite Bartolf, sat as he would sit anywhere, a medium-sized man in every way, not distinguished, an ordinary fellow, after all, with his arms folded, his head tilted, a smile on his face, a sharp, clear look in his eyes, attentive, reposed, utterly and fully confident in his almost illimitable powers — as the old bard of Camden would say: "... looking with side-curved head, curious what will come next."

That Harry could save the kingdom, should the kingdom require saving, was never in doubt for Bartolf, for Harry, or for anyone who knew him.

Bartolf came rapidly to the point. He had, of course, apprised himself of Harry's situation. And now, if you please, hold on to your seat. Bartolf had come to offer him a job. Yes, a job! To put Harry's name and the word "job" into the same sentence seems like a most unnatural thing to do. But this was the fact, although we must give credit to Bartolf that he never used such an opprobrious term; he called it instead simply an "offer." And in this case the "offer" — yes, you guessed it — was for Harry to do nothing, come back to Palm Beach, come back specifically to the club, and begin doing again what he always did anyway: just be who he was.

In his absence, the club had suffered. People had become abrasive; some stopped coming. Without Harry, Bartolf said, the club would go "belly-up" — yes, "belly-up," like a huge dying sailfish in the Gulf Stream offshore. And if it went "belly-up," what else would not go "belly-up" along with it — persons, marriages, families, the whole society?

Harry demurred just a bit. Bartolf took note of that and raised one corpulent hand, spreading his heavily bejeweled fingers as if to dispel objections. "You will have a room at the club — yes, even a small apartment there, if you so wish. We already have such quarters for some of our staff. And a salary ..."

"A salary?" Harry interrupted.

Does one offer a fellow like Harry a salary?

Certainly not.

"A stipend," Bartolf corrected himself. "Or call it a 'royalty.' Or a 'remittance.'"

"And its terms?"

"To do what you did."

"Which was ...?"

"To do nothing. And, oh yes, to park your Rolls outside the club in its usual place. It's important that people know you're there."

"And what other inducement is to lure me away from these most inimitably luxuriant surroundings?"

"A sense of duty to your old friends. A sense of duty to the world itself. For if you can regard destitution as a luxury, the rest of us know in our hearts that luxury is a destitution—arguably the worst destitution in the world. Anyway, you can come back here whenever you want: a short vacation, as it were, from the demands of not having any demands made on you at all."

The problem was clear enough. Harry, of course, had been a habitué of the Dolphin Beach Club—quite regular, in fact, occupying *his* table in a corner of the cocktail lounge, nursing a drink that never seemed to disappear, engaging in idle chitchat with all comers, telling stories, exchanging gossip, filled with an inexhaustible fund of information about all sectors of the leisured life, from horse tackle to fishing lures, from exquisite beverages to the high cuisine of all times and places and seasons. About fine art and fine music of all kinds, about antiques and cinema and oriental rugs and a dozen other things about which he seemed to know everything there was to know. He could talk about everything—not always as learnedly as a scholar might talk but always well—as long as it touched upon all those good things that eased the human soul and salved its wounds.

Moreover, and most importantly, he liked almost everybody and found them superbly interesting, for some reason or another. Each person was special and different. As the old bard of Camden would say (and pardon me if I'm impelled to cite Walt Whitman once again): "Clear and sweet is my soul, and clear and sweet is all that is not my soul." Now and then, a few unfortunates, unwary of what they were doing and incited by their own aggressiveness, would invade Harry's repose and challenge his gentleness and imperturbability. But they always found him serenely unassailable. Soon enough, the edge of their aggression, and its all-too-apparent discomfort even for themselves, had been blunted, to their own infinite satisfaction.

In short, people came to the Dolphin Beach Club to be there with Harry, even if they didn't actually speak with him. Just to see him at his table made them feel all right with the world, feel it was okay just, for a while, to be — yes, just to be; *to be a being.* How odd to say something so obvious, and so unremarkable: *to be a being.* Just to watch and look and take things in. To witness and to wait.

With a single glance Harry could dispel all regrets, calm all anger, heal all sorrow, resolve all tension. For above all, Harry was, in his own somewhat complicated way, a truly simple man; and he brought out in all those who sought him a kind of simple happiness. To be affixed, if only for a moment, in Harry's invariably appreciative and ingenuous gaze was to bask for that moment in the recognition that one mattered, that your very *being as a being* mattered as much as anything else mattered in this all-too-troubled, all-too-cluttered world. Harry, indeed, was the Dolphin Beach Club's most valued member. He was, indeed, the Dolphin Beach Club itself.

Well, I shall not belabor you with the details of his reinstallation at the club. Saying goodbye to his fellow members of the diminutive swamp flotilla was, as ever, easy to do — he would be back quite regularly. And since he'd never unpacked the old Rolls-Royce, departure presented no particularly strenuous exertions. The spiders and other such creatures could move back into their preferred quarters, and the pelican would have to fend for itself for a while, as it usually did. Soon, the great, black-coached car headed back for Palm Beach and over the Flagler Bridge, spanning Lake Worth. At North County Road, it turned left and arrived withal at the pretentious pink portals of the Dolphin Beach Club itself.

But now it's time to interject, if I may, my long-deferred disquisition. I implore my readers' patience in this matter; please do not shun my words but attend to what I have to say, for it applies to you and yours, no matter how vigorously you deny it.

Fourscore and who knows how many years ago, our forefathers came to this bounteous land so that they could suspend a hammock between two trees and take a long siesta.

Okay, okay, I hear that clamor of voices raised in truculent objection. But I tell you that all those "huddled masses" came, still come, to our shores so that their toil would bear fruit and that, therefore, they would not have to toil anymore — no imperious earl or baron, no angular party functionary, no scrofulous commissar to wrench away their hard-won gains. They would suspend their hammocks from the trees, suspend them from coast to coast across the undulating heartlands, and sway in those hammocks in the soothing breezes of prosperity.

Sure, the dream didn't work out like that for most, and many were denied that dream from the start; many others discovered it was more difficult than they had expected; and many more had not anticipated those who, from boundless private greed or from lofty public aims, had developed a voluminous appetite for harvesting fields that others had planted.

But that was the dream.

That was our dream.

For America is the perennial vision of the Peaceable Kingdom, the vision of still waters and green meadows, "every man under his vine and under his fig tree." America works as ardently as it does so that it doesn't have to work anymore. It's a place where we work in order to "retire" — and the younger that retirement, the better. Who else other than that founding patriarch Thomas Paine could enunciate more succinctly the highest purpose of our polity when he said, "Every man wishes to pursue his occupation and enjoy the fruits of his labors and the produce of his property in peace and safety and with the least possible expense. When these things are accomplished all objects for which governments ought to be established are accomplished."

And where else in the world, one wonders, does the twenty-two-year-old, in applying for that first serious job, make inquiries about the retirement plan? And why, when we retire, do people "congratulate" us as if we have achieved something, when, in fact, we're achieving nothing except the opportunity to reap the harvest of a redolent cornucopia that amounts, finally, to nothing much at all? To sit back — the front porch, the rocking chair, the sunlit street—and to watch the parade of life that thumps and blares, with flags and drums and twirling batons, down Main Street; to bundle up in the hammock in the yard, suspended between two great cool, leafy trees: that's who we are.

Yes, despite our frenzy of making and buying and selling, that's who we really are: the fisherman half-dozing on a sunny wharf, the beachcomber kicking up sprockets of sand into a waggish breeze, the sprinkler of flowers and the watcher of baseball games and the swinger of golf clubs and the browser in old bookstores. Add to this the habitué of the barbershop hypnotized by the black ceiling fan sluggishly stirring a breeze on a hot afternoon, the motorcyclist reclining backward in the wide saddle of his Harley, the inveterate putterer organizing an entire day around hammering a single nail into a shabby barn door, and the elderly tyke finding final consolation amid the bright lights of glitzy casinos and in the cool depths of lush, tropical cocktail lounges.

In that sense, Florida can be construed, in its own distinct way, as the quintessence of America; Palm Beach the quintessence of Florida; the Dolphin Beach Club the quintessence of Palm Beach; and, as we have already noted, Harry the quintessence of the Dolphin Beach Club.

So why do we need old Harry Wiedenhausen?

Because he points the way with a clarity, a sureness, and a resolution we all must envy (though no one in this world would ever really envy Harry himself). No backsliding for Harry, no doubts, no guilt. To do nothing but gaze at things is what it's all about. *To be a being.*

Now there he sits, as he once did, in the bar of the Dolphin Beach Club, sublimely doing nothing, looking out at everything with still, untroubled, lucid eyes—not the sleepy, watery eyes of the dissipated, nor the ingratiating, predatory eyes of the seducer and the confidence man—but with the eyes of the lover beholding his beloved.

He watches and he waits. He lets things happen. He knows that someday Juliana, too, having survived her pre-senescent fling, will join him at his table, as she did in the past, in the early evening—the two of them giving just the right tone to the dinner hour that follows. It's good to be there, because he's there.

The "good-for-nothing lout" turns out to be the one who is, conversely, "good for everything." As the old bard of Camden would say (and I beg the indulgence of my readers if once again I quote Walt Whitman, who knew us all so well): "I'm satisfied—I see, dance, laugh, sing."

What else is there to do?

Moving Out

I guess I thought it would be easy. No, I guess I thought it would be *easier*. I would give myself plenty of time, be meticulously organized, proceed step by step, sort things out, put them in order. I've been telling my colleagues — those few whom I can, or will, communicate with — that I planned an orderly retreat. I would marshal my resources, chart my route with deliberation, make transitions smooth and elegant. I might even enjoy this opportunity, at long last, to assemble a final inventory of things and dispose of them properly. The one thing I would not do, under any circumstances, is transfer disorder from one locale to another — from, for example, my office to my attic at home.

So much for good intentions!

I sit in my office at my desk. It's close to the door so I can pay some attention to the traffic in the hallway from time to time. I generally keep my door open — it's an accepted practice and one I feel sympathetic with. It lets people know you're "available." Further, we're discouraged from being "alone" with students, and I'm very glad to have had a good excuse over the years not to be alone with them and to be able to explain that I'm complying with college policy regarding this matter, especially when a student has rather made a point of closing the door after entering and I've had to ask for the door to be reopened.

It's also good not to be "closeted" with fellow faculty; all business conducted on campus should be, in some sense, public business. Pockets of secrecy tend to be seditious.

Other advantages have accrued from the practice of positioning my desk near the door; it helps me have advance warning of who's coming by and who might do me the disfavor of dropping in for a surprise visit. I've learned, over the years, to recognize the footsteps of my colleagues from quite a distance.

As always, my desk is littered with piles of stuff. Cardboard boxes packed with books are stacked along one wall and are ready to go. Movers will arrive later this morning to cart off the heavier things — the college picks up the tab for this, not as a favor but to make sure that we don't linger and do actually vacate the premises in a timely fashion. It doesn't even matter that you've been around since, roughly, the Pleistocene age. When you're out, they want you out, period, and the faster, the better.

I've already closed and locked my filing cabinets: they'll be transported, along with all their contents, to that attic at home that I've already mentioned. I gave up trying to organize them several days ago. Somehow, I know that I'll never open them again and that an ill-fated scion of mine, after my demise, shall have to haul them out to the middle of a snowy field, empty out their contents, and set fire to it all — a fate not as glorious, perhaps, as Beowulf's fiery incineration on a headland looking over the sea, but not as ignominious, anyway, as being trucked off to the city dump.

Still, the impulse to preserve all this stuff is powerful. What treasure shall be lost to posterity should it vanish, one is tempted to think. Why do I think like that? *Why do we all think like that?* We just can't get used to the idea that what's important to us is of little or no importance to others.

Well, maybe instead of being consumed in some splendid conflagration, it will get recycled; my lecture notes — for example, my Chaucer notes, so artfully fine-tuned over the years — may one day be a container for Cheerios; the filing cabinets themselves may end up as a fender on a Ford convertible. That's better than nothing. Those things will eventually be trashed, too, and recycled in their turn. Life as a perpetual recycling of trash — an interesting analogy, I must say, a cycle of creation and destruction, repeated over and over again. There's something vaguely Hindu about that, or Stoic, or whatever. Meanwhile, I glance about me. Shelves, desk drawers, cabinets, wire baskets, boxes, dusty corners: all filled with junk. Whatever will I do with it?

I know a lot of stuff accumulates in thirty years, but being a person who's generally prompt, even precipitous, in throwing things out, I wasn't prepared for this much stuff, nor for the impatience that has so soon emerged in dealing with it, nor for the rapid resurfacing of habits that explain this lack of order in the first place.

What I've put off once, I shall put off again—and for a few good reasons, actually. I've found that reducing chaos to order is, more often than not, simply to reproduce chaos all over again, and perhaps in an even more pernicious guise than before—maybe more pernicious because at least it was, formerly, a chaos you understood.

Its prior haphazardness had the benefit of a history.

The new haphazardness conferred upon it will involve largely specious categories whose recently, and hastily, devised principles will be soon forgotten. On top of that, it's not just stuff; it's your life, in a way, or at least part of it. It resists careful definition as it unfolds itself to your prying eyes and hands roughly in the way it happened, one thing after the other, though in reverse, the older things lying deeper in the debris and coming later.

Then there's the emotional side. I thought I might be upset. But I'm not. Well, yes, I am. I'm upset because I'm not upset. I'm upset by my apathy. I'm upset because I can shrug off all those years so easily, without regret. I am, by and large, a sentimental person, but here I feel no sentiment, no waves of nostalgia, no fond memories. I'm upset by my emotional numbness.

I see myself as a person getting ready to leave a hospital after an extended illness: I want to go, but whatever put me here in the first place is still holding me down, impeding me, making movement difficult, and I don't know if I can tolerate the possibility of health waiting for me at the brightly lit end of some narrow corridor, where the wheelchair will bump into a doorsill and I'll have to get up and fend for myself. Illness has its consolations and convalescence its sorrows. Still, it's a relief just to think that I don't have to care about any of this anymore. Yet that's the most appalling thing, after all:

I don't have to care. So why did I ever care? I'm reminded of Feste's song at the end of *Twelfth Night*:

> *When that I was but a tiny little child*
> *With a hey, ho, the wind and the rain,*
> *A childish thing was but a toy*
> *For the rain it raineth every day.*

If you'd ever told me, when I was a quasi-deranged undergraduate so long ago, that I would spend the prime of my life in the office of an English department at a college somewhere, I would have been astonished. It's the one thing I would never have considered doing. While in college, I even avoided taking courses in English literature because, so consistently, those courses violated my own experience of the literary works we read. What got said about them had nothing to do with why they were so good, so enjoyable to read, such a pleasure to apprehend. At the time, I couldn't have explained my reasons; and I won't try here to retrace the uncertain and erratic steps that, later on, led me to such a momentous dislocation.

For I, like so many others, belong to the unwholesome "tribe of temporizers." We "temporize" with our lives. We live not in real time but in the "meantime." The problem is that when the "meantime" ends, if it ever ends, real time has ended too.

I once saw in the shadowy air shaft of a library annex a tall, almost impossibly narrow tree, surrounded on all sides by sooty concrete walls and glassy windows streaked with whatever it was that rain washed off those hideous concrete slabs. The tree, an evergreen of some kind, bent and twisted its way thinly and agonizingly upward toward the sky and the sun above. It was a living, rounded, palpable thing among all those flat inorganic surfaces yet was reduced to a mere thread of itself by its brutalized environment.

"Trying to get out," I thought.

If I was really thinking, I would have thought: "It can't get out" (at least not until someone uproots it and drags it out — "roots first," I might say in a more macabre moment, if I were so inclined). Yet even I, with all my reservations, even with all my aversions, had no idea what I should have really been having reservations about, what I should really be averse to.

I could never regret, or renounce, or reproach that sirens' song, whose beauty was true and good, whose beauty remains that way for me, even to this day. But I had no idea of the whirlpool at the bottom of those cliffs whither their song had led me.

Don't get me wrong! In principle, the whole conception was right, is right, will ever be right. A haunted grove. A sanctuary. A sacred temple. A place consecrated to savor, again and again, the presences of those earthly gods whose measured dance confers, out of the ages, its boundless delight. A place to be right and just and reverential to those things whose sheer splendor compels just such a response.

But that's not how it is.

If it exists for any purpose beyond the display of its own garish blandishments, which is doubtful, it exists to suppress exactly that. As an undergraduate I knew this somehow. I just didn't know yet what the big picture really was, and I certainly didn't know the details.

It's an implacable proliferation of verbiage. It's textbooks, articles, journals, student papers, syllabi, pamphlets, brochures, letters, dossiers, announcements, research notes and lecture notes, reports, minutes of meetings, class handouts, textbook solicitations and advertisements, newsletters, bulletins, memoranda, committee findings, class rosters, recommendation forms, grade sheets, teaching assessments, job applications, new course proposals, audio-visual requisition slips, library and bookstore order blanks, advisory sheets, calendars and schedules, surveys, press catalogues, registration forms, student-advisory files, workshop descriptions, conference flyers, exams, blue books, curricula vitae, get-well cards (perpetually to sign — myriad and sundry diseases flourish in academia), requests for donations, invitations to faculty and student functions, room reservation forms (with eight layers of carbon copies). It's a virtual landscape of paper, with rivers and oceans, cordilleras and jagged peaks towering over sluggish glaciers that wind down through valleys to the sea.

Add to this a stack of slippery computer disks two feet high, a hard drive jammed with documents, e-mail messages backed up by the hundreds, voicemail lights on your multibutton telephone console blinking shamelessly in the early-morning glow as, still bleary-eyed and with a hot plastic coffee cup nestled precariously in hand, you stumble through your office door.

And the talk—the talk, talk, talk: lectures, seminars, meetings, colloquia, student advising, committee deliberations and hearings, canvassing for votes and heading off imminent and brainless policy decisions by frantically "buttonholing" everyone you can contact in advance, fundraising projects, conferences with administrative officials who issue peremptory summons and then make it impossible to get an appointment, interviews, telephone conversations, fending off a dozen kinds of solicitations with a dozen kinds of prevarication, lunchtime gossip, and the eternal intrigues and scandals bruited about in private offices and secretive groups huddled together in hallways. All of this perpetually regurgitated from the fecund maw of academia, like Spenser's allegorical monster *Orgoglio*. Arrogance. Presumption. Willful and intractable ignorance.

"Ivory tower"? "Sacred garden of the muses"?

Scarcely.

Shall I miss the shady campus; the old granite buildings; the bronze statues of august scholars and somber divines of yore; the false-front, neo-Gothic façade of the library; the Latin inscriptions over arched doorways; the students strolling by, dressed for the beach resort or the cruise ship or the hiking trail or the shopping mall, chatting on their cell phones: "Hi, Mandy, come on over and have pizza with us at six"; or "Hey, Roger, you won't believe how many six-packs we ...."?

Shall I miss it?

No.

Believe me, I say no.

Nor will I miss the faculty conversations either: automobile insurance, house renovations, decks being eternally constructed in backyards, weather, good deals on airplane tickets (like the ancient sophists, modern academics are drifters, always coming and going), washing machines breaking down, ethnic restaurants, parking problems, movies, abominable popular fiction taken very seriously, health clubs and diets, vegetable gardens, complaints about everybody and everything, sports, news items, political asides of the most whimsical sort, picked up and authoritatively parroting glib Public Radio commentators heard while driving into the campus that morning.

Nothing—nothing, other than what the rest of the population talks about all the time.

Anything—anything, but what might touch upon the life of the intellect, the life of learning.

Because, of course, there's no common ground, except for certain fashionable trends that sweep from time to time through academia like epidemics of cholera causing cranial dehydration and voluminous logorrhea. Even within a department you can expect very little in the way of serious exchange except for the mutual reinforcement of the powerful prejudices that underscore the self-understanding of many disciplines.

Other than that—there's little to be said. Mind you, these are, for the most part, very nice people; amiable, generous, kind; they've done the best they can in an environment that makes no sense at all. One on one, and face to face, they're open and considerate; but in a crowd they're like all other crowds: members of predatory gangs with 90 percent of their brains switched conveniently off.

And where internal community—what little there is of it—implodes, external management explodes.

In this college, as elsewhere, while the number of students and faculty has more or less stayed the same for the last thirty years, management has expanded 300 or 400 percent. Even the computer phenomenon, which should have cut down on the need for such labor, has served only to swell, immensely, its profusion.

Yet academic management is an alien presence on campus: another world, in a sense, whose interests are diametrically opposed to what, in principle anyway, the university has been for centuries.

If I didn't feel sorry for the administrative personnel, and personally like a goodly number of them, I might feel some resentment about their sitting aimlessly in their offices, stroking their goatees or twisting their ponytails, staring hypnotically at goofy screen-saver images floating across their range of vision, and thinking somehow that their job is to transform society.

They live in a world of outrageous rhetoric combined with equally outrageous drudgery. Their work is to figure out how to make more work for everybody else; they do that quite effectively, for they're the primary fountainheads, prolific and inexhaustible, of the flood of paper that washes perpetually downward through academia like the four inky rivers that cascaded from the higher to the lower strata of ancient Hades. If they had their way, what little is left, ever so tenuously, of the art of teaching would be smothered forever under a blanket of bureaucratic formulas and assessment procedures (though many in the faculty are all too obliging to help them out in this).

Moreover, if these administrators went into classrooms each day, they would never believe their own rhetoric. Well before most college students get to college, they're hardened into a form as tough as reinforced concrete. Our adolescent entertainment and consumer culture has shaped them in a way no educational institution could ever emulate, even if it tried as hard as it could (and sometimes it seems to be trying to emulate precisely that culture, and little else). So, there is no transformation for those students; not in any way at all. That's just as well, I guess, given what the transformers have in mind. It's just as well, too, because, beneath the youthful intemperance and the mild-mannered dishonesty with which they so faithfully ape the adults in their lives, most students are still possessed of some basic human decency and reserves of common sense. It won't last much longer for them. So let it be for now.

As I said, I've thrown it out routinely—all this printed matter—about as fast as it comes in, 95 percent of it, ignoring it as I slide it, in thick slag heaps, conscientiously to the edge of my desk, allowing it to hover at the brink momentarily, tip, and avalanche downward, with a satisfying crash, into the recycling bin that's now conveniently located at the side of my and every other faculty desk. It's amazing how I've become convinced that the recycling of waste is a socially meritorious act. Hence, in a strange way I welcome it. The more I get to trash, the more gratification I can take in having trashed it. The other stuff, the electronic stuff, merely awaits getting around to the puncture of the Delete key. How I love to jab at that key with the simulated ferocity of an angry child exploding balloons!

And the talk—most of that talk, little of it serious anyway—is readily forgotten, though it depletes your energy and saps your strength, even as so often it insidiously debases the things being spoken about, reducing them to articles of use, of leverage in a contest of power and will.

Footsteps. I don't recognize them. Someone not in my department. Ah—Simon Evans it is. History Department. He comes to my door, peeks in, smiles. "Moving out, huh?" he says. There's genuine warmth in his smile. I'm a little surprised by that. "We'll miss ya," he adds. I believe him. I think he means it, even though he said "we" instead of "I" and "ya" instead of "you" (both standard ways of indicating overt insincerity—but he's shy and has tried to mask his sincerity behind a formula of insincerity).

He hasn't said anything to me in a long time (except for his cheerful salutations as we pass by one another on the campus), not since we had lunch together—was it about five years ago? He says: "That was a great lunch we had together. We never did finish the conversation we were having."

"I guess we didn't," I answer. Funny, but I could take up that particular conversation even now exactly at the point where we dropped it. I imagine he could do so as well. It was one of those rare forays into what might be considered a "serious" conversation.

I wonder if he remembers that it was so long ago—academic life extinguishes any sense of passing time, of real time; we live in the "meantime," as I said. The shaping of our thought for, and the perpetual address of our sensibilities to, the adolescent and immature mind, whose revolving constituency keeps it the same age decade after decade, has a way of freezing us in time, of settling us into a persistent and undesirable youthfulness that never grows but that teeters, from its onset, at the brink of a doddering senility.

Simon is a young fellow, a social historian. He had written and published an item on an historical event that, in my partially accursed youth, I'd actually lived through and had witnessed, had known firsthand, though superficially, a few of the people involved. I've made it a matter of courtesy to read the publications of colleagues whenever possible and to mention that to them—a courtesy that was rarely returned (actually, it was never returned, now that I think of it). In this case, I thought Simon might be pleased to have lunch together and to talk with someone who had that firsthand knowledge. Initially he was—pleased and complimented; until he began to realize from what I was saying that he might have gotten almost the entire historical event dead wrong. Mind you, I didn't ever contradict his thesis or his facts—you don't do that, at least not face-to-face, in academia; if you did, the entire code of academic forbearance, its pseudo-urbane cocktail-party mentality, would ignominiously collapse. I was just providing, in the most tentative way possible, something supplemental, a personal perspective, a different angle; I even flattered myself to think that he might find it exciting to discover a new and as yet untapped "primary" source, an actual eyewitness. Naturally I know that an eyewitness account which is not subjected to rigorous cross-examination is close to worthless, and I was ready and willing to be cross-examined, knowing that my memory can be fallible too.

But he drew, I assume, his own conclusions from whatever I may have said. I'll admit that I didn't know what was going on in his mind at that time: maybe he knew, right from the start, that he'd made the whole thing up and had forgotten he did and didn't expect to run into a person who had actually been there; or maybe he surmised that I was the one who was deliberately fabricating an alternative version, trying to upstage and humiliate him; or maybe my account of the event underscored for him just how arbitrary the writing of history can be, and a recognition of that sort at the moment was simply too frustrating for him to countenance. At any rate, as soon as he fully recognized what my having "been there" could entail, he gulped down the rest of his sandwich and fled (an appointment with a student was suddenly recalled — a routine escape canard) with a promise to continue the discussion some other day. I think that in this case he may have meant it, but it was the end of the discussion. It was never renewed.

Anyway, that was just one of dozens of interrupted and deferred conversations. As soon as one of them becomes serious and not just an exercise in genteel flattery, shut it down! A critique of a position assumes a standard of truth; if there's no such standard, then a critique is merely an insolent nuisance.

I lean forward a bit and watch Simon walk down the hall and go up the stairs. Maybe he'll actually miss me, though I can't imagine why. Someone once told me that leaving a place often draws out people who appreciated you for some bizarre reason, and you never realized that before, and they never tell you until you're more or less out the door.

What's in this drawer? A plastic pencil sharpener, stuffed with pencil shavings. The stub of a candle — why the hell would I have a stub of a candle?

Dozens of ballpoint pen caps—but no pens for them to cap. A miniature screwdriver for fixing eyeglasses. A small plastic shamrock, green with gold edges (for St. Patrick's Day?). Scissors. A letter opener with a handle intricately carved from Indian rosewood. A list of new parking regulations (now very outdated—such regulations need to be scrupulously observed, for the campus police regard faculty, perhaps justifiably so, as a particularly dangerous quasi-criminal subclass). A bottle of aspirin—only two aspirin left in it. Paper clips. A postcard from a student who went into the Peace Corps after graduation: it shows a monastery in Armenia. A magnifying glass for use with the department's Oxford Unabridged, Small Print. The magnifying glass that came with it and had its own little drawer on the top of the boxed volumes was stolen years ago from the department office and never replaced, so I had to have one of my own. (I don't share it, by the way, and I don't need to share it because now I have my own Unabridged at home and haven't needed to consult the department copy for years anyway.) Ah, a wad of Dunkin' Donuts napkins stuck together by a single coffee stain that has penetrated through all of them. A knot of rubber bands. More paper clips. A nickel and some pennies. A print, badly wrinkled, of the Globe Theater. Two leather eyeglass cases, black, both dried out and discolored. A seashell. What on earth is a seashell doing in here? A pair of wooden chopsticks in cellophane wrapping (what guest lecturer did we subject to the gustatory horror of the local Chinese restaurant?). Highlighter pens: pale green, yellow, pink, orange. A set of loose-leaf dividers.

A clipboard. I went through a clipboard phase once. I had a dozen of them, all labeled and suspended from hooks on the wall near my desk, with disheveled wads of paper clamped askew under each clip, rather like leafage dangling from the muzzles of a small herd of giraffes. It looked as if I were a shipping clerk in a department store, but it was an attempt to be organized. Organized? Anytime I bent a clip back to shove in a new piece of paper, all the rest of the paper fell out in a shower over my desk and floor. The worst thing was, I wouldn't bother to pick it up, until eventually, after a week or so, the cleaning lady would come to my office door, stand there silently with hands on hips, and glare at me. I was, still am, totally terrified of the cleaning lady. She's the only person around here you can take fully seriously.

Anyway, a large, framed print of Samuel Johnson now occupies the space once covered with clipboards. He gazes at me with a tilted head and a bewildered expression on his face. I don't blame him. He asks the same question I ask: "What, sir, if I may have the effrontery to inquire, are you doing occupying these disreputable premises?" But I'm very fond of my engraving of Samuel Johnson. He's one of my patron saints. As long as his icon is there, I feel safe.

Footsteps again. Do I ever know who this is! Dick Bennet, our department chair, whisks by, jovial as ever, nodding his head as he passes and twitching the bushy squirrel's tail he obviously doesn't (but should) have. He's glad to see me leave, if for no other reason than it gives him the opportunity (so he thinks) to hire someone for my place. He loves the hiring process, all the cringing and obsequiousness and condescension that goes along with it, the round of appointments, the campus tours, the lunches, the applicants dressed so nattily, though often rank and soiled with nervous sweat. He loves to talk of "level-playing fields" and "opening up issues" but believes none of this. The questions he asks applicants are gauged to elicit very specific answers. He always gets the answers he wants, for the applicants are marvelously well programmed to provide them. Though they come from many different universities and graduate programs, they're trained to think exactly alike but to present their thoughts as if they were the results of a great deal of independent reflection. They're all resolutely conformist adherents of so-called critical thinking while being incapable of critical thinking themselves and blissfully unaware that the "critical thinking" movement represents one of the most phenomenal frauds to appear among all the other frauds that academia is so prolific in producing.

Dick doesn't know, fully anyway, that I've been one step ahead of him. Having been dysfunctional in the department for quite a few years now, I was able to convince the dean that I don't need to be replaced. The dean agreed. There are few things he would be more ready to agree with. His job is to make sure that the faculty is as sparse as it can be without the institution collapsing (every new multimillion-dollar building they put up is always accompanied by a small reduction in faculty and by a sizable augmentation of staff). Getting rid of a tenured faculty member—especially a decade or more before he's normally scheduled for delivery to the ossuary and not having to replace him or her—is a gift from the gods. It's what deans dream about at night after a hearty dinner, and blubber about at the faculty club bar during "happy hour" when a trifle deep in their cups.

Dick doesn't know this yet; he thinks that my replacement has simply been put off for a year. Of course, I may be partially replaced by one of these so-called lecturers or other personnel who now constitute the itinerant and rootless indentured servants of the modern university system.

More paper clips. A postage stamp, very old, never used, with T. S. Eliot's picture on it—I wonder if I could still use it (though I would have to add more stamps to meet the necessary postage). A collection of keys—I have no idea what to. A watch with a broken wristband, dead in a way only a dead watch can be, time frozen for the last—fifteen or so?—years at, what is it? 11:21. Some photographic slides of the Unicorn Tapestries at the Cloisters in New York. (Why do I have these? Uh oh. I guess I never returned them to the art library—ten years ago maybe. And they never missed them?) A pair of reading glasses with one ear hook missing. A piece of duct tape I must have used to try to reattach that missing ear hook—unsuccessfully, I figure. A box full of paper clips. A razor. A spoon, almost bent backward on itself (what happened?). A printer cord (what printer?). Several pieces of chalk, fractured and broken.

An old gradebook. I look in it—dozens and dozens of names no longer attached to faces. I used to have stacks of these around. I carefully guarded them because I didn't want to let it get out how I graded students. That old myth about professors throwing student exams or papers down the stairs and seeing where they land has more of a certain symbolic truth to it than one might want to concede.

More pen caps without pens. A ruler. Crumbs. A calendar (about fourteen years old). A gadget for punching holes in paper. Another postcard—sent to me when I was a child by my father when he was interned in an enemy alien camp in North Dakota during World War II (near Bismarck, of all places!) The postcard shows a buffalo and a teepee and has a big "Censored" stamped on it. (Why do I have this here? Is it to have reminded me, at some point in my "career," that I, too, was an "enemy alien," an innocuous presence, yet considered highly dangerous, with "Censored" stamped across my forehead? I put the postcard aside, away from the other stuff.)

More paper clips. Ah, here's my old pipe—a calabash pipe with a porcelain bowl. I haven't seen it for years. It takes me back a long way to when I'd envisaged using one in class so that I could imitate those blank, presumably meditative stares that professors were famous for while packing, lighting, or puffing on pipes. I never got far with that: the pipe made me nauseated, a calabash pipe looked idiotic in a classroom (it's a kind of pipe associated with popular images of Sherlock Holmes), and I hardly ever used it. Anyway, pipes are *objecta non grata* these days: smoky, old-fashioned, reminiscent of crusty male enclaves and prerogatives. And here—oh yes—a box of unused pipe cleaners. But no tobacco? Alas. But I wouldn't smoke it anyway.

CLOMP, CLOMP, CLOMP. Who could this be? Is it Paul Bunyan returning from the Northwoods in his hobnail boots? Or could it be his fabulous blue ox with his mighty hooves? No, it's Miranda Stimson in her stiletto heels striding stridently past, tiny, thin, and taut, a flinty visage peaked in front like the steel wedge that a lumberjack uses to shatter a log. She doesn't like high heels—too suggestive of feminine oppression—but she wears them anyway so that at least she'll break five feet in height, and she keeps the stiletto points razor sharp, ever ready, should the need arise, to puncture and kill—something male, preferably. Maybe she specializes in impaling squirming male mice to the floor. She doesn't look in, head bent forward, keeps her eyes always focused ahead of her, is perpetually angry, on the defensive, hates me and everyone else on principle, even most women, it would appear, a frightful synthesis of Grendel's Dam, Lady Macbeth, Goneril and Regan, Duessa, Madame Defarge, and Big Nurse wrapped into a single miniature ferocious force, ready to skewer the entire universe—should it have the misfortune to come her way. Too bad—I hear she's very good at what she does, whatever that is.

A professor I had in graduate school once told me: "Don't think you'll ever teach anyone anything. Sometimes you will, of course, but more by accident than on purpose. It's by accident because the student who learns something from you will learn it by deciding to learn from you, but you have no control over that decision and no ability to predict when and where and how long it will happen. Beyond that, even in the best of circumstances, you'll take most of what you know to the grave, and no one but you will ever know it — or know you ever knew it. Rejoice and be glad that you know what you know. It's a treasure that only you will appreciate."

When I first heard that, I refused to believe it. Now I do.

Truly good students come along now and then, two or three a year. You recognize them because, once they know that you know something, they *insist* on learning it from you. They appear, suddenly and inexplicably, like luminous spirits out of the dense fogs of Acheron and Styx and grope their way through the shrieking rabble of the modern university like Dante and Virgil clambering across the rancid ditches of the lower Inferno. The Circles of Fraud. The circles of Swift's Aeolists busy at their loathsome work. Hamlet's "foul and pestilent congregation of vapors." It's amazing that these students survive at all. Some don't.

Curiously, though, as I reflect upon it, in my later years I've tended to draw more students than usual — but not, frankly, through any merit of my own, as far as I can see. I can't help but think that my being dysfunctional at the college had something to do with that. Perhaps my condition, in some way, echoed their condition, my estrangement mirrored their estrangement. It's curious, too, how sagacious I suddenly became in their eyes when word got around that I was on my way out. Maybe the explanation of that was simply because my departure was interpreted as the sort of divestment that, under the circumstances, any intelligent person would make. In any case, I've become a wise man, one of the Magi of old, dismantling his tent, packing his camel, and preparing to disappear into the desert twilight.

In general, students are transients, passing through, treated like vaguely unwelcome guests who are both watched with painful scrutiny and ignored as if they weren't around, pampered like children but herded into compounds like prisoners of war, referred to as "kids" and called by their first names but subjected to occasional kangaroo judicial procedures that would make most totalitarian regimes blush with shame, coddled as valued customers but charged prices so high that it amounts to criminal extortion, profoundly dispossessed of what is ostensibly conveyed to them as their special possession (their own intellects) by reducing all intellectual growth to "negotiating your own identity," i.e., positioning it so as to gain whatever maximal cash flow and social prominence might ensue from that, as if that were the only kind of personal identity that mattered.

That's what their professors have done with their own lives, and that's what they're teaching their students to do. Why be interested in truth, beauty, and wisdom when you can be interested more profitably in your ever so sovereign self?

Furthermore, anxiety is induced in students by a terminus (graduation) that's drawing ever closer at all times. Somehow the conclusion of something unintelligible is the most unintelligible thing of all, for it concludes what, by definition, cannot have a conclusion. Hence, graduation, despite its grandiose trappings and ceremonial hype, is an arbitrary benchmark that leads from nothing into nothing. Students develop fearful intimations of sheering off into an inexplicable void in which whatever shards of authentic learning they may have garnered, having already been rendered more or less meaningless by the collegiate experience, will be rendered even more meaningless by an ambient popular culture, abetted by an ambient "elite" culture, whose pervasive intellectual shallowness, moral debasement, and aesthetic vacuity do everything they can to impoverish that learning. I think the students found some comfort in consulting with someone who may have understood part of what they were experiencing.

You don't understand the modern university until you recognize that it reverses whatever motto it claimed for itself in the past. If the motto is in Latin, add a *non* to it. I think of that ancient edifice of Oxford — "*Dominus [non] illuminatio mea.*" How about Harvard: *[Non] Veritas.* Or Yale: *[Non] lux et [non] veritas.* Or Brown: *In deo [non] speramus.* Or Princeton: *Dei sub numine [non] viget.* Well, you could go on for a while with this. (On the other hand, there's the motto of my esteemed undergraduate alma mater, *Vox clamantis in deserto*, which, unaltered and unadulterated, perfectly describes the kind of experience I had there.)

I wonder how many parents give a thought to what they're sending their children to. Most don't know, most wouldn't care, most are satisfied by, even proud of, thinking their children are climbing the ladder to social advancement and economic success. A bare handful might think that their children have begun a life of self-cultivation, of *Bildung*, of nurturing their minds and spirits in what is true and beautiful and good: the beginning of a lifelong flowering of their intellects and sensibilities. They're unaware that they have consigned their progeny to asylums of multiple social pathologies.

A sliding, shuffling, devious walk. Hesitant, then aggressive. Brace up! Get ready! Dave Atkins sticks his head through the door. I never especially like it when Dave Atkins comes by. His academic specialty is intrigue. He's the department Iago. He slithers into my office, a big grin, short, even teeth all aglitter, eyes cocked jauntily to the side. He props himself against the door on one elbow. "Hey, guess who's going to get your office?" he says in his raspy way, a sound no more endearing than the faint clatter of a rattlesnake coiled at the base of a distant Sonoma cactus.

Damn him! The exact, the precise, the perfect stab. He gets me just where I can be got. I do regret giving up the office; it's the only regret I have. I'm oddly, perversely jealous about it—my lair, my niche, my space, my retreat. More to the point, I'm possessive about my window, about the view I have through it, a view—a grove of Norwegian pines and white birches, a woodland pool at the center of it—that belongs to me alone. Some design peccadillo of a contemporary (and possibly blind?) architect has ensured that no other office window in the building gets that view. It's my secret. I've meditated it a hundred thousand times, in all seasons of the year, as bright scarlet leaves fall from the birches or as eddies of fresh snowflakes whirl in countless shimmering patterns in a winter twilight glowing through the dark branches of the pines. I don't want anyone else to claim possession of that view—it's the one thing I'm pained to give up.

Dave—Iago—he got it on the button!

"So, who's going to get my office?" I ask. He *would* turn this into a riddle. He always does, the backbiting, backstabbing, jealousy-mongering, treacherous son of a bitch. Raise suspicions about everyone! He wants me mentally to pass in review all the members of the department. He stares at me with a malicious grin.

I repeat my question: "Well, Iag ... ah, Dave, who gets it?"

"NOBODY!" he shouts. He buckles over with laughter. He holds the sides of the door with both hands and laughs and laughs.

I don't laugh. "So, who is nobody?" I ask, presuming that "nobody" may be a code word for somebody. For English professors, everything is a code; nothing means what it seems to mean; that's how they destroy the value of literature for just about everyone, including themselves.

"Nobody is nobody," he answers, still holding himself firm against his own gales of laughter. I have the impression that in his wild hilarity he may actually climb up on the door and start swinging back and forth on it.

"Nobody has done this to me," I respond, echoing Polyphemus in the *Odyssey* and feeling very much like that blinded Cyclops, staggering through primordial darkness with a great blazing stake poked in his singular eye.

"They're going to turn your office into a storeroom—a place for keeping computer stuff."

I don't know whether to feel pleased or offended. It enhances my own sense of utter uselessness: "They don't even need my vacancy." In a sense, even the emptiness I leave behind will stay empty. Somehow, I'd thought there might be some competition for my office, a scramble to see who would get it. No one else has a view like that. Then again, most people don't know I have this view. Even those few who have been far enough into the office to be able to see out the window don't notice it. Academic people, by and large, are studiously taught to construct mental "paradigms" in their heads, conceptual chimeras, epiphenomenal word-worlds, but not to look at actual things. On the other hand, I'm relieved by this information; I can't begrudge a stack of computer equipment gaping out of my beloved window.

Dave departs, thank God, waving behind him: "I'll see you at the retirement dinner."

Retirement dinner! I'll tell you one person who wouldn't be at my retirement dinner, if there were one. That's me. What kind of nonsense speeches would they make about me? What would they memorialize me for? What would be on my list of achievements that some eulogist would recount? I can just hear it now. "After years of persistent effort and a long, lonely battle, our distinguished colleague, whom we honor this evening, succeeded in getting the Buildings and Grounds Department to mount a coat hook on the inside of the men's room door on the second floor of Hoyden Hall." Applause. A few people jump to their feet while applauding. A few more jump to their feet—including Iago. Then, though a bit reluctantly, a full standing ovation. A sea of smiling, excited, malevolent faces and clapping hands. Embarrassed acknowledgment from me as I stiffly screw my head up sideways and force a bitter, disembodied smile. Everyone sits down again.

Time for the Master of Ceremonies to tell a joke. He tells it. Slightly ribald, off-color, toilet humor—appropriate for the nature of the achievement. Laughter. Academics take a special delight in off-color jokes; it helps them assuage their feelings that they're not "of the people," whom, of course, they proclaim to love but actually despise. Meanwhile, I lean forward over my dessert and fork into my mouth some dry, unpalatable morsel of cake conjured up by the dining hall staff for the event.

What my august colleagues won't ever understand is that it really did take a lot of work to get that coat hook mounted on the men's room door. I could have done it myself—gone to a hardware store, purchased what was necessary, and put it up in a few minutes with a screwdriver and a drill. But then I would have been accused somehow of defacing college property, unjustly "privileging" that particular facility (why didn't everyone else get a coat hook too?), as well as violating several other rules. Anyway, it seems as though I had to fill out a thousand forms in triplicate and testify at hearings before a dozen recalcitrant, nitpicking committees—to say nothing of the unseemly wrestling match I had to conduct in the hallway with the surly carpenter dispatched, finally, to do the job. I would hope they all would appreciate that!

But there won't be a retirement dinner. Allison Berglund is in charge of such affairs, and I got to her at least a year ago in order to forestall such a monstrosity. I threatened to kill her if it happened. Not really! I did make some kind of simulated threat, bouncing around and waving my arms like a psychopathic gorilla or something to that effect; but all in fun—Allison is a delightful person who understood at once what the problem was and assured me that I had nothing to fear. She organizes all the retirement dinners—she's a so-called social "resource" person and hence just as dysfunctional as I am—and abhors these affairs even more than I do. She would find some excuse—such as the *hors d'oeuvre* caterer's being scheduled for a heart attack about that time of year—that would make it impossible.

I also managed, through a sequence of the most punctilious maneuvers, to deflect the prospect of a departmental retirement gift. I've always regarded the extracting and imposing of compulsory gifts among people for institutional reasons as one of the most loathsome things in the world. But I couldn't avoid, as hard as I tried, the faux-colonial Windsor chair, engraved with the retiree's name, that the personnel department, in its egalitarian frenzy, gives to everyone, from the janitors to the periodically vanishing college presidents.

They asked me where to deliver it. I said I didn't want it. They said I had to take it, whether I wanted it or not. I said I wasn't retiring; I was resigning. No difference. I still had to take it. Somehow the personnel computer, when signaled by some finance office computer that an account is soon to be dropped from the payroll, is programmed to order and send these chairs out, and any human or other android interference with the system might cause a massive electronic breakdown, both here and along the entire grid of the Eastern Seaboard of North America. So I gave them delivery instructions to the firewood pile in my backyard.

As for egalitarianism, I'm all for it. Too bad it doesn't prevent academia from becoming ever more and more embedded in its obsession with rank, status, public image, and privilege. In fact, that's all it cares about (except for money, which is the real heart of the matter — Thorstein Veblen got that right over a hundred years ago when he wrote a book about the university). Also, I really do object to giving the same reward to people who work reasonably hard, such as janitors, and to people whose function it is to pull the wool over people's eyes persistently and systematically, such as college presidents. But I guess I should appreciate them. They achieve a marvelous equipoise between the mendacity they practice and the mendicity they pursue.

Hmm. A plastic serrated knife — probably intended (though in vain) to slice one of those detestable chunks of rock-hard processed cheese that grace all academic functions. Tickets to some college performance I never went to. I learned, through hard experience, to avoid performances given by professional groups on campus. They know that college audiences consist not of the students who never go anyway or of the faculty who can't be dragged away from their television talk shows but rather of the local "academic" or quasi-academic demimonde who've been bred to have an undiscriminating adulation of "high art" and of the "artist" and will, invariably, give an enthusiastic reception (and always a standing ovation) to the most incompetent performance. At colleges, professional groups provide such performances accordingly and get the customary paroxysms of sycophantic applause. Indeed, the audiences seem to regard their function as needing to be approved by, rather than to approve of, the performers.

A name tag with a safety pin. I always had a way of sticking myself with those safety pins. Another name tag, this one with a sort of chain to put around your neck. (How I've always hated name tags. I don't like complete strangers to know what my name is without having had some kind of personal introduction or interaction first, however minimal. And I don't like people squinting at some location on my chest to find out. I should have followed Odysseus's example and always had "Nobody" written on the name tag.)

A comb. An old automobile repair bill. Several more automobile repair bills. (Few things in my life, I should say, have been more terrifying in anticipation and more financially crippling in outcome than automobile repair bills. A goodly portion of my life has been impaired by my sequence of automobiles and their insatiable demands on my time and resources.) A small box filled with paper clips. Another box filled with paper clips. A card showing a dentist's appointment (about eight years ago).

A paperweight — a small chunk of granite marked with colored chalk — a gift from my daughter when she was in kindergarten. I like this. I hold it tenderly in my hand for a while, the way you would hold a child's hand. I put it to the side with my father's postcard. I never used it much. In my office, the only thing that could operate as a functional paperweight would be the Rock of Gibraltar.

A bottle of ink (all dried up now). A stapler — jammed and broken like most staplers I've known in my life. A bottle of Tums for the tummy — just in case, never opened. Pink, blue, and white index cards. Thumbtacks for the bulletin board posted outside my office door. A large box filled to the brim with paper clips. *Why all these damned paper clips?* Pennies. A get-well card sent to me when I was having a knee operation, signed by the whole department (of that time — many of whom are gone now, expelled into outer darkness, living, presumably, on skid row, which is the next step down after academia. Have you ever been the recipient of a lecture given to you by a derelict? They can discourse most copiously on all kinds of esoteric and idiotic subjects. That's because so many of them are former professors.) A chocolate-bar wrapper. A gold tassel detached from the tam cap of my academic commencement outfit (the cap, gown, and hood of which have been useful most of these years as providing a base for Halloween costumes of various kinds for my children — you know: witches, vampires, zombies, and other sundry ghouls for whom academic regalia is especially appropriate). A map of the London Underground. A small light bulb. A blues harmonica (never got much beyond "Swanee River" with that). An announcement, written by a former secretary, that I would not be keeping office hours that day. Two or three Earl Gray tea bags. A business card from a textbook salesman. A flashlight. (Does it still work? No, it doesn't — they never do when you need them, though right now I don't need it anyway.) Matches (for the candle stub? For the pipe?).

Yes, remnants of my "in case I'm trapped in my office by a blizzard" kit: a small hot plate, a tiny pot for making coffee or soup, some Lipton dried soups, granola bars, a bottle of water, a towel, other stuff. I never had to use it. Lucky I didn't. I heard once that, if a professor were discovered bunking down in his office during the night, for any reason whatsoever, even if it were to protect his life from some mass murderer roaming about the campus, he would be dragged out to a remote area behind the gymnasium and riddled with bullets. The campus police routinely burst into all the offices every night with huge flashlights to make sure this doesn't happen.

Ah, a small Russian black-lacquer box, a tourist item, picked up on a trip to Russia, adorned with a painting on its lid of a boy and a horse caught in a snowstorm (how appropriate; but, anyway, here it is — my wife has been looking for it for years). It rattles. What's in it? I pry off the top. Some cuff links. A tiny piece of flint purloined from a prehistoric site in Brittany (the only time I ever stooped to that execrable practice — but it had something to do with one of my medieval courses, something about monks being turned into stone by a sorcerer, and I wanted to show my students a shard of petrified monk), a brass button from a blazer, a lapel button with Shakespeare's image and "Happy Birthday, Shakespeare" imprinted on it.

Shakespeare has something like the status of a rock star in academia; everyone worships him—not for the right reasons, as I see it—but few actually read his work. He's a "cultural icon," and that's about it. They worship him because they worship celebrity (he occupies a status more or less equal to that of John Lennon among the younger faculty). I pick up the lapel button and throw it away. I close the box and put it with my father's postcard and my daughter's paperweight.

A box of staples—for use in my jammed stapler? A corkscrew. A corkscrew! All alcoholic beverages *strengst verboten* in academic offices! Heroin, cocaine, and marijuana okay, I guess, but not a drop of Benedictine or Grand Marnier. One more way to get riddled with bullets behind the gymnasium. Red and green ink pens. (Red ink used for correcting papers is perceived nowadays as "threatening" to students; green ink, for some reason, is not. A light pencil, barely pressed to the paper with minute, cautious lettering, is even better—it lends a certain "apologetic" tone to your comments.) A Christmas tree ornament given to me as a gift by a student—a lavender Victorian bulb with a little sleigh etched on the side. I appreciated that. It goes with the special items: my father's postcard, my daughter's colored rock, my Russian lacquer box.

More footsteps. Blithe, lissome. I know who this is. Louise Lindsey swishes past, swinging her arms in her provocative way, then stops, pirouettes on the heels of her dainty shoes, and tilts her pretty head through the doorway. She waggles her fingers at me as if to wish a kind of temporary goodbye. But not really. It's her way of engaging in some quite innocent, make-believe flirting. Her academic specialty is Renaissance drama. She's a recent addition to our faculty.

I made a strong case for hiring her for a number of reasons, but most of all, in my own mind, I pressed her case because she, everything else having been more or less equal (which they usually are, so-called credentials being either downright deceptive or almost meaningless), was the most beautiful applicant we had had for years, and her beauty, in some curiously insidious way, was being held against her by a few members of the department. In addition, she's poised, modest, courageous, astute, self-possessed, ingenuously appreciative of the homage so rightfully conferred upon her, an "Athena of the flashing eyes," a consummate though unintentional source of wonder and threat to men and to women (though for different reasons) because, in being the most perfectly natural thing she is, she, like all perfectly natural things, is a prodigy, a miracle. (Of course, it's considered anathema in academia to say something like this — we're not supposed to think in such "gender" terms, even as we're pressured constantly to do nothing but that.)

And I knew the delightful havoc she would create. Beauty — real beauty — is a shocking, disruptive thing. One beauty breaks open the way to another beauty. How better to awaken students to the beauty of Shakespeare's verse than to have them uttered rhythmically and perspicaciously ("trippingly on the tongue," as Hamlet would have it) by those glorious lips. Students would fall into a stupefied, awed love of her, and she, like Dante's Beatrice, would cause them to aspire to divine wisdom.

Well, not really, I guess, but, as I understand, it has worked now and then. Students would actually divest themselves of their tickets to a football game and instead go to a performance of *Othello* so they would have an excuse to visit her office and tell her about it and evaluate, as she would do, the quality of the performance.

I wave back to her and emit a bestial grunt, rather like an old boar whose tusks are stuck in a rotten log and whose hooves are frantically slipping backward in the mud as he tries to dislodge them. She whinnies sweetly and prances down the hall like a palomino filly, full of vigor and pride.

A few minutes later, Barry O'Sullivan "pops" in. He reminds me of a piece of popcorn, "fluffy" and always "popping" up here and there. His fluffy blond hair also pops up all over the place. He's a specialist in James Joyce. "We'll catch ya later!" he says, seeing that I'm busy (note the "we" and the "ya"; but I'm only pretending to be busy and grovel about in my enormous collection of paper clips, having recognized his little step-dancing jig in the hallway before he appeared at my door).

The hell he will "catch me later"! He'll scrupulously avoid me. There was a time when he wouldn't speak to me or even look at me — it lasted for almost three years. For the first six months or so, I didn't know why. After making some inquiries, I found out that a snitch in one of my classes had reported to him that I'd cited, with unqualified approbation, Lawrence Durrell's rather allusive aspersion against Joyce's literary style: "stream-of-pompousness."

So I dared to say something negative about James Joyce! Although there are passages of incomparable and luminescent beauty in his work, much of his writing is what the modern university is: pretentious, self-assuming, atomized, irresponsible, incorrigibly shallow, erudite in an idiosyncratic and sloppy sort of way, mannerism and posturing gone berserk, fundamentally uncouth in taste and judgment, a colossal waste of truly prodigious talent. Anyway, it took a long time for Barry to forgive me for that.

Inviolable Rule Number God Only Knows What: don't bash, don't even nudge other people's specialties (especially if they have some kind of ethnic loyalty to it—though I've never understood why Irishmen would have an attachment to Joyce; I'm not sure he had much of an attachment to them except to use his contempt for them as grist for his literary mill).

Have an opinion about everything in the universe—the less you know about an item, the stronger your opinion can be—and broadcast it about relentlessly, especially in circumstances where it's totally inappropriate to do so. But, heaven forbid, don't have a considered opinion about the worth of an author—the one thing English professors might actually be supposed to know something about, but they have no problem acceding to enormously exaggerated and uncritical claims made about so many of the "canonical" authors.

Barry's brain is a mountain of disconnected trivia about James Joyce, which is to have a mountain of disconnected trivia about a mountain of disconnected trivia. It all pops about in there like the popcorn inside those huge glassy poppers you see in movie-theater lobbies. I don't think he knows anything else about literature. He certainly doesn't know the dozen or so languages Joyce knew, which was at least one saving grace for that renegade bard, though in the end Joyce figured out how to abuse that too. Barry goes popping down the hall.

Phew! He's gone. Actually, he's a nice guy, when he's not popping off about Joyce. I've had a few pints of Guinness with him, in better times, in the local pub, and his stories about Galway are too precious for words. What he doesn't know is that he can tell a story much better than Joyce can. In his own way, he's a better literary artist than Joyce was. But that's not so surprising; in my lifetime I've run into dozens of ordinary folk whose literary abilities, more often expressed in oral than written form, are remarkably superior to those of many famous authors. A fellow I know at my town dump is about as great a master of figurative language as Shakespeare was (unfortunately, most of it is obscene). The anonymity of greatness, in this and in all other matters, is a mystery we can hardly begin to fathom. How many stupendous minds and talents have there been in history, and we know nothing about them!

Telephone ringing! Telephone ringing in the adjoining office! Someone is calling *him*? Usually, he's the one who's calling. He isn't in today, Felix Gommerz, so the telephone gives up ringing after ten or so tries. I'm so glad he isn't in, especially on my final day. Several times a week he shows up, office door wide ajar, his enormous bulk squeezed into that treacherously squeaking, tipping chair behind his desk, as he engages in his interminable telephone monologues. I don't know to whom he's talking, but I do know that, when he's speaking to a man, his voice is loud, coarse, rebarbative, but when he speaks to a woman, he slips into this slow, deliberate, quavering, slightly falsetto, "lovey-dovey" voice. Does he think he's being seductive? He drones on and on, relentlessly. Apparently, the people on the other end never have anything to say.

Despite the courses in late-nineteenth-century British fiction that he teaches, his real, though partially clandestine, specialization is Victorian and Edwardian erotica, both literary and photographic. He prides himself on his collection, which he claims is the most comprehensive this side of the "pond" (on the other side of the "pond," he says, only the British Museum can rival him). He always has a little secretive bundle of pictures he wants to show around, his "recent acquisitions," as he calls them, and on occasion he stealthily tiptoes (yes, I said "tiptoes") over to my office like a brontosaurus *sur les pointes* to coax me into looking at them. Despite his efforts, I adamantly refuse. He goes tiptoeing away. (Also, for some reason, he's terrified by my print of Samuel Johnson and constantly has to avert his eyes to keep from noticing it.)

Sometimes his telephone monologues are interrupted by students, begging, as it were, admittance to his office. They only come to ask about grades, and he responds with a pretext of "crunching the numbers." This is his way of shifting the responsibility for the students' grades from himself to his computer. The computer always does the crunching but hasn't gotten around to it yet, so the students' anxieties cannot be addressed. I can't help but think that Felix is fantasizing about crunching something else, for he's as close a modern approximation to a middle-Paleolithic anthropophagic ogre as is possible, and, I figure, he may have correlative untoward tendencies. Let everyone be warned!

What's this? A report of some kind. A faculty report on students' use of research papers purloined from the Internet. I never read it fully. I stopped assigning research papers years ago. Ask for something that tends to increase students' dependence on sources whose reliability they're as yet unable to judge, and you will get something that is, by and large, apishly dependent. The result: students uncritically parrot their sources so that, in effect, a whole culture of indirect plagiarizing ensues. So why did I keep that faculty report? I remember thinking that the report itself was plagiarized (and from the Internet, no less), and I wanted to make a point about that to somebody or other. I never did.

I remove the paper clip and toss the report into the paper recycling bin. *So that's it! That's why I have so many paper clips!* I compulsively remove paper clips from documents and add them to my hoard. Why? I ask myself. I never reuse them. Now I know. Yes, I think I know. I don't want to mix paper recycling waste with metallic recycling waste. My social conscience won't let me! "Thus [social] conscience does make cowards of us all!" (My apologies to Hamlet for adding that word "social.") I have an obsession with this.

And yet I don't worry about metal staples, do I? Oh no, not me! Good grief! Worry about staples? Are you kidding? I may be as exemplary as a recycled version of Young Goodman Brown on this recycling business, but it doesn't go as far as staples. (Good heavens! what dark implications can be read into my literary allusion here! Has the Witches' Sabbath, to which I've been lured, wittingly or unwittingly, of which I've been an appalled witness, and in which I've been an even more appalled participant, been something real, or has it been a grotesque and evil phantasm produced by some demonic force? How could anything so absurd and so perverse actually be real?)

Colin Andrews. Abruptly he's there, framed by my office door. No footsteps. Ever. Apparently, he floats just above the ground. Whenever he comes by, he always appears in the doorway silently from out of nowhere, stands there like a ghost or a mirage and smokes his cigarette, swiveling his head around mechanically (like one of those ventriloquist dolls) to exhale the smoke backward into the hallway rather than into the office, though it curls around his head and wafts in anyway, drawn over me and my desk by the draft of my beloved window. Actually, for some reason, I don't mind the smoke; I appreciate its curiously "fumigating" effect, though I know I'm supposed to suspect him of trying to murder me with it. Colin's academic specialty is modern American drama. He also moderates the student drama club.

He's a few years older than I am: an old war horse like me, but cool, svelte, intensely cynical, looking askance at the pretensions not only of the collegiate world but also of the theatrical world. I enjoy him; I enjoy his wry comments; I enjoy his unassuming ways as well as his intelligent, technical, high-standard, no-nonsense reverence for the drama. He's spent much of his life enacting the role of a thespian matador, deflecting with his subtle, politic cape the delirious lunges of innumerable stagestruck zealots. After properly incensing the air with his cigarette, he speaks: "So what was the best thing about these thirty years," he says to me, "the fondest memory, what made it all worthwhile?" He inhales his cigarette and holds the smoke in, with the cigarette propped up by quivering fingers in front of his face, as if he's waiting for my reply as the right moment to exhale.

That doesn't give me much time. I admire him, and I don't want him to die of asphyxiation. I mentally review the applicants in quick order. The department barbecues (to which I went only once and never again after I discovered that watching a group of college professors play volleyball is possibly the most depressing spectacle in the world)? The collegiate functions, each one more tedious and insufferable than the last? The core curriculum wars, which produced, predictably, outcomes that professors refuse (covertly) to teach and that students refuse (overtly) to learn? The mix of collective self-pity and outrage, the shrill hilarity, self-promotion, and sycophantic congratulations that went on at department meetings?

"There were some students," I say, "who made it worth it. There were some colleagues, too, just a few. Like yourself."

He smiles, still holding his smoke, though some of it leaks out in little wisps from the corners of his mouth. He's still waiting.

"But it was the company I kept that really mattered: Chaucer and Shakespeare and Milton, Fielding and Austen and James, Jonson and Donne and Swift, and so many others, and not just in English: Dante, Virgil, Rilke, Tolstoy, Cervantes, Villon, the first and still the greatest, Homer—where can I stop? And in those glorious, all too glorious languages, each one with a tang and texture of its own. Masterworks of dazzling, inimitable utterance that I've read again and again and again, so that they've become my life's blood. It makes me happy just to think about them."

He smiles again. He bevels his head around and releases an immense cloud of smoke into the hallway. It rushes in great torrents downward from his nose and his mouth. I even have the impression that it's coming out of his ears and from some hole in the top of his head. He rotates his face back in my direction. The smoke streams in from behind him, through the office, over me, and out my window. "That's plenty," he says. "That's plenty to be thankful for. Those are friends we would all be thankful for. Would that the rest of us would have that much to say in the end!"

He goes the way he came, vanishing, drifting like the ghost of Hamlet's father, silently, along some imaginary battlements into the smoky mist.

More paper clips! I throw them away. *Oh my God, I throw them away!* I even throw them into the paper bin!

The movers have arrived. They thump down the hall in heavy shoes—two burly fellows and one as thin as a piano wire (and probably as strong). They squeeze into my office, smelling of packing tape and fresh air. They look around, mystified. What kind of weird place is this? I don't blame them. *What kind of weird place is this, after all?* They gaze at Sam Johnson's picture on the wall over the desk. Who's that? they wonder. What's he doing, presiding over this mess? Good question.

Sam Johnson looks back at them with his puzzled expression. "May I exhort you, sir, to remove me from these insufferable premises with all due alacrity!" he seems to say to them from his eighteenth-century engraving.

The piano-wire man peers out the window and says: "Nice view you got here, Prof." First person ever to notice that, or at least to mention it!

They wait for instructions. What are all these piles of junk? What story do they tell? What summary statement can I give to these fellows, something that says it all?

"The horror! The horror!" I almost cry out, wanting to reach up desperately to them like Kurtz, like Mistah Kurtz himself, out of an inexorable Heart of Darkness.

But I don't.

I almost do, but I don't. I'm not dead yet, and I'm not about to die. Instead, I say, quoting Saint Augustine:

"Sero te amavi, pulchritudo tam antiqua et tam nova."

"What?" asks the piano-wire man. He looks at me as if I'm crazy.

I repeat:

"Late have I loved thee, Beauty so ancient and so new ..."

Time to go. I'm ready to go. Spin that old wheelchair down the hall and let it bump me out at the doorsill! I'll land on my feet. Well, not really; it's not over yet, but I think you get the idea. I'll invoke Feste's song once again:

> *A great while ago the world begun,*
> *With hey, ho, the wind and the rain,*
> *But that's all one, our play is done,*
> *And we'll strive to please you every day.*

Arthur Glenhope

A rthur Glenhope wasn't what you might ordinarily call a "gifted child," for, if reading a serious biography of Henry Ford at the age of ten could be regarded as unusual, even precocious, Arthur came to it not out of some extraordinary intellectual acumen but rather out of the fascination that many a young boy has for automobiles. His love of Ford motorcars caused him, quite accidentally, to notice that book, a weighty tome, to say the least, on a shelf of the local library. That he read it, cover to cover, soon thereafter, was a signal event in his life. He would soon immerse himself in the biographies of other great manufacturers, financiers, and captains of industry. John D. Rockefeller and Bernard Baruch and J. P. Morgan and a dozen others of that ilk were the paragons of his youth and played complex roles in his fantasies and dreams.

He had little time for the usual heroes of boyhood: athletes, soldiers, explorers, conquerors. While most of his classmates longed for trips across the Hudson River to Yankee Stadium for baseball games or to Madison Square Garden for basketball or a circus or a rodeo, Arthur was happy, as soon as he was in his early teens, to take a bus from his New Jersey suburb across the George Washington Bridge into Manhattan and then ride a subway to Wall Street, where he wandered about the cavernous streets, his imagination aflame with plans and ambitions, not the least of which depicted for him a majestic skyscraper that would one day rise from some block now consisting of old lofts and seedy Chinese restaurants and would bear upon its brassy portals the imposing title "The Arthur Glenhope Building."

He himself was already a tall, raw-boned, stately young man, even in his early adolescence, and his powerful visage—marked by a firm jaw and aquiline eyes and capped by strawberry-blond hair—towered above the crowd that scurried to and fro along the avenues. Arthur loved it all: he loved the energy, the productivity, the wealth, the conglomerate of huge buildings and soaring bridges, ships being drawn into harbor by tooting tugboats and airplanes droning overhead, vehicular traffic streaming endlessly along the raised highways, the screech of subways beneath the pavements, and the multitudinous institutions of culture and refinement that prospered in the midst of such an inexhaustible cornucopia of industrial prowess and technological advance. He wanted to be part of it, indeed at the very center and heart of it. If anyone can ever be said to have had a "calling" in life, then Arthur had just such a calling.

Arthur had a friend—probably his only real friend—whose name was Sammy Ungar. Sammy was—well, I hate to say it—a "goofy" sort of fellow. A later age would have used somewhat more incisive language to describe him: "nerd" maybe or "dork." He was, according to some standards, very smart in that sort of limited technological way that some people have. He was always fumbling around with some sort of gadget and fancied himself an "inventor," rather a bit in the mode made popular in those days by the newspaper comics and the movies—strange, short fellows with bug eyes framed by colossal, horn-rimmed spectacles, with tousled sandy hair and loose pants held up by suspenders. Such fellows perpetually had light bulbs in little bubbles going off over their heads and big, silly grins on their faces. Come to think of it, Sammy did look rather like that comic-book image.

Sammy's first "invention" resulted from the fortuitous sliding of a pencil through the spirals of a notebook. Now, what bored fifth grader, sitting at a desk during an interminable afternoon at school, doesn't do that at least once or twice in his or her life, accompanied by whatever fantasy it takes to make it interesting? But Sammy saw momentous potentialities in this relationship—a light bulb, as it were, clicked on in (or above?) his as-yet nascently inventive brain. He detached the metal spiral from his notebook—which was almost empty of paper anyway—and tailored it to fit the length of the pencil. He now had a pencil that would not slide around in his fingers, should his fingers, under the duress of taking a test or of an overheated classroom, happen to become sweaty. He'd invented what he called a "nonslip" pencil.

Now, since Sammy, even as a fifth grader, was aware of his friend Arthur's burgeoning business interests, he took the idea to Arthur for potential mass production and marketing. Arthur considered it for a bit (a minute or so) and didn't think it would "float." He turned it down. Sammy would, in time, get used to such rejections—of which there were many but which never dimmed his unalloyed admiration for Arthur and his ever eager and cheerful solicitation of his advice.

Arthur, for his part, appreciated his friend's persistent, if futile, ingenuity. Sammy sometimes invoked for Arthur an image of Henry Ford at an early stage in his career, fumbling around with some primitive gasoline engine in a garden shed. It would have been better, as things turned out, if Arthur had paid closer attention to that fanciful image. Also, Sammy's and Arthur's interests oddly converged in their mutual absorption in miniature electric trains, fueled by the elaborate miniature train layout in Sammy's basement. Sammy, of course, loved the technicalities; Arthur loved the fantasy of trains and grain elevators and oil and chemical rigs and lumberyards and all the other paraphernalia that went along with it.

Otherwise, they simply enjoyed each other's company.

In the early years of high school, when, during homeroom at the onset of the school day, the schoolmaster would read a passage from a Pauline epistle and lead the class in the Lord's Prayer (yes, such practices once existed even in secular schools), Arthur and Sammy would exchange amused glances every time the schoolmaster raised his voice predictably on his carefully chosen and frequently repeated phrases and admonitions: "I have fought the good fight," the schoolmaster would intone with trembling voice, bracing his brood for the perils that lay ahead in their lives, "I have finished the race. I have kept the faith ..."

Arthur, meanwhile, fashioned a future for himself as perfectly planned and orchestrated as such things can be. Until he graduated from high school, he was a financial manager for every organization in the school that he could get connected to; he ran bazaars and fundraising events, sold hot dogs at the football games, bought and resold at a substantial profit all the varied accoutrements of student life (from sports equipment to fountain pens to well-worn trots for Latin translations), figured out how to bring in a large public for student dramatic productions, and organized book sales for the library. Well, of course, a person who does that kind of thing is bound to run into jealous and suspicious accusations from others. But Arthur was always a model of integrity—even if his deft, though rather liberal, reallocations of money from one student-fund account to another tended to alarm the more fastidious faculty advisors—and he survived quite well those few ugly incidents that did arise.

When he graduated from high school, all the accounts of student organizations he'd been associated with had been enriched enormously by his activity. Arthur himself took nothing, except the prominence it gave him—a prominence that carried him on to prestigious schools and the threshold of an outstanding career. He went to Yale for his undergraduate work in economics and to Wharton for business school, repeating at these schools the same kinds of extracurricular activity that had marked his high school years. During the summers, he worked for a variety of investment firms and businesses, mainly in downtown New York but in other locations as well.

One summer, after completing his freshman year at Yale, he worked as a courier for a firm in Manhattan, a job that had him doing the rather menial work of running about the busy streets carrying armloads of papers and files and briefs from one office to another. But he loved the job, for it allowed him to gain entry to and see a great deal of the business and financial world of New York.

On a particularly hot day, he was making his way down Fifth Avenue carrying a bundle of files when he was stopped momentarily by a traffic light. He took this time to turn around and gaze upward at a majestic old building, the Cosmopolitan Club, one of the most exclusive clubs in New York, going back a century at least. At that moment he saw an elderly gentleman, tall and large-framed like himself, dressed elegantly in a perfectly tailored three-piece suit, standing at one of the lofty ornate windows on the slightly elevated first floor of the club, watching in bemused silence the crowded street just beneath him. For what may have been only a second or two, their eyes met, and Arthur stared with wonderment at this august figure framed in such lofty and secluded splendor. Then, quite by chance, the elderly man nodded cordially in salutation, as if to say: "I, too, was once where you are; someday you will be where I am." The traffic light changed, and Arthur was off on his errand again, his heart lifted, his mind and imagination ablaze with his prospects for the future.

"Someday," he thought, "I'll stand there and look out that window and bestow that same salutation, that same blessing, on someone like me." Indeed, it may be said that that dream, that aspiration, would haunt him for the rest of his life — to stand at that window someday as the august representative of a world he loved with such passion.

Now, as for Sammy Ungar, he continued to fiddle with his gadgets and play with his electric trains. In his high school years, he was one of those kids who hang around the science labs and build what are inevitably regarded as "weird" contraptions and run "experiments" that mystify (if not mortify) the science teachers. Among the frequent flickerings of mental light bulbs that occurred in his adolescence, only one showed any promise at all and it involved, ironically, light bulbs. He invented a mechanism to cool down a hot light bulb rapidly without shattering it, so that you wouldn't have to wait so long before unscrewing it from its socket and replacing it with a new one. Such a dramatically time-saving device would, no doubt, be indispensable for all light-bulb changers throughout the world.

Sammy, as usual, proposed this idea to Arthur. Arthur gave it some thought (about half a minute), didn't think it would "float," and turned it down. Anyway, after finishing high school, Sammy went to a local New Jersey technical institute for college and continued to live at home, ever expanding his electric train network and transforming his attic into a laboratory for testing his ever more outlandish inventions.

After graduating from Wharton, Arthur embarked upon his career. From the very beginning, Arthur's abilities were recognized, and he was swept up into the higher echelons of ruling cadres and influential cliques. His youth, his vitality, his intelligence, his imposing personal presence made him the perfect operative for risky missions in the business world, a quick-witted and savvy emissary to be sent into troublesome situations. Arthur found himself almost at once in the thick of mighty deals and multimillion-dollar negotiations conducted among industrial giants. He learned the ins and outs of corporate power, shifting stock prices, mergers, public relations crises, buyouts and acquisitions, internal struggles over command and control, congressional hearings, and SEC investigations. He entered into interminable debates with corporate lawyers, signed and broke contracts with public relations firms, initiated great advertising programs. He knew what it was like to win big and to lose everything just as rapidly. He witnessed the rise and fall of great financiers, the triumph and disgrace, the tensions that threatened defeat at every turn, and the resolutions where the payoffs were beyond all telling of it.

If ever a man delighted in what he was doing, it was Arthur Glenhope. Before him he kept the images of the giants he emulated, the visions of enormous wealth, and the kingdoms it would bring with it. And whenever he hurried down Fifth Avenue by the Cosmopolitan Club in a taxi to a meeting downtown or just walked by on his way to a business luncheon, he saw himself standing one day behind one of those windows, just like that gentleman he'd seen years before, in magnificent repose, surveying the busy scene just below.

In contrast, not much happened in Sammy Ungar's life. After finishing college, he still lived at home. His expenses were few, but he brought in a small income by fixing high-tech bicycles and working at an electric train hobby outlet. In later decades he developed a lively and astute interest in computers, and his inventions grew ever more sophisticated. He even invented a computer-driven home radar system, connected to strategically located and electronically activated spray cans, for detecting and destroying unwary mosquitoes that ventured across a yard.

It was, in fact, quite a marvel, and Sammy was convinced it would revolutionize mosquito control throughout the world but especially in New Jersey, where the need for such backyard control is ever particularly urgent. He contacted Arthur and proposed the idea to him, but Arthur was much too busy to give the proposal much more than about fifteen seconds' thought, didn't think it would "float," and turned it down.

Sammy later made some interesting adaptations to his mosquito defense system. Again, he contacted Arthur. But, even if Arthur had been interested, he was immersed in so many complex legal and financial entanglements that he had no time at all to consider it.

Now, at this point I wish I could say that things went well, finally, for Arthur Glenhope, after all his sedulous preparations and his even more extravagant expectations. In a way, things did go very well, if, like some purists, you insist that the real joy of heeding a call is the exercise of the activity itself, rather than the results that ensue from it. But Arthur had more than his fair share of disappointments. Among other disagreeable things, Arthur found out what it was like to uncover massive fraud at the highest levels and then become the fall guy for a dishonest and incompetent boss, taking the rap while the boss escaped with a fortune. Other things also didn't work out well. Arthur shifted from enterprise to enterprise—from banking to insurance to manufacturing to service industries, from working for others, to working with others in elaborate partnerships, to setting up his own operations and then seeing them go down into bankruptcy because someone at city hall, at the behest of whatever crony, rewrote a regulation that destroyed the companies overnight.

He knew the humiliation of being fired; he knew the horror of being the one appointed to do the firing, especially when the one being fired was the most reliable person around and that was why the person was being fired. Arthur conducted his business life with unflinching probity and resolute intelligence; yet all of his ventures, for reasons beyond his control, collapsed into unfathomable ruin.

Sammy, on the other hand, did manage to sell an enormously upgraded and retooled version of his original mosquito control apparatus. He'd somehow transformed it into a way to detect, deflect, and destroy short-range surface-to-surface missiles as well as ordinance, including even mortar shells and rocket-propelled grenades. It resulted in one of the most lucrative contracts ever issued by the Pentagon. Sammy had no idea what to do with the proceeds, so he gave them over to a broker who invested in technology stocks and who then sold everything before the great technology bubble burst. Sammy became an enormously rich man, but he continued to live at home, tinker in his attic, and play in his cellar. He had no need for any of that money. He didn't even know what to do with it.

At the urging and referral of his broker, he became a member of the prestigious Cosmopolitan Club (the club was short of money and was eagerly recruiting new wealth). But he had no use for the club and never took advantage of the many privileges that his yearly dues and generous donations made available for him.

Meanwhile, Arthur had long ago moved out of New York. He'd worked in a variety of other cities. At one time he was a partner in a meat-processing plant in Omaha. Another time he worked for a shipping company in Long Beach, California, and managed a fleet of refrigerator ships bringing fresh produce from Chile. He owned a hotel in Acapulco and invested in local airlines for the tourist trade.

Again and again, he ran afoul of whatever there was to run afoul of. His own efforts at a family life were destroyed several times over, as he engaged in conflicts with former spouses, avaricious and duplicitous women who were angry about his failures and acrimonious about alimonies and childcare. He could no longer count how many different houses he had lived in, how many lawsuits he'd lost, how many real estate ventures he'd been forced to abandon. Yet he never gave up.

Reduced, at the age of fifty-eight, to living in a single room in New Orleans, he scraped together enough money to buy himself a brand-new, perfectly tailored suit of elegant material. Then he began to look for a job once more, playing very much the part of a prominent businessman. It would soon be the Christmas season, and businesses might need help. But he could find no work in New Orleans and was, for all purposes, broke.

In late November of that year and as a last resort, he telephoned Sammy and asked if he could come and stay with him for a while. He knew that Sammy, an aging bachelor by now, still lived in the old frame house of his parents, now deceased, just across the Hudson River from New York. Arthur felt that, if he could live with Sammy, he might get a foothold again in the New York business world and have a chance to rebuild his career. He didn't know about Sammy's enormous financial success, for Sammy never talked about it to anyone. But Sammy was, as ever, delighted to speak to Arthur and glad to have a chance to renew a friendship he'd always treasured.

Sammy, in turn, didn't realize how desperate Arthur's situation was. Then he had a wonderful idea: although Sammy had plenty of room in his house, most of it had been taken up by his ever-expanding electric train system. So he suggested that Arthur be his guest at the Cosmopolitan Club. He would have a private room there, have access to all the dining facilities and other amenities, and find it convenient to downtown locations and appointments. Since Arthur would be a guest, Sammy would pick up the tab for all expenses.

Arthur was a bit surprised and even embarrassed by this suggestion; he had no idea that Sammy was a member of the club, and, knowing that in his present condition he could never afford to stay in such a place, he found it difficult to accept the generous offer. But Sammy, in his cheerful and eager way, insisted, and Arthur agreed.

He remembered the Cosmopolitan Club well from earlier years, though he'd never seen it except from the outside, and he would be most honored to stay there. He was glad he had his new suit, so that he would be properly attired for his sojourn at the club. He would arrive in New York the Monday before Christmas and, at Sammy's suggestion, go directly to the club, get "settled in," and embark upon his job search. Sammy would join him for dinner on Friday evening, which also was Christmas Eve. On the following day, Christmas, Arthur would be invited to join Sammy to view (and presumably to play with) the electric train set that now ran throughout the house and into the yard and that could coordinate, from a central computerized control panel, dozens of trains in simultaneous motion as well as load and unload timber, grain, and other industrial products. Tiny cameras inside the engine windows transmitted images of the moving trains to a large bank of television monitors mounted over the control panel. Sammy told Arthur all about this, and Arthur was, this time, truly curious to see it.

It's strange how so many of us, when encountering a place we've never known before, suddenly feel as if we have, at last, come home. I know a middle-aged lady who, having just stepped out onto the balcony of her room at a Swiss hotel, gazed for the first time upon those regal mountains, breathed for the first time that mountain air, and knew immediately she had finally come home, even though she'd never been in Switzerland before in her life and would be leaving in just a few days. I've known others who have had that same experience in the cloisters of medieval monasteries, in an Irish pub on some misty island, or while looking down from an olive grove at the glistening Bay of Corinth far below.

So it was with Arthur Glenhope. Entering the portals of that solemn club was a homecoming for him. Though he'd never been inside before, he seemed to be familiar with its every detail—its magnificent front hall, its Great Reading Room with the windows looking out over Fifth Avenue, its billiard and smoking rooms, its oaken bar so redolent with leather and tobacco and fine spirits, its sumptuous private restaurant provided with liveried footmen and waiters. Everything was appointed with the choicest furniture and carpets, lamps and chandeliers—muted, somber, substantial, tasteful; and the vast oak-paneled walls were covered by portraits of the great business personages of New York's incomparable history, the giants of industry and finance themselves, assuming the poses of statesmen and imperial commanders. A pair of gilded elevators took their privileged passengers to ornate, impeccably clean rooms on the upper floors, spacious rooms provided with large, old-fashioned bathrooms and every convenience you ever could think of.

Life was easy here; one of the many rules of the club forbade any exchange of cash; likewise, tipping was expressly forbidden—which was fortunate for Arthur, for in just a few days tipping alone could have vanquished what was left of his reserves. Another rule required formal attire and quiet deportment at all times in the public rooms. To discuss or conduct business on the premises was frowned upon, and even the use of telephones, except in private rooms or in a special enclave reserved for that purpose, was discouraged. Meanwhile, the footmen delivered messages and brought coffee or tea or an aperitif, if it was so desired. It was a place Arthur Glenhope was always meant to be, his proper home, his niche prepared for him from the beginning of his days, determined for him from the beginning of the world by the inexorable powers that be.

He soon eased into a way of life that was, from his perspective, flawless. He took breakfast in the restaurant at about nine in the morning. Then he moved to the Great Reading Room, where a large Christmas tree had been set up and where a fire ever dazzled in the huge hearth. There he would sit in a capacious leather wing chair by the window, read the *Wall Street Journal* from cover to cover, and watch the vibrant holiday crowds swarm along Fifth Avenue just beneath him.

It was a colorful scene, since all the stores were alit with Christmas decor and the people, entering and exiting the department store on the other side of Fifth Avenue, immediately opposite the club, displayed the excitement and good cheer of the season as they carried shopping bags crammed with gift-wrapped packages through the crowd. Yellow-orange taxis raced by, darting in and out of traffic, and buses, jammed with shoppers, rolled up in front of the club's windows discharging their tumultuous cargo from the rear door, even as a new crowd of travelers jostled their way through the front door. Policemen in their trim blue uniforms and mounted on sleek horses threaded their way through the traffic and blew their whistles; Santa Clauses at the corners clanged their bells and collected money in little, red-painted iron pots suspended from white birch tripods, while men with garish and steamy metallic carts at the curbs sold hot bratwurst and roasted chestnuts.

It was all too wonderful for Arthur—all this buying and selling, all this eagerness and joy, all this life of a robust and commercial world unfolding before his eyes as he sat in repose in the Great Reading Room, its age and solemnity and seclusion gathered in a mystical silence around him.

During the holiday season, members made very little use of the club, preferring to be at home this time of year, so Arthur almost had the club to himself, and his initial anxieties about running into a familiar face or a potentially embarrassing conversation were soon put to rest. One evening, in the bar, alone except for a small knot of men at the far end of the room, he recognized a voice from the distant past, a railing, sour voice to which he could no longer attach a name, and which was voluble in an expression of outrage. The bartender, who, like the other staff of the club, was remarkably adept at enforcing club rules without humiliating the members, eventually approached that person and asked him to lower his voice. The person complied, and Arthur made his escape from the bar without calling attention to himself.

During that entire week, however, Arthur had no inclination to pursue the business that had brought him to New York, to make appointments, to look up old colleagues (as reluctant as he was to do that anyway), or to read the job classifieds. After a modest luncheon, he might go for a stroll up Fifth Avenue to the Plaza Hotel and Central Park, or down to Rockefeller Center to watch the skaters, or over to Park Avenue to look at the expensive cars exhibited in the various imported automobile showrooms. He returned to the Great Reading Room for the evening hours. He felt comfortable there among the faintly illuminated portraits of industrialists, whose success he'd not had but whose grandeur of vision he'd shared, whose enterprise and verve and audacity he'd again and again emulated, whose acumen he knew and also, in a way, possessed.

After a leisurely and solitary dinner, he would retire for the night, sometimes reading in bed until rather late — on this occasion, it was a book about the capricious fortunes of the lobster fisheries in Maine. He was sure that he would soon again venture into the great world of business enterprise, but he didn't search out anything that week. He needed to rest, to compose himself before he set out again. And the Cosmopolitan Club was the best imaginable place to do that. In the meantime, the staff of the Club had come to know and like him and were pleased to run his errands and bring his requests on small silver plates and respond to him deferentially with "Yes, sir, right away, Mr. Glenhope."

On Friday, the day he would meet with Sammy for dinner, Arthur resumed his usual routine. In the early evening, while waiting for Sammy, he once again sat in his leather wing chair and gazed out at the milling crowds just below the window. It was Christmas Eve, and the pace was frenetic. At one point he stood up at the window for a while so that he could look at what was going on directly beneath him on the sidewalk. A street musician was stationed there and played a rather melancholy version of "Joy to the World" on a wounded, wheezing old accordion. But the crowd was pleased and stopped to listen and threw him a goodly amount of loose change. If Arthur had known how to open the window, he would also have tossed him some loose change, even though, as Arthur sadly reflected, his own financial condition might not be much better than that of the destitute man below. Yet what a world seemed to separate them.

At that moment, Arthur noticed a young man in the crowd clutching an attaché case to his chest with both arms and staring directly up at him in glazed admiration. Arthur pulled himself up straight in his fine tailored suit and smiled benevolently down at him, nodding gently his approval. "Take heart, young man," he seemed to say, "The aim is noble and the vision good." The young man nodded in return and disappeared into the crowd and into the dazzling evening darkness. Arthur sat down again in the wing chair. He recalled that similar encounter so many years before, when he'd been a young man looking up into those very same windows. He smiled. Never had he felt so good in his life, never so fulfilled, so complete, so happy.

Is this all he'd ever really wanted—to be able to stand there, in that window, and confer upon someone, as had been conferred upon him, a solemn blessing, a word of hope and life? "I have fought the good fight," he murmured to himself, echoing some words once tendered to him in a context he could no longer remember, "I have finished the race. I have kept the faith ..." He could remember no more of those words. In some way he knew that what he'd done, in spite of everything, had been the right thing. Bounty, increase, prosperity, the good life—were not these also proper ends for mankind, a blessing for all nations?

A kind of heavy drowsiness came over him, though his lids were half open and still vaguely taking in the bright lights of the whirring traffic and the brightly lit stores beyond the window, all so luminous and blurred against the deepening night. A comforting balm, a honey-like ointment, began to drip down through the weary and wasted interstices of his soul, down through its rusty girders, its dark chambers and corridors, soothing and easing the rawness, blunting the sharpened edges, coating the damp and the crust and the mold.

Soft, shadowy images flitted through his mind, images now muted and mellowed—images of deadlines and closures, of abusive depositions, of harassing calls in the middle of the night, of unnecessary tax audits conducted by aggressive attorneys looking for promotions, of bills paid at the last moment, of payroll checks issued against his orders even while the bank loans necessary to cover the checks were still pending, of embittered and traitorous partners, of backstabbing and talebearing, of libelous rumors let loose by malcontents, of confrontations with deranged and fraudulent associates, of leaks to the press or to the competition, of foreclosures, of regulatory commissions hounding, pursuing, cutting down, impounding accounts, slapping liens on your cars, your house, your very existence. He fell deeper into his comforting sleep—all of those images now erased, forgotten, dissolved in a beneficent and pervasive warmth. A few flakes of snow began to drift down on the busy scene outside the window.

Sammy arrived directly at six and was pointed by the concierge toward the far end of the Great Reading Room, where he could find Arthur. He shook the light snowflakes from his overcoat, gave the coat to the cloakroom attendant, and hurried in his usual cheerful manner to where he saw Arthur in his chair by the window. Arthur seemed to be asleep. His noble, stately head leaned to the side and rested against the tall chair. There was a smile on his face. His hands were folded neatly in his lap. Sammy shook Arthur by the shoulder to wake him up. There was no reaction. He shook him again. And then Sammy understood.

Arthur Glenhope was dead.

A Keeper of Keys

He was, verily, a keeper of keys. Be patient, my dear readers, and soon enough I shall explain what I mean.

Having heard, in all too many guises and circumstances, what you may loosely call a "reunion" story, I hesitate, with good reason, I believe, to offer one of my own. This is not to say that such stories cannot be, at times, without distinction; furthermore, you can justly claim, in their defense, that all genres of story have been mined again and again for whatever resources they can yield.

I speak here not only of the story that gives an account of what we conventionally think of as a "reunion" — the family or collegiate or regimental affair (to name but a few) where old associates come together to celebrate a relationship they shared sometime in the past. I also speak of the personal reunion — the encounter with an individual whose path we've crossed at some juncture in our lives and whose memory, for whatever reason, is worthy of treasuring and, at times, renewing — if that's at all possible, which it rarely is.

The problem with a reunion account is that, in its own way, it has too predictable a plot — after all, we change with time, and so do our relationships and perceptions. Therein lies the plot, if we can call it that, packaged and ready for use. Even more compelling is the fact that so often we don't change with time. Therein reside the painful complications into which the plot may, and frequently does, devolve.

I think, for example, of my own experiences (and thus of the accounts I've given of them) in actively seeking out a "reunion" with a person who once had a significant impact on my life, who opened a door for me in the traditional metaphorical sense of that phrase, who made me aware of new vistas of life to be explored and of momentous actions to be emulated. Such persons are frequently teachers, though not always in the technical sense of the word "teacher," being understood as someone standing in front of a classroom and steering the occasionally eager student through the intricacies of some academic pursuit. For most of our teachers, in the broader and truer sense, were parents, friends, coaches, neighbors, siblings, spouses, our own children, and others too innumerable to list.

What they all had in common is that they held forth a potentiality, a way to go, a direction to be pursued — some more feasible than others; moreover, if my own life is any indication of what generally happens, such potentialities, garnered from so many different sources, accumulate at such a rate that it would take not a lifetime but a dozen lifetimes to fulfill but a small measure of them.

But I also address myself here, as I deem I must, to reunions with persons who once opened dazzling possibilities for us but whom we discover, at the time of our attempted renewal, to be anything but possibility — to represent to us, to our shock and inconsolable distress, an evacuated intellect, a shriveled life, a maimed and blocked and not too infrequently embittered existence that has made so many exclusions that life itself seems to have been the final object of exclusion.

Which, my dear readers, if you've managed to survive such a prolonged and abstruse prolegomenon, brings me to my story at last, a *paradeigma*, in a sense, as the classical rhetoricians would be quick to point out, of the utter wretchedness to which such a human life may descend. But I speak here not just of an example but of a real person. Billy Landor, I shall call him: not his real name, I must add, for I wish to protect his anonymity, especially since his life has become devoted to being anonymous, even among the people who were, long in the past, closest to him. This is not the Billy Landor I once knew, of course — the ever spirited, ever surprising, ever generous Billy Landor.

When, after an interval of more than thirty-five years, I finally sought him out, I recognized immediately that the Billy Landor of my former acquaintance no longer seemed to exist. For suspended from his belt was a key chain with more keys attached to it than I would think could be functional in the life of ten human beings. There must have been hundreds of keys attached to that chain. And, if I saw correctly, additional key chains were linked to a "parent" key chain, as it were, forming an entire cascade of such chains, each bearing its own cluster of chains, so that it resembled a grapevine with its heavily laden clusters of grapes drooped down over a burdened trellis. The entire apparatus jangled and swung its remarkable weight as he walked. I'd never — still have never — seen anything quite like it. It called so much attention to itself that Billy seemed to disappear behind it, as if the key chain was Billy himself, as if it had subsumed and devoured his very identity.

As I would soon discover, it had, in some sense, done precisely that. The Billy I recalled from a former life swung a single car key on a tiny clip that he sometimes looped around his index finger; he would twirl the key around until it flew off his finger and up into the sunlight and then he, on its descent, would snatch it out of the air with a laugh. He had, at that time, no other keys that I was aware of. I don't think he ever locked anything up. But now he was different. If you were to have asked me, at the moment of our first recognition after such a long absence, who this man was, I would have said: "He's a keeper of keys."

I don't really know what brought us together originally. All friendships, maybe all human relationships, have a factor of mystery about them. They defy much rational analysis. For as much admiration as I'm able to confer upon the great treatises of the past that aim to explore what friendship is, I've never found them too convincing.

When I think of Billy Landor, I think of the college reception where I first ran into him. We just happened to be the first two freshmen to show up at that reception and therefore really had no other option but to introduce ourselves and talk to one another. If a third person had been there, would we have ever become friends? An astute observer might point out that our mutual propensity to arrive early for social occasions was already an indication of broader aspects of character we could share. Incidentally (and I rather consciously use that word "incidentally" as descriptive of a great number of important things that happen to us in our lives), our early arrival made possible our subsequent role of being spectators of, and commentators on, the later arrivals.

Both of us knew, for example, independently of one another and even before the end of "freshmen week," which the college in question set aside for all its excessively belabored "orientation" activities, that we had made a terrible mistake. College wasn't going to be what we had expected it to be, and we had chosen the wrong college (without much of a sense, however, of what would have been the right one). That's not an altogether unusual sentiment for incoming freshmen, and it happens for various reasons. Our common witnessing of the unwholesome parade of new students into the so-designated "commons" and the social behavior that quickly emerged confirmed what we'd already discerned in the few days we'd been on campus: that a presidium for the pursuit of wisdom and knowledge is not where we now found ourselves. Even despite the eminently "elite" status of our institution, we would be struck, again and again, and at every level, by its inexorable shabbiness, by its lack of definition and purpose, by the glaring hypocrisy and pompousness of its official declarations. I shall not pursue this issue at the moment—it's simply too complex and too given to manifold misunderstandings. It's sufficient here to point out that nothing binds two souls together as quickly and as firmly as disaffection with an environment; and we had plenty of that.

As for Billy Landor himself—well, I would describe him as being somewhat short and stocky, with black wavy hair, a very large forehead and large black eyes in a broad, placid face, often expressionless except for the occasional tilting backward with a slight jolt and an "ah!" when something presumably enlightening had registered, a countenance cheerful enough but with a random dark mood that would pass over it like the shadow of a fleeting cloud on a hillside. I knew when such a mood passed over him, for he would knit his brows momentarily and stare somewhat distractedly into the space in front of him. He dressed in ordinary clothes almost to a fault—a checkered flannel shirt and khaki pants being like a uniform for him.

Billy had been, I was told by someone or other, a reasonably successful high school athlete, although in an unusual way: he was strong and fast, and, though he did just about everything wrong in the various sports he participated in, his rare and sporadic successes more than made up for his errors. In baseball, for example, he could be counted on to strike out quite consistently while at bat, but, when he did make contact with the ball, it was largely futile to try to recover it from whatever distant place it returned to earth. Yes, he knocked it "out of the ballpark," not figuratively but literally. He didn't continue sports at college, but I can't help but think that the expression "knocking it out of the ballpark" did apply to Billy Landor in a most figurative way as well. Where that figurative ball landed no one shall ever know.

The best I can do to describe the range and focus of Billy's interests is to give some vague collocation of items, a cluster, a constellation of things he thought and talked about. I wish I could do better than that, but that I can do as much as I can is evidence of the impact Billy had on me in those years. His main interest was, I guess you could say, "physics." He was interested in everything, but "physics" was his focus. I put the term in quotation marks because it wasn't exactly the same "physics" studied in the department of that name in the college, though Billy did his share of work in that regard.

His "physics" involved taking Aristotle's ancient work on physics as seriously as that of Albert Einstein, or Arnold Sommerfeld, or Werner Heisenberg, or Wolfgang Pauli, or Niels Bohr, all of whom, but especially Einstein, Billy seemed to have known well by the time he entered college as a freshman. It involved, as well, a concern for principles that would illuminate principles, make them intelligible as the principles they were, what the ancients called the study of "metaphysics" — not in any sense a religious concern, as is so often imputed to it, incorrectly, by many moderns but rather a physics beyond physics: the physics of physics itself, a meta-physics, the science of science. He discovered quickly that those who he thought might share his interests didn't; and that, more than once, the apparently august luminaries of the world he sought to penetrate angrily repelled his inquiries by asserting dogmatically, "We don't ask questions like that!"

"Why not?" Billy might rejoin, not in class (at least not in those early days) but in a late evening discussion with me. "If you keep using a term over and over again, isn't it reasonable to inquire about what that term actually means? A mathematical correlation, as brilliant as such correlations can be, tells us very little about the actual identity of those things that are correlated and the terms that are used to refer to them. Hence, everything remains arbitrary in the end. Exactness of calculation is mistaken for rigor and sophistication of thought; calculation deals only with what is calculable inside a system whose unity as a system remains utterly as unknown as it ever was."

As for metaphysics, you might as well have expected that someone, or some department, at the college was given to the study of medieval alchemy as to have expected there something so arcane as the study of metaphysics, though Billy would have rejected such an analogy most vigorously. I can hear to this day what he might have said: "Alchemy! But that's what they're doing! They're technicians, not scientists. They're magicians and content to be so, to manipulate the forces of nature, not to understand them, and to do it while uttering their mantras and formulas, as has been the perennial task of magicians! It's they who dally with the occult, having no other context in which to put things. Only when science, through metaphysics, can address the whole domain of truth will it be enabled to do its own task properly."

I confess I was surprised by all of this; I'd concluded, from my own studies, that the license to remain in a deliberate state of ignorance about the terms of a discipline, and about the larger context in which it belonged, was a privilege reserved for the literary scholars among whom I groped my exasperated way, though at the time I could have scarcely articulated the problem as I've just done now.

But in all of this I don't want to give the impression that Billy was one of those students, all too common at the so-called elite schools, who, though very bright, peak intellectually about a year before they arrive at college with a mind made up about everything and who, having achieved the entrance they desired, are unable to listen to or to learn anything more.

Nor was Billy one of those sharp-eyed, self-satisfied, cynical sharks who circle around in the murky waters of academic fora and who like to embarrass a potential prey with impertinent and sophistical inquiries. Billy, to the contrary, was, in his own way, a novice of the finest sort; he had a plethora of questions and a boundless willingness to listen and to learn, but the very character and quality of his questions already put him far ahead of and far above the intellects of his professors.

In consequence, we had a companionship of the aggrieved, but really much more than that. I'm not sure that I did much for Billy—about that I can't speculate. But Billy made the world a more meaningful place for me, for Billy had a vision of the universe that sparkled like an iridescent jewel, aflame with light and movement, a jewel that bore within it both the principles of cohesion and freedom, of luminous intelligibility and perpetual gratuitousness, determinate, purposeful, and unpredictable at the same time.

Frankly, the universe he saw was not unlike those poems I loved and which I'd read over and over again, not so much for what they said (because they didn't actually say very much) but for what they were: delicately contoured fabrics of speech whose dynamics of verbal form could be experienced again and again, just as you can listen to the same piece of music or look at the same painting innumerable times and still continue to enjoy it.

I'll admit that I'm not qualified to comment on the scientific soundness of Billy's understanding. He was, ever and ever more during his college years, treated as an eccentric among his peers; his ideas were rejected and ridiculed; he was ostracized as hopelessly out of touch with his time and ill-equipped for pursuing any advancement to a professional status in his field. His rejoinders, no longer reserved to the dorm discussions, touched off angry remonstrations from professors who found their class agendas derailed by them and their commitments challenged. The adjustments, the compromises Billy needed to correct this situation were simply not possible for him. That he even managed to graduate with a degree from the institution was almost a miracle. Further studies, except for those he undertook himself, were debarred for him.

All of this might give you some hesitation about Billy; but it happened some time ago, and what I did learn from him and read at his behest has made me reasonably able to follow, at least as presented at the popular level, some of the developments in his field that have occurred since then and to be able to surmise that, had Billy entered the scene several decades later, he may have found a more suitable venue for the exercise of his intellect. He simply came along quite a bit too soon. In his time, in his youth, there was no such thing as "theoretical physics" in a full and proper sense. Now there is, or at least it's called that, though it still may not — not yet anyway — correspond to the threshold Billy had already, possibly, crossed over in his own work, crossed over a very long time ago.

What then did, finally, shut poor Billy down? Was it just one too many "we don't ask that kind of question" thrown at him by a narrow technician whose scientific jargon was his own protection against the world and against actually knowing anything about it? Was it the deepening solitude and estrangement in which Billy found himself year after year as he haunted the alcoves of great libraries, discovering in their vaults the voices of obscure but gargantuan minds now unknown, and perhaps even unknowable to the present generation, and whose works were sometimes penned amid the fury of revolutions or in rat-infested trenches or amid bleak internment camps?

Or were there deeper explanations? Did the shadow that sometimes crossed his face — now presumably growing longer, more frequent, darker than ever before — have roots that predated any of his intellectual attainments, ones we shall never quite understand? What other factors had entered Billy's life since I'd known him? I can't answer any of these questions: soon after college, I lost touch with Billy Landor. What little I came to know about him later trickled down to me through the infrequent and wholly fortuitous sightings that acquaintances we once had in common could pass on to me. Eventually, Billy disappeared altogether.

Then one day I chose to seek him out.

I don't know what made me do that. I do know that at some transitions in life you feel a need to pause for a moment and to pick up threads long since either broken or discarded. I started to seek out various people I'd known in the past. With Billy Landor, more than a quarter century had passed. I shall not submit you to the baroque convolutions I had to go through to track him down, the clues I followed, the people I spoke to. His withdrawal had been about as complete as you could make it. If it was by accident that I found him in the first place, it was largely by accident that I found him again. I made arrangements to meet him. I was surprised that he consented.

We met in a dilapidated diner near his home. It was the kind of roughshod place we would go to when we were college students, though the menus, even in such places, now are replete with exotic items we would never have heard of back then. That's where I saw him with his enormous key chain. He looked older, of course, perpetually distracted, his eyes rolling about for no reason, his brow wrinkled and taut, and yet youthful in another sense — the same person, in a way, with hair still pitch black and wavy, his head still susceptible to little jerks and sudden exclamations. His attire was familiar: the same sort of checkered flannel shirt and khaki pants.

I did most of the talking, to my embarrassment; I wanted to find out about him, but he was deadly silent, which forced me to do that talking: to talk about family, former friends, my profession. He rarely looked at me through all of this. Yet I knew he wanted to hear it, so I continued babbling on and on, and he would roll his eyes around and look out the window and sometimes at me and sporadically jerk his head backward when I said something presumably surprising. He never touched the food he'd ordered. I would sometimes ask him a question, but he wouldn't answer.

Billy offered then, oddly, to bring me to his home. There was something he wanted to show me. His house, a run-down brick townhouse in a shabby neighborhood, wasn't far from the restaurant. He unlocked an old garden gate. We passed through it, and he locked it again behind us. We entered through the basement and then passed through several doors, some of which had three or four locks that had to be negotiated. Billy spent a great deal of time sorting through his keys as he did this, finding just the right key like plucking the perfect apple from a copious tree. His attention to the locking and unlocking was intense and obviously a source of great concern to him. We traversed several corridors, all locked from the outside and then relocked from the inside. They were crammed with books, not lined up on bookshelves but stacked in piles that reached up to the ceiling. Some of these piles had collapsed, and we had to step over them as we went.

After some effort making our way up staircases crowded with books heaped on every step, we finally entered, on the second floor of the building, into a room that appeared to be something like an office. I think it had four or five locks on the door that had to be painstakingly operated before we could enter. The blinds were drawn, and even though it was midday, the room was very dark. He turned on a light. Filing cabinets, all with multiple locks on them, and a bank of small safes surrounded us. In the middle was a writing table. Pens and mounds of paper were scattered all over its surface.

There was also a wall of computer monitors and electronic equipment with wires exposed, crisscrossing the wall at strange angles, bundled up into tangled nests at some places and drooping loosely elsewhere. Hundreds of tiny red and blue and green lights blinked on and off.

There was a single chair. He asked me to be seated. He turned to his files and began unlocking some of them, looking briefly through them, and then methodically relocking them. Finally, he withdrew a small metallic strongbox from one of the cabinets. He placed it on the desk in front of me. He made no motion to unlock and open it; he just pointed at it. Finally, he spoke.

"It's in there. It's the conclusion of my work, at this stage anyway," he said.

I didn't know what to say, so I said nothing.

His brow wrinkled. His eyes rolled. "I've tried to answer a few questions no one else wanted to ask," he said. "But they won't want to hear the answers. Generally, people don't like to hear answers to questions they don't want to ask."

"Maybe they will," I contended, "maybe now they will. I think some things have changed."

He stood there silently for a while, looking not at me but over my right shoulder.

He spoke again: "You mustn't think I'm out of touch with what's going on. I'm very much in touch. I know what's going on; I know it in detail."

He gestured to his computers. "You're right to say that things have changed, but they still haven't changed enough. Please don't tell anyone about my work. It's very secret. It would be dangerous for you to tell anyone about this. I keep it carefully under lock and key. But I wanted you to know, only you. I wanted at least one person to know that the foundational work has been completed. I'm now working on some of the implications of that work."

I realized, as he replaced the strongbox in the filing cabinet, that our meeting was over. He now escorted me out of his house, through lock after lock, like a jailer, except he was locking me out, rather than in, and soon would be locking himself in, rather than out. At the garden gate, he said goodbye to me. I think he'd been glad to see me and was sorry to see me go; but I had to go, in any event, and he returned to his many-chambered dungeon of locked enclosures.

I've not seen Billy Landor again. I often wonder what secret he has locked up inside that box of his. Could it be something substantive, something that really could reshape everything we know about the universe in our time? Could it be, in itself, a key that unlocked, or could unlock for us, a boundless treasury of knowledge? Or could it be something that's just one more locked-up thing, the product of a locked-up mind, a point of departure into an infinite series of locks, diminishing finally into the nothingness of a lock for which no corresponding key exists? Most of us would—and for good reasons, I suppose—jump to the conclusion that it's the latter, a manifestation of madness, the sorry extinction of a brilliant and original mind. We'd prejudge the potentiality of the work by the actuality of the person who produced it.

In a way, I wish I could accept that conclusion. Most people would accept it—of that, I'm sure. But I can't. At the risk of sounding mad myself, I suspect that locked inside that box is evidence that Billy accomplished exactly what he set out to do. I know that that's an extraordinary thing to say, especially about something that no one is ever likely to read. But it will take someone else—someone, either now or in the future, who will tread the same ground that Billy trod and who will arrive, independently, at the same discoveries—who, in effect, will have to arrive at them all over again before some future generation will know about them and be able to take them seriously.

For (with a clarity few of us will ever attain), Billy Landor had a vision of a world dominated by two irreconcilable views: polarities arrayed in fierce and intransigent opposition to each other. The first is so steeped in willful blindness, aimlessness, and randomness that not even a limitless number of locks and keys could ever suffice to confine it or protect us from it. Infinitely and finally lawless, it ever threatens, at any moment, to collapse inward and onto us its entire weight, leaving behind nothing but a wisp of smoke . . . and maybe not even that. Today, and in our world, no better exemplar of it can be found than subsists in the moral chaos in which those persons ostensibly most dedicated to learning are the ones most doggedly opposed to it.

But you can readily surmise that Billy Landor would never have embraced that way of life. To have done so would have transformed him into a fellow traveler, a self-satisfied habitué of that specialized cavern of shadows wherein you can entertain the comfortable idea that if ultimately the universe makes no sense at all, then you might as well just rock back and forth interminably and in peace on your technological hobbyhorse, alongside your peers, without asking disagreeable questions about where you're going or what anything means. Spiritually, Billy would have become like someone in a fitness gym who huffs and puffs on a treadmill while going absolutely nowhere at all. His mantra, too, would have become: "We don't ask questions like that."

More likely, Billy Landor had deepened his knowledge of that other universe of which in his youth he'd already had such rich intimations: a world too full, too resplendent, too meaningful (as he would have thought) to expose to the raillery of others, to eyes and mouths whose inveterate vulgarity would debase and denigrate what he knew was worthy of boundless wonder. He'd encountered neither a random universe fundamentally unintelligible to the human intellect nor one mechanical and soulless, limited aspects of which could be controlled for human utility by imposing upon them nominalistic brackets and Procrustean reductions, merely quantitative formulas and equations. In fact, he saw and could understand some of the principles of that which the ancients understood originally by "physics"—by the Greek term *physis* itself, the word for "nature": a perpetual action of achieving, in the whole and in every detail, an ever greater and greater internal and variable determinateness, recursive and progressive at the same time, a dynamic thrust into a cosmic plenum that no one could anticipate or predict and which was constantly attaining its end (part of its end being the sheer attaining of it); and that would again and again, as a perpetual genesis, blossom into the being of Being as pure and substantive gift.

Physis: bloom, prosper, manifest, attain, actuate, *dunamis, energeia,* as Hopkins said in his poem about that marvelous bird, the windhover, and by implication about the entire creation—the "*achieve* of, the mastery of the thing."

Could this be precisely what he felt he had to lock away until the time, if ever, would be right for its disclosure?

It's perhaps appropriate for me to add that, if I've taken the proper measure of what I've here proposed and as I've temerariously, perhaps even precipitously, presumed to represent it, then how ironic it is that Billy Landor, the most liberated among us, should seem be the most incarcerated; that he, the most authentically *convivial* among us — alive and connected with the whole universe in the true Latinate meaning of that ancient term — should appear to be the most alone, though never less alone than when alone (*nunquam minus solus, quam cum solus,* as the ancient sages used to say), while the rest of us live out our lives secluded in our own collective but nonetheless isolated caverns, staring at and applauding the shadows that we ourselves project upon the walls of our captivity.

Yet I'm jealous, in a way, of that old friend of mine whom I've called Billy Landor. I wish I had a key chain just like his, with all those keys on it. I would like to have a key chain with a hundred million keys on it. Rather than weighing me down, it would raise me up. I would go around the world and unlock all the locks that people lock. I would unlock Billy Landor's locks. I would do what Billy Landor was meant to do, what he once did for me, so that he could do it once again, in the way that only he distinctly was meant to do — to unlock something for himself and thereby for all the rest of us.

I would like, verily, to be a keeper of keys.

Millicent

O Millicent, Millicent, Millicent!
O Millicent the magnificent, the ineffable, the sublime!
O vale of Paradise, O palace of wonders, O bejeweled
  blossom among flowers,
O graceful swan among graceful swans!
How thoughts of you flow like honeyed nectar through
  my veins!
How I would cast myself down before you! How I would
  worship you!
O sweetness, O bliss, O solace beyond compare,
O succulent savor of life for me,
How can I forget you?
O Millicent, Millicent, Millicent!
How I adore you.

Ah, René Tarmione! After all, you do know René! I mean, who doesn't know René Tarmione—if that's actually his name?

"*É bien, mon ami! Comme vous voulez!*" René declaims with a sweeping gesture, and with no less than an ominous squeak, as he ushers me to a table in the restaurant. I sit down in a chair—it's upholstered with pink plastic stuff, stiff, uncomfortable—at the outside of the table. He slides himself—I don't know how—into the similarly upholstered bench along the wall behind the table. But René is famous for squeezing into narrow places—and, even more miraculously, squeezing back out of them.

He has summoned me to a "conference." That's another thing he's famous for—his clandestine "conferences." If all of this sounds just a bit portentous to you, if not pretentious as well, I assure you it's both. It's always portentous for "these people," though René is not really one of "these people," any more than I am, though he's willing to play the role assigned to him by others (as well as to him by himself, no less), whereas I'm—well, was—not willing to be quite so cooperative.

The act of summoning itself, of course, was enveloped in the most arcane procedures imaginable: in this case, a slip of paper carefully inserted into the folds of the wrapper of a chocolate bar, which chocolate bar was subsequently slipped, ever so deftly and ever so surreptitiously, into my galoshes—the one for the left foot, by the way; that's a rule—where they'd been sluffed off at the entrance of my place of work. I found the message later that day by pulling on the galoshes and, to my astonishment, discovering the chocolate bar as a lump under my left foot.

I mean, really, it's been at least a year and a half now since "these people" have been in touch with me. The message contained a single number and six letters—in this case, a 7 and the letters KDWFTR—don't try to figure it out, my puzzled readers! It said, in effect, "12:30 at Ignacio's Pizzeria on Friday." I won't try to explain. I still know this sort of thing, or at least I still know one of the codes passed on to me during that brief time I was in contact with "these people." This particular code, no doubt, is by now defunct, but René would know that I wouldn't be updated on these matters and used this presumably now older code deliberately. I should add, in all fairness, that when René issues one of his summonses, he does overdo it a bit, and his exquisite excesses in these matters are his way of expressing his invariable contempt for the entire procedure itself.

Naturally I must attend the "conference"; one always does (though I don't really need to—I'm not and never was actually one of "these people"—but in this case sheer curiosity got the better of me, and, anyway, I had a pretty strong premonition about what it was going to concern, and I could scarcely have left *that* alone, I must say). Telephones, the mail, other media of communication are considered much too dangerous to use, too subject to the exhaustive and apparently inexhaustible surveillance assumed to be exercised day and night by the authorities who have, it appears, nothing better to do than monitor the lives of a small band of revolutionaries who missed their chance about fifty years ago — or something like that, though most of "them" whom I knew were not even born fifty years ago. (But the young have a singular genius for living in the past, especially in a past they know nothing about — may even be inclined to do so more than the old, who, if it's to be believed, have more wisdom than to do that. How strange!)

But in the Movement (as I shall call "these people" henceforth, somewhat glorifying it by conferring a capital "M" upon it), even the most trivial directives — no matter how short and no matter how far the distance to be traversed in order to impart them — must always be passed through a face-to-face meeting in a public place.

Why this is considered to be the ultimate act of secrecy I don't know. Perhaps it leaves no documentation, no records, no "paper trail" behind. It does provide a great deal of opportunity for travel, for "slinking" around generally (as I would put it), and for copious indulgence in food and drink on company time and at company expense (though there's no actual company that I'm aware of, there is and never was such a thing as company time, and nowadays company funds are pretty much depleted).

Another consideration also arises: why there was, or had been, or ever would be some secret thing between René and me, I'll never know. But, in its own way, as I'm sure will become transparent soon enough, the meeting is portentous, at least for me in a very personal way; and it's just as well that it's kept as secret as it is, at least from "these people," who, however resolutely they relish every act of betrayal, would not relish this particular one.

A few words about René, in case you don't remember him too well (though I don't really believe that's possible — nobody forgets René). Well, you do remember how very portly he is — I can see that in the expressions you have just assumed, in the way you widen your eyes and puff out your cheeks.

Actually, some of that portliness is a bit deceptive. It's mainly his neck, if you know what I mean; he doesn't have one. René is one of those people who have a small, refined face peering fretfully out of an enormous mass of flesh that encases and entraps it. In René, the mass begins at a kind of peak on the top of his head and widens out in one unbroken sweep down over his chest somewhere. In the middle of this fleshy cascade is a tiny, delicate face—lonely, as it were, isolated in the midst of such an alien environment.

And what an environment it is—ravaged, scarred, pockmarked, discolored, a mountainside eroded by however many storms of life, and with crevasses and ridges tucked away in the flesh that sometimes yawn open as the great gelatinous mass shifts from side to side, revealing long, thin seams of grayish-black beard, still encrusted with shaving cream, which the morning's razor unhappily, but understandably, missed.

All of this is emphasized by René's most unfortunate propensity to lean to the side as he talks, his head tipping rather decidedly and thereby stretching out and exposing the immensity of this fleshy mass to maximum disadvantage. Yet that nervous little face chatters away, his little eyes darting about, his lips puffing and pooh-poohing with continuous exclamations in French—a language I do not know well, though I, and apparently everyone else, always seem to know what he's saying.

About the rest of his physique, I shall have little to say, though it's shaped a bit like an upside-down light bulb: thin shoulders, an enormous spread at the hips, and all of this, in turn, balanced precariously on two short, spindly, knock-kneed legs that manage, quite miraculously, to guide this ungainly bulk around with the most astonishing grace. The peak of his head—to return for the moment to that remarkable protuberance—is usually capped with a small black beret, making the entire conglomerate look like a large onion-domed cupcake or muffin with a tiny chocolate drop mounted at its utmost spire.

I don't know how René started out in life: he may have begun—if you'll forgive the absurdity of such a thought—as a normal American boy looking for that new frontier that our national mythology, taking its cue from Huckleberry Finn, assumes that all normal American boys somehow or other crave. René Tarmione found his new frontier while on a student year in Paris, where he quickly gave up his study of Molière and Racine for an involvement in the student radical movements of the time. After his return to the United States, so I've been told, he was forever talking of "popular fronts" (invariably rising to meet the threat of "national fronts"), infra-party squabbles, demonstrations, esoteric enclaves and societies, the police, double agents, international conspiracies of innumerable kinds, secret pamphlets, distribution of incendiary leaflets, dead drops, and all the rest. He himself became specialized in the Movement as a kind of courier, a curiously neutral link between various splinter groups who used him to communicate with one another.

René himself couldn't have asked for anything better in life. He lived, I presume, off an inheritance produced by his father's prosperous hardware store in the Midwest somewhere—capitalist lucre, to be sure, but handy for a bona fide revolutionary, even if René really were one.

He wasn't. He just loved the drama of it, the interminable gossip and backbiting and illusions of power-brokering that went along with it, the sense that minor quarrels among its members had repercussions that impacted the future of mankind. He loved, too, the ability of the Movement to supply a limitless parade of personalities, disordered and disaffected as they were in a multitude of ways, that you could, justly and delectably, hold in the most blistering contempt. I don't know why and when and how he picked up his habit of sprinkling French phrases throughout his discourse, though sometimes I think he may have resolved, at some early stage of his largely self-fictionalized career, to imitate Dostoyevsky's cultured but renegade revolutionary, the elder Verkhovensky. Or, to the contrary, he may have come to such a disposition quite on his own. I rather suspect he did the latter, trumping Dostoyevsky, not *avant* but *après la lettre*, not before but after the fact (if that's possible), but I suppose we'll never know.

So where do René and I begin our ever so surreptitious—I suppose I should call it—*tête-à-tête*? Ah, yes, where it makes sense to begin—with Millicent's wedding. First, we order our pizzas. That takes a while. The combination of pizza toppings must be chosen with the most excruciating solicitude. René asks the waiter many questions about how fresh this item is or what the provenance of that item may be. You might think we were in some kind of gourmet establishment, instead of the dump we occupy—located not far off Second Avenue in the East Village. But you'll soon understand why this attention to the toppings is so important. René also orders what seems to me to be an immense vat of ginger ale with which to wash down his pizza.

Subsequently, René turns to the business at hand. René's primary job in life is, after delivering messages, to annoy people; or rather, we might say, his primary job in life is to annoy people *while* delivering messages. He is reasonably good at it. He knows that an account of Millicent's wedding will annoy me to no end. He knows that I was once emotionally devastated by my love for Millicent. He knows that there was nothing more important in my life than my love for Millicent. He assumes that that's still the case.

And, as you know all too well, my dear readers (having, I assume, waded through my idiotically prolix and rhapsodic prelude), he's dead right about this. And he knows (*malheureusement*, I would say, if I were he) that he's right, too, for he knows that I would not have shown up for something as absurd as a "conference" with him if that were not the situation.

If you're wondering how I got to know a person like René, how I got involved in the Movement in the first place, you now have your answer. I actually met Millicent in the Metropolitan Museum of Art, where we both had become mutually absorbed, for a moment, in a landscape by the Dutch painter Hobbema. Of course you laugh! After all, the Metropolitan Museum of Art is one of the standard pickup joints for a certain class of New Yorkers.

Anyway, a moment later, we were mutually absorbed in one another — I in the most beautiful woman I'd ever seen: tall, winsome, her lovely visage framed by an aureole of amber hair flowing in great waves down over her shoulders. Meanwhile, she, you can safely assume, was absorbed in the fact of my absorption itself, my instantaneous and unutterable adoration. One thing led to another (as it conventionally does).

Frankly, I would have followed Millicent into the jaws of Hell. I just about did that — into the periphery of the Movement, that is, where I served a brief stint as a startled and uneasy spectator. Later, she abandoned me, quite unexpectedly, in that ungainly spot in the Movement and rushed off to marry an ineffectual boob — a boob named Bib, by the way.

"Aha," I can hear you mutter, dear readers, with the spittle between your lips frothing demurely, "a jot of jealousy, huh?" Look, I know a boob when I see one, and this fellow is a boob. Life has been torture for me ever since.

"*Alors,* you missed nothing at all, *rien de tout,*" René assures me at the onset of his account of the wedding. Does he think I actually wanted to be there? But even this prelude, as dismissive as it apparently is, lets me know that René truly enjoyed himself at the wedding—which meant the wedding must have really been awful. René enjoys only consummately "tacky" things, for they give him boundless license for expressing his contempt once again; and contempt is what René is all about.

"In the first place," he continues, "they rented for the occasion the most broken-down old union hall in the city—most likely abandoned years ago by whatever union used it, its members being much too busy these days with their luxury pickup trucks and hunting rifles and scuba diving in the islands. The hall was cold; it was musty; its bathrooms would make a sewer in Calcutta look positively antiseptic by comparison."

I nod sympathetically. I know and he knows that Millicent could have rented the most expensive hotel ballroom downtown if she'd wanted to. She comes from an enormously wealthy family who live in one of those mammoth mansions in Greenwich. She's in rebellion against all that—or so she lets on.

"She purchased a gown at Goodwill—a great fluffy, odious thing: an item meant flawlessly to violate, at every level of sensibility, her own otherwise flawless taste; her idea, I guess, of quintessential proletarian chic. The ceremony was performed by a justice of the peace who's also a member of the Movement. Music was provided by a cadaverous oaf with a tattered accordion. He played some Yiddish songs. For a quarter of an hour, we were all the bittersweet denizens of some impoverished *shtetl* in what is now Belarus as it may have been, say, about 1900. Our musician then cranked out a few Mexican ditties, and we transformed ourselves instantaneously into revolutionary *campañeros* for the nonce, clacking our clackers and pretending thereby to shoot priests and nuns in order to spice things just up a bit. Later we became fishermen from the Aran Islands.

"How very protean we are, don't you think? We are the people; we are everyone: everyone, that is, rather than someone, which is why we are no one. A few of the more boisterous comrades, naturally, tried a bit of dancing, if you choose to regard dancing as leaping clumsily about while viciously snapping your fingers in other people's faces. As for food, a long harvest board was set out for the repast, such as it was. It was, *mon ami*, a potluck affair, each guest bringing a contribution, if you really want to call it that."

"How did 'that,' or whatever it was, turn out?" I ask, not really either wanting or needing to know. I know already about such things. The whole idea is to be as gruesome as possible. You, my dear readers, have probably been to such affairs, and you know what I'm talking about. No doubt the very thought of it makes you nauseated. (Or maybe not; do I see you drooling?)

René tilts so far over to one side as he speaks that you'd think he would finally roll over and off his comfy perch, rather like Humpty Dumpty or something to that effect, though he would land not with a crack and a fracturing into pieces but with a deadening thump and a spreading over the floor in a thick porcine pool, with that face of his floating about in it, his eyes twinkling, his pursed lips tweeting, in French, "*Au secours, au secours!*" Yet that never happens, and, for all what appears to be progressive tilting, he never goes anywhere—like the Leaning Tower of Pisa, except in the format of Yankee Stadium. I guess he's wedged too tightly into his seat to topple over.

"How did 'that,' or whatever it was, turn out?" he cries. "*Abominable, abominable!* Utterly *dégoûtant*—only what an antibourgeois bourgeois would conceive as the *haute cuisine* of the *ouvriers*, if the *ouvriers* had an *haute cuisine*. At least thirty versions of a pasta salad, each one more revolting than the last! Only Satan himself, in all his unbounded scropulificence, could come up with such an inferno of gustatory monstrosities! I do loathe pasta salads—don't you?"

"Actually, I haven't given it much thought."

"Well, I have."

He smacks his lips when he says that. "Now, when I was a youngster, by some common acknowledgment—yes, common acknowledgment—the vilest comestible on earth was what was called a 'noodle salad.' Surely you recall such opprobrious items in the 'deli' sections of markets, an abhorrent mass of elbow noodles immersed in a yellowish mayonnaise sauce and ordinarily contained in a stainless-steel tray. It was some poor fool's job to scoop that scruffy stuff into a cardboard carton for customers whose tasting faculties had clearly been impaired at birth by some congenital defect.

"Now, tell me how it happened that, by substituting the word 'pasta' for the word 'noodle,' one opened the floodgates for an inundation of the most infinitely variable, if not infinitely revolting, concoctions the world has ever seen. Damp, gluey, insipid, horrifying things! The wedding feast, I'm sorry to say, was a pageant of such concoctions lined up one after the other, each vying assiduously to look like the worst conceivable excrescence to be discovered at the base of an ancient Roman *vomitorium*—which venerable institution, *sans doute*, was the source and origin of the so-called pasta salad to begin with. But such a *faux-proletariat* dish—you know: cheap, disgusting, and *exotique* at the same time—was just the right sort of thing for the occasion.

"In any event, some angel in disguise, unknowingly saving my life (for I should have been starved without it), had the basic human or angelic decency to contribute to this mass horror a tiny platter of prosciutto and melon, the total contents of which I gobbled up, single-mouthedly, so to speak, before anyone else had a chance to get to it. I don't believe in this 'sharing' business—none of us do, no matter how much we talk about it. Our purpose is not to save society but to loot it. Note that wherever we succeed, the first thing we do is move into the houses of the rich, drink up their wine reserves, and gorge ourselves on our favorite junk food served up on their luxurious dinnerware—what better venue could there be from which to conduct our high-minded kleptocracy! In any case, our pasta salads are eloquent symbols of what we have in mind for the future of mankind. *Ce que tu manges, ce que tu es!* If you eat pasta salads, you're a pasta salad."

"Did Millicent deign to touch any of it?"

"Millicent! Deign to touch it! Allow it to pass through though those lips as delicate as flower petals! *Mais non!* Millicent does not eat proletariat food, no matter how garishly *exotique* it pretends to be and no matter how exquisitely *déclassé* she presents herself. She smiled benignly over it all, as is her way, smiling in that wealthy suburban hostess way we all love so much, repressing the need to gag, I imagine; but her obeisant subjects, each one fawning over her ever more obsequiously than the last, stuffed themselves with the foul array.

"I believe she ate a tomato. Yes, one of those miniature cherry tomatoes that squirt across the table when you bite into them. Her marriage banquet consisted of that sole tomato—lucky tomato, so privileged as it was to glide down her swan-like throat, whole and unmolested by her glistering white but potentially offending teeth. So considerate she is, as everyone thought, so self-sacrificing—even at her own wedding, saving food for others in need! In need of what? one wonders. Meanwhile, what *had* she breakfasted on before coming to the wedding feast? Eggs Benedict at Petrossian's, no doubt, with a side order of the very best Beluga caviar!"

"I, actually, would doubt that very much—"

"Of course, of course—how could I forget that our abstemious Millicent abhors the gormandizing as well as gourmet proclivities of the *haute bourgeoisie*? Show her a person who eats gourmet food, and she'll show you a person, so she thinks, who's eating up the substance of the people. But she does rather overlook—or seems to overlook—the same gormandizing, though hardly gourmet, proclivities in all the other classes, including the motley assemblage at her wedding who were gobbling up that revolting swill as ravenously as a herd of swine."

"And who were they, if I may ask?"

"Oh—the whole *potpourri* of them: the Wanhopes, Ottocar von Tworf, Hadleyson Burrell, Lothar and Wanda Cootbill (the 'Abominable Couple,' as we affectionately call them these days), the Klingheuler twins—male and female twins are so charming, don't you think, but, in this case, it's impossible to know which one is which, not because they're identical twins, which obviously they're not, but because they trade genders back and forth from time to time as they see fit. And then Boris and Imogen Kabernikov (*noms de révolution*, of course; I don't know what their actual name is, but I think it's Jones), Wong-Lung Chu, Allesandro Vinagretto ..."

"Ah, yes, whom they call the 'Catanian Cockroach.'"

"*Bien sûre!* And then Mahood ibn Saladin; Maisie Tuttle with Hank, her ever slaveringly salacious spouse, pawing at every woman, or facsimile thereof, in the room; Rory van der Wopple; Dr. Emil Sarcophagus entwined in his venomous nest of indigent invalids; Somadevi Ramasitaravana—I tell you, the dreadful circus in its entirety: happy clowns and sad clowns, quarrelsome dwarfs, phlegmatic giants lolling about with cavernous crocks of beer dandled fondly in their hairy forearms, bearded ladies expectorating gobs of chewing tobacco into plastic cups, epicene gentlemen applying their mascara. If Jacques *le violent* and his *bombe plastique* had made an untimely, or perhaps timely appearance, he should have divested the world of the largest congress of the most unimportant, though self-important, people in it. And … and … in the center of it all, as if lifted high above the madding crowd on the trunk of a huge, bedizened circus elephant was Millicent herself, dazzling, iridescent, blazing in white, an angel, a queen, worshipped by one and all."

"But where was her husband?"

"Her husband? You mean Bib?"

"Bib the boob. Wasn't he there? Wasn't Bib there? At his own wedding?"

"Of course, Bib was 'there,' insofar as it's ever possible for him to be wherever 'there' is. Don't you know how dancing elephants perch on big circus barrels, their legs coyly pressed together at the base in a kind of upside-down triangle?"

"So he was the elephant."

"No, he was the barrel."

René's face shifts again in a little arc, moving from left to right this time through the mass of flesh, leaving a few shy ripples behind. His tiny teeth sparkle with delight. The tip of his tongue darts out between his lips and flickers momentarily like the tongue of a lizard before it's just as rapidly withdrawn.

Our pizzas have arrived. They're covered with mounds of steaming mushrooms, olives, anchovies, and cheese.

Conversation lapses until this matter of the pizzas can be resolved. This is done, by René, with inordinate dispatch. I take time out for a moment to warn you, my thus far presumably indulgent readers, that what you're about to witness is one of the most improbable and therewithal revolting displays of gastrointestinal ingestion known to mankind. If you're of fastidious disposition, I suggest that you either skip over the following paragraph or else take this opportunity to visit the men's or ladies' room for the duration. Meanwhile, fidelity to my account requires that I forge ahead and return to René.

Rocking his inner face gently back and forth until it's centered more or less in the middle of his outer face, he cautiously lifts his pizza — the entire thing—to the tiny aperture of his lips, as if taking careful aim for the action that will soon ensue. His lips widen, and his teeth protrude and start whirring and chattering with the most alarming high-speed mechanical sound as they grip onto edge of the pizza, lifting lightly the cheesy mass on top and drawing it in. Quite remarkably, the whole surface of the pizza begins to move, becomes slowly detached from its crusty subsurface, and undulates in slow ripples over the crust, contracting and narrowing gradually at one end into high, steaming ridges and funneling into his mouth. It's like a layer of fuming lava that slides sluggishly over a landscape and, thinned at last by passing through a steep defile, plummets downward into the sea. In a few seconds it's over. The entire surface of the pizza, with all its mushrooms, olives, anchovies, and cheese, has vanished in a single draw down his throat, leaving behind the white, denuded crust, as pockmarked as his face and still vaporous with heat. He replaces the crust on the metallic pizza plate. He doesn't eat the crust—that's why this "topping" issue is so vital.

I can't understand why he hasn't burned his mouth and throat irreparably in this feat. Perhaps the huge vat of cold ginger ale that he swallows in a few gulps immediately thereafter helps out somewhat. In any event, he's soon ready to converse again. I have, meanwhile, lost my appetite.

"I don't know how you do that without burning yourself, René," I try tactfully to observe. (Anyway, welcome back to the story, those of you who, understandably, absented yourself for a while.)

"I do burn myself," René wails. "But I can cope with burns. I used to be a fire-eater in my youth, you know."

"Ah, a high roller, a *bon vivant*, a gay blade, a sower of wild oats!"

"I may have been all that too—depending on how you define it. No, I was literally a fire-eater, going about to county fairs, raising money for the Movement. It made us feel so frightfully prole to hobnob with carnival people! And we are, after all, just like carnival people, each with our own little tricks; except that carnival people don't end up, when the performances are over, shooting one another in the back of the head, whereas we are rather favorably inclined, once the shooting has begun, to do just that."

"I thought you had plenty of money."

"I do. But I would never give a cent of that money to the Movement. It's capitalist lucre, not fit to support the Movement but fit, nevertheless, to support me."

"Millicent yields none of her monumental trust fund to the Movement either."

"*Ça va sans dire.* She has more brains than to do that. But it's a source of limitless power for her. The Tantalus effect, you might call it. Keep it just out of reach, and you will get everybody relentlessly clawing at you! How charming it is to be clawed at. Don't you just love to be clawed at? That's why people own cats."

René now goes through what I understand to be his customary post-prandial ritual, wiping himself with his napkin, coughing, snorting, burping, wheezing, gurgling, blowing his nose, shaking his jowls, rubbing his hands.

"You come, obviously, as an emissary?" I say finally.

"*Absolument!*"

"And you come as an emissary from Millicent?"

"*Absolument!*"

"And what does Millicent want of me?"

René is silent for a bit, his now rather fretful eyes darting about the room, occasionally alighting upon me, occasionally upon my as-yet-untouched pizza, occasionally upon the waiter, who now eyes us curiously from a distance, occasionally upon the glass doors of the pizzeria. What is he looking for? — spies, stalkers, informers, a possible murderous intent on my part, a possible repeat performance of his fire-eater act with my pizza? In any case, he's preparing to get down to business. His inner face recedes deeply into his outer face. Then, from out of that bulbous crevasse, he solemnly pronounces, though in a husky whisper. "*Elle voudrait prendre un rendez-vous avec toi!*"

Pardon me, dear readers, and look away for a moment as the blood rushes to my head, my pulse explodes, my heart thumps wildly in my chest, my hands quiver uncontrollably, my eyes are blinded, my ears are filled with a surging roar. In boundless desperation, in boundless hope, I grasp for a moment of reprieve, of collecting myself. I pretend not to understand him. "What?" I cry. "What did you say! Say it in English!"

He glances nervously around the room. Again, he speaks in a whisper: "She wants to meet with you."

I'm thrilled, and I'm horrified. It's what I'd expected to hear, it's what I wanted to hear, yet hearing it jolts me immeasurably. I'm not surprised because one of René's functions in the Movement is to meet with people to set up meetings. I'm also not surprised because I'd figured somehow that Millicent would, someday, try to get in touch with me and that it would be done in just this way—secretly, with an emissary involved, even with René involved, because only he could be trusted, paradoxically, with such an overtly traitorous mission. But I'm astonished that it's so soon—so soon after her marriage! Just one year, almost to the exact day!

"When? Where? How?" I gasp, covering up all the while with my napkin the fact that I'm gasping.

"My task is to deliver the message, not to describe the specifics. I'm commissioned only to communicate back to her your consent or lack of consent. A yes or a no."

"I haven't seen her for well over a year and a half now, well before her marriage," I say, or think I say. I can hardly hear myself talking. My throat is contracted, my voice high and squeaky, my ears still filled with the roar of overextended capillaries. Further, I could have said "a year, five months, twenty-two days, and sixteen hours," but that would have given away too much, and, though I did not, do not, have my wits about me, I have enough not to say that.

How could I forget that last conversation with her in the Hungarian restaurant, my tongue smarting from the goulash I'd burned myself with (unlike René, I can't tolerate such things) and Millicent's beautiful eyes drilling huge holes through my skull? That's when she rejected my proposal and announced her engagement to Bib.

"*Oui, je sais,*" he says, nonchalantly.

"I don't understand why she wants to meet me," I lie. I know why she wants to meet me. He demurs, sucks in his lips as if reversing them, and kisses himself inside his own mouth—a repulsive gesture that only he knows how to execute. But it gives me a moment to catch my breath. I stop gasping. I proceed: "But you can conjecture. I've never known you not to be full of conjectures."

"Well, *c'est bien facile, n'est-pas?* She misses you."

"But she got rid of me … went off and married that boob Bib."

"*Peut-être* she doesn't miss you. But she misses, you can be sure, your worship of her, your adulation, your adoration. And, as you know, *mon ami*, she thrives on worship. The purpose of her life is to be worshipped—well, in any event, that's one of its purposes, though, *certainement*, its main purpose."

"She has the right to be worshipped. If you were a goddess, you'd insist on being worshipped too. But my worship was clearly not enough for her," I added.

"*Eh bien sûr, mon vieux.* Everyone else worships her too. The Movement worships her. Even I—yes, even I—in my own sort of way, worship her. That she's a goddess I shall not gainsay. And nobody thinks that more than she does. She has something that few others have—she has, if you excuse the ridiculous expression, class. You note that I use the expression, in this context, to mean distinction of person, rather than social standing, and rather positively."

"More than class, René—an aura. There's nothing like it in anyone else I've ever known. Intelligence, beauty, imagination, taste, passion, sensuousness—she radiates it all. But she preferred their worship to my worship?"

"*Comment épouser un soldat, on qui aime tout le régiment?*"

"What! What a vile thing to say!" I shout. I refuse to translate this comment for you, my joyfully snickering readers. Its obscene implications are all too obvious. But I know Millicent too well. She would never …

"*Pas de toute! Pas de toute!* You misunderstand me. I make no implications. As I've said, Millicent thrives on their worship. How else could she put up with such a repellent lot?"

"But my worship is just so much deeper, so much …"

"*Naturellement. Mais vous n'avez pas raison* … Ah, you're wrong to assume that she made a choice between your worship and their worship. She wanted both, *vous voyez*. She knew she could depend on yours—that yours would survive whatever she did. That's a great compliment to you—to your steadfastness, to your seriousness, to your loyalty.

"*Mais les autres!* About that she could not know. If she'd gone to you, their affections would possibly have been lost. Consequently, she secured their worship by marrying one of the most nondescript among them — one who simply served to set her off even more remarkably from the crowd and who could never, under any circumstances, command her (or anybody else's) affections. Her affections were reserved solely for you. She has, no doubt, special plans for you."

"And how will I meet her — when, where?" I ask again.

"You will be contacted."

"Contacted? Ah, I see, some enchanted evening I'll bump into a stranger on a lurching bus who, without my even seeing him, apologizes and then is gone. Moments later I'll find the instructions neatly folded and inserted into my lapel pocket. They'll be written in code, I suppose."

"That well may all happen, but I doubt that it will be written in code. This, *mon ami,* is top secret and therefore will not be written in code so that potential interceptors will be fooled into thinking that it's a code, one that they can't break because you can't break what is, in principle, unbreakable since it's not a code."

"Why are we hiding this? Of what possible interest could this have for the wardens of national and international security?"

"None at all. We're hiding this from the Movement."

"I should have guessed."

"The Movement would not at all approve of Millicent's engaging in secret communications with you."

"But they don't have to be secret!"

"All communications are, by definition, secret. Anyway, they need to be secret. As you're well aware, the members of the Movement spend most of their time spying on each other — with good reason, of course. Once this betrayal business gets going, there's no stopping it. One just keeps betraying — anybody, anything, for any reason at all. A liaison between Millicent and you, if it became known, would certainly be viewed as a betrayal of the cause. Under those circumstances, some members of the Movement just might cease to worship her."

"In any event, it would be a betrayal of her husband."

"That would not, *au fond,* matter much to them. As they interpret things, Millicent has betrayed (so they think) her own social class by joining with them. That's one of the reasons they worship her. She also makes them feel that somehow her presence actually inducts them into the class she has betrayed, which is where they've always wanted to be in the first place. But none of that matters too much. The cause is built on betrayal — through and through. The problem might be to *renége* too much on your betrayals: that's what could be seen as intolerable in some cases."

"And what about this husband of hers, this Bib — this boob? What about him? I guess I don't need to say that no matter how big a boob Bib may be, he has his rights, which neither I nor anyone else has the privilege to violate. You know I'm not a religious man, but I have no impulse to covet another man's wife or to commit adultery with her."

René begins to giggle; giggles turn into jiggles; jiggles turn into wiggles; and finally wiggles turn into massive tectonic convulsions rocking back and forth across his outer face, his inner face riding the storm with all the dexterity of a well-piloted schooner breasting great rollers in a hurricane. "Covet?" he shrieks in his laughter. "Covet you do, and covet you shall!"

If I weren't so offended by his statement, I'd be worried about his safety. Is it possible to die of laughter?

"No!" I cry back. "It's just too dishonorable!"

"As for adultery," he goes on, "you should know from prior experience that you're not likely to get that far before this drama reaches its predetermined conclusion. Millicent doesn't do procreation. Everything even remotely associated with procreation disgusts her. That's one of the reasons she married Bib. No procreation with him, I can assure you. He won't even try. Nor with you, no matter how much you try."

He calms down. He remarks, "Ah, so full of noble sentiments — so typical of you — all of which compunction shall vanish like the most volatile tinder once subjected to the first flame of rekindled passion. Well, I've not much to say about Bib. You have, I'm sure, correctly described him as a boob — whatever that means, and I don't have the slightest idea what that means. He's one of those people who does what he does, not in order to do it but in order to remember, at some later time, having done it. Meanwhile, to jog his memory in that future senescence to which he has devoted his life, he continues, sedulously, to assemble the most tiresome, multivolume scrapbook you could imagine, preserving every shred of information about his life: a kind of history in the making, a living chronicle of the most boring life ever lived. I don't think he stops to reflect that one day he might very well pop off before he ever has the chance to pass such a grand review before his eyes, and some caitiff *pauvre* will be saddled with the unpleasant task of hauling all of that dreadful stuff to the city dump. Another way of saying this is that he spends his life writing his own encyclopedic obituary—one that no one will ever read, of course."

"He did do one exceptional thing, regardless of what you say. He did marry the most remarkable woman in this, or any other, universe, if I dare say so!"

"If that's true, he certainly doesn't know it, and it wasn't, at least, *his* achievement. She chose him as the suitable partner, an accessory to her person, rather like trotting into Tiffany's and picking out some hideous brooch—the more hideous, the better. I'm sure he never saw what was coming; even now he probably hasn't much awareness of what happened, though his scrapbook will certainly have a whole section devoted to it, replete with photographs and other souvenirs."

"But why that choice, René? It confounds me!"

"*Hélas, hélas,* whom else should she have chosen? The Catanian Cockroach?"

"Well, no ..."

"The male Klingheuler twin—provided she could pin down for a day or two which one it was?"

"Of course not!"

"Or Ottocar von Tworf with his *pince-nez* tilted so jauntily on that horny beak that passes as a nose and with his pretentious, foot-long cigarette holder perpetually tipped upward between his steely teeth at what we're to assume is a most jaunty and becoming angle? Just because he spends part of the year in what was once East Berlin, rubbing shoulders in some seedy tavern with the old-timers at a revolutionary's *Stammtisch*, he feels he has the right to be particularly obnoxious."

"She should've chosen me!"

"She did. She did choose you. She chose Bib because she chose you."

"That's insane, René; it doesn't make any sense!"

"She chose a husband who could not (and never would) have or make any claim upon her; who secures for her the position in the Movement that she wants to have, safeguarding her meanwhile from disagreeable approaches and unwanted proposals; who, at the same time, excludes you from the Movement, so that she doesn't have to deal with all the problems you would've created for her among the others ..."

"Problems?"

"Scads of them. *Une multitude véritable.* You were a great source of embarrassment for her, you know. I mean, it's quite all right to feel contempt for the whole lot. Who, in their right mind, would not? But it's not all right to show it *si évidement* in front of them. Especially, from a fellow as *outré* as you are! Also, you should know, they suspected you were a mole, an undercover agent, even an *agent provocateur.*"

"How absurd!"

"Of course how absurd! The more absurd the charge, the deeper and the more delectable the suspicion. You *are* rather a *roué*, a most provocative rascal, you know, *mon vieux.*"

René attempts to mimic what he takes to be a provocative look, sidling his inner face to the upper right corner of his outer face and glancing at me while coquettishly batting his tiny little eyelashes. I refuse to be provoked. He laughs vigorously at his own little joke, a wave of flesh again, but with less disruption than before, rolling back and forth jovially across his outer face.

Becalming himself a bit, he goes on: "Then, by virtue of your exclusion, she can find in you a reprieve, a refuge, from the tastelessness of the Movement, a tastelessness that she truly abhors, and a true companion for all that's good and luminous in her soul. For you, *mon frére*, worship the educated, the cultivated Millicent, the Millicent of polished style and inimitable elegance, the precocious princess who was worshipped by her parents and at all the fancy schools she ever went to.

"The Movement, to the contrary, worships the role she's created for them — the disaffected aristocrat who confers upon them acceptance from what they think is the *haut monde* and which they so desperately crave. They even rather appreciate the *hauteur*, the disdainful reserve they detect in her, because at heart they're all contented slaves, cultivating and luxuriating in their sense of intractable inferiority. *Alors*, Millicent gets everything she wants; she continues to be worshipped by the Movement and she continues to be worshipped by you. It's all really quite an astonishing variation on the traditional *ménage à trois*, don't you think?"

"I can endure everything about you, René, except your occasional little flirtations with obscenity!"

"*Je suis desolé, je m'excuse, je m'excuse!*" René squeals as he leans toward me, his fine-featured inner face stretching forward as if ready to burst asunder from its outer, gelatinous imprisonment: "*Mon ami!*" he twitters archly, "she loves you! She adores you! You alone worship her with all the boundless adoration she deserves. You're her life, her breath, her being, her all! She has made the consummate sacrifice for you! She married the most insipid man — in this, or any other, universe (to use your own words) — so that she could nurture her love for you and you alone! For the sake of appearances, of course, she had to wait a year or so before she could put her plan into action."

"But she's put me through hell!"

He relaxes. His inner face recedes back into his outer face. He nods benignly. It's remarkable how his inner face can jog up and down a bit sometimes while his outer face remains immobile. He mutters: "She had to test you somehow. We test everybody, you know."

"That's inhuman!"

"*Par pitié, par amour pour l'humanité, soyez inhumains!*"

"So, which of your beloved Jacobins, your endearingly beneficent butchers, is responsible for that particularly repellent imprecation? Robespierre, Danton, St. Just ..."

"I don't recall. You're right. It was one of them."

"And did he enunciate it before or after his head was lopped off?"

"*C'est bien amusant, ça!*"

"And your role in this little intrigue?"

"My job is also to report back to her ... the state of your affections. I see you have not changed. She expected that. She'll like that."

"But she's betrayed me nevertheless," I exclaim. "She betrayed our love for each other. She betrayed her own affections. She's betraying the Movement right now. She's betraying her husband by sending you here. She's betraying me again by luring me into an illicit liaison that she knows I could scarcely resist but that can only humiliate me further, that will have to be conducted with maximum secrecy, and yet all of that will be a ludicrous game, a charade, that makes a mockery of any desire I might have for a genuine marriage, a life of intimacy with the woman I love, a desire for children with her, that ..."

"Such an outmoded bourgeois ideal!"

"Such a natural thing for any man to want!"

"Such a foolish thing for any man to want ... especially with a woman like Millicent!"

"Explain!"

"I may do just that ... in the course of time! You won't want to hear it."

"Do it now!"

"*Silénce, silénce!*" René whispers. "You'll find out, soon enough. Anyway, you're arousing suspicions." He looks around at the adjoining tables. He smiles and adds, "*Mon vieux*, don't you understand by now? Betrayal, treason, *le trahison*: that's who we are, that's why we exist. Treachery is fun. It makes us feel important. Relax and enjoy it."

"Then you're telling me that Millicent has a traitorous heart!"

"You're the one who has said it," he asserts, blinking his eyes at me. He begins to make motions to leave; and what motions they are, the very embodiment of some primeval seismic force vibrating through his colossal mountain of flesh! His custom is always to leave first. He squeezes himself inward while exhaling, like an accordion being squashed together. He wiggles his thin little legs frantically. He slides somehow from behind the table, stands up on those impossible legs bowed precariously at the knees, and, with an enormous inhalation, reinflates and expands his imposing magnitude. He stares down at me. He prepares to address me with authority.

"You know, *mon ami*," he says, "my mission has, at this point, been discharged. But you have not answered my question, and your failure to provide a negative reply entails, undoubtedly, a positive response. I take it you consent to a meeting. But, come to think of it, I do have a few other *bon mots* to share with you before I depart, if you don't mind."

"Why should you do that?" I ask.

"Because I rather like you," he answers. "And you know me. I practically don't like anyone—except myself, and I'm not always too sure about that. Regard this as an honor of sorts."

He decides to sit down again. He pulls out a chair from the neighboring table and lowers himself into it. Then his inner face, after churning around a bit in his outer face, focuses on me rather in the way it had focused on his pizza. "You at least, *mon camarade manqué*, were sufficiently faithful to your own intelligence to reject the Movement in your heart, despite the asinine and utterly ineffectual acrobatics you went through to look as if you were interested in it and despite the fact that your rejection meant giving up what you loved most in this world—though it appears now that, through no fault of your own, you may be able to recover what you lost ... well, recover it in a way. But I trust you will not deviate, in any event, from that original fidelity. I admire people who refuse to be stupid, and you, *mon ami*, have, by and large, refused to be stupid—at least in reference to the Movement and its sundry waggeries."

He pauses. He seems to be thinking. It's odd to see him like this. He continues: "In reference to Millicent? Well, about that I shall reserve judgment for the moment. In my own treacherous heart, I also admire your fidelity, even as I now venture to cross a whole new threshold of treachery altogether by betraying Millicent herself. For, as you yourself declaimed, and I make haste to confirm, she's the very soul of treason. You can never know what to expect of her, except that your expectations will somehow be subverted. I simply wish to warn you of that, if you don't know it by now.

"You, I, the Movement, for all our worship, are finally nothing to her: she rides us like the expensive horses she rode in her privileged youth. The rest of us may be of dubious provenance—old nags, if you will—but you're the thoroughbred, the treasured mount, the trophy of distinction. That doesn't mean, however, that, when she has finished with you, you won't end up at the same *abattoir*, ground into dog food like the rest of us. She is, *vraiment*, a member of her class—the ruling class, the managerial class, after all, those who regard their mission in life as being born to command and to control other people's lives—and, accordingly, she deserves to be, in the final analysis, *tiré*."

"*Tiré?*"

"*Bien sûr, tiré.*"

"SHOT? You mean, SHOT?"

"SHOT!"

René purses his lips as he says this and perpetrates another one of his internal kisses with a sickening smack that bears an astonishing resemblance to the report of a small-caliber pistol. Customers at nearby tables in the pizzeria look up from their luridly steaming platters with a jolt and stare over at us.

I resume. "But if she loves me as deeply as you say, how can she betray me?"

"Betraying someone you deeply love—someone, moreover, who's deeply lovable, as I presume, in some sense, she thinks you must be—is the most passionate betrayal of all. Moreover, can you imagine how inwardly humiliating it must be for her to feel so subject to a passion as bourgeois as personal love? It violates both her aristocratic dignity as well as her revolutionary fervor. Just imagine: if she actually married you, she might even find something good about life itself. But then she would have to renounce all her sacrifices for the great cause. Anyway, she's betrayed you once already. She'll do it again."

I protest. "Revolutionary fervor! The great cause? You just told me the Movement means nothing to Millicent."

"The Movement means nothing to her indeed, but the cause means everything. She knows the rest of us—whom we narcissistically call the Movement—as the trivial, play-acting buffoons we are; she's deadly serious, ready to embrace the logical consequences of what she's chosen to act on."

I rise to her defense. "Millicent is just too complex for us mere mortals to understand. Her irreproachable divinity circumscribes entire universes! She's a 'wondrous many,' not a 'dull-witted oneness.' Her apparent contradictions encompass all the acquired wisdom of the ages!"

He tilts his head to the left. The mass of flesh shifts accordingly. His little eyes twinkle intently at me. "So, her name is 'legion,' is that correct?"

"No, I don't say that at all. You hypocrite, how you revolutionaries love to cite Scripture!"

"That makes us no different from everybody else, including, as is so often said, *Monsieur le Diable* himself. And you must not suppose that I'm illiterate in matters *théologique*. In fact, I've rather cultivated them. But all of this is beside the point. What then is it that you want to say about Millicent?"

"Millicent is a labyrinth, a sublime labyrinth, a multilayered, multifaceted labyrinth, too transcendent for us to grasp in our petty sublunar ways!"

"Ah, *je vois, mon cher. Mais, souviens-toi*, at the core of every labyrinth, no matter how sublime, no matter how marvelously contrived and intrinsically convoluted it may be, dwells a raging beast, a minotaur, a hybrid creature, a voracious monster who will take its pleasure in consuming you, heart and soul."

"But I thought you said you worshipped her too."

"I do. I worship beasts. The more bestial they are, the more I worship them. Millicent's indisputably superlative qualities make her beastliness all the worse for just that. But you—you who profess to know her so well, who claim to know her better than any of us do—hardly understand the real Millicent after all. For example, you don't really credit her intelligence as much as you seem to, despite how much you extol it. Millicent is an incomparable genius, a woman of brilliance. That's why she appears enigmatic to us 'mere mortals,' *comme vous l'avez dit.*"

"You see!" I shout in interruption. "You agree with me after all. Millicent is a deeply thoughtful woman. Where could you find someone more thoughtful than she?"

"Thoughtful? Did I say thoughtful?" he chides. "I said brilliant. She doesn't think; she constructs. What's remarkable about her is the remorseless, irrefragable logic she can apply to those putative thoughts, those constructions, however brilliant, working out their implications to the proverbial nth degree. Her logic has grasped, as fully as can be grasped and as few others manage to do, the depth of beastliness that must be plumbed in order to eradicate the created order of things.

"Every bond of affection must be broken, every loyalty extirpated, so that only one bond of affection, one loyalty, can be sustained—and that's to the universal imperium that's to come—the imperium, if I may say so, and if I may wax *théologique* for the nonce, of the Anti-Christ, of the Non-God, of the Un-Doer of the Universe, of Universal Extinction."

"How you insult her, how you impugn her motives, her ..."

"*Pardon, monsieur*, impugn her motives? *Certainement non!* Her ideals are the highest and her motives the purest conceivable."

"What good does all of this do for the Movement?"

"*Rien de toute!* Do you think we revolutionaries actually want the revolution to happen? Of course not! If it should happen, then what on earth would we do with ourselves? We don't know how to do anything other than be revolutionaries. We would have to cease feeling hounded and persecuted—which would be a calamity for us. There's no greater joy than the joy of considering yourself to be a victim. It justifies anything that you want to do.

"Moreover, we'd also be the first group to be eliminated, for the leadership of the revolution would know that among self-indulgent social parasites, we're the worst, making absolutely no contribution to the public weal at all, being, as we are, inveterate miscreants, *flâneurs*, shams, *fainéants*, self-serving loafers, you name it. How on earth could the new order of things transmogrify us—us, of all people—into the efficient little tools that it wishes to make of everybody else?

"And should the revolution ever succeed, we won't go to our summary liquidation with our heads held high, I can assure you of that. We will go out groveling at the feet of our liquidators, clutching the barrels of their rifles and sticking them in our eye sockets as we thank them and instruct them when and how to pull the trigger and tell them they're doing the right thing."

"*La révolution dévore ses enfants*," I interject, mimicking my interlocutor, *en français* no less.

"How very sweet of you to say that," he chirps.

"I learned the expression from you, René, sometime or other, in our shady past. I was under the impression that you rather relished the 'devour' part."

"How not so very sweet of you to say that," he purls. "But we digress. In any case, our adorable Millicent won't be one of those devoured. *Hélas, hélas, mon pauvre*, just imagine what it's like for her to be in love with you. Like a medieval saint in a cloister who must struggle for years to bring some final weakness under control, some residual lust or anger or envy, so in the vast and hollow cauldron of her heart Millicent must struggle to extinguish the final burning flame of love that lingers on inside her, perhaps even some recalcitrant and horrifying impulse to find in you the seed of life and a source of birth within herself, all of which would be a scorching reproach to her mind and conscience.

"Source of birth! *Mon Dieu!* And all the exclusive love that that entails! A love that longs to cherish and preserve what is unique and particular! Horrors! Yet she must nourish that love as well, for it furnishes her with the immense internal struggle out of which all true spiritual heroism is forged. And she'll do it, mind you, she'll controvert that love as thoroughly as it can be controverted. If to love is, among other things, to will the good of the beloved, then she has forced herself to will your perdition and has calculated every move to make that happen.

"She can, *mon ami*, predict everything you will do and control how you will do it. She'll reduce you to a beast by inducing you to hate her—she whom you love above all things—and to betray her. She'll turn you into an image of herself. It will be the culminating point of her life, the most successful thing in it, a mark of insuperable superiority, the point of honor to which every true aristocrat deeply aspires. Further, she recognizes, in her impeccable logic, that as a member of the ruling class, as progeny of the capitalist rich, she, too, deserves to be shot. Getting shot in the end will enshrine her martyrdom in all its immemorial splendor."

"And who, René, if I may be so bold to ask, will shoot her?"

"*TOI, mon ami, c'est toi même*," he squeals.

"*MOI?*" I squeal—I mean, I scream back. "*As-tu perdu la tête?*"

Did I scream that too? And in French? Yes, I did. "Have you lost your head?" I scream again, in my own idiom this time.

"It will be you—yes, you who will have that exquisite privilege. It will be you who will shoot her! She doesn't want life implanted in her from you, she wants death."

"René, sometimes I think—"

"You will have your fling, your *petit cinq-à-sept*, your *affaire*—as far as that will go, and it won't go very far, no further than it did the last time. How could you resist? You have consented to it already, even without having said so. But you will drink the cup of humiliation to its dregs. She'll do everything in her power to get you to shoot her. And you, *mon ami*, will comply with her wishes."

"That's nonsense!"

"*Quand on aime tellement une femme, on est bien près de la détester!*"

"I don't understand that. Say it in English!"

"I don't need to. You will say it yourself, soon enough, in English or who knows what language. And what do you love about her anyway? Her adornments? Her qualities? *Peut-être.* But about her soul you know close to nothing. And besides, *mon ami*, you're already betraying her. Of course, you have only done what it was planned you should do."

"And just how am I . . . ?"

". . . betraying her? Listen to yourself! You're doing it right now by exposing this confidential *tête-à-tête* to the public by letting the cat—or is it the rat—out of the bag, so to speak, by passing on these horrid little secrets I've told you to your freakishly prying friends, your 'dear readers', as you presumptuously call them, as you're doing right now!

"Just look at them! How they cuddle up there in their armchairs like rhesus monkeys, their knees drawn up to their ears, chattering and giggling, their tails wrapped around their necks like nooses, with slobbering grins on their faces and eyes pinched and *moiré* with malignant glee! Meanwhile, *c'est toi* whom they laugh at, *le crétin*, the starry-eyed Pierrot in love, the harlequin, whose hopeless passion will not defray the cost when it finally comes in, your steaming entrails gorged on by the glistering teeth of that lion-woman, by that ravenous, claw-baring Sphinx herself, under the clear and all so dispassionate moonlight. That she loves you, as she does, makes it all the worse, makes her beastliness shine out with unalloyed brilliance.

"But she must also figure that among your readers there are a select few who won't laugh, who will truly grasp the significance of what will have been done—the ultimate sacrifice she'll have made, the self-oblation, the model, the paragon of the heroic vanguard who will follow her and enshrine her memory. She'll have shown to the doubters among her class that it can be done, that, in the service of unbounded hate, no renunciation ever need be spared. She'll have shown that there are no depths to which one cannot descend, once one has resolved that elevating oneself above everything else — above absolutely everything in the universe, including the universe itself — demands, unremittingly and irrevocably, extirpating the universe itself and all it holds dear.

"But that's not the final victory yet. For she'll achieve all of this, as I've said, by transforming you — you, the unassailable, the irreproachable, the incorruptible, the chivalrous and intrepid lover — into a beast yourself, which aim shall triumph at last when you deposit that dainty little slug into the dainty little cerebellum at the back of her dainty, but not so little, brain. She is, as you say, a goddess, even more so in her own eyes than in yours, and she insists on her rights as a goddess. She's Ishtar the Destroyer, the goddess supreme of all the tawdry Babylons this world has ever spawned, the goddess who devours her lover and devours him ever more rapturously the more he is beloved.

"Then, the deed done — done just as she willed it to be done, as the police cordon tightens around you, as the baying hounds of pursuit close in upon you and you inhale their hot, rancorous breath, you will know how, out of the depth of her love, she has bequeathed to you a depth of hatred you'd never thought could exist in the human heart. In that hate you will find the eternal communion with her that she has willed for you, the hate-bond, the *Liebes-Tod* in reverse that you crave.

"And do not think for a moment that you will escape the fate she's designed for you. Your unbounded adoration of her will short-circuit what little is left of your reason, to say nothing of all your better instincts. Meanwhile, she'll have achieved everything she wanted: to be worshipped, forever and ever, as the destroyer of a world that should never have been created in the first place, a world that she hates because it was not made the way she wanted it to be, a world where she could change stones into bread at her command, where she would never dash her foot against a stone, where all the kingdoms and nations of the earth would be under her dominion.

"*Bonne chance, tovarish,* you will need it! *Au révoir!*"

My dear readers, how he insults you! You're not a bunch of ghoulishly grimacing monkeys — are you?

Well, . . . are you?

Stop all that hooting and drooling and answer me!

And how he insults me! And how he insults her—her, her, Millicent, the divine Millicent herself!

He rises from his chair, spins himself about on his skimpy, tippy-toe feet, and whirrs merrily out of Ignacio's at a tilt, like a child's top, though not without glancing over his shoulder at the waiter and wondering whether he'll be followed. He obviously wants to be followed. He leaves me to pay the bill. I'm not surprised. He always leaves other people to pay the bill. That's another one of his trademarks! And I haven't even eaten my pizza yet. It still sits in front of me, sodden, shriveled, and cold.

> *O Millicent, Millicent, Millicent!*
> *O Millicent the malignant, the deplorable, the defiled!*
> *O pit of pestilence, O dungeon of darkness,*
> *O vile weed among vilest weeds,*
> *O scorpion among scorpions!*
> *How thoughts of you flow like scorching poison through*
>   *my veins!*
> *How I would flee from you! How I would shun you!*
> *O bitterness, O horror, O desolation beyond compare,*
> *O acrid taste of death for me,*
> *How can I forget you?*
> *O Millicent, Millicent, Millicent!*
> *HOW I ADORE YOU!*

Leviathan

Leviathan was a horse: a large white horse with a long white mane that drooped down below his neck and a long white tail that swayed back and forth in the prairie winds. He wasn't an especially beautiful horse. He was old and had a sagging belly and knobby knees; his mane and tail were unkempt and dirty and snarled with burrs and shreds of grass; his fetlocks and hooves were encrusted with dried mud; there was dust and grit all over his body. His right ear was oddly torn and always seemed to tilt backward on his head like an ear of corn partially broken off at its base and hanging, just barely, from its stalk.

But his neck was as strong and as firm as an arch of antique marble and he had enormous blue eyes, as bright as sapphires. He loved to gaze at things with those glowing eyes, gaze at all kinds of things for a long time, as if he understood them, as if he'd known them all his life. His eyes were like orbs plucked from the deep-blue Wyoming sky and dropped from their heights into his sculpted and noble head.

Nobody knew where Leviathan came from. He just showed up one day, trailing along after a herd of cattle in one of the southeast pastures of the Pronghorn spread. One of us saw him there, Riley it was, when he was laying down some salt licks for the herds in that area. Riley told us about him, and as soon as we could make the arrangements, some of us borrowed his car to look for him. I don't know why. There were plenty of other horses around: in the ranch corrals and stables; in the pastures; in the upland woods where we went to hew down trees and haul them back for wooden fence posts. Sometimes we even saw wild horses grazing along the edge of the high escarpment that ran for miles along one side of the valley.

These were all fine and beautiful horses, filled with energy and life, but not like old Leviathan. Not like him at all. We went to see Leviathan because, as Riley had said, there was nothing quite like him. He looked like a creature from another age, another place, another world altogether. We could never fully explain this impression, but that's what he looked like. One of us, Jon, who was a literary type, called him Leviathan because he reminded Jon of the white whale named Moby Dick, and "leviathan" is taken to mean "whale" in the Bible. Just like Moby Dick, this creature seemed to come from that other world that was more this world than this world seems to be. How can I explain that?

At our insistence, Mr. Garret, the ranch owner, made some inquiries. None of the other ranchers up and down the valley could identify the horse. Some had seen him wander by in recent weeks, stop by their pastures, sniff at a few items, move on. No one came looking for him; there were no notices for lost horses and no signs that anyone owned him or wanted him back. He was apparently not shy of human beings; indeed, he was friendly and docile and appreciated a human approaching him, petting him, looking him over, and wondering who he was.

He appeared to have the ability to get in and out of fenced-in pastures, to join up for a while with a herd of cattle and then leave, even gathering together with some fellow horses for a bit now and then before showing up somewhere else a few miles farther up the valley. Did he have the ability to open gates—and then to close them, most considerately, behind himself when he left?

As you would expect, Mr. Garret was pretty puzzled. He figured that Leviathan might have been a packhorse—the sort that some outlanders use for hauling supplies when heading off into the mountains for a hunting safari. Perhaps Leviathan had been lost; perhaps he'd just drifted off from some encampment during the night and nobody especially noticed or cared. It was curious that he had no bridle or halter on him, nothing to indicate a human claim. Maybe he was just set loose and shooed off so that an original owner wouldn't have to cart him from the high country of Wyoming back to Cheyenne or Omaha or Denver or wherever he came from. Lots of people did that sort of thing with their dogs and cats and other animals: just left them someplace rural, thinking that they were being given their "freedom" and could survive perfectly fine in the wild, though what, in fact, these people were doing was leaving their pets to die difficult and lonely deaths.

Whatever Mr. Garret thought about Leviathan's origins, he was initially resistant when we proposed that we venture into the valley lowlands, find Leviathan, "capture" him, in a sense, and lead him back to the ranch. His argument in opposition was very simple and could be summarized in two words: "Then what?" But we were young, and the chain of reasoning that began with "Then what?" hadn't been too perfectly branded on our brains yet. The future could take care of itself. I think, in retrospect, that it probably did; but we were lucky that it did. Anyway, Mr. Garret consented, much to our surprise, issuing in the meantime a number of curtly framed caveats. The horse, under any circumstances, was not to be a nuisance, either to the ranch personnel or to property or to other livestock. We agreed to assume all responsibility.

Including Riley, there were nine of us at the ranch that year. We were "the summer help," recruited with ads put in a number of newspapers, to assist the regular staff of ranch hands from June through the end of August. We came from everywhere—from the East, from California, from several Midwestern states. The ranch was located in one of those high valleys in Wyoming that cut through treeless grasslands, ascending upward through foothills and plateaus, and terminating in dense conifer forests and in the towering, snowcapped peaks of the Absaroka Range. The valleys have rivers of various sizes flowing through them, bordered sometimes by marshes and groves of aspen and cottonwood. The valleys also have, here and there, wide, lush hayfields.

During the summer, the cattle are driven up to the higher pastures in the foothills and even to the narrower valleys in the mountains while the fields below are harvested for their hay. The herds return to the lower valleys for the winter. Our job was to mow, rake, buck, and stack the hay, which would provide winter fodder for the herds. It was a demanding physical job requiring long days and many-sided operations. We were glad to get whatever leisure we could. Leviathan was a diversion that several of us — Jon, Walt, and I — would welcome. For a week or two before we sought him out, we talked endlessly about him and what we would do once we had him in our keeping.

The "hunting" and "capture" of Leviathan, if I may dignify our expedition with such expressions, turned out to be more daunting than we had expected. It had rained heavily during the night, so the fields were soaked, and we couldn't engage in the haying operation until things had dried out somewhat. So we had the day off. We would devote it to the pursuit of Leviathan. I should say that Leviathan himself was the easy part. When we finally found him, he welcomed us as if we'd been long-lost friends. Tracking him down was the hard part. Having seen him as an incongruous member of a cattle herd several days prior to our search led us to believe that we should have no trouble at all in spotting him in open country. Obviously, Leviathan, in the meantime, had ambled off, in his slow, measured way, into the marshlands of the river bottom.

After several hours of driving around in Riley's car and finally concluding that that's where he may have gone, we decided that our search required abandoning the car and sloshing around in knee-deep mud for hours, pushing brambles and razor-sharp thistles out of our way, being attacked by billows of aggressive mosquitoes more copious we ever imagined could exist, tripping over submerged roots and landing face down in the mud, and being deceived again and again by a species of white flowering bush whose mirage of attaining our goal produced an endless series of disappointments.

When we did find Leviathan, it was something of a shock. First, we encountered a white apparition hovering in the underbrush close to us. We decided not to be fooled once more by one of those flowering bushes. Then suddenly the white apparition reared its massive head upward through the branches, and he was there, right in front of us, looking at us through the foliage with those great blue eyes and seeming to say: "Where were you? I've been here all this time waiting for you to show up. Goodness, what a mess you've made of yourselves." Well, he wasn't all that pristine himself. A small armada of dragonflies circled around him and finished off any mosquitoes so impudent as to invade his territory. It was also shocking to be so close to what we'd seen previously only at a great distance. Leviathan was much larger than we had expected. There was also something bizarre about him, as if we'd stumbled upon a unicorn standing in the middle of a primeval Druids' grove.

We had a halter and a rope with us, and he took to those without the slightest protest. But it wasn't so easy to lead him out of the swamp: he had to struggle as much as we did with the difficult footing and the deep mud. It might have looked rather comical to an observer: Leviathan and the three of us, like four clowns together, fumbling through the muck, falling and rising, pushing our way through the dense brush, and bumping into one another and pulling each other down, though Leviathan was the most stable and provided our support on many an awkward occasion.

Gradually we learned that he should be leading us, rather than vice versa. And he did. We followed him toward the river, and there we cleaned ourselves off, splashing water on each other and washing off Leviathan, even though the water was bitterly cold, as these snowfield run-off rivers usually are. We walked along the shallow edge of the river until we found a place where we could get back up to high ground again without having to traverse the marsh. Then two of us returned with him to the ranch. It was a long walk but well worth it. Jon found the car and drove it back. We had, at last, our Leviathan.

Did we ever clean him up! What an act of grooming, currying, clipping, washing, rubbing, and polishing went on! By the time we finished, he looked like a great chalk horse carved out of the side of some ancient Britannic hillside. He looked like a horse fit to be ridden by Marcus Aurelius on the summit of the Capitoline Hill. He looked like one of those Lipizzaner stallions ready to perform in front of the Viennese court accompanied by the music of Johann Strauss. He looked as grand and as mysterious as the great white whale after whom he was, indirectly, named. We were proud of our job, and he was proud of it too.

I admit that Mr. Garret, to say nothing of the sundry ranch hands, was puzzled by this treatment but not unappreciative. I mean, after all was said and done, Leviathan was still an old "nag" who had wandered in from the prairies.

Initially we bedded Leviathan down in a small, dilapidated stable not far from the main compound of buildings that comprised the Pronghorn Ranch. We brought him plenty of fresh water, hay, some oats now and then, gave him the exercise he needed, swept out his stall, and kept him immaculately groomed. An elderly, mostly retired cowboy—the only fellow at the ranch, from what we could make out, who actually would use that term to refer to himself and who would dress accordingly—was our consultant about how to take care of Leviathan: to look after health problems, teeth, hooves, and the like. He took a lot of pleasure in advising us "greenhorns" about what to do. For our part, we had never imagined that so much work was involved in taking care of a horse.

It's difficult to know what Leviathan thought about all this fussing that went on about him. I think he liked it, but he made it clear, before too long, that he didn't really need it. He started, quite regularly, to get out of his enclosure. We didn't know how he did it. He would do it in the middle of the night when no one could see. During the day, he would mosey around the ranch and the adjoining pastures, on his "own recognizance" as it were, minding his own business in a way, even as he was, in fact, rather busily minding everybody else's. He watched old Frank, the mechanic, fix broken tractors; he watched Mrs. Carter, the cook, select vegetables from the kitchen garden for the evening chow (and always offering him a carrot or two); and he watched Olaf Swenson, who spent his life sharpening things and liked to sing as he whirled his millstone while the sparks flew in every direction.

Funny thing, too, but everybody talked to Leviathan just as a matter of course. We wanted to talk to him because he was the only thing around that seemed to care and would actually listen. How often I talked to him, telling him everything I was planning to do in my life. He was so understanding and so patient. Did the amused and skeptical glint in his eyes show that he knew already that I would never actually do any of it?

Anyway, he followed us around, doing his own thing, coming and going when he felt like it, often ambling after our great wobbling processions of machinery as we moved from field to field over rough ground, harvesting and stacking the hay. Finally, we gave up trying to keep him in his little stable.

We never knew where he spent the night. He didn't bother anyone, and we just let him do what he wanted to do. Even Mr. Garret didn't seem to mind, though Leviathan and we were violating some of his rules.

Eventually we borrowed a saddle and put it on Leviathan and took turns riding him. These were not particularly adventurous rides, for it was difficult to prod him to move much faster than a slow canter, and even that would last for only a short time. Walt preferred to ride him bareback; Walt was a kind of gymnast and could do all kinds of dexterous things. Leviathan was amenable to anything we wanted to do. He enjoyed our company, and I have to admit that often, when I went out for a ride, I did it more for his entertainment than for mine. We did enjoy following deer paths through the many ravines that provided access from the lower valley up through riffs in the escarpment. Then we would ride along the edge of the escarpment. I don't know if horses take pleasure in things like "views"; I've always rather doubted that they do. When they stand someplace for a while, they avert and shake their heads in that bored, impatient way that indicates they would rather be doing something else.

But Leviathan certainly seemed to like the scenery, if that doesn't sound too absurd, and he could watch over the distant canyons and cloud formations for long periods of time with what looked like rapt attention. In fact, he paid more attention to things than do most human beings I know. As for averting the head in a bored, impatient way, well, that describes just as many of my friends as any horses I know.

We did have fun, on a few occasions, finding suitable shelter from sudden cloudbursts that swept over the mountains and descended into the valleys like golden eagles swooping down on their prey. The claps of thunder and the streaks of lightning fragmenting the sky were more frightening to me than they were to Leviathan. I always let him lead the way and find the best refuge, which he did, often seconds before the first wave of colossal hailstones ripped through the air like what I imagine a discharge of musket shot would have been in a Civil War battle, followed by huge, isolated raindrops smacking into your face like the big wet kisses that many a child doesn't particularly want to have. As we watched the storm pass over us, I'd whisper "the thunderbird" into Leviathan's sagging ear, and he would shake his head in understanding, as if he were one mythical critter acknowledging the domain and authority of another.

One time, when we were making our way up a ravine and passing through a clump of brush and pine trees, we startled some mule deer. A stag and three does jumped out of the grove, bounced up the ravine in a zigzag pattern for about fifty yards through some sagebrush, then turned to stare at us. We stared back, just as surprised as they were, and continued on our way up the ravine. They continued to watch us. Soon the does were grazing on some patches of grass, even as we passed close by, and had no further concern. The stag continued to eye us but without anxiety. He seemed to say: "So it's you, after all. Did you have to give us a start like that? And who's that goofball sitting on your back?"

I think that Leviathan was pleased by these encounters with his feral brethren. He also seemed to know some of the mustangs that lived on the plateau beyond the escarpment. Once we were rambling along a stretch of prairie when a pronghorn antelope showed up in the distance. The antelope moved up to about fifty yards behind us and followed us for several miles, or for about half an hour, before it finally cavorted off across the prairie and disappeared. During this little pageant, Leviathan would sometimes stop, swish his head around, and look at the antelope before proceeding further. I began to wonder if they were friends too and I was the "third party" making old ties between them difficult to renew.

As I said, Walt liked to ride Leviathan bareback. One evening, after a difficult day in the fields, we went out to join Leviathan for a little after-dinner company. Walt got the idea of riding Leviathan around in a circle inside a training corral. He managed to get Leviathan up to his customary slow canter. Then, just as a silly stunt, I suppose, and with no little bravado, Walt crouched on Leviathan's back and then stood up there. I couldn't believe what I was seeing. Leviathan was prancing around in a circle with Walt standing on his back. What was even more unbelievable — and sometimes I think it must have been more my imagination than real — Leviathan's gait became wonderfully elegant and measured. He looked as if he was dancing, lifting his legs in an odd sort of way. He looked as if he was doing what he was meant to do. It occurred to me then, and I still think about it now, that Leviathan, in some part of his past, may have been a circus horse.

All of this didn't last very long. Walt attempted to flip upside down and do a handstand on Leviathan's back and almost immediately fell off. Leviathan ceased his trot and looked around at Walt with a kindly but somewhat reproachful glance. After all, Leviathan had done what he was supposed to do; why had Walt not lived up to his part of the bargain?

It never happened again. Sometimes I wonder if inadvertently we had penetrated some treasured but inviolate secret that Leviathan harbored in the depths of his heart, one of those memories that are finally too precious to reveal except in the momentary but capricious display of them. I'll never know the answer to this, but I'll also never lose my memory of what went on in my mind at the time: the sense of a circus band, the big tent, the ringmaster, beautiful young women in glittering array under the lights, a thousand laughing, cheering children, and Leviathan at the center of it, looking out at it all, enjoying every minute of it.

Leviathan — hadn't I known it all along? — was, in the end, not just a performer but also a spectator, a spectator of spectators, in love with the razzle-dazzle of the world, inside and outside of a gorgeous circus tent.

There's one special event regarding Leviathan that merits attention. Each day, Mr. Garret would have to decide which field the crew would go to for the day's work. Then something like a mechanized military column would assemble in the ranch compound and advance out to the designated hay-field. All told, a column might consist of seven or eight tractors of different sizes bearing different kinds of attachments. There were also several trucks as well as Mr. Garret's somewhat antiquated Land Rover and a huge, movable catapult-like rig for building haystacks as tall as a three-story building.

Some of these fields were difficult to get to. The procession might have to ford the river several times, pass through circuitous and hazardous cutbacks, and negotiate an occasional treacherous bog (I once saw three tractors get embedded in the same bog — the ranch bulldozer had to be sent for to get them out), long stretches through wooded lanes where boughs and fallen trees might have to be cleared out of the way, and gates whose rusty locks and joints required nothing less than crowbars to get us through.

The only one who had an easier time getting to a worksite was Leviathan, who simply walked straight to it, crossing over whatever needed crossing over, and not paying attention to what our heavy machines demanded of us. Sometimes he arrived at a worksite before we did, and we could not figure out how he could have known where we were going.

On this occasion, the usual process was set up. It took four men to build a stack, and we "temporary" ranch hands often got stuck with this dirty, physically exhausting, and often dangerous job. The four men would stand at each corner of where the stack was projected to be, tear apart with their pitchforks an immense swath of hay that was dumped in the middle of them by the hay rig, and drag hay over to the sides to build up the corners. Gradually the stack would rise beneath them. It was dirty work because each swath of hay would land on the stack with a huge puff of dust and chaff, and the abrasiveness of tromping around in the hay could wear out a new pair of dungarees in two weeks, to say nothing of what it did to a pair of boots. It was dangerous work because the stack buckled and swayed as it was constructed and, as I mentioned, was close to three stories tall by the time in was finished. Falling off the stack was always a threat.

Well, one day, one of us fell off. It was Josh—I haven't mentioned him yet. He was a star football player from some Southern school who thought that ranch work would toughen him up for the coming football season. He was tough enough, I would reckon. But when he fell off the stack and then discovered that two tines of his pitchfork had penetrated the palm of his right hand and had exited out the back, he fainted dead away. I don't blame him. I probably would have done the same.

The problem now was how to get him to an emergency room. The closest hospital was sixty miles away at least. But that could happen only after we got him out to the nearest road. That was the real problem. The journey into the field that morning had been excruciating. The journey out, to someone in his condition, would be even worse. There was a road only a mile away as the crow flies, but it was a three-mile trip through unbelievable obstacles if done by machine.

Leviathan to the rescue! I'm not kidding. Who would ever have thought it?

Leviathan just moved into position on his own. Josh did regain consciousness but wasn't able to do much. It was quite an effort for a few of us to lift Josh's big defensive-tackle hulk onto Leviathan's back while one person braced that pitchfork still dangling from his hand (we didn't dare to pull it out ourselves). Then, holding on to Josh from both sides, we walked alongside Leviathan and allowed him to find the shortest, most convenient route to the road. He carried his burden with the utmost care, stepping gently over obstacles and avoiding sudden movements of any kind.

By the time we reached the road, Mr. Garret had brought the Land Rover from the field by hurtling wildly over the uneven terrain of the "bucking bronco" trail (as he later described it) and was able to load Josh into the passenger seat and rush him to the hospital. But first, figuring that leaving the pitchfork in the hand until it could be removed by a professional health provider probably entailed greater risks than removing it himself, he yanked it out of Josh's hand and wrapped a first-aid bandage around the wound. Oddly, there was little blood. Josh let out a yelp none of us were likely ever to forget and once again fainted away.

Immediately afterward, before getting into the Land Rover, Mr. Garret strolled quickly over to Leviathan, slapped him firmly on his neck, and proclaimed: "Good job, old boy!" Even those of us who were "summer help" knew by now that Mr. Garret never said "good job" to anyone who had done a good job. He said it only to someone who had done a spectacular job.

Of course, summer came to an end. That's when Mr. Garrett's initial admonition "Then what?" came back to us with a great deal more than its original force. We had to depart. We had to go home. What would happen to Leviathan?

During those final weeks, we discussed, consulted, pleaded, lamented, and agonized over what we were going to do. It was the old, retired cowboy who finally settled it for us. He told us to let Leviathan decide for himself. We asked him if a horse could actually decide for itself. He said he didn't know; but, if it could, Leviathan was the one who could do it, and he would certainly know what to do.

Two days before we left, I rode Leviathan, bareback this time, out to a high, rocky hill about five miles from the ranch. Jon and Walt followed along in the Land Rover. About five hundred yards from the summit of the hill, they stopped the vehicle, disembarked, and accompanied us on foot to the summit. There we all stood for a while, looking out over the panorama before us: the prairies, the hills, the forests, the mountains. Then we removed the halter from Leviathan, said our goodbyes, and walked back down to the Land Rover.

We were very sad about this and could hardly talk to one another. We couldn't help but wonder if, like an original owner, we were not leaving Leviathan to a sad and lonely death. We had heard a great deal about how long and bitter were the Wyoming winters. But Leviathan continued to gaze out over the landscape. Soon it would be autumn and the herds would return to the lower valleys. Would Leviathan be with them? We got into the Land Rover. Before we started up the engine, we saw Leviathan sweep his neck in our direction and look at us for a moment with his brilliant blue eyes. He seemed to be saying, "Thank you." Then he turned back again to face the wilderness, walked slowly away, and disappeared over the crest of the hill.

We knew, of course, that we were the ones who really had to be thankful. And we were. We started the engine and drove back to the ranch. Leviathan didn't show up the next morning, as we thought he might possibly do. On the following day, the three of us, plus Riley, were heading in Riley's car eastward out of the valley. We were on our way home—home to the Mississippi valley, to the Atlantic coast. We couldn't help but keep a lookout for a solitary white horse somewhere up in the rangeland around us. But we didn't see anything.

The following spring, I wrote a letter to Mr. Garret asking him if he, or anyone else, had seen Leviathan or heard anything about him. He wrote back telling me that Leviathan had vanished—indeed, had vanished that very day we had taken him out to the hill where we had left him, had vanished back into the prairies whence he, on some curious day in the past, had mysteriously come and now had just as mysteriously gone. I should have felt worried, I guess; but I didn't.

I'm confident that Leviathan is out there somewhere, doing what he always does, taking care of himself, his long white tail swooshing in the prairie winds, his great blue eyes affixed patiently, lovingly, on the far horizon.

Tutelary Presences: A Triptych

1

Brünnhilde

I think she merited the soubriquet Brünnhilde, among various other reasons, because wherever she went, she never seemed to walk. Like Brünnhilde, *prima donna* of the tempestuous Valkyries, she flew. She flew into rooms, even as she flew out of them when it was time to leave. She flew around them while she was in them, except for those moments, now and then, when she alighted upon a chair or sofa or piano stool like a short, stocky eaglet upon a branch or rocky outcrop, arching her neck slightly forward, flexing her muscular wings, fixing her gaze upon a target, and waiting to swoop once again. She flew up and down staircases. She flew along the streets and in and out of buildings. She didn't, of course, fly upon a six-legged horse and bear the shades of slain warriors into Valhalla, but she could fly, with unparalleled energy, over the keys of a pianoforte and bear thereupon, with enthusiasm and devotion, the sublime spirits of the grand opera into the high empyrean of hearts and souls. She flew, in a sense, into my life, even as later she flew out of it.

She resided in an old five-story edifice on Central Park South close to Columbus Circle with a magisterially sculpted façade and a gorgeous view of Central Park—a proper nest for the Muses (and for Valkyries) if there ever was one. Therein she waged, for decades, a cosmic war against a band of real estate developers who, if they could finally succeed in dislodging her from her studio loft on the fourth floor, would be able to vacate the building of its final tenant and tear it down, replacing it, as Fáfnir and Fasolt would certainly have done, with yet another shimmering titanic spear puncturing the firmament over Manhattan. But she had an unbreakable rental contract from decades earlier—one of those sacrosanct bonds that quasi-divine figures so often seem to have—and a character as tenacious and well-accoutered in psychic panoply as any other Valkyrie in this world could ever boast. That lovely building is gone now, and she has gone, too, in the only way she would have ever consented to go, chanting until the end of time, as I would imagine, her joyous death song as she flew to whatever ring of flames, upon whatever mountain peak, shall in our memories be pleased to blaze around her.

I should say up front that my relationship to her was scarcely as dramatic as all that. After all, I was only twelve years old at the time. Each year she took—condescended, perhaps, to take—a limited number of students for music lessons. These were, in some sense, "special" students, though I could never figure out what was special about me, and I could never get over the feeling that, whoever and whatever it was that made the recommendation necessary for my entry into her minuscule but ever so elite *conservatoire*, had sorely miscalculated the level of my abilities, and even more the level of my motivation. That selection may have hinged more upon Brünnhilde's friendship with one of my aunts than upon any putative talent that I might have displayed in some momentary and largely gratuitous skid into virtuosity.

My aunt's meteoric rise and fall so many years before as an international opera singer had peaked in the small opera houses of Cremona and Mantua and bottomed out before a half-empty house at Covent Garden. Although Brünnhilde had been her coach and guardian, efficacious and sheltering, in this finally hapless trajectory of events, she wasn't able to protect my aunt from all those serendipitous consequences that affect the lives and careers of even the greatest artists.

For all of this, as I said, she flew into my first lesson and flew out of my last: the former with boundless hope and the latter with boundless grief. But there was no point, for her, in regretting what regrets could not repair. When it was appropriate (as well as expedient), she could be tragic, but she had no regrets. Quite candidly, I, too, have few regrets about all of this, though I do have some regrets about having few regrets. I don't doubt that the proper judgment was made in the end; it was she who was disappointed, and I didn't enjoy disappointing such a formidable spirit. If my destiny had lain in that direction, it would have been a beneficent destiny, and her guidance would have been the best thing about it. If she knew—knew better than anyone else I've ever known—the heights to which great artistry can rise, she also knew—knew better than anyone else I've ever known—the stupendous labor without which all great artistry cannot flourish. She knew, and made a point of emphasizing again and again, that the fineness of the fine arts resides in the maximum of precision and control.

She stood, as firmly and strongly as the Valkyrie she was, against the "expressionist" understanding of the arts that prevails in so much of modernity, though many of those who knew her would regard her as the most expressive person they had ever encountered. And she was; but she could distinguish clearly between what it means to express a real passion (a passion about something and for something) and what it means to express an artistically controlled imitation of a passion (i.e., to be passionate about the skill of pretending to be passionate). And if anyone knew what it meant to be passionate, about anything, it was Brünnhilde.

Most people didn't see the laborious and painstaking tasks she submitted herself to—they saw only the Valkyrie result, the exuberant, stormy side of her, not appreciating that Valkyries are what they are because of the enormously pedestrian preparation they put into what they do. I suppose it was that part of it that I couldn't, in the end, abide, at least in regard to this particular pursuit, and that made my efforts futile and worthless. There's no point in hankering after supernal beauty when you can't discipline yourself to spend hours a day doing finger exercises and counting out beats in measure until you're ready to keel over with exhaustion.

I'll never know, of course, since I was too young at the time, how big the world of opera was that surrounded Brünnhilde in those days. She seemed to know everyone in that world, all the singers and musicians, the performances, the ins and outs of the opera stage, what was going on all over Europe and the United States. She'd been born in the American South, in Alabama, I think, and spoke with a heavy Southern drawl. But her early years in Europe taught her Italian, French, and German. She could imitate the accents of each of these languages in English (which she often did in a most comical way); she could speak the languages fluently as well as speak (again, for comic effect) in elaborate, nonsense mimicries of these languages. It would appear that she'd been in every great opera house in the world, at La Scala and Bayreuth and Vienna and Glyndebourne and everywhere else (I imagined her flying from one locale to the next on her winged, mythic six-legged horse).

It was to the Metropolitan Opera House in New York that the steed of her professional life was most closely tethered, and much of her work was calibrated to its repertoire and ambiance. She'd been a piano accompanist to a myriad of singers, a few great and most otherwise, and she'd performed with them on their tours and recitals. She had an encyclopedic knowledge of operatic scores and librettos and could, on the spur of the moment and if offered a piano worthy of her robust renditions, regale the guests at a social occasion with the most dazzling stories drawn from the entire range of operatic literature, so much of which she seemed to know by memory, and which she could embellish with endless anecdotes about what this diva had done with such and such a passage and how that *Heldentenor* had faltered at just the wrong moment in *Tristan und Isolde*. All of this was reinforced, naturally, by her virtuoso playing on the piano as accompaniment to herself and her vivid storytelling.

She wasn't a singer herself but developed an ability to speak the words of an aria dramatically as she played its stirring music on the piano; the effect was beyond description. She could assume all the roles in a libretto, acting them out in sequence as she proceeded through the text (usually abridged, of course, to high points only). Her lively narrative filled in the scenic details and the stagecraft. What's more, she could present all of this with enthusiasm and humor, making people laugh at what is inveterately funny about opera (and especially about opera librettos) even as they sighed over what is great. She could turn high seriousness into high comedy with a single note—a single note played flat and out of key. She could mock what she loved, making it just that much more lovable. She was, almost, as it were, in such a situation, an entire operatic performance encompassed in a single person.

She even did this sort of thing professionally, I should add, occasionally renting out one of the ballrooms in a downtown hotel for the purpose. But I never attended one of those professional afternoon entertainments. I was too young for that and would have been too out of place among the well-heeled, matronly entourage for whom they were intended. My viewings were private—yes, private, if you can envisage that. On several big family occasions, she was there and would sometimes demonstrate some small portion of what she could do. My aunt, retaining after many years some measure of her former abilities, might help out here and there. But at my lessons, after what always was a grueling session, my tears were brushed away by a modest offering of chocolates and little maple-sugar soldiers and by her playing a selection from an opera.

In my time with her I must have been presented with, albeit in pieces and fragments, just about all of *Aida* and *Don Giovanni* and *Lohengrin*. I cannot attend to these operas to this day without thinking of her, without thinking of the ceremonial Egyptian beard she made out of something or other and attached at times to her chin when she was being the pharaoh, or of the sheaf of papers she brandished in her hand between snatches of Leporello's catalogue aria. And her recitation of "In fernem Land," the piano swelling with Wagnerian cadences, shall resonate with me for all my days. It was almost too good to be true.

There were many other sides to Brünnhilde's life that I knew practically nothing about—as is true about everybody we know, even those we know most intimately. She'd spent several years in Milan when she was young—my aunt told me about that—and there had been a young, gallant military officer in her life. Mussolini's contribution to the war had cut that marriage tragically short. Her husband responded to his mobilization orders, as he felt his military oath and regimental fealty required him to do, even as she departed for home until things should get "back to normal" again. Things never got—generally never do get—"back to normal." He was killed in Africa. Nevertheless, she proudly bore his Italianate surname as her own surname for the rest of her life.

Her Italian years had endowed her with a knowledge of Italian cuisine, especially Northern Italian cuisine, long before it became widely known in the United States, and among her many operatic friends her loft on Central Park South was noted for its fine Italian fare. Her specialty was a beef brisket simmered in a fragrant sauce, served *con patate*, and what *patate* they were! I had it once at a family occasion.

But the configurations of our lives change, like the changing forms of a kaleidoscope as it's slowly turned — the pieces staying the same, in a way, the relationships altering moment by moment, sorting into new patterns with every turn. So, as time passed, her piece for me slid into some obscure spot at the edge, I suppose — still there, but no longer as prominent as it once was.

To this day, I can't help but think of Brünnhilde soaring off somewhere in the exuberance of her flight. I can't help but think of her asleep upon that fire-moated mountain until, as in one of the greatest moments in opera, encased in her glittering armor, her Valkyrie eyes widen again, as luminous as the luminosity they gaze upon, her very words in that magical awakening being everything that she was in life for me and for so many others:

> *Hail to thee, O Sun!*
> *Hail to thee, O Light!*
> *Hail to thee, O brightening Day!*

2

The Sandhog

So how was I supposed to know he wasn't the janitor? It wouldn't have made any difference anyway. I wouldn't have interacted with him in any other way than I did. I'd completed my first day at work at the university and was on my way out to the parking lot. He was swabbing the hallway floor with a huge wet mop, with a long-legged swagger and a long-armed swing that made me have to bolt into a hop and a skip to dodge around him. He begged my pardon when he noticed I was there. We exchanged some comments. I said he looked like a sailor swabbing the deck. He said he was, indeed, a sailor swabbing the deck. I laughed. He laughed. I continued down the hall; he continued to swab, once again absorbed in his work. Clearly, he took this swabbing very seriously.

Next day I would see him again at my first official faculty meeting. I discovered that the same man, the sailor with the mop, was also the associate dean of the graduate school.

How could I mistake him when I saw him again? He recognized me at once and nodded at me with a smile, as if he were an old friend. He was the classic leptomorph type, a beanpole, the lank, rawboned sort of man I associate, for some obscure reason (perhaps because he'd quipped he was a sailor), with nets and harpoons and choppy seas: a body so tall, straight, and lean that his head looked like a finial on a post or a knob on a spar, especially when it was rounded off by the tight little woolen naval watch cap he often wore.

Over the course of time, as I came to know him better, I realized that that long-staffed prominence was a position well-suited for his head, for the expression on his face looked inquisitive, puzzled, and urgent, like that of a watchman who sees something over the heads of a crowd, or who, from the peak of a tower or a mast, scans something on the far horizon that he cannot identify at first and that he feels is important and needs to tell everyone about but doesn't know yet what to say or how to say it. He often blinked as if continuous peering into the distance had strained his eyes, and, when he wasn't wearing his cap, a sprig of gray hair dangled down over his forehead and was being perpetually brushed aside. Although he was well advanced in age, he had the demeanor of a man twenty years younger.

He was as cheerful a fellow as one could ever meet: every problem for him was a puzzle to be solved; every hardship, a challenge; every disappointment, a nudge, kindly and well-intentioned, to reconsider a little bit more what you were doing. His expectations were always modest—so modest that sometimes he drove others almost crazy by his modesty. In any debate he always seemed to have the last word—but by default, I should say, always by listening carefully, with that puzzled look on his face, by waiting until just about everything had been said and then by isolating and rearticulating the strongest point in the position of his interlocutors, though in a provisional and inquiring mode, and by presenting their argument with deference and circumspection, while trying to be sure that he understood them correctly.

That's why he drove people crazy—unintentionally, of course. The clarity of his cautious summarizing of other people's positions all too often brought to the fore—made explicit, you might say—the latent, the implicit, illogic of the position he so carefully explicated; and the position, without further argument, would, typically, collapse. He always felt that the most important person or persons he had to convince were those who had made the initial proposal. They usually ended up withdrawing it of their own accord. Case closed.

Naturally, as dean, he had to advance his own proposals from time to time, but always with such reserve and restraint, always with such due consideration for the interests of all who had to be involved, that they found ready acceptance. There was rarely anything to object to. Once again, case closed.

Some people called him "the Sandhog" — an odd designation, certainly, for someone of his shape and disposition. I suppose it suggested a person who hunkers down and digs in and is impossible to dislodge from a position. That was hardly the Sandhog at all. It might also suggest a person who tunnels underneath a mighty fortification, a "sapper" who brings impregnable walls hurtling down. But I never knew the Sandhog to have a single catastrophic inclination in his bones. Life was full of problems, but you couldn't solve them by generating brand-new problems out of them. Injustice was never to be rectified by initiating new injustices. In any event, the origin of the name was much simpler than that. The Sandhog had once been a bona fide "sandhog." I'll tell you how I learned that. He told me himself.

I was sitting at a table in a faculty lounge having lunch one day and was, incidentally, joined by the Sandhog and, a bit later, by another fellow whom I'll call Barry. Barry plopped down at the table, plopped down his cup of coffee, and plopped into our conversation without trying to find out what it was we were talking about. He normally did that, and we weren't surprised by it. Well, Barry was always full of steam, chugging around the campus like the "little steam engine that could" and letting off, as you can well guess, a lot of that steam, interspersed now and then with a sequence of short, shrill whistles.

He complained about everything. He was a political sort of person, and every source of complaint had a hypothetical political source and explanation. I won't go into the details of this, for even the modalities and targets of complaint shifted from time to time. Usually he complained about a supposedly global "system," run by a well-organized, well-funded, and malicious cabal, that made everyone miserable most of the time. If you spilled coffee on your pants leg, the "system" was responsible for deliberately manufacturing unbalanced cups that tipped over on you. It was responsible for the mercenary fraud that hoodwinked you into drinking coffee in the first place and caused your caffeine addiction; it was also responsible for coffee plantations in Brazil that were, according to him, still staffed by slave labor. It was responsible for wasting energy by heating up water that then singed your leg when you spilled it. And so forth.

The "system" was often referred to by the sinister and opprobrious term "it." "It" was responsible for everything bad. Of course, none of these considerations prevented Barry from drinking his coffee.

On this particular day, Barry railed against landlords of every stripe. *"Rentiers"* (as he called them, appropriating for the occasion a term of wider disapproval) were generically despicable people. Countless millions of lives had been destroyed by them. Overcrowding, disease, crime, mental illnesses, social dysfunctions of all kinds were caused by landlords. They should all—yes, he used language like this—be rounded up and executed. As suddenly as he arrived, and without waiting for a response from either of us, Barry jumped up from the table and left, leaving a metaphorically hot stream of metaphorically steamy froth behind him. What was important to him was that he had said what he had to say, not that we had heard what we had to hear. He forgot his steamy coffee cup. What would he blame that particular oversight on? How did "it" manage to do "that"?

Now, the Sandhog had his usual puzzled look on his face during this rant. After Barry had steamed off, he nodded his head sympathetically. He didn't in any way try to repudiate or object to anything Barry said. But he made it clear that he had grown up in the circumstances Barry had described, circumstances of grinding and oppressive poverty, part of which was contending with difficult and negligent landlords. But there was more to the picture than Barry let on; indeed, it was clear that Barry himself had never experienced any of the things he'd so vividly decried.

But the Sandhog had. The Sandhog acknowledged that he'd been perhaps, as he figured, lucky in escaping the consequences Barry had outlined. He'd lived as a child in a two-room apartment in the Bronx, an apartment that had nine other people living in it: his parents, six siblings, and a maternal grandmother. It was one of those—what they called in those days—"cold water flats." Heating in the winter was provided by dangerously incendiary kerosene stoves. Summer was spent dragging tattered mattresses out onto the fire escapes and sleeping there. Plumbing was inadequate and often broke down; infestations of cockroaches and rats were common; hallways and stairwells were a shambles—ill-lit and filled with trash.

The survival of his family during the Depression years was a constant daily trial. He'd had to find odd jobs from his earliest years. But he told me all about this in the same way that people recount "fond memories." The hardships gave meaning, purpose, and strength to his life and to the lives of those around him; they bound people he knew together in a common effort. He attended the local parochial school, then one of the Catholic high schools in New York City, and finally went to college at Fordham.

Now, this is where the "sandhog" bit came in. He worked his way through college and graduate school by taking an evening shift in excavations deep underground in the city, much deeper than the subways, and in pressurized caissons under the rivers where the installation of vital equipment for the life of the city took place. Such work was considered unusually demanding and dangerous. The people who did this kind of work were called "sandhogs." They drilled, day and night, through bedrock in unwholesome tunnels hundreds of feet below the city, doing work almost totally unknown to the rest of the population. But he was glad to have work and to be able to pay for his university tuition. It also paid for his regular attendance as a "standee" in the back row at operatic and philharmonic performances. Somehow, he even landed an occasional job as an "extra" in crowd scenes performed at the Metropolitan Opera, where he could walk about wearing a helmet and carrying a spear and listen to the singers only a few feet away from him. Several times he'd acted as one of the porters who bore the ailing Amfortas into the temple of the Holy Grail on Monsalvat.

He was glad to have worked with the people he worked with. He regarded himself as having been granted a privileged life, and he was deeply grateful for it. Years later, some of his colleagues in the rural university where he and I now were had learned of his past and, taking into account some of his more eccentric habits, began to call him "the Sandhog." For him, it was an honorific title. He was proud to have been a sandhog.

While still living in New York, and after a stint in the Navy (or, more specifically, in the Brooklyn Naval Yard, and hence the source of his somewhat threadbare naval peacoat and watch cap he wore during the winter as well as of his self-identification as a sailor), the Sandhog became associated with the so-called Catholic Worker movement. He was a friend of its early founders, contributed to its newspaper, and participated in its charitable activities. When he left New York City, he took many of its ideals with him. He founded an agricultural commune not far from our university by arranging for the purchase of an old, run-down farm and converting its house and barn into a kind of monastic enclosure. It was a house of prayer as well as a house of work—*ora et labora*, the ideal of the Benedictine Order from the early Middle Ages.

The commune prospered. It raised its own food, chopped its own wood, dug its own wells, built additional lodgings and a spacious refectory for common meals, entertained guests from around the country, helped out the local poor, sheltered the emotionally crippled and the homeless spirits of all classes of society who manage to grope their way to such places, sold its cider to tourists for the cash it raised, then gave that cash away, and everyone who lived there and had an outside job pooled their resources into a common fund. Many students from the university, both young men and women, opted to live there during their student years, contributing their work to the community. They also got to participate in the vital intellectual and musical life of the inhabitants—a resource of which, being open to the public and inviting anyone from the outside, I was able to take maximum advantage of for many years. There was nothing quite like it. The commune was a kind of miniature university itself, more devoted to an ideal of knowledge than the actual university where I worked. Some of its people were even married and raised their families in the commune.

In his job at the university, the Sandhog sought to illustrate his ideals among the faculty by what he did. He felt that everyone should be willing to take modest emoluments and often deflected his pay raises into scholarship funds. He also had this altogether bizarre conviction that faculty should participate in the physical maintenance of the campus. The aim was, among other things, to bring down some of the prohibitive costs for students. He thought that the students should participate as well. He also was convinced that communal physical work was good for the soul and good for the well-being of people who worked intellectually together.

Naturally, these ideas were not taken very seriously by his colleagues. Nonetheless, he insisted on living up to what he urged others to do. His swabbing of the floor I'd seen on my first day was just one instance of this. He attended to a dozen other little jobs, such as planting grape arbors and nurturing a small rose garden outside the dean's office where his philosophical club could meet from time to time and foster their symposia.

I guess I should add one other detail. How can we discuss such an academic person without mentioning his area of specialization? What was it, after all? That wasn't altogether easy to find out, for the Sandhog didn't put it on display. There were his courses listed in the catalogue; we heard students and colleagues talking about him; we took stock of the sort of references and comments he made in certain situations such as academic lectures and colloquia. The Sandhog, it seemed, had burrowed into everything. Absolutely everything. There was no academic specialization that he didn't seem to know something about. I think that's why he may have been appointed to be a graduate dean.

But he had a tool with which to do this. His area of specialization, I eventually figured out from all these sources, was logic: in particular, the *organon* of Aristotelian logic that he knew in detail in the original Greek. He also was intimately familiar with the great medieval treatises on logic as well as modern developments of logical theory. He could transmute, spontaneously and instantly, the terms of the most everyday argument into the formulations of contemporary symbolic logic and work out, in his head, its inferences and connections. He was in possession, you could say, of the science of thinking, of the science of thinking about thought itself.

I've never known anyone who came even close to knowing as much about logic, and how to apply it, as did the Sandhog. This is the reason he had such an unassailable position in faculty powwows of various kinds—he could, in the most gracious manner and with the most flawless accuracy, demonstrate the logic, or (more often) the lack thereof, in the position of an interlocutor.

Yet he always insisted, and acted upon the understanding, that there's something prior to logic without which logic itself will not and cannot work: the "being of being," as he would say, and the sheer unmediated apprehension of it by the intelligence, the scanning of the far horizon for the thing you cannot yet identify, and letting that thing announce itself, present itself as an incipient whole before its parts come into focus, and gradually shape our minds with the crystalline, multivalent distinctiveness of its form.

Starting with that pre-logical understanding, you might claim, the Sandhog had burrowed, like the sandhog he was, into the logical center of the classic syllogism—the "middle term," the scientific definition, the ontological insight—and he saw the world from there; and therewithal, like a sandhog, he burrowed into the center of the world itself, whose structure so astonishingly and miraculously corresponds with the logical and mathematical systems that the human mind devises to encapsulate its findings.

And what a world he saw!—a world in which the Logos of the world itself, at yet another level, was encamped, embodied, enlivened; the center and core of meaningfulness; a Logos "full of grace and truth." For him the universe was a fact; but not just a fact: it was also a Voice; and he knew that the more accurately and rigorously we apprehend a fact, the more powerfully we can hear that Voice speaking to us, if we only take the time to listen.

I shall not forget too readily the swagger and swing of that genteel man, detached and cheerful and solemn, the tall man with the long mop, the man whom they called the Sandhog.

3

Fleur-de-Lis

A colossal woman, hefty but not obese; a swart face grooved deep with age and labor; brown, black-splotched skin as sere as a cordillera of parched equatorial mountains; short, ragged hair sticking up in little patches amid glossy bald spots; a huge wen pendant from her lower lip; a snaggle of discolored teeth; tatterdemalion, garish garments of homemade origin draped in loose folds from her massive frame; a rolling limp in her heavy gait; muscular, bare arms, as tough and groined as mahogany boughs; impeccably clean and wearing some eau-de-cologne she was very proud of. She came from Haiti, spoke English with a heavy Creole accent, lived in Brooklyn somewhere — we never knew where — walked across the Brooklyn Bridge in the morning to Manhattan, caught the subway to the 186th Street bus terminal, and rode a bus across the George Washington Bridge five days a week, sometimes six, when necessary, to our domicile in New Jersey, where she took care of us; took care of us in so many ways.

Her name?

Fleur-de-Lis.

We were pampered people. How many people did we know who were not? Fleur-de-Lis made breakfast, lunch, and supper for us, cleaned our rooms, did our laundry, mended our torn seams, changed our diapers, supervised our playpens and backyards, looked after our dog and cat (both of whom loved her more than they loved us), and in due season even did a bit of gardening for us—raising tomatoes and greens and onions for our salads and sundry flowers for our vases.

She did much more than that. She took it upon herself to answer the phone, startling, no doubt, the unwary caller by her perplexing mix of Haitian rural accent and a ceremonious elegance apposite, somehow, for the court of Louis the Fourteenth, though you could be fairly sure she'd never heard of the Sun King or the golden age of Versailles.

Actually, she answered both phones, including the one with a separate number that my father used to run his medical practice partially out of our house. She took messages for him, canceled or confirmed appointments, made lists of infirmities and complaints, and—we'll never know how much she did this—proffered her own medical advice by prescribing for "*les malades*," as she referred to them, her own version of Haitian folk remedies.

Did it matter?

Apparently, they worked. Patients began calling her, rather than my father. Those remedies certainly worked when administered, surreptitiously, to us.

But more than that. She made sure our family was a family—a task my parents were not, for whatever reasons, wholly capable of. My father was too busy and too tired: interminable house calls and hospital emergencies were working him to death. Soon enough he died from them—perhaps from one too many meningitis cases in a child, keeping him up all night until the initial crisis passed. My mother was too preoccupied by whatever it was that kept her preoccupied: her club, her social engagements, her daily crossword puzzle in the *Times*, her fashionable publications, including the weekly *New Yorker* magazine, her fingernails. We never quite knew.

I wouldn't say that all aspects of Fleur-de-Lis' interaction in our lives were necessarily pleasant. If she consoled and nurtured, she also cajoled and scolded, insisting that certain rules be followed and certain boundaries never be transgressed. She lectured, too, holding forth with the grandiloquence of a Bossuet or a Fénelon or a Fontenelle on proper decorum and gracious manners. About this, there were no compromises: what would have been right, as we could infer in retrospect from her speech and deportment, for the court of Louis the Fourteenth (had she known about it) was equally right for the tin-roofed shack in Haiti, for the garrulous tenement in Brooklyn, and for the luxurious suburban mansion, where, more than anywhere else, you could grow slack, dissolute, locked into the privacy of your own intractable and self-absorbed fantasies.

Had I the presence of mind in those days, which I certainly didn't, I would have kept a record of all those proverbs and sayings that dropped perpetually from her mouth. I remember only one. One of my siblings had risen in outraged protest against some obligation she'd reminded him of. He didn't, so he claimed, have to do anything he didn't want to do. Her answer—and how I wish I could remember her very choice of words and inflection—was that the only time a person didn't have to do what he didn't want to do was when he was dead. An obvious enough observation, I suppose, except for what it said about her life and what it may have said about life itself, indicating that you're dead already, while still alive, if you refuse to meet your obligations.

One incident, in particular, lives in my memory with astonishing vividness. We had a swimming pool—an old-fashioned one built back in the twenties, very deep, surrounded by a terrace and high trellised walls covered with old rose vines whose flowers bloomed all summer long and whose gigantic thorns sometimes ripped into us when we were careless in our running along the edge of the pool during our water games. We also took care of emptying the pool at regular intervals (this was before the days of filters) to scrub it out and fill it with fresh water.

One time we had drained the pool, went off to have lunch, and returned to begin the scrubbing when we discovered at the deep end of the pool an enormous and very vicious possum that must have scrambled out of the nearby brush somewhere and tumbled in. It cowered at the deepest end of the pool. Approaching from the shallow end in a faux-phalanx of backyard warriors, my brothers and I made various efforts to assault it with rakes and other paraphernalia with which we thought to subdue it, only to be propelled, again and again, into a panicked retreat by a snarling attack.

In due course, Fleur-de-Lis became apprised of our distress. She lurched resolutely to the pool area, leapt down into the shallow end of the pool with a vigor that utterly surprised us, and limped clumsily but unhesitatingly down the incline toward the possum. It didn't have time to attack. In probably the fastest motion I've ever witnessed in my life, she'd grabbed the possum by the tail and the next moment the poor critter went sailing over the rose trellises and into the woods beyond. We heard it scurrying off to safety. Fleur-de-Lis exited the pool as if nothing more extraordinary had happened than peeling an onion or filleting a fish.

I think you could also say that Fleur-de-Lis was somewhat of a seer. She liked to tell fortunes, and we found that rather funny. She would predict the outcome of the various athletic contests we were in at school; she was often right, though I don't remember how often. She was also subject, according to her own accounts, to spectacular visionary experiences that sometimes made her very worried and morose. One day, while she was crossing over the Brooklyn Bridge toward Manhattan, she saw two tall identical glass buildings raging with flame and smoke and bringing death and desolation to many innocent people. She was terribly upset by this vision. She told this to my mother. My mother, of course, dismissed it; no two such buildings existed and probably never would. The tip of Manhattan already had too many buildings. Fleur-de-Lis was comforted by that. I've always wondered whether she lived long enough to see those two tall identical buildings erected in later years.

In the final years of his life, my father was diagnosed with a terminal disease. He was given about four years to live. All of us refused to believe this; I don't even know if he believed it, and some of the specialists that he consulted were of different opinions about it. Anyway, one year he decided to join several colleagues on a trip to Zurich, Switzerland, to attend an international conference on the treatment of prematurely born babies. He would be gone for about a week. Halfway through the week, he suddenly and unexpectedly took ill, was rushed to a hospital, and within an hour passed away. There was no time to inform anybody.

He died at 11:32 at night, Swiss time. Shortly after 5:32 that evening, the equivalent time on the Eastern Seaboard, Fleur-de-Lis entered the living room and asked my mother if any changes should be made to the menu for the evening meal. When my father was away, we often had a simpler fare than usual. Fleur-de-Lis wanted to know whether to change the menu now that my father had come home. My mother was a bit flustered by such a curious misapprehension. She told Fleur-de-Lis that he wasn't expected until the end of the week. Fleur-de-Lis told my mother that she'd seen the "doctor" walking around the house, peeking into every room as if saying hello and making sure everything was fine. My mother didn't pay much attention and went back to her *New Yorker*.

Fleur-de-Lis returned to the kitchen and wept. She'd realized that the "doctor" wasn't saying "hello" but rather "goodbye."

The telephone call from Switzerland came a few minutes later.

After my father's death, my mother "abandoned ship." Don't ask me what this is all about—it's too complicated and it's too tedious, and no one in their right mind would believe it.

Fleur-de-Lis somehow foresaw what was coming, all the disaster that it would entail: there's no other way to explain the grief she expressed when we took our final departure from her. We sold the house in New Jersey and moved to Los Angeles. We wanted her to come with us, but she had too many ties in Brooklyn and even in Haiti, a shorter plane ride from New York, to permit her changing her residence.

My mother, soon thereafter, took up with a man who stayed home all day and helped her with her crossword puzzles and her fingernails.

We never saw Fleur-de-Lis again.

About the Author

Johann M. Moser was born in Cambridge, Massachusetts, in 1940. He grew up in New York City and later in New Jersey. At Dartmouth College he majored in philosophy and studied with the poet Richard Eberhart. In 1970, he received a Ph.D. in comparative literature from the Catholic University of America in Washington, D.C., where he specialized in poetics and medieval literature. From 1970 until his retirement in 2000, he taught literature and philosophy at St. Anselm College in Manchester, New Hampshire.

Moser published a volume of verse titled *Most Ancient of All Splendors* with Sophia Institute Press in 1989, as well as edited and translated for the press both an anthology of classical Nativity verse and, in collaboration with a colleague, Robert Anderson, an edition of St. Thomas Aquinas's hymns and prayers.

Although familiar with many areas of the United States and having lived several years abroad, Moser spent his early summers in the Lakes Region of central New Hampshire, where he has now resided for over half a century. In these decades, he has formed an intimate bond with northern New England, whose mountains and lakes and lively populace have been a source of inspiration for him, even as he has devoted himself to a sustained pursuit and emulation of world literature in all its dense historicity and its universal aesthetic achievements.

www.ingramcontent.com/pod-product-compliance
Lightning Source LLC
Chambersburg PA
CBHW030120010826
48973CB00002B/346